I0728974

Division One: Texas Rangers

by Stephanie Osborn

Chromosphere Press

Huntsville, AL

Texas Rangers

© 2018 Stephanie Osborn

ISBN 978-1-947530-02-7 (print)

ISBN 978-1-947530-01-0 (ebook)

Cover art © 2018 Darrell Osborn

Fiction

First electronic edition 2018

All rights reserved. No part of this publication may be reproduced, stored in a retrieval system, or transmitted, in any form or by any means without the prior written permission of the publisher, nor be circulated in any form of binding or cover other than that in which it is published without a similar condition being imposed on the subsequent publisher. All trademarks are property of their respective owners.

This is a work of fiction. All concepts, characters and events portrayed in this book are used fictitiously and any resemblance to real people or events is purely coincidental.

Chromosphere Press
P.O. Box 3412
Huntsville, AL 35810
www.chromospherepress.com

Table of Contents

Chapter 1

"...And that's it, guys," the trim, athletic blonde in the black Suit, standing behind the podium at the front of the lecture hall, said with a smile. "The only reason I scheduled one last meeting after the final exam was to see if any of you had questions about anything I didn't cover, or suggestions for how to make the course better. Unlike the typical university class, you all passed with the proverbial flying colors. Not that I expected any differently from this bunch."

"You did great, Meg," India, the junior partner of the Alpha Two team, and the Alpha Line department medic, said. "I can't think of anything I was curious about that you didn't cover, or answer when someone asked it in class. And the latter largely because you sorta led us into it, like you intended us to ask those things, to get us thinking."

"Yeah," Romeo, India's partner—in the Alpha Line department, and in life—agreed. "I wadn' sure what t' expect, an' I never was one f'r a lotta science stuff, but this was interesting in th' good way."

"Well, I didn't expect for most of Alpha Line to take the class," Omega said with a laugh. "Echo, are you sure you didn't coerce 'em, Ace?"

"I swear I did NOT," the tall, rugged, senior member of the Division One's Alpha One team said, quite serious. "But everybody in the department knows your background, and they know you know your stuff. I think we all just wanted to take advantage of a different sorta class with a teacher we all knew and respected."

"Indeed, Professor Omega," Agency Director Fox decreed. "You even taught this old desert fox a thing or two, and you know I've been around the galactic spiral a time or twelve."

"They're right, old girl," Madrid, head of Weapons Development, agreed. "I can't think when I enjoyed a course more."

Murmurs of consent went around the packed lecture hall, and Omega blushed at the praise as she smiled again.

"Good, then," she said. "So everybody liked the way I laid out the structure of the course?"

Another murmur of agreement rose.

"Any questions?"

A hand went up toward the back; it was Love, of the Alpha Five team.

"Yes, ma'am. Are you gonna have a follow-on course?"

"Probably, eventually," Omega said. "I know what I want to do for it already, I just have to have time around missions, administrative duties, and what-all, to pull it together. Is there anything y'all would like me to do as a course? You know, kind of a request for a course?"

Alpha Eight team member Monkey raised his hand.

"I'd like to see something on ground-based observational astronomy," he said. "You kinda got me interested in it as a serious hobby, maybe. I dunno if that would be better suited to a one-on-one practicum, or a lecture-type thing, though."

"Oh, I could see that being a lecture with lab," Omega brainstormed, "where the lab is actually working with a telescope and learning to make observations."

"I'm there," Dog noted; he was a recent transfer into the Alpha Line department, and Echo and Omega both considered him a damn fine starship pilot.

"Fox, anything in particular you think needs to be in the curriculum?" Omega wondered.

"If suggestions are what you're looking for, meyn khaverte," Fox said, considering, "come by my office later; I think I can help you populate the curriculum. I'd like to see several things, such as a course on navigational hazards from the astrophysics perspective—WHY they're hazards; how to best handle new discoveries on a mission; how the classic interstellar drive works, and several things like that."

Oohs and aahs went around the room.

"Then I'll try and come talk to you at some point," Omega

agreed. "Or you and Zebra can come to dinner some evening after shift and we can brainstorm then."

"Even better," Fox averred.

"Professor Omega?" one of Madrid's subordinates from the Weapons Development department asked, raising a hand.

"Yes, November?"

"Back when you were showing us how to visualize space-time and run calculations in it..."

"Yes?"

"Is it true that you can actually SEE it? I mean," November tried to explain, "I've heard the rumors that you set a speed record on the tesseract puzzle in Alpha Line qualifications testing..."

Omega's eyes went wide; she had not expected a personal question. She felt her face heat with a flush, and she dropped her gaze, uncertain what to say. Abruptly a tall, familiar body in black materialized at her side, as a strong, affectionate hand came down gently on her shoulder.

"She can, and she did," Echo said, voice quiet, as he stood beside her and gazed at the class. "But before any of you start in wondering how much of her intellect and abilities were given to her by a certain deceased alien psychopath, I want you all to know something that not even Meg herself knows yet, because I haven't told her."

The room grew silent, and a puzzled Omega looked up at her partner, waiting for him to continue his statement.

"I dug into Omega's educational history in the months since we found out about that whole pile of shit," Echo told them. "It took a while, but I decided it was worth it. I knew how much it all bothered her, and I wanted to try to see for myself how much of it was innate, and how much of it was what she and I call, 'Slug's tinkering.' So, since we always download all the records on a new agent before they get removed from the outside world, I dug deep into her elementary school records."

"Oh? What did you find?" Fox wondered, and Omega stared at Echo, surprised.

"What I found was that Meg is just that damn smart," her partner declared. "They tested her early on for school—IQ, problem solving, all kinds of shit like that—because they needed to know if they should send her to a special program or something...or even if they had a program they could send her to, I think. The school shrink was shocked, judging by his reports; it seems she pretty much went out the top of all their tests, and kept going. You don't even wanna know what her IQ is."

"Do you know, Meg?" India wondered.

"No, I don't," Omega murmured, wishing her face would cool down. "I only asked a couple of times, out of simple curiosity, but the counselor wouldn't tell me. Seemed to think I'd get a swelled head if I knew, or something, I guess. It was never really that important to me, so I never pushed it."

"What was her record on the tesseract test?" November pressed. "Or is that classified?"

"It's not classified, though only Omega can agree to reveal it," Fox said. "Four of us were there to witness it, however. Omega?"

She shrugged, realizing she was about to get even more embarrassed.

"Nineteen and a half minutes or thereabouts, if memory serves," Fox informed them, and a collective gasp went up from the room. "Echo, what about that particular ability?"

"That one's a little harder, Fox," Echo admitted. "I can't say for sure that Slug didn't enhance that one, because your typical school systems don't really have testing that can measure that kinda thing. But I'm ninety-nine—with a whole lotta nines after the decimal—percent sure that he didn't CREATE that ability in her."

"So she had it already, Slug jus' maybe bumped it up a little?" Romeo wondered.

"That would be my take," Echo agreed. "Meg? Can you remember being able to do that before the...abduction?"

Omega stared at him for a moment, then cupped her hand

around her mouth and chin and thought back to her childhood.

"No, I can remember being able to do it," she finally acknowledged. "Probably not as well as I can now, but the ability was there. I think...I think maybe he must have just enhanced it. Maybe not all that much, either. I mean, I'm pretty sure he enhanced it some, but no, you're right...he didn't CREATE it."

"That's what I thought," Echo said, intense satisfaction written all over his face. "Professor Omega has some serious gray matter, no matter how you stack it."

The room erupted in raucous cheering, and she gave Echo a sheepish grin, feeling the deep blush that even made her ears burn. He returned to his seat in the front row, and she held up her hands for silence...which took a few moments to achieve, as the students from Alpha Line were trying to set up a wave through the class. Unfortunately, the room wasn't quite big enough, so eventually they settled down.

"Any other questions, comments or suggestions?" Omega wondered. "Preferably about the CLASSWORK this time?"

The room remained silent; several heads shook in the negative.

"All right, then. Division One University's first Astronomy 101 class is dismissed for the final time. Congratulations, everybody."

They all filed out, laughing and cheerful.

* * *

"C'mon, Meg," Echo said, coming to her side, as did Fox. "We need to check in at the Alpha Line Room, then go do a patrol."

"Anything up?" she asked.

"No, not particularly," Fox noted. "Things have been pretty quiet since we got the whole Cortian mess settled. It's only a routine patrol that I asked for Alpha One to perform, just in case. If there IS anything out there, you two will see it. Or hear about it."

"Speaking of the Cortians: How's that coming?" Echo wondered.

"Corta is still quarantined and blockaded," Fox said. "A few of the various nation-states on the planet have asked for material on other types of governments, and the Pan-Galactic Coalition has provided it. There's indication those guys are studying it, because observations from the blockading ships say small changes are being made. But in the main, they're still pretty damn screwed up."

"Well, from what you showed us of the reports, it's no wonder, Fox," Omega pointed out. "Their planet has next to nothing in the way of resources. It's dog eat dog, down there."

"True. Which is why the Coalition is trying to work out a way to offload part of the population to a suitable, uninhabited world that's been discovered nearby, and that has abundant natural resources for them to work with...for a change."

"Ooo, that would be good," she decided. "It might halfway give 'em a fighting chance to learn how to be useful members of galactic society, instead of a bunch of rogue pirates and slavers, marauding around."

"Exactly." Fox paused as they reached the Core. "Well, meyn khbrim, this is where I get off. I'll see you two later." He headed up the ramp to his office.

"Meg, I saw you brought your book bag for the last class," Echo noted. "Do you want to run home and dump it off, or just leave it in the Alpha Line Room? It's time we hit the road for our patrol."

"Oh, I think I'll just leave it in the Alpha Line Room," she decided. "I can pick it up and take it back to my quarters later."

"C'mon, then, let's go," he said. "I'll check email while you stash it in your desk, then we'll get the Corvette and head out."

"I'm all over that. Can we maybe get first lunch while we're out? I was so excited and nervous to see what folks thought of the class, I didn't really eat much for breakfast."

"Yeah, I noticed; it worried me until I figured out what was up. Okay. That works for me."

* * *

"Hey, what do you want to do tonight—er, in the morning—after work, Meg?" Echo asked his partner as they completed their routine patrol through New York's busy streets, quite some hours later.

Said 'routine patrol' had ended up with Alpha One nabbing two petty thieves from offworld who were foolishly trying to hold up the gift shop of the Central Park Zoo; busting a Kochavi prostitution ring located in one of the most affluent areas of Midtown; and rescuing a small Erikian child who had managed to get on the wrong side of the railing on the walking path of the Robert F. Kennedy Bridge and was dangling in a very precarious position. After a good bit of maneuvering, with the lighter Omega climbing out over the edge of the platform to reach the child while Echo anchored her with his own body weight and a firm grip on her ankles, they were eventually able to bring the child back to safety and return the little one to her parents.

In no wise could it have been called an uneventful patrol, even if it WAS routine, and both Agents were tired by the time they were en route back to Headquarters. They managed first lunch only because they stopped by the deli down the street right after leaving Headquarters; the sun was now only an hour from setting, so in addition to Omega's breakfast, they had missed second lunch—what most New York denizens would have termed dinner, except Alpha One's shift ran from 8am to 8am—and it was only two more hours until time for first snack. Both Agents were starved.

So it was no surprise when the platinum blonde in the Corvette's passenger seat sighed—a very tired sound—before answering.

"Actually, Echo, I think I just wanna go for a walk outside," she responded, and he nodded.

"Central Park? Or we could wander over toward McCarren Park; it's closer, if not quite as green. Or we could meander through one of the riverside parks..."

She shrugged, slightly discouraged.

"No, I mean the real outside. But I guess that'll do."

"The real outside? What does that mean?"

"I mean they're landscaped to hell and back. Echo, I'm not a city person, like most people seem to think. Remember, I spent almost the first twenty years of my life on a farm in Alabama, and the bulk of the next ten commuting in to either Huntsville or Houston from at least the suburbs. But I've been stuck in the middle of the Big Apple—Brooklyn, specifically—already for...for..."

"Going on a year and a half, now." Echo watched his partner out of the corner of his eye, a knowing half-smile on his face. "Sounds like somebody could use a vacation."

"Do Division One agents really get vacations?"

"Of course, Meg. You can't give a hundred and ten percent on a 48-hours-a-day, 7-days-a-week, 182-and-a-half-weeks-a-year kind of schedule, like we do, without the occasional break. If you want to put in for some extended leave, I think I can guarantee Alpha Line's department chief will approve it, and do his damnedest to get it through Fox."

Omega smiled and poked him in the shoulder.

"One of the perks of being partnered with the department chief, huh?"

"Yeah, you might say that." Echo grinned. "Let's make sure there's nothing on tap that Fox will need us for, and then I say let's head for the hills. And soon."

"That sounds good to me!"

* * *

A few days later, Echo and Omega sat in the Alpha Line Room just off the Core. "Well, looks like Alpha Line's number-one team is due some extended leave time," Echo remarked, looking at the notification that had popped up on his computer screen. "Fox just approved our vacation application. I'll put Romeo and India on call in our place, while we're gone. We have two weeks, beginning the end of this work period—which, unfortunately, just started—so we have several days to prep."

"Great!" Omega responded, pleased. "I didn't know you

put in, too, Echo."

"Figured I might as well take advantage of the opportunity, Meg. Not much I can do with my partner gone, anyway."

"I doubt that," she gave him a respectful, if amused, glance. "You're way too experienced an Agent to get away with a remark like that. Where are you going?"

"Where are YOU going?"

"I asked you first." Omega grinned.

"No. I mean, I can't answer you until I know where we're going."

"Oh. You're coming with me?"

"Yeah. You think I'm gonna let you go running off alone, Ms. Trouble-Magnet? You'd probably head off to L.A. and find yourself in the middle of a riot or an earthquake or a wildfire or something," Echo teased, a mischievous twinkle in the brown eyes.

"Well, at least I'd know what to do, I guess. And you can't ever claim life with me is boring," Omega shot back.

"No, that's true..."

"You mean you're really coming along?"

"Yup, I pretty much got to, to tell the truth. New policy," Echo told her. "After Sierra was murdered last fall vacationing alone, Fox got together with all the department heads—it was before you got made assistant chief, so I guess I just forgot to pass on the info, and we haven't really had occasion to talk about it, you and me—anyway, us leads all discussed it. And we decided partners should stick together whenever possible—including vacations. You may be on leave, but that doesn't mean your enemies are."

"Good point," Omega said, brow suddenly furrowed.

"What's wrong, Meg? Had you rather I NOT come along?" Echo asked, sobering as he watched her reaction. "Want to get away from me for a while?"

Well, shit, he thought, dismayed, and fighting against whatever it was in his chest threatening to crack. *She looks downright anxious. It never even occurred to her that we could take a vacay TOGETHER, even after all my hints back after the first of the year. I wonder if she even heard it, given everything else that was going on in that head, at the time. Or maybe she didn't WANT to hear it. And now I'm not sure she likes the idea. At all. Only...I'd hoped to try to, I dunno, maybe reach out, let her know I'm interested, and see if maybe we couldn't have a...closer...relationship by the time we got home. Dammit.*

* * *

Huh? There's a slightly...bleak look around his eyes, Omega thought, watching Echo. *Is he worried I don't want him around? No, no. I'd have him beside me around the clock...as close as I can get him...if I only thought he'd be willing. But that face sure looks like he thinks I don't want him along. I need to fix that.*

"Oh, no, it's not that at all, hon. I never get tired of having my best friend around." Omega gave Echo a warm, welcoming smile then, and he returned it briefly, then studied her intently as she continued. "But do you really want to come along? Or are you only doing it because of the policy? I don't want you to be bored, Ace."

* * *

"Well, I probably wouldn't have put in for leave myself, I'll admit...but it has been several years since I've had any real time off. I sure can't say the idea doesn't appeal. And after all the shit with the Cortians..." Echo shrugged, then tried a reminder. "You might not remember, given all that was going on back then, but we actually discussed it briefly, before that all went down—back just before the supposed 'first contact' and all."

"Oh. Yeah, we did, didn't we? And you'd sorta indicated maybe a joint vacay, then, too. I mean, I liked the idea, it's just...well. After...everything else that went down right after that, I, um...kinda forgot. Sorry." Omega pulled a wry face. Echo, secretly relieved, nodded.

"That's okay, baby. Given 'everything else that went down,' I think you're entitled. So like I said, where are we go-

10

ing?"

* * *

"Okay, lessee...drop back and punt," Omega murmured, thinking hard.

"Why?"

"I really don't want you to be bored..."

"Meg, just tell me what you were going to do," Echo said, spreading his hands. "Whatever, it'll be fine with me, I swear. You should know that, by now. If you think it'll be fun and restful, chances are, so will I. Anyway, we gotta start setting it up and arranging transportation an' shit."

"Um, I was going to pack up the new portable telescope and a laptop, and head back to Texas someplace. Spend some time outdoors observing, maybe do some camping—or not, if there's a nice place to stay close by—and spend lots more time generally roamin' around. I used to have this rancher buddy who let me stay there and observe. Remember when we met?"

"Yeah. Okay. Sounds relaxing, but not boring. That'll work. We'll go to the Ranch. You can teach me the finer points of astronomical observing, and I can teach you to ride a horse."

"No, you won't," Omega told her partner. Echo glanced at her, startled.

"Why not? You afraid of horses?"

"Hardly," she laughed. "You'll see."

* * *

On Alpha One's next day off, Omega woke up early, finding herself eager to start setting up for the upcoming vacation, and curious about Echo's proposed destination. Since the apartment next door remained dark—though a thin sliver of light was just visible under the bedroom door, evidence that Echo was up, but not yet dressed or ready for what they jokingly referred to as 'public viewing'—a hungry Omega grabbed a breakfast bar and wandered into her study, sitting down and booting the computer before logging into the Agency intranet.

A quick perusal of Agency field stations gave her the approximate location of the Ranch—west Texas, not very far from the Pecos River.

"Huh," she muttered. "That's not too far at all from where I used to go observing, let alone where Echo and I met. Cool."

Then an idea struck.

Hey, you don't suppose he chose it BECAUSE it's close to where we met, do ya? she wondered to herself. *That might almost come across as...sentimental. And THAT...might...*

Omega smiled slightly, wistful, then caught herself and shook her head.

Stop it, girl, she told herself sternly. *You're looking for any excuse to indicate that he cares. In THAT way. When you already know he doesn't...because he's never gotten over Chase. Those dreams during and right after our spaceship crash, back in the spring, told me that much. I guess you don't get over the love of your life. Which bodes ill for me. Never mind my, er, 'augmentations' thrown into the mix. No. Just stop it.*

"Hey, baby," Echo said, coming into her study just then, casually dressed in black jeans and matching tee. "Whatcha doin'?"

"Oh, I'm just scopin' out the Ranch and the area around it," she told him, trying to quickly shift mental gears.

"Found anything interesting?"

"No, not yet. Well," she corrected herself, "it all looks interesting, and awfully pretty. I guess I've gotten used to thinking of 'interesting' in the mission sense. But this isn't a mission. And from what I can see of the website for the 'guest ranch' there, I think I'm gonna have a lotta fun."

"Excited about the vacation trip, huh?"

"Yeah, I am! I'm really looking forward to it. Have you put in the paperwork to Fox yet?"

"Well, I submitted for the time off for Alpha One, and he approved it," Echo reminded her. "But I thought we'd tag up with him personally to set up the destination. That okay with you?"

"Yeah, but...I mean, what if there's no room left? It's a guest ranch, right? And they maintain a cover as a REGULAR guest ranch, so...they could book up before we even get our request in there."

"Nah," Echo said, giving her a wry grin. "Don't sweat it, Meg. That won't be a problem."

"But..."

"Trust me. I have an 'in' with the place. I've, uh, been there a few times, let's just say."

"Okay..."

"Look, remember when we met? When my perp ran over your telescope?"

"Oh HELL yeah." She snorted. "I was just thinking about that, actually. I realized, when I saw the location, that it's pretty close to there."

"Right. Well, that's...where I was staying for that mission. Me an' the Ranch go...way back."

"Aha. All right, then. I'll just let you handle it, I guess."

"Exactly, an' that's fine. Speaking of our trip, I need to run out and get some stuff. I thought I'd run over to the mall and grab some jeans that aren't threadbare, junk like that," he told her. "I'd put a request through Supplies' Personal Wardrobe branch, but I don't know if there's time for it to go through in triplicate and get approved an' junk, let alone get what I need here before we leave." He shook his head. "Bureaucracy is bureaucracy, the galaxy over, I guess."

"So you're gonna just run out and get some? Aren't we supposed to wear certain kinds of stuff, even off-duty? Like, to make sure we don't stand out?"

"Well, yeah, but it isn't like I haven't been around this place long enough to know what the requirements are," Echo said, grinning. "So. You wanna go with? You can help me pick out the pair that makes my ass look best," he teased.

"Pssht! As good as that ass looks? An' as hard as you work on it? Just get a pair that fits that ass halfway decently, and it'll look great." Omega's eyes twinkled as she chuckled.

"So you like my ass, huh?" Echo grinned wider.

"I'm a healthy hetero semi-sorta-human female, the last I

checked, and you're a well-built human male, more or less," she riposted, unsuccessfully stifling another snort of amusement. "Besides, I think I've told you once or twice that you have a cute butt. What, do you need me to tell you every day, so you know?"

"All right, all right," he laughed. "Are you gonna go shopping with me or not?"

"Oh. Well, crap. Decisions, decisions. Normally I would, yeah, but I just got started here, and I'm kinda curious about the area..."

"Okay. It's no big deal. I can get the stuff on my own; we just seem to really hit a synergy when we do stuff like that together. Wanna meet for a late first lunch instead? Then we can finish any other shopping we need to do, and do THAT together. And it'll give you time to scope out our destination, in the meantime," he added. "And get a feel for what you need to get when we DO go shopping, I suppose."

"That'll work." She offered him a smile, and he returned it.

Then Echo was off, and Omega returned to her researches.

* * *

It wasn't so much that Omega didn't know about the western Texas region; after all, as Echo pointed out, she had once spent the odd weekend here and there observing in the area, whenever she could get away from her work at NASA. And while it might be possible to run into someone who recognized her, it was unlikely the person would associate her face with Megan McAllister, since she had tended to keep to herself whenever she had been in the area.

No, it was more a case of worrying about Alpha One giving themselves away by being in the wrong place at the wrong time and running into someone who might recognize Echo.

Because that's near his old stomping grounds too and, after all, he was almost of age when he got 'drafted,' she thought. *So his features were pretty much established. Oh, I suppose he filled out some, because most guys with his build are pretty gangly as teenagers, and develop a fuller, more muscular, more mature figure as they settle into adulthood. And damn, but his is full and muscular! Some days I gotta work hard not to drool. Especially in the gym. Whoa, girl.* She broke off and mentally shook herself, regaining her train of thought. *But his face would have been essentially set, as would his height, I expect. And he played football at a high enough level to get a college scholarship, so he wasn't exactly skinny, even then. And that means that even today, he'd be recognizable by anybody who knew him well, back in the day. So while I'm sure HE knows who and what to look out for, I gotta make sure that I don't screw up and give him away.*

So a cautious Omega was trying to locate any living relatives, as well as what close friends might still be in the area. A few quick searches served to put paid to worries of old classmates.

"Okay, that works," she decided. "The Ranch is kind of isolated, and there's plenty of land around the main house. Plus, it's damn near fifty miles to his home town. I doubt we'll run into any old school chums or girlfriends. Now family...you never know..."

She knew Echo's father had died before he became an agent, and his father's parents had died when Echo was very young; that put paid to that consideration, and he had no siblings. But she thought she recalled that his mother was still alive, and he had had a grandfather living with them through most of his youth. So Omega set to, in an effort to locate them.

"Aw," she murmured a few minutes later, disappointed upon finding Echo's Apache grandfather's obituary from nearly ten years prior, in a Mescalero, New Mexico newspaper archive. "I was looking forward to meeting Shiitsooyee some day. I shoulda asked Ace about him, I guess. The fact that he didn't say anything should have been a clue, though, and I didn't pick up on it. Well, let's see if I can find his mom. She's the one I'm worried about, anyway. Moms have a kind of seventh or eighth sense or something about their kids, I swear."

So she dug back into her researches, starting with Shiit-sooyee, who had been Echo's mother's father, and branching off from there. It took surprisingly little time before a familiar name popped up, and she read the short article associated with it, then pushed back from the desk, feeling some of the blood drain from her face.

"Oh no," Omega murmured, staring at the article on her laptop screen. "No no no. Tell me I've got the names wrong."

Swiftly she pulled up another tab on her browser, dug into the classified personnel file archive of the Agency, searched on a particular code name, and entered a password. A directory popped up, and she scrolled down through it before finding the file she wanted and opening it.

"Nalin Iyaaye Bryant," she murmured. "Dammit. I was afraid of that." She shook her head. "I need to talk to Fox about this, right away. WITHOUT Echo."

* * *

Va'du'sha'ā was the fourth planet orbiting Zeta^2 Reticuli, a star not unlike Sol. It orbited well inside the Kuiper belt of that star. It was a lovely blue-green world, with lush vegetation, plenty of geological resources, and an advanced culture. It had three moons of various sizes, two of which had atmospheres, and all of which had colonies and settlements, as did most of the other planets in the Zeta^2 Reticuli system.

But the Zeta Reticuli system was a distant binary, and while Zeta^1 Reticuli was a star similar to its sibling, its system was far less noteworthy. What planets it had were small, mean things, undetectable from Earth by that planet's most sophisticated innate technology, and possessed of little of value save real estate, and that rather less than prime. The one planet of any significant size was remote from all others; it was uninhabited and nearly uninhabitable. Zeta^1 Reticuli had long since boiled away any atmosphere it may have once possessed; it was pockmarked with craters, tidally locked with the star, far too close to Zeta^1 Reticuli for any practical use...

...Save one.

* * *

The three cloaked spacecraft landed on the anti-starward side of the planet, which the Glu'gu'ik called Or'da'sha, in a tight cluster within a small crater in the northern hemisphere.

There were two saucers and one bullet-shaped ship. After nearly an hour of apparent inactivity—not that anyone was watching—a hatch on one saucer opened. It was followed by hatches on the other two spaceships opening.

Eight beings, of five different alien races, emerged, clad in spacesuits of varying sorts.

"Anything?" one of the two Glu'gu'ik asked the other. The second Glu'g'ik waved around a scanner of some sort.

"Nothing," he said.

"Good," the first Glu'g'ik said. "You—the Aves. What do you sense?"

"My name is Trrlpk," the Aves said, offended.

"But we call him Birdy," the Delzantian smirked, "because none of us can pronounce his real name."

"Right," the Glu'g'ik noted. "Birdy, if you please."

The Aves put a gauntleted hand to his helmeted temple and closed his large eyes. After a few moments of silence, he opened his eyes and looked at the lead Glu'g'ik.

"Nothing," he reported. "I detect no sentients other than ourselves anywhere near."

"Good."

"Why are we even here?" the Delzantian grumbled.

"Because this was a likely rendezvous spot," the lead Glu'g'ik declared, "and because I wanted to get a good look at the lot of you before we embark on this little mission."

"And?" the female Zargothian demanded, nose in the air. "Do we meet with your high and mighty scrutiny, oh lord of the Glu'gu'ik?"

"You'll do," the lead Glu'g'ik decided. "Provided you do what you're told, when you're told to do it."

"You have a lot of nerve," she snarled. "I think I'll just..."

"Do what you're told, if you know what's good for you,"

the lead Glu'g'ik noted, calm. "Don't forget what I know. Do you really want that to get around to the proper authorities?"

The female Zargothian abruptly silenced. Several sets of eyes rolled; everyone in the group knew about her proclivities, and it didn't take a genius to guess what kind of information the Glu'g'ik had on her.

"What's in it for you?" the Aves wondered.

"Revenge," the Glu'g'ik told him. "The human Division One Agency has something that rightfully belongs to Va'du'sha'ā. Something that rightfully belongs to ME."

"You weren't kidding," one of the male Zargothians said to the female. "He really is a lord of the Glu'gu'ik."

"Or thinks he is," the female replied, tone dripping scorn. "This one actually thinks he should be Emperor of Va'du'sha'ā. That's how he introduced himself, to get past the security of House Zznndt."

"You don't mean the F'al of Va'du'sha'ā, do you?" Birdy wondered, addressing the Glu'g'ik.

"Indeed. That is precisely what I mean," the lead Glu'g'ik said, drawing himself up to his full height of four feet and a couple of inches. "I am Eb'vuv Ub'he'tae'la, of Clan Ab'ra'kud'un, the direct descendant of the Last Crown, Emperor Ma'dre'le'er."

"Whoopee," one of the Zargothian males muttered, and Eb'vuv shot him an angry glare.

"So? Take it back," the Delzantian said, wagging his head from side to side in his equivalent of a shrug. "Find that...F'al thingie...and go home with it."

"We cannot," Eb'vuv said. "They have hidden it so deeply it cannot be found, even with our quantum senses. And rumor has it that they have a rogue Glu'g'ik of their own, no less a one than a hidden member of the royal stewards, Clan Hou'd'ni, to control it for them."

"I have no idea what you're wabbling on about," the Delzantian complained.

"Never mind," Eb'vuv said, irritated. "At least you have

the answer to your question."

"What about you?" the female Zargothian asked the second Glu'g'ik.

"I'm with him," the other Glu'g'ik shrugged. "We're in this together, he and I."

"My right hand," Eb'vuv remarked with a smirk. "Are you all ready?"

"I suppose," sighed the Botanoid; it was the first thing he had said. "It was fruiting season at home, and I shall have to miss it. But the pay rate is good, as usual. Where do we rendezvous when we arrive in the system?"

"I'll send you the coordinates in a ciphered blip when we drop into normal space inside the Sol system," Eb'vuv noted, and started to turn back toward his ship.

"Payment?" the Aves said, curt, and the Glu'g'ik halted.

"You have already had your deposit," Eb'vuv noted. "I presume you all used it to outfit yourselves for this mission. I don't intend to provide each of you with your own equipment."

Heads nodded.

"Good. You will get the rest upon completion of the mission."

"Which is?" the Delzantian asked.

"Why, the same as it was in Terran 1963," Eb'vuv replied, smug.

Grins spread around the group.

"Let's go," the female Zargothian declared.

They all turned back to their vessels.

* * *

Moments after the last sentient had ingressed and the hatches all closed, the ships vanished.

Slight disturbances, from atmosphere that shouldn't have been there, stirred the soil of Or'da'sha, then died away.

* * *

"...And she WAS in the Mescalero Indian Hospital," Omega told Fox, alone with the Director in his office. "But evidently that's a real small facility, so they've airlifted her to the

Eastern New Mexico Medical Center in Roswell."

Since Echo had decided to go shopping on his own for the morning, a badly-worried Omega had gone straight to Fox's office. It proved to be the perfect opportunity for Omega to see Fox on the sly, and she took it without hesitation.

"Oh, gronk and abdab," Fox murmured, when she finished explaining. "Echo's mother? You're certain?"

"As certain as I'm sitting here, Fox," Omega sighed. "Damn, but I wish I was wrong."

"Merde." Fox raked a hand across his face, disturbed.

"And you didn't know?"

"No, I didn't," Fox said, shaking his head. "I guess we need to keep closer tabs on things like that, for our agents. What kind of cancer is it? Did the article in the tribal newsletter say?"

"Yeah. Pancreatic."

Fox winced.

"Yeah, I know, Fox," Omega agreed, subdued. "That one's got a bad prognosis."

"How far along is she?"

"Well, I'm not sure. The announcement was from not quite three weeks ago—say, seventeen or eighteen Earth days—and indicated that she'd only just been diagnosed. But," Omega added, "I immediately started looking up stuff on pancreatic cancer, and it seems it's awful hard to detect until it gets past a certain point. So if they've detected it, she's already a ways along."

"Exactly. I've talked to Zebra about such things before. Our after-dinner small talk can get technical. And graphic." Fox gave a rueful chuckle. "I expect you and Echo know how that works."

"Oh yeah. I know how THAT goes."

"Now, did the article mention what stage?"

"Yeah. Stage II-B. Whatever that means; I didn't have a chance to look up cancer stages an' related matters yet. And while I got that biology degree, I'm not a physician, let alone an oncologist."

"Mm. I know a bit more, then, from discussions with Zebra—she keeps an eye on me, because of all the shit I was exposed to in the concentration camp, then roaming around Europe as a homeless street kid and the like; it looks as if the various regens Pulgey put me through while I was working for him have taken care of it, but she likes to be careful. So I'm pretty sure what that means is, it's gotten outside the pancreas proper, but hasn't metastasized yet."

"Which means," Omega tried, "that the neighboring organs are starting to be affected, but it hasn't...like, floated around to the lungs or the brain or something?"

"Pretty much. Isn't that your take?"

"I...dunno, really. I was kind of guessing with my answer. For my biology degree, I tended to focus on studying bacteria and viruses and things like that, because that's more in line with what NASA expects to be the first discovery of life elsewhere—never mind the Coalition. I'm afraid I'm just not that familiar with medical stuff, and boy, do I regret it, in this job. I mean, I think that's what it means, but..." Omega shrugged.

"Right. We could use more information," Fox considered. "I'd really like to know how much time she's got left, before I tell Echo about it."

"Well...do you want me to make a quick reconnoiter?" Omega asked. "If you can come up with an excuse to split me off from Echo on an errand for you, maybe a couple days' worth, I can buzz down there, see what I can find out, and come back and report to you."

"I think that's a good idea, Omega. And yes, I believe I can find the cover you need to do it."

* * *

The next morning, after Alpha One had gotten done with their off-duty errands—which had been difficult, given Omega's efforts to keep something from her partner that she didn't truly want to keep from him, but which she knew would cause him pain—as soon as they arrived in the Core, the lighting between the floor tiles began blinking yellow.

"Fox wants us," Omega noted, already knowing more or less why.

"Yup," Echo agreed. "Let's go."

* * *

"There you are," Fox said as Alpha One entered his office. "Echo, this isn't really an assignment for you, but as the department chief, I need your approval for it."

"Huh? What's up, Fox?" Echo wondered.

"I have a little assignment I need to use Omega for," Fox noted. "I'd need to send her away from Headquarters for a day or two. It's nothing dangerous, or I'd send you both. It's really more of an errand than anything."

"Can't you use someone else, Fox?" Echo said, scrunching his face. "I'm expecting that new batch of Alpha Line applications, and as head of training for the department, she's pretty essential to the evaluations..."

"No, zun, I can't," Fox said. "I'm sorry, but I need someone of her skills and abilities."

"What's up, then? What's it all about?" Echo turned to his partner. "Meg? Do you know what this is?"

"Um, I have a suspicion, maybe," Omega said. "Fox, is this that thing you called me in to mention yesterday?"

"Yes, Omega, it is. And Echo, it's a private matter. I'll tell you about it soon, I swear, but for right now, trust me to know that Omega is the best candidate for this errand."

"Can I at least know why it needs my assistant chief?"

"Because it may possibly pertain to the Director's security?" Fox offered. Echo blinked.

"Oh," Echo said then, mollified. "Well, we wanna keep you safe. I guess I'll just hold off evaluating the forms until Meg gets back. When does she need to leave?"

"I was hoping she could grab her kit and head out in the next couple of hours," Fox said. "Omega?"

"Unless there's something Echo needs me to do before I go, I think I can manage that, Fox," Omega agreed.

"No, just the applicants," Echo said. "And that'll wait until you get back."

"Okay. Fox, how do you want me to travel?"

"I have a slot set for you on the maglev, and an Agency car waiting at the maglev station on the other end."

"All right. I'll run back to my quarters and grab my kit bag, then head for Grand Central. Pop the gate info to me on my cell phone."

"Will do."

"See you later, Ace," Omega said, rising from her chair and heading for the door.

Once she was gone, Echo slumped a bit in his chair.

"Easy there, alter khaver," Fox murmured with a grin. "One might almost think you were going to miss her while she's gone."

"No shit," Echo grumbled.

"No, zun, it won't do. You were willing to go off for several WEEKS with the Cortians, and leave HER behind. Now you know what it feels like."

"Yeah, I guess. But I don't have to like it."

"Neither did she."

Echo gazed at the Director thoughtfully.

"Yeah," he finally admitted. "I guess you're right." Then he shrugged. "I won't be doing that, ever again. If it's a mission, Meg goes wherever I go, from now on."

"Good. And don't worry. After all, you'll be taking a nice long vacation together soon." He waved a hand at the door. "Now go get back to it. And thank you for the loan of your partner."

A glum Echo headed for the Alpha Line Room alone.

* * *

In about an hour and a half of swift travel, the maglev took Omega to the Dallas Office, where a loaner vehicle, an Infiniti Q60 duly modified to Agency specs, awaited her. Omega accepted the vehicle, threw her kit in the passenger seat, punched up the Division One version of GPS, and headed out of the

23

Dallas-Fort Worth metroplex, aimed generally west on Interstate 20.

As soon as she got out of the city proper, she took the exit for 'Highway 281/Mineral Wells' and headed north. Once she crossed the Brazos River, she turned onto a gravel ranch road, got well away from the highway, and pulled behind a copse of trees. There, she activated the passive cloaking on the Infiniti, morphed, and took off, headed west.

* * *

It took about four more hours of airborne travel for the morphed Infiniti to reach Roswell, New Mexico from the Dallas-Fort Worth metroplex. Omega arrived around 1pm local time; the first thing she did was to pop by the Agency's Roswell Station to check in and notify Fox that she had arrived in Roswell. Then she ran by a florist's shop to pick up a small bouquet of fresh flowers—she already knew, from past conversations with Echo, that his mother loved flowers of almost any variety, and these were commercially-grown bluebonnets, one of her favorites—and headed straight for the hospital in which Echo's mother lay.

Omega pulled up to the hospital in the loaner car Fox had provided, located a visitor's parking space, and pulled into it. Getting out, she hit the button that activated the VERY special security system on the Infiniti, and headed into the hospital.

A brief query at the reception/information desk sent her to the oncology wing of the hospital, which unlike most big city hospitals, was relatively low and spread out. When she reached the oncology wing, Omega stopped off at the nurse's station, explaining that she was an old friend of Mrs. Bryant's deceased son, and had heard of her illness.

"Oh, that's wonderful," the head nurse remarked. "She hasn't had any visitors, and we've felt bad for her. Thank you for coming by. She's in room 312."

Omega thanked the nurse and headed for room 312.

* * *

When she knocked on the door, Omega heard a faint,

"Come in," from the other side. She opened the door and slipped inside, setting the small vase of flowers on a side table just to the left of the door.

There, in the hospital bed, was a frail older woman. She had high, wide cheekbones, a slightly aquiline nose, and generally strong facial structure—the same structure she had bequeathed to her handsome son—under a deep bronze complexion, slightly weather-beaten skin, and silver-gray hair. Piercing chocolate-brown eyes, so like her son's, gazed at Omega under a prominent, high brow. This was a woman who had been beautiful before cancer struck; now she was wasting away rapidly.

The thick, straight gray hair was long and formerly lush, now somewhat dry and straw-like, reaching partway down her back and at that moment, loose, though the woman's thin hands were endeavoring to braid it with only limited success.

She was relatively tall for a woman, close to but not quite Omega's height, she adjudged; but the ill woman was considerably under weight for her height, a condition Omega presumed to be due to her disease. As their eyes met, Omega smiled.

"Mrs. Bryant? Nalin Bryant?"

"Yes? You are not the nurse..."

"No, I'm not. My name is Meg Blake."

"I am very pleased to meet you, Meg Blake," Mrs. Bryant said, cocking one eyebrow in a quizzical fashion. "But to what do I owe this visit?"

"Oh, I'm an old school chum of Echo's, I mean Alex's," Omega said with a smile. "Everyone called him by his nickname so much, it's still a habit after all this time, I'm afraid. It's been years; I doubt you'd remember me. He and I had a falling out in our senior year, when I started dating a guy on the rival football team."

"Oh dear," Nalin Bryant said with a slight smile, and continued attempting to bring order to her hair, trying to braid it. After a few moments, weary arms dropped back to the bed. Instinctively, Omega reached out and smoothed the other woman's hair, then began to braid it for her. Mrs. Bryant's smile widened, though it remained rueful, in reference to their conversation. "I had forgotten all about that nickname of his. Yes, he was always an excellent mimic, particularly of animal sounds, though he could imitate people's speech patterns almost as well. You say you dated a rival football player? That would have done it, all right. I...do hope you made up the breach, before...well, before he...didn't have a chance to do so."

Omega sobered.

"Yes, ma'am, we did," she murmured, hating to have to lie; hating even more to have caused hurt to the mother of the man she loved more than life. "I understood, and never, um, felt hard at him. We...always got along well, except for that."

"Well, good," Mrs. Bryant decided, allowing the younger woman to work with her hair. "Alex was a good boy. Sometimes a bit too curious for his own good, or anybody else around him, when folks were busy. But he was smart, and a hard worker, and not afraid of responsibility. He...had so much potential." The older woman sighed.

"I know," Omega said, subdued. *And he still is, to all of that,* she added mentally, wishing she could say it. She picked up the hair tie on the tray by the bed, and fastened off the completed braid. "There you are."

"Thank you," Mrs. Bryant said simply. "That is much better. I was constantly getting it tangled, and sitting on it, and whatnot. And your own braid is quite pretty, so I am sure it looks very nice."

"Aw, thanks," Omega said with a smile. Tentatively she covered the other woman's hand with her own, squeezing gently. Nalin Bryant promptly turned that hand palm up and wrapped her fingers around Omega's hand, returning the squeeze.

"You are a nice young woman," Mrs. Bryant decided. "The sort I would have hoped Alex would take notice of, one day."

"Oh! Thank you, ma'am," Omega said, trying not to flush.

"What makes you say that? He already had a girlfriend, if I remember right."

"Yes, and she was nice enough, I guess. Alex liked her," Mrs. Bryant said, "but somehow, I never thought she was the one for him."

"Were they serious?"

"More or less, I suppose, for that age. He intended going to the university, and she did not. But he let me know that, if the relationship held up long enough for him to complete his degree, he would probably come back and marry her, and settle down on our ranchero. But," she sighed, "he never made it to the university."

"Yes, I...I heard about the...incident...that took him from you."

"Ah well. That was many years ago now. Forgive an old, dying woman her moments of melancholy. Surely you are not here to reminisce about my son, long gone as he is," Mrs. Bryant said. "What can I do for you? I am sorry I cannot welcome you more properly," she waved her free hand at the bed in which she lay, "but it seems I may be joining the rest of my family soon."

Omega blinked.

"You sound...like you almost welcome it," she observed.

"Well, in a way, I suppose I do," Mrs. Bryant decided. "James is long gone, and Alex, and even Shitaá..."

"Um, Shitaá?"

"Oh! My father," Mrs. Bryant explained. "Forgive me; I think of him in the Apache language, and I forgot for a moment that you would not know the word. Alex called him Shi-itsooyee."

"Oh yes, I remember that!" Omega exclaimed. "I guess that is an Apache word for 'grandfather,' and Shi- Shitaá," she tried, stumbling over the unfamiliar word, "means 'father'?"

"Just so," Mrs. Bryant confirmed. "But in any case, Ma died long, long ago, when I was a little girl..."

"Ma? I've heard—uh, I used to hear Echo call you that."

"Yes, it is a Lipan word for 'mother.' I suspect it was derived from either English or Spanish, but it is used quite often, as is 'dadí' for father. So it is not...'original'...to the language, I do not believe."

"I see. And you have no siblings?"

"Oh yes," Mrs. Bryant gave a soft, wistful smile, "I have three sisters; but they married, left the reservation, and moved far away. I have not seen or heard from them in many years; not since Shitaá died." She sighed. "I am tired, you see. I have been alone for a long time, now...nearly two decades, really. I have had my work, of course, and I am sad to leave the healing. It has been a blessing to me, as much as to those I treated."

"I'm sure," Omega murmured, gesturing to the older woman to continue, glad to give her the opportunity to reminisce, and gleaning information from her remarks.

"Shitaá was a healer—what you would call a medicine man—and he encouraged me to study Western medicine at the university, since I rather took after him, and he trained me in the various medicine ceremonies in addition to my academic studies," Mrs. Bryant explained. "Then I met Alex's father at university, and James and I fell in love and were married after we both graduated. Shitaá decided to come live with us when I had some minor difficulties during my pregnancy; he tended me and got me through the problem, then stayed to watch Alex grow up and help teach him the Lipan ways—which, I might add, James was very proud of. I cannot speak for other branches of the family, but the Bryants of which James was descended had no problems respecting the ways of the local peoples, though sometimes invaders moved in and caused trouble for everybody, all around."

"You know about the Bryant family history?"

"Yes, yes, James told me a good bit about his family history! Alex had the benefit of a strong Lipan cultural upbringing, AND a strong Celtic Texican upbringing; we thought it would be beneficial, and give him a more open mind and a broader sense of who he is. Unfortunately, the doctor in town was not like that; he was moderately biased against Natives, and when Shitaá began to develop some chronic conditions as he aged—arthritis, pre-diabetes, and such—he found he could not get good treatment, for the doctor gave him short shrift at the best of times. And as a nurse, not a physician, I could only do so much."

"So you urged him to come back here, to the reservation?"

"I did. He had a younger brother alive at the time, you see; my uncle, whose family could assist in his care. And then I came back myself, when I...lost Alex."

"And the brother?"

"Oh, he smoked too much." Nalin Bryant waved a dismissive hand. "Tobacco is a sacred medicine herb, not a thing to be abused. It was a constant bone of contention between Shitaá and Uncle. And so it killed him...AND his wife. The children, like my sisters, scattered to the four winds." She shrugged. "At any rate, since I returned, I have worked at the hospital during the week, and prepared herbal medicines and such on the weekends, for my patients who chose that way. Only," she added sadly, "I cannot do it any more. I no longer have the strength. And thus the last scrap of my life has been taken from me. It is as well. There is nothing anyone can do. I will be glad to see my family again."

"If...some of that...could be returned to you, would you want to try?"

"What do you mean?"

"I, um, I work with a group that does, uh, that develops experimental medical treatments and other such things," Omega hedged. "When I heard that Echo's mom was ill, I mentioned it to my supervisors, and, and well..." She broke off, because she had not actually suggested this to Fox, and wasn't entirely sure how he would react. "I thought you might make a good candidate for an experimental cancer treatment we have. For me, it's, it's kind of a thing to do for Echo, you know, in his memory, sort of. But they—my supervisors—wanted more information. And that's why I'm here—to find out what I can, and see if there's anything we can do for you. I can't promise anything," she noted, glad to find a way not to lie, "'cause I don't even know if you're a candidate yet, but it might just work for you, if you turn out to be a good candidate. Or...it might not." She paused, then met Nalin Bryant's gaze, direct. "Would you be interested in trying?"

"It would eliminate the cancer?"

"If you're a candidate, yes. Almost certainly."

"And I would be able to return to my healing work?"

"You would." *And then some, if Fox will just approve what I have in mind,* she thought.

Mrs. Bryant considered for long moments.

"Well, it will not hurt to try," she decided. "Talk to your supervisors and see if I am a candidate. If I am, and if the treatment works, I will be able to help more people before my time arrives. If it does not, then I will be where I am now. And I am ready to go now, if that is the will of the Creator." She hit the buzzer for the nurse on duty. "Wait, and I will see you have copies of my medical records to take with you."

Chapter 2

"...You want to EUTHANIZE her?!" Fox exclaimed in his office when Omega reported in upon her return. The windows were opaqued, the door closed and locked, and she had debriefed to Fox on Mrs. Bryant's physical and mental states, then proposed her idea. "I'm sorry, Omega. Aside from the fact that Echo would never forgive you, neither Zebra nor Zarnix would be happy with that idea!"

"Oh! No no NO! Oh geez oh geez oh geez!" Omega exclaimed, putting both hands to her head in horror. "It sounds the same! I didn't think about that! No! It's a totally made-up word! No, Fox, youth! 'Youthen'! I meant 'youthen,' like in make younger! Like Pulgey and Doron did for you! I thought, if we brought her in and put her in the regen pod, we could not only heal her cancer, we could shave a few years off, so she feels better and has a little more stamina. Youthen-ize, not euthanize!"

Fox smeared a hand across his face; it was the exact same gesture Echo sometimes used, and a distracted Omega briefly wondered which had picked it up from the other. Then the Director started to laugh.

"Oy! All right, my dear," he finally chuckled. "That was a brief comedy of errors. Thank HaShem it was VERY brief."

"Amen to that!"

"But I'm afraid we still can't do it," Fox sighed, sobering. "If we did it for Echo's mother, then every agent who had a sick family member would want to have them treated. And while Zebra and I have been thinking about how to set up an 'experimental clinic' much as you used in your cover story, we don't have one yet, and haven't even brainstormed all the details. We'd be inundated."

"But Fox—"

"No, Omega. Not even for Echo. I'm sorry. More than I

can say, I am sorry." He drew a deep breath and let it out in a long, sad sigh. "You never heard this, tekhter..."

"Heard what?" Omega said, feigning innocence.

"Right. Now, you might have figured it out anyway, but... given how we met, and the circumstances of our working together, and the fact that Pulgey looked to me to ensure Echo was well-mentored...not to mention my mental and physical age at the time...well, Echo is as near to my own son as I'm ever likely to get, at least in the near future."

"What about you and Zebra...?"

"We've discussed it, I'll admit," Fox confessed, flushing a bit. Omega decided a blushing Fox was cute, though she was careful not to say as much, or even let it show on her face—the only person apt to dislike the appellation more than Echo would be Fox. "And—you're the first to know—she and I are merging our quarters into one, in the next few weeks. We're determining where we want everything now. Once that's done, I plan on shooting a certain bit of paperwork to Pul for approval—since I'm Director for the Division, that approval authority gets bumped all the way up."

"Life partnership?!" Omega exclaimed in delight, clapping her hands.

"Exactly. But that is as between us. Oh, I suppose you can tell Echo. But still, he is the son of my..." he broke off, made a wry face, then continued, "relative youth. Not genetic, of course. But as near as may be, otherwise. So it truly does hurt me to have to turn down your request on his behalf. I know how much it pained him to be separated from his mother, especially so soon after his biological father's death."

"Well, Fox, I have an idea about that," Omega said, "if you'll just hear me out, and be open to the idea."

Fox raised a skeptical eyebrow, and met her gaze with a stern glance.

"I'm listening," he said.

* * *

"She's a nurse?" Fox said, surprised. "I never knew that.

32

How did I never find out that?"

"Not just a nurse, Fox, a nurse practitioner," Omega elaborated. "She even went back and picked up a doctorate in clinical nursing after Echo supposedly died. And she's worked in something like three different fields—gynecology and obstetrics, emergency medicine, and general practice. Plus she's a highly skilled herbalist, and could maybe pull double duty in the chaplaincy, for the agents from southwestern tribes—her father, Echo's grandfather, trained her in most of the spiritual techniques he practiced." Then she played her trump card. "And you know you and Zarnix have been scrambling to build the Medical department back up, even a couple years after the Klydonian invasion though it's been."

"Yes, and it does sound like she would make a promising medtech," Fox agreed. "If she was willing."

"AND...it would give Echo back to her," Omega added. "And her back to Echo."

Fox sat back, astounded.

"My dear girl," he declared, "you may have just killed half a dozen birds with one well-thought-out, beautifully-aimed stone." He reached for his phone. "Let me call bubeleh."

* * *

"I don't know, Fox," Zebra admitted. "It sounds like she's awfully far down the drain already. And we've never had to try setting up the regen fluid composition for cancer before."

"I was farther along than she is," Omega pointed out. "And y'all pulled me outta the drain."

"Yes, but Doron was here then," Zebra noted. "And you didn't have cancer. You just got the hell fried out of you. It was more a case of regrowing parts."

"The technique cured MY cancer, way back when," Fox protested.

"And again, Doron worked on you," Zebra reminded him.

"Bubeleh, don't sell yourself short like this. You are a brilliant physician, or you wouldn't be where you are. And you'll have Zarnix and all of Medical to back you. After all he has given the Agency, isn't it right to at least TRY to do this for Echo?"

"Well, yeah, but..." Zebra sighed, uncertain. "Does he know yet? About his mom?"

Fox glanced at Omega; she shook her head. He sighed.

"No, he doesn't," he said. "Which means we'll have to tell him."

Omega blanched. Fox saw.

"You're afraid to tell him?" the Director wondered.

"Not...afraid, exactly," Omega confessed. "It's just...I don't wanna see the look on his face. In fact, I'm dreading it. He'll be...worried, to say the least."

"And I'm about to make it harder," Zebra said, unhappy.

"How so, bubeleh?"

"I don't want you to tell him that we're gonna try to re-gen her," Zebra declared. "I can't come close to guaranteeing a good outcome, let alone a successful one, and I don't want Echo to get his hopes up, only to have her die anyway, despite all we can do."

"So...all we can tell him is, 'Your mom has cancer, and she's dying'?" Omega asked, patently horrified.

"Yes."

"That's the only condition under which you'll try it?" Fox asked, also shocked.

"Right." Zebra was upset, herself, but firm on the matter. "If you want me to try this, Echo can't know I'm doing it."

Fox and Omega stared at each other.

"Oy vey," Fox murmured.

"That," Omega agreed. "Lotsa that."

* * *

"...And here's the information I need you to find out," Zebra said. "Stick your tablet over here."

Fox fished his tablet out of a pocket—Omega had long since decided that he'd been the one to introduce Echo to warp pockets, though Echo had evidently developed it to a fine art—and extended the electronic device in hand; Zebra lightly bumped her own tablet to it.

"There. That file has the list of questions I need answered, along with check boxes and text blocks for you to fill out," she told him. "Fill it out as you ask her, it'll relay back to me, and I'll have the completed file by the time you finish interviewing her."

"You are on top of things as usual, bubeleh," Fox murmured, opening the file and studying it. "And should I not understand something?"

"Text me on the fly. I'll be sitting here watching the data come in, 'cause I've got an alert on it. Let me know the day and the approximate time you expect to see her, and I'll be sitting at my desk, staring at the screen, waiting."

"Got it," Fox decided. "Tomorrow, Omega?"

"We can do that," Omega agreed. "Maybe you oughta pop Echo a message, letting him know you're using me again."

"You can't tell him why!" Zebra exclaimed, throwing out a warning hand.

"No, no, my dear," Fox soothed. "We already set up a little cover story, when Omega went to reconnoiter the situation."

"Oh? What did you tell him?" a curious Zebra wondered. Omega grinned hugely, and the physician blinked, uncertain. "Uh-oh. I dunno if I like the looks of that..."

"Let us just say that, of the entire Agency, these two know about our upcoming paperwork," Fox said, flushing. "And the cover story is that Omega has been working for me on the pretext of planning for that."

"Oh," Zebra said, joining her lover in turning red-faced. "Well, okay. You two are as near family as we've got, I guess."

"Exactly, bubeleh." Fox agreed. "And they aren't going to tell anyone until we are ready to do so."

"Right," Omega verified. "It's okay, Zebra, I swear. Your secret is safe with me, and I haven't even told Echo yet—so far, I haven't needed to, though I expect that to change at some point. Now, Fox, let's get Echo notified that he's on his own again tomorrow, and then we can start lining up some other stuff."

"On it," Fox said, already setting up the travel arrangements on his tablet.

* * *

"Mrs. Bryant?" Omega said, knocking on the hospital room door just before peering in. "Mrs. Bryant, it's Meg Blake. Are you awake?"

"Mm, what? Oh, yes dear, I'm awake," Mrs. Bryant said, perking up and turning her attention from the television, which was muted. "Please come in."

Omega slipped inside, then went to Bryant's side and gave her a gentle hug. Mrs. Bryant smiled and hugged her in return, though her grip was feeble.

"Mrs. Bryant, I have someone I'd like you to meet," Omega told the older woman. "He's my supervisor, Mr. Fritz Aufteilung. He's waiting just outside in the hall. May I ask him in?"

"By all means."

Omega turned and motioned through the partly-open door, and Fox entered the room.

"Hello, Mrs. Bryant," he murmured, offering a hand. The ill woman took it and shook. "I'm very pleased to meet you. Ms. Blake, here, has spoken a great deal about you and your family, very highly I might add, and I'm glad that we may have the opportunity to help you."

"Yes, this experimental procedure," Mrs. Bryant recalled. "I have some questions I'd like to ask, and I'm sure you need more information for your screening procedures..."

* * *

"All right. You're not claustrophobic, you aren't afraid of water," Fox enumerated, working on the form on his tablet. "You have no support structure left other than your team of doctors and nurses."

"And me," Omega murmured, and Mrs. Bryant smiled slightly.

"Yes, my dear, and thank you for that."

"And you say you have had no other chronic or pre-existing conditions, until the cancer caused blood sugar issues?"

"That's correct," Mrs. Bryant confirmed. "It rather seems as if everything has gone haywire since, but I had had my annual physical not six months prior to discovering the cancer, and everything appeared to be fine at that time. Blood pressure excellent, stress test good, carotid sonogram clear, colonoscopy fine." She shook her head. "And then the bottom fell out."

Fox used his stylus to scribble notes on the electronic form, aware that Zebra was reading it back at Headquarters as soon as he could spell out the words.

"No diabetes, pre-diabetes, pre-existing renal insufficiency, cardiovascular or coronary artery disease?"

"No, sir. Not that anyone is aware of, at least."

Fox x'ed NO on each line.

"What medications are you on? How long have you been on them?"

"I haven't been on any medications until this."

"Chemotherapy?"

"We are trying to determine the best course of action," Mrs. Bryant said. "Dr. Begay thinks I should try a combination of chemo and radiation, with some palliative care to help support me through it, though I am pushing for surgery to remove as much of the diseased tissue as possible, first."

"So you haven't started on a formal treatment as yet?" Omega asked.

"No," Mrs. Bryant affirmed. "It really has not been that long since the cancer was detected, even less time since it was verified, and the insurance has been...difficult."

"Oh, I see," Omega murmured, shooting a worried glance at Fox.

"I know," Mrs. Bryant sighed. "It should have been started already."

"No, that's really very good for our purposes," Omega explained. "The chemotherapy could actually interfere with our treatment, effectively poisoning it. That was one thing we were very concerned about."

"Huh," Mrs. Bryant grunted. "I suppose there is a positive side to everything."

"Do you understand the nature of your disease, the stage, the side effects of the various treatments, and what is required of you?" Fox continued the questioning.

"Oh, yes." She gave them a wry grin. "I have worked with oncology patients before. I'm quite aware of the situation...and its probable outcome."

"Are you willing to follow our instructions for the clinical trial we are proposing?"

"Whatever I need to do."

Fox glanced up at Omega and nodded, pleased.

"That's all we need from you, Mrs. Bryant," he told her. "Now what questions do you have?"

* * *

A few minutes of discussion, and a couple of text message queries to Zebra, served to put paid to Nalin Bryant's questions and concerns.

"Anything else?" Omega wondered.

"No, I can think of nothing at the moment," Mrs. Bryant said, running a hand over her hair, in a gesture very similar to the way Echo sometimes raked his fingers through his own hair. "I'm sure I'll think of something else..."

"That won't be a problem," Fox noted. "We'll make sure to leave contact information in case you have further questions. Now, may we speak to your principal physician?"

* * *

"No, there's very little we can do, at this point," Dr. Yazzie Begay noted. "Since the cancer has already spread outside the pancreas, removal of that organ doesn't really get us very far, though we'll probably do it anyway—surgically excise as much of the diseased tissues as we can get. We have been weighing the options of chemo versus radiation treatments, but if you have a clinical trial she qualifies for, which looks promising and would produce less post-procedure sickness, that's a definite option, too. To be honest, I'm a little concerned about her ability to come through either radiation or chemo, because of the after-effects. I'm sure you've noticed, Ms. Blake, how frail she's grown."

"Yes, I had," Omega said. "I...remember...her as much stronger and more robust."

"Exactly. Pancreatic tumors are notoriously difficult to detect, and usually by the time they're symptomatic, things are pretty far along. And that's what happened with Mrs. Bryant."

"Dr. Begay, while I'm not a physician myself, my...work... ensures that I am reasonably fluent in medical matters," Fox offered smoothly; in point of fact, it was his relationship with Zebra that ensured said fluency. "And I assume the role of the pancreas in blood glucose regulation, and the subsequent effects of the cancer, is the main reason for her weakened physical condition?"

"In large measure, yes," Begay agreed. "When the nutrients aren't being properly handled by the body, then the body suffers. The fact that there are starting to be some other organs involved, all in the digestive system, isn't helping that situation at all."

"Mm," Fox said, annotating the electronic form on his tablet to ensure Zebra got that information.

"Can I ask what sort of treatment you're offering?" Begay wondered. "I could better advise you, and her, if I knew."

"I'm sure you'll understand that details are proprietary," Fox said. "But the general concept is an attempt at restructuring the cells, beginning at the genetic level. It's an effort to reverse the mutations that caused the cells to become cancerous in the first place."

"Wow, that's some seriously advanced biochem," Begay decided, eyebrows flying upward. "And have you had much success with it?"

"Yes, we've treated several patients successfully," Fox allowed. "Offhand, I don't have the statistics on it, because the doctors are holding matters close to their vests until the research papers come out..."

"Oh, right; I get that," Begay said with a nod. "That sounds really promising, then, and just the sort of treatment that I've long wanted to see developed. But I thought it was gonna be science fiction for some decades yet."

"No, we're developing it here and now," Omega declared. "I'm really proud to be associated with the organization doing it."

"And we're glad to have you in our organization, Meg," Fox said with a slight smile; he and his Agent had just communicated appreciation to each other, completely honestly, without the physician having a clue that they were NOT talking about a biomedical research firm.

"Well, then what I think I'll advise Mrs. Bryant is that she enter your clinical trial, and if that doesn't work, or isn't fully successful, we can bring her back and do a round of radiation, and maybe follow it up with chemo," Begay decided. "Do you know when you'll have a feel for whether she's a good candidate?"

"Within a few days," Fox said, "well less than a week. Likely in the next day or two. I've already emailed the information to the physician in charge, Dr. Zelda Giatros, and she'll be reviewing it as we speak."

"Very good. We'll wait to hear from you, then."

* * *

Back at Headquarters, Fox and Omega stopped off at Medical before going anywhere else.

"I don't know yet," Zebra told them before they had a chance to ask. "I'm still reviewing the information you two got...which was positively exhaustive, Fox. You done good, sweetheart."

"I do try," Fox noted. "And our various ongoing conversations in recent years have helped that, because now I know more than any diplomat or bureaucrat rightly ought to, about medical matters."

"Well, you're really brilliant, honey, and I rubbed off,"

Zebra said, allowing herself a small smile, though her forehead was still puckered in worry. "So I'm not at all surprised. Now, have you two told Echo about his mom?"

"No," Omega exhaled the word.

"Then don't you think you ought to go do that?"

"Come with me to my office, Omega," Fox decided, "and let's figure out how we're going to do this."

* * *

A bit of planning between Omega and Fox in his office—with the windows opaqued—resulted in the decision for the revelation to come from Fox exclusively, with Omega feigning ignorance of the situation, and providing emotional support for her partner.

"What he'll let me give, at any rate," she said, morose. "I know exactly what he'll do. He'll turn white, go all monosyllabic on us while he gives you whatever info he thinks you'll need, then bottle it all up and hold us at a distance."

"Most likely," Fox agreed. "Still, he may surprise you, mayn teyere. The two of you are quite close, and—you may not fully realize this—he thinks the world of you, my dear." It was as broad a hint as Fox dared, in the circumstances.

"Maybe," Omega hedged, but he saw her slight flush. "I still don't think he's gonna let me in far enough to help much."

"More than you may think, or be aware. I have known him since the beginning of this formal organization, Omega, and he was barely more than a boy then; I've watched him grow and mature, and I know what kind of man he is now, and what helps him, and what hurts. So please believe me when I say that you are good for him."

"I try," she sighed.

"You DO," Fox corrected. "Now, run on to see him. I'll call Alpha One in for the notification in a few hours. Try to act surprised, when I do."

"All over it, Boss," she murmured, rising and leaving his office.

* * *

41

The Alpha Line Room was empty of all but Echo when Omega entered it. He was sitting at his desk in the corner, doing paperwork, but when she entered, he laid it down and focused his attention on her with patent curiosity.

"What the hell are you and Fox up to?" he wondered. "Sending you off on 'errands' alone, or going with you, gone for a day or two at a go, and barely back for a few hours in between..." He shook his head. "And not telling me a word."

"Oh," Omega said, and initiated the cover story she and Fox had devised. "I thought he'd have told you already. Maybe he's just embarrassed; Fox can get cute when he's embarrassed, only it's so rare to see him like that. Just don't tell him I said that! He actually blushed when he told me, and he needed my help."

"Told you WHAT?"

"I wonder if I should—wait, he said I could tell you, but nobody else," she remembered. "So you gotta not tell ANYBODY."

"All right, I swear I won't tell anybody else...what?" Echo responded instantly. "What is he up to?"

"Okay, he and Zebra are...well, they're not 'tying the knot' so much as signing the paperwork..."

"Life partners?" Echo exclaimed, pleased. "That's great! But what do you have to do with it?"

"Several things, actually," Omega said. "First off, they're trying to merge their quarters, and he's trying to understand some of her wants and needs in that respect."

"Okay, a woman's touch," Echo said, nodding.

"Right. Second, he wants to get her a...huh. I guess we'll call it a wedding present. Kind of like how Romeo had me helping him pick out India's Christmas present last year."

"Oh, I get it. So yet more of a case of, 'trusted woman friend giving advice.'"

"Yup. And last of all, he wants a private retreat for 'em someplace. But because he's the Director, and she's the assistant chief of Medical, it has to be a really secure location, with fast, easy access, and very VERY private. So," Omega shrugged, grinning, "since Alpha Line's chief is too busy and too important to send out on something like that, the assistant chief gets to play real estate agent."

* * *

"That's...a cool idea," Echo decided, wondering if he and Omega might one day make similar plans. "So...am I supposed to know any of this? Like, you said that HE said you could tell me about the life partnership, but what about the rest?"

"Um, like I said, he told me I could tell you...pretty much all of it, as I understood it," Omega said, sitting down at her own desk. "But when he gets around to telling you himself... eh. Maybe act surprised, a little bit."

"Got it."

"Hand me that new batch of Alpha Line applications, and I'll get 'em organized for you, like I promised before I headed out the first time."

"Okay." Echo handed over the rather hefty stack. "I'm probably not gonna do much with 'em at this point until we get back from our vacation, though."

"All right, I can live with that. But I can still go ahead and get 'em organized."

* * *

Huh, Echo thought, as he turned back to his paperwork. *That's an odd sort of thing for Fox to ask Meg to do. And a bit out of character for the Fox I know. I wonder if there's something she isn't telling me. Meg and Fox would...MEG and FOX. No, surely not. Especially not if that bit about a life partnership were true. And why would they use that for a cover for an affair? If it got back to Zebra, she'd KNOW it wasn't true. Nah.* Echo mentally shook his head, hard. *And as well as I know both of those two, Fox and Meg, no way would they pull a stunt like that. Not behind people's backs. Not when Meg knows Zebra loves Fox, and Fox knows I love Meg. Even if there was attraction there, and I haven't seen ANY sign of it, neither of 'em would act on it. Get a grip, Echo.* He drew a deep breath.

On the other hand, I DO have a birthday coming up. And she knows it. I wouldn't put it past Meg cooking up a surprise, and roping Fox into helping her execute it. In which case, it's FOX covering for MEG, not the other way 'round. And THAT... would be in character for both of 'em. I kinda hope she doesn't, though. I think I'd rather not have a big deal made out of it. He glanced at her briefly, looking for any indication that he'd hit on the solution.

But if she WAS planning something, Omega gave him no sign.

* * *

Two hours after they went to the deli down the street for second lunch, the summons arrived from Fox.

Omega felt her gut clench, but slapped a nonchalant expression on her face, thankful for her old community theater experience, back in the days when she'd had time for such hobbies. Then she rose and followed Echo across the Core, toward the ramp to Fox's office.

Oh man, she thought, dread wrapping about her like a cloak. *This isn't gonna be any kind of fun. Watching Echo internalize all that pain? I'm already hurting for him, and he doesn't even KNOW yet. Then again, I wouldn't want to see him vent all that pain, either, because it'd tell me exactly how bad it really is; he just doesn't DO that! Dammit. I'd rather it was another mission with the Cortians than this.*

* * *

A very pale Echo listened in shocked silence as Fox outlined his mother's condition and prognosis. Omega watched, saying nothing, simply taking in her partner's pain and trying to avoid flinging her arms around him in a hug, knowing that she would certainly lose it if she did, and afraid that it would cause him to lose it as well. *And I don't think any of us could handle THAT,* she thought, seeing the tautness in Fox's face, knowing it was reflected in her own.

Finally, Fox finished the litany of symptoms and likely disease progression. He paused, and Omega could see the sympathetic pain on the older man's face, as well. But Fox very deliberately avoided meeting her eyes; neither of them was comfortable with the omission they were being forced to make, but they also understood Zebra's reluctance to negate that omission.

So we press on, and do the best we can with what we got, Omega thought.

"Zun? Are you handling this all right?" Fox asked then, watching Echo's face, drawn in pain he was trying hard to hide...but not quite succeeding, at least not with these two.

Anybody else in the entire Agency isn't gonna see what we see, Omega realized. *Other than the fact he's pale—which would be expected, given the situation—he would just look like he was determined to get through it.*

"Yeah, Fox."

Monosyllables, she thought, increasingly worried. *Exactly like I was afraid of. He's pulling in.*

"What do you want to do about the situation?" Fox pressed.

"What is there to d—?" Echo began, but his voice suddenly cracked, and he stopped. The Alpha Line chief dropped his gaze to the floor, staring, unseeing; then he closed his eyes, and simply sat there for long moments. When his shoulders slumped, Omega bit her lip.

Fox and Omega exchanged pained glances. He waved a hand at her, as if to say, *Do something.*

Omega shrugged and shook her head. *What can I do?*

Fox sighed soundlessly and shook his own head. *I don't know.*

Omega returned her attention to Echo, studying him, knowing him too well to think the pain did not run deep. As much as she felt for him, she could not help but feel his pain as well, and it was in that moment that she reacted on instinct.

Echo's hands were resting on his thighs as he sat in the visitor chair across the desk from Fox, and as matters had become clear to him—when he had realized his mother was dying, and he was powerless to help, or to stop it—those hands had balled into fists. *White-knuckled fists, at that,* she noted.

Now Omega, without conscious thought, reached out and covered his near hand with her own, letting her hand fit itself to the contours of his fist, offering what comfort she had to give. The gesture sent a message—*You're not alone; I'm here. I care. I'll stick with you.*

Echo reacted to that soft touch. The tight, hard fist melted, his hand opening to wrap around hers, holding it in a fierce, strong grip. He drew in a sudden, deep breath, and let it out in something that sounded vaguely like a choked-off dry sob, or perhaps only a hiccup. Then he nodded once without looking up, squeezed her hand briefly, and managed to force out the statement he had aborted moments earlier.

"What is there to do, Fox?"

"I can arrange for you to go see her, one last time, alter khaver. And you wouldn't have to brain-bleach her, or make up a cover story this time."

"I...hm. It's a thought," he considered.

He opened his eyes, but still did not look up, merely continued staring at the floor with that same unseeing gaze; Omega had a strong suspicion that memories were flitting past those chocolate-brown eyes. But he also kept holding her hand in that same fierce grip.

"I can go with you, if you want me to," Omega breathed. "Or not. It's your call. I'm here for you, Ace, however you need me to be. Whatever you want me to do."

* * *

He squeezed her hand again and nodded, but did not speak, and he didn't try to look at her. *I don't dare,* he thought. *One look at those big blue eyes of hers, and the sympathy and caring there, an' I'll lose it. There's no telling what I'd say or do. Babble like an idiot, most likely. Cry like a baby, maybe. None of it is a good plan right now. Especially given I'm supposed to be Mr. Alpha Line Chief Badass. I need to hold it together as much as I can. But...damn. When she took my hand, it was... it was like I suddenly got stronger, somehow. Maybe that's...*

46

what having a spouse is about, kinda. At least partly. I wish Meg really—

"Echo?" he heard Fox's voice, seeming to come from a distance, interrupt his musings. "What do you want us to do, zun? Shall I set up an opportunity for you to visit your mother one more time?"

Briefly Echo envisioned his mother's shock and delighted surprise at discovering her son, alive, healthy, a strong adult in a secret organization, taking care of the entire planet...and more. And suddenly his mind envisioned that powerful shock causing her already-weakened bodily systems to crash, as his mother died in his arms before he could say another word. He very nearly gasped in horror.

"What's wrong?" Omega asked in alarm.

"No-nothing," he got out. "I just...it just hit me, how big a shock it would be to her, seeing me after all this time thinking I was dead. And," he added, "I think maybe I better not go see her, Fox. That kind of shock...if she's as weak as you say, it might...it might..."

For some reason, the phrase, "kill her," simply would not come out of his mouth. For that matter, it would barely form in his brain.

* * *

It was Omega's turn to squeeze Echo's hand.

"It's okay, Ace," she murmured. "I'm gonna stick close by you through all this. And if you change your mind, we'll go see her. I don't have to go in with you, if you don't want me to, but I can and will stand guard while you see her, if you decide you DO want to."

"I know, baby," he breathed. "Right beside me through thick and thin, like always."

"Yup. If that's where you want me to be."

"It is."

"Good. So...do you wanna go see her? We can take India or something, just in case..."

"No, I think—much though I hate it—I want Ma to have

47

as much time left as she can, to...to do what needs doing. Getting her affairs in order an' stuff. And that means me not showing up and shocking her." Echo finally looked up at his partner. "But you know what?"

"What?"

"I think I REALLY need that vacation now."

"Yeah, hon," Omega sighed, "I think we both do."

"Then go wind up what you need to," Fox told them. "You've only got 'til the end of this work period, anyway, and that's just a few more days. And get me whatever destination you've settled on. I'll set things up for you if you need me to. Echo, I'll have an open file on your mother, and I'll keep an eye on things. If there's anything I need to know...?"

"Call me," Echo said simply. "Off the top of my head, I dunno what might come up, or I'd tell you now. And...keep me posted."

"Of course."

* * *

The next morning, Omega slipped down to the medlab, on the pretext of helping Zebra and Fox work out negotiating some housing details. Fox met her there, and they closeted themselves in Zebra's office. Omega placed a call to the hospital, requesting Mrs. Bryant's room, and she was patched straight through. Echo's mother answered.

"Hello?"

"Hello, Mrs. Bryant. This is Echo's old friend, Meg Blake," Omega said.

"Ah yes, I remember. Thank you for getting back with me. Do you have word?"

"I do," Omega answered. "My supervisor, Fritz, is here, too, and the doctor."

"Good morning, Mrs. Bryant," Fox said. "The word is good. We cannot guarantee anything, but you appear to be a good candidate for our procedure, and we will gladly take you into our program."

"What insurance do you accept?"

"Oh, don't worry about that," Fox said. "There will be no fee. I will see to it that you have proper paperwork to that effect, duly signed and dated. For us, this is about saving lives. You do understand it is something of an experimental procedure?"

"Yes, Mr. Aufteilung, I do." Mrs. Bryant's voice sounded firm, as if her decision had been made.

"Then Mrs. Bryant, let me introduce your physician for the clinical trial, Dr. Zelda Giatros," Fox said, nodding at Zebra.

"Hello, Mrs. Bryant," Zebra said. "This is Dr. Giatros. I'm looking forward to meeting you."

"As am I."

"We'll come to transfer you to our facility the day after tomorrow," Zebra said. "That will give you and your doctors there some time to get all the appropriate paperwork handled."

"That sounds excellent. I hope your procedure will help me somewhat. I do not have hopes of full healing, you understand; I am a nurse of some experience, and I know the realities of what I face. But if you can extend my life a few more years, so that I can be of service to others, it would be a good thing, I think. If you cannot, I am accepting of my fate, so all is well, either way."

"Then I'll see you at 10 a.m. the day after tomorrow, with Mr. Aufteilung," Zebra said.

"Meg? Will you be coming with them?" Mrs. Bryant wondered.

"No, ma'am, not this time," Omega said. "I'm afraid I couldn't shake loose from other commitments. But I'll try to come by your room, once you've arrived."

"I look forward to it."

"We'll see you then," Fox said. "Goodbye, Mrs. Bryant."

"Goodbye, Mr. Aufteilung."

* * *

One full Division day later, Omega got a brief text on her cell phone from Fox.

Gift arrived.

> *Roger. Need me for the delivery?*

Negative. All under control.

Omega glanced at Echo where he sat at his desk, working on the computer, then turned back to evaluating the applicants for Alpha Line.

* * *

"This is a very unusual medical facility," Nalin Bryant noted, as Zebra saw her settled into a room in the medlab. "I have never seen anything like it."

"That's because it's not like anything you've ever seen before, Mrs. Bryant," Zebra told her, as Fox entered the room. "Oh, there you are, hon."

"And well timed, by the sound," Fox said. "Mrs. Bryant, there are a few things you need to know, and a proposition we'd like to put before you."

"What? This sounds...odd," Mrs. Bryant murmured, perturbed.

"It is, a bit," Fox admitted. "I'm afraid we approached you under a bit of a false flag, but we do have your well-being at heart, I promise you. As well as that of your son, Echo."

"My son has not been a concern in many years, Mr. Aufteilung. The dead do not raise concerns."

"Well, that's just the point," Fox said, shooting a wary look at Zebra, who nodded behind the other woman's back, ready for any adverse reaction. "Your son isn't dead."

"WHAT?! How dare you??" Mrs. Bryant was incensed.

"Calm down, Mrs. Bryant," Zebra murmured, injecting a small dose of mild sedative into the IV, as well as a galactic pharmaceutical that would help the sick woman withstand the shock of the revelation that was coming. "Let him explain. This...gets complicated."

Annoyed and perturbed, Nalin Bryant shook her head.

"Very well. I'm listening. But it had best be good."

* * *

"...Oh, dear God," Mrs. Bryant murmured, nearly a quarter of an hour later, staring at the identification photo of Echo that Fox had given her. "And you mean to tell me that my boy is still alive, and working for you in this...organization?"

"He is," Fox averred. "That's him, right there. That photo isn't more than six months old."

"Yes, that's him! Oh! He is so handsome! He looks a lot like James, but also like Shitaá, when he was young and I was small. May I see him?!"

"Not yet," Zebra soothed. "He's been made aware of your illness, but has been afraid to visit you, for fear of what the shock might do, your finding out he was still alive. And in your condition, that's a valid concern. That's why we waited to tell you until I could ensure you had medication to keep you from stressing while we explained."

"Then how do I know what you say is true?" Mrs. Bryant declared, still skeptical. "This photograph could be faked." She tossed the printed image onto the bedclothes.

Zebra touched the intercom on the wall.

"Zarnix, could you grab Dr. Rglfrz and come to Mrs. Bryant's room for a few moments?"

"Certainly, Zebra. Are we having a bit of a problem convincing her?"

"Exactly."

"We'll be there momentarily."

While Zebra was having that conversation, Fox pulled out his electronic tablet and began to work on it. After a few moments, he handed it to Nalin Bryant.

"Here," he said. "I told you that Echo headed up a department, the Alpha Line special forces department. Here is the department office, as viewed through one of our security cameras; I'm sure you'll recognize the man at the corner desk."

Mrs. Bryant took the tablet Fox proffered and stared at the live video on the screen, complete with a small timestamp in the corner to demonstrate its current activity, then gasped. There was no audio to go with it, but an obviously-living Echo sat there; it was equally obvious he was working at a computer.

Other Agents came and went in the frame, occasionally reporting to Echo, sometimes getting paperwork from him and carrying it away, sometimes handing over paperwork. Several came by to get coffee from the pod brewer on the credenza along the back wall, and apparently offer greetings. On the other end of the back wall was a second desk; a familiar woman with a long, platinum-blonde braid sat there, her back to the camera.

"What...I mean...is that...?" Mrs. Bryant tried, staring at the blonde woman.

Just then the woman turned, rolled her desk chair across the room, and handed a stack of papers to Echo, who nodded, smiled, and accepted them. She smirked and said something to Echo, who laughed, shook his head, and put the stack of papers on the corner of his desk.

"It is! That's Meg Blake!" Mrs. Bryant exclaimed.

"Well, that's the name she used, and a lot of the agents—including Echo—do nickname her Meg," Fox confirmed. "But her code name is Omega. She's Echo's partner. It was her idea to do this...for you, and for him."

"She got him to laugh," Zebra observed.

"Yes, she did, Zebra," Fox agreed. "I saw that, and am glad to see it. We both felt that might be good for him. She and I had a talk, and she is trying her best to keep his spirits up. He's very worried about his mother, because he doesn't know she's here, or that you're working on her. And Omega...is very worried about HIM."

"Aw," Mrs. Bryant breathed.

* * *

Just then, Zarnix came in with Dr. Rglfrz, a Kardorian physician temporarily assigned to Division One Headquarters for an exchange of medical techniques.

Zarnix, being a Chesharilzi, sported his normal bright purple hair, orange eyes, and slightly blue-tinged skin. At a glance, he was simply an eccentric human with a taste for odd hair dye. However, a keen observer would also have noticed that his large eyes were somewhat wider-set than the average human, his jaw slightly longer, mouth a bit wider, his ears a little more pointed. The overall effect was somewhat elf-like; there was speculation among the anthropologists in the Sciences department that some of the myths of fae beings—most notably, the Tuatha de Danann—might have been based on the earliest Chesharilzi visitors to Earth.

Rglfrz, like most Kardorians, looked like nothing so much as a long-armed velociraptor; his skin was brightly colored and patterned in shades of red, orange, and green, and his skull, neck, and upper back were adorned with a spiky, pinfeather-like plume of brilliant blue. A powerful tail extended from beneath the lab coat he wore; his scrubs were especially tailored to permit the extra appendage, as well as to fit his long arms and thick, powerful legs appropriately.

"Oh, dear Lord!" Mrs. Bryant exclaimed, staring at the pair. "I...don't know what to say."

"Say what you are thinking," Zarnix declared, and Rglfrz nodded agreement. "We understand what you are dealing with, and we fully expected this, Rglfrz, Zebra and I. You will not offend us."

"Well, it wasn't very diplomatic, but what almost came out was, 'Neither of you is human, are you?'" Mrs. Bryant said, a slightly sheepish grin on her face. The expression reminded the others strongly of Echo.

"No, we are not," Rglfrz said, cheerful. "And that is fine by us. The more we all know about the different peoples of the galaxy, the better we are able to help everyone."

* * *

The two alien physicians chatted a bit more with Mrs. Bryant, who admired Zarnix's hair and Rglfrz's plume, then went back to their rounds; Zebra and Fox returned their attention to Bryant.

"So, are you more convinced now?" Fox wondered.

"Yes," Mrs. Bryant said, with a firm nod. "But I still cannot yet see my son face to face, and speak with him?"

"Well, like I was saying earlier," Zebra noted, "he doesn't

know you're here, because we weren't sure if we could get everything lined up to do this. And I think..."

"That he would be upset even more to see me in my current condition," Bryant noted, shrewd and self-aware. "I know that I have deteriorated rapidly in the last month."

"I wasn't going to say so," Zebra confessed, "but you do look rather frail, and I'm betting that's NOT your normal state, what with your professional history. So what do you say that we get you as well as we can, as quickly as we can, and then surprise him?"

"Oh, I think that sounds like a good plan," Mrs. Bryant said with a wobbly smile. "And...you would like for me to work in this facility, once I am well?"

"This facility, or whatever one of the Division One Offices you choose, if you had rather be closer to home," Fox confirmed. "There is even a small station in Roswell, not so far from the reservation...though that might be bad, in case someone recognized you and put two and two together."

"I'm betting we could figure out a way to make it work, Fox," Zebra said. "It could get a little complicated, but we could, for instance, have her working for us at the Roswell Station because she survived the experimental procedure and got better. Or she could be her own distant cousin, or something."

"Yes, but she would have to walk a fine line, bubeleh, remembering not to let out the nature of the work she will do for us. Even Echo, our top Agent, thought that was a pain in the tokhes. And he only did it for a few months."

"True. But since she's apt to look younger when we're done, she could be that distant cousin."

"Still risky. We'd need to set up an identity, complete with history, for said cousin."

"Yeah. Besides, here, she could see Echo more often." Zebra nodded.

"Would I be working under you?" Mrs. Bryant asked Zebra.

"Quite probably, at least initially," Zebra said with a smile.

"And I'm what you might call the deputy chief of staff for the Medical department, so even if we were to assign you to a different physician, I'd still be here."

"And you say this Meg person is my son's partner?"

"That's right," Fox said. "Her code name is Omega, as I think I mentioned earlier; but Echo often calls her Meg, as do several of the other Agents she's close to. She's one of my top agents, second only to your son. Between them, I can't count how many times they've saved cities, countries, and a few times, the entire planet. Not to mention prevented at least one interstellar war from breaking out. The two of them truly make an amazing team."

Nalin Bryant's jaw dropped slightly at the enumeration, and she paused to consider for long moments. Finally she looked up at the two of them.

"Then," she decided, "I think you have a deal."

"Excellent," Fox declared with a smile. "Zebra, please prepare our newest medtech for the regeneration chamber."

"On it, Fox," Zebra averred.

* * *

Omega dropped down to the medlab on the pretext of restocking Alpha One's supply of Rejuvic, the all-purpose healing solution that, Fox had finally revealed a couple of months earlier, had been loosely based on the Edeptan healer Doron's regeneration fluid from years ago. As much as the pair tended to use it to doctor what they called their 'boo-boos' after a mission, Echo had no problems with his partner ensuring they had a fresh supply before heading out on vacation.

Echo's mother was in her hospital room in the bed, as Zebra and several medtechs hovered around her, preparing her to enter the regen pod later that afternoon. Mrs. Bryant looked up and smiled as the door opened.

"Hello, Omega," she greeted the Agent. "I want to thank you for this incredible opportunity."

"Hi there, Mrs. Bryant," Omega said, beaming. "I'm so glad not to have to fudge my back story around you any more!"

55

They laughed.

"Well, but I can now understand why you did so," Mrs. Bryant said, waving a hand around her. "At first, I thought that I had gotten in with some crazy people, or perhaps a scam, insurance fraud or the like, when Zebra and Fox initially began to explain! But I have now seen a good deal of the equipment, and Zebra has introduced me to some of your, um, I think the term is 'offworld' physicians, and I know it for truth now."

"Yup, it's pretty cool," Omega agreed. "I used to work for NASA; I was an astronaut and astronomer, and what I'm doing now is what I always dreamed of doing."

"And you really are my son's partner?"

"I really am. And later on, I can introduce you to another of his past partners, who wound up getting injured and falling in love with his doctor, so now THEY'RE partners, and I work with Echo."

"How many has he had?"

"Three. His first, the guy who took him under his wing when he first got sucked into the Agency, was code-named X-ray, and they worked together for...I dunno, twelve, maybe fifteen years or so. But X-ray died a few years ago, in a fight with an alien criminal. He and Fox did their best to mentor your son, and look out for him, until he was experienced enough to do it for himself. If you mention him to Echo, go easy; he still grieves X-ray a little bit."

"Ah. That is good information to have. Thank you. I would not hurt him for anything, especially after so long apart."

"Are you mad at him for that?"

"No; I think I understand better, now. Though if I am honest, I have some emotions to work through about it," Mrs. Bryant confessed.

"That's understandable. Are you ready for the regen process?"

"Ooo! Sort of," the older woman said, giving Omega a rueful smile. "It's kind of like prepping for major surgery. I am a little bit afraid of it."

"Don't be," Omega soothed. "It saved my life this past winter. I was in it for quite a while, and I'd have died without it."

"You have experienced it?"

"Yeah. I was in it for several weeks. I was...badly burned," Omega admitted. "It's a long story that I won't bore you with right now, but I was...missing entire chunks of me. And you see how I turned out," she said, stepping back and turning slowly, holding her arms out so Mrs. Bryant could see. "And Echo was in one for a couple days in the spring, after we had an accident with our spacecraft. We crashed on an alien world and he busted both legs, see, and it turned out to be faster and less painful to just stick him in for about two days and run the regen process on him. It really is pretty comfortable, when you get down to it. Nothing at all like the aftermath of major surgery— I was in a lot of pain, until they put me into the pod, and then the pain went away and I could relax. I slept a lot, and you probably will, too."

"Even Fox has been in one, years ago," Zebra added. "And he had cancer, and you see how healthy he is, now."

"Yes, and did you not say that he is considerably older than he looks?"

"That's right," Zebra affirmed. "He'd be at least as old as your father would be now, and maybe some older. When there's cancer involved, one of the best ways to defeat the cancer is to regress the age, and remove all of the mutations that led to the cancerous cells developing in the first place. Of course," she added, "it's possible to simply regress the age, without needing to cure any particular disease, too. But that's one of the reasons I've taken the blood samples and run some genetic testing on you, to try to ascertain how far we would need to regress your age to ensure we remove the cancerous mutations."

"Oh, I see." Mrs. Bryant nodded. "That makes very good sense. And this will mean I will also look and feel younger, with more energy and more flexibility, when I emerge?"

"Exactly. Arthritis, blood sugar issues, any tendency to

cardiovascular disease...all gone. We're planning on trying to fix everything we can find, and getting you in the best possible shape we can, as much as we can. I can't promise we'll get everything, but we're gonna try. But first, we're gonna see about licking that cancer. I'm figuring we're going to need to shave off a couple of decades, there—and I'm sure you won't mind THAT at all."

"Not in the least!" Mrs. Bryant fairly lit up.

"I thought so!" A smiling Zebra turned to Omega. "Honey, I'm gonna have to shoo you outta here now. We're going to be putting Mrs. Bryant into the pod in about ten minutes, and we need to sedate her and strip her down first, so the process won't be alarming, and the fluid can get to her whole body easily. I'm sure she'd like some privacy for all that."

"No problem," Omega said with a smile. "But before I go, I need to ask Mrs. Bryant a very personal question, so I can double-check something..."

"Oh?" Nalin Bryant murmured, raising an eyebrow.

* * *

"That's great," Omega said, grinning, some five minutes later.

"But can you have it done in time?" Mrs. Bryant wondered.

"Oh yeah, that won't be a problem at all! I got connections, and I had it in work weeks ago," Omega gave her a mischievous grin. "I only wanted to make sure it was right. Thanks, though. That's perfect."

"That sounds wonderful. I am eager to see," Mrs. Bryant observed, and Omega's grin grew wider.

"Okay, Omega, I kinda need to get busy with Echo's mom, here," Zebra reminded.

"Right. Gettin' outta the way." Omega took Mrs. Bryant's hand and squeezed it gently. "You take care, now, and just worry about getting well. I'll be looking after Echo while you're doing that, and then we'll just surprise the hell outta him. How does that sound?"

"Utterly delightful," Mrs. Bryant said, beaming. "I can't wait."

* * *

Omega stopped by the medlab pharmacy on her way out and picked up a fresh bottle of Rejuvic, then headed home to her quarters.

Echo never knew she'd made a side visit.

* * *

Echo's birthday morning arrived a couple of days later, and he woke up to the smell of breakfast already cooking, delicious odors wafting through the back door all the way to the bedroom. He glanced at the alarm clock: it read 5:02 AM.

What the hell? he wondered, trying to get his wits about him. *The earliest we ever get up is 6:00, unless something weird and bad is goin' down. But it's three hours before we have to be on duty today. And, per Fox's orders, even that's squishy, given...everything...going on.* He couldn't bring himself to think, "because Ma's dying." Then he very deliberately added, *AND we're getting ready for a vacation.*

He hauled himself out of bed, stuck his feet in his moccasins, and wrapped his naked body in his robe, wondering what on earth had possessed Omega to start the day so early. He was too groggy—and recent years had provided too few reasons—to remember the day. It didn't help that he was anything but awake at that time of the morning.

"Meg? What's up with...?" he began, wandering through the back door and toward her kitchen. "It's not even time to get up yet..." He glanced at the dining table, already set for two, and blinked several times, trying to focus his eyes. Then he rubbed his fists in them and tried again; it didn't help.

"Oh! You're up!" Omega exclaimed, coming to the kitchen door. She was dressed, but casually, in jeans and t-shirt, rather than her usual Suit. "You're not supposed to be up yet!"

"Huh?"

"Shoo! Go on back to bed with you! I'm not ready yet!"

"Meg, what the hell are you going on about?" Echo wondered, thoroughly confused. He raked a hand through his hair, briefly standing it on end.

"Echo!" Omega waved her hands at him. "Don't tell me you don't even know what I'm talking about. Shoo!"

"Okay, I won't tell you, but I don't."

"Agh!" she cried, hitting her forehead with the palm of her hand. "Are you even awake yet?"

"Not really."

"Go. Back. To. Bed," she told him, firm. "Get some more sleep. Don't worry about me. Everything's okay, I just wanted to do something a little...different...today."

"Okay, whatever," he grumbled in sleepy annoyance, turning and heading back the way he'd come. "When WILL you be ready for me to get up?"

"I can give you another couple hours, Ace. You want me to come in and wake you when I'm ready?"

"Uh, um, well..."

"You're back to sleepin' in the buff again, huh?"

Echo sighed; he'd been caught.

"I been bustin' my ass, tryin' to get used to sleeping in the boxers," he told her. "Honest, I have. I've even tried getting all different kinds of material—silk, silk knit, that bamboo-fiber shit, all of it."

"None of it is working?"

"Not yet." He sighed again. "I decided I'd like to actually have one night of uninterrupted sleep without feelin' like my manhood was bein' strangled, so I didn't put 'em on last night."

"Okay," she accepted his statement. "Then how about I come knock on the door when I'm ready? Be forewarned, though, if you don't get up when I knock, I WILL come in and GET you up. Buck naked or not."

"Uhhh..." Echo's sleepy brain took that in, and somehow decided not to object—much. "I gotta get up and get dressed, or at least shower, or somethin'..."

"Nope. You don't. Just grab your robe and come on. I have my reasons, Ace. Trust me. Just go back to bed, and I'll come bang on the bedroom door when it's time for you to get up."

"Okay, if you say so."

A long-suffering Echo headed back to his bedroom, where he closed the door and stuffed a towel under it, to keep the delectable smells from making him drool in his sleep.

* * *

Echo was sound asleep again when the sharp knock came on his bedroom door. He was dreaming a somewhat disturbing dream, in which he and Omega were attending a funeral for someone outside the Agency. Omega clung to his arm and wept, occasionally hugging him tightly, but for some reason Echo only felt numb, though he expected for some reason that he should be much more emotionally distraught.

But the knock roused him from sleep, and he immediately knew what the dream was about. *Ma,* he thought, his heart doing a nose-dive.

A strong fist pounded on the door again. He pried one eyelid open far enough to focus on the alarm clock; it read 7:34 AM, and he pushed up, in alarm of his own.

"Dammit! Didn' mean t' sleep THAT long," he griped, shoving himself out of bed and reaching for his bathrobe, as Omega had instructed him earlier. "There's squishy, an' then there's just plain late."

* * *

"Echo!" Omega called, raising her fist to rap hard on the bedroom door for the third time. "Time to get up, Ace! Breakfast is ready! Don't make me come in there!"

She started to hammer hard on the door again, when the door swung open abruptly and Echo filled it.

"All right, already," he declared, grumpy. "I'm awake. LATE, I might add. What the hell were you doing, waiting so late to get me up? There's no way I can get ready and get to the Core until nearly nine o' clock, now. Well, I could, but I'd have to skip breakfast and really rush..."

"No, you're not! It's okay, Ace," Omega said, grinning from ear to ear. "Fox knows, and he's okay with it. After all, it's a special day."

"There you go again. What the blazes are you talking about?"

"C'mon into my quarters and you'll see, Ace."

* * *

Echo followed Omega through the back door and into her quarters.

There, on the dining table, was a monumentally big Southern-style breakfast of eggs, bacon, sausage, country ham, shrimp and grits, homemade biscuits, sawmill gravy, and fried cinnamon apples. Two places had been set with Omega's mother's Sunday china and flatware; a carafe of freshly-brewed coffee sat on a warmer to one side, the savory aroma of chicory wafting from it.

A large package, wrapped in blue paper and adorned with a bright yellow bow, sat next to one of the place settings. Echo blinked.

"Happy birthday, Ace!" Omega cried, and gave him a big hug.

"Well, damn, Meg," he declared, starting to grin, as he finally understood. "I completely forgot." He hugged her in return, secretly relishing the rare opportunity.

"I actually believe you," she told him.

* * *

She wouldn't let him open the package until they were finished with breakfast.

"Well, but we need to eat and get to the office," he pointed out. "We can worry with the present later."

"No, we don't, and yes, you do. Fox gave Alpha One special dispensation to come in late today. Alpha Two is in the Alpha Line Room handling things while we're celebrating."

"This isn't gonna be some sorta surprise party thing, is it?" he wondered, suspicious and not liking the idea. Given matters with his mother, he flatly did not feel like a big group celebration. A little personal thing with Omega, this special meal she'd prepared, was one thing. Being inundated with cheers and congratulations was, at the moment, quite another. "Like, as soon as we show up in the Alpha Line Room, the whole damn department comes outta the woodwork or something?"

"No," Omega said, sobering. "I didn't think this was...the right time for it," she admitted. "Plus I knew you wouldn't like that much attention, anyway." She met his eyes. "I've had this little private celebration planned for a while, and I even had to get special dispensation for that," she pointed at the gift. "Fox and I both thought it might be a nice way for you to start the day."

"Do Romeo and India know? About...any of it?"

"Yeah," Omega confessed. "They know it's your birthday, 'cause Romeo already knew that from when he was your partner. So I can't promise that they won't have a present for ya, and I can't promise that Fox and Zebra won't. I dunno; I never asked."

"What about the rest of the department?"

"That, I got no clue. If word got out it's your birthday, some of 'em might. But I didn't tell anybody."

"All right. What about...the other thing?"

"Your mom?"

"...Yeah."

"I think Fox decided, in the circumstances, that Alpha Two oughta know about your mom's condition, too. But nobody else knows. Well," she added, "I think he consulted with Zebra, sorta. But then, Zebra's his life partner, or about to be."

"Uh-huh."

"Is...that okay?"

"Yeah, I guess so, baby. I get that you and Fox are...worried about me, and trying to take care of me. I suppose having Alpha Two and Zebra helping out in that is probably a good thing, taken all together. And I appreciate it, even if I don't say much, or don't show it."

"You do show it, Ace," she told him. "I see it, and I think Fox sees it. Maybe nobody else would, 'cept maybe Romeo, but we do see it. It's subtle, but it's there. It's okay."

"Good. So...let's eat this ginormous breakfast you cooked for me, and then head to work, and I can open your present later," Echo decided.

"No, no, no! You gotta open it after we eat breakfast, Ace! Trust me on this! After all I did to make this just right, and get Fox's approval and everything, you gotta do this in the proper order!"

"Okay, okay," he capitulated. "Hand me another biscuit, would ya? Where'd the gravy go? Oh, there it is..."

* * *

Once he had gotten it in his head that Alpha Two was covering for them, Echo relaxed a little and took his time over breakfast, then helped Omega hand-wash the dishes and put them away; the china was bordering on antique, one of her most treasured possessions, and it couldn't be put into the dishwasher. The fact that she had broken it out for their breakfast spoke volumes to him about how much this little celebration of his birthday meant to her, and he felt warmed by her caring. Then she led him over to the couch, sat him down, and bore the brightly-wrapped gift to him.

"There," she said with a huge grin, plunking it into his lap. "NOW open it."

His first reaction was to pat down his pockets for his knife, but since he wasn't dressed yet, it wasn't in his bathrobe pockets. Echo tore off the paper by hand to expose a large cardboard box, a good two feet on a side and some eight inches high. He slipped the lid off the box...

...And gaped at the contents.

Inside was a pair of custom-made cowboy boots in black leather. They had moderate stacked heels, not-quite-pointed toes in the traditional shape sometimes known as an 'R toe,' and subtle black stitching across the instep.

But a couple of inches up the shaft from the ankle was an explosion of color, as multicolored leather pieces stitched together to depict a design: a low brown mountain stood against a deep blue night sky, while an elliptical pool at the mountain's base reflected the sky. Overhead, a silver leather moon was crossed by the Native American four directions, narrow wedges of yellow, red, blue, and white; a triple row of silver-stitched 'moonbeams' extended to right and left. Angling in from the outside top was a silver, four-pointed star, trailing a golden wake behind it. Scrollwork fancy stitching framed the image, the scrollwork itself a repetitive outline of the identifying brand for a certain Texas ranch of Echo's intimate familiarity.

"Dear Lord," Echo whispered, stunned. "Meteor Mountain Ranch."

"Exactly," Omega said, grinning hugely, and clapping her hands in delight like a child. "The boy from Texas done got his cowboy boots, with his own ranch on 'em! I mean, I dunno myself what it looks like, but you've told me all about it and the naming of the ranch. Given it was the site of the First Contact, I guess I probably ought not to have had 'em fill in the crater with water, but I was afraid it wouldn't show up otherwise. And you told me it did sometimes fill with rainwater."

"Baby, they're beautiful," Echo said, deeply touched. "But I can't possibly wear 'em. They don't fit our dress code."

"You sure can, and they definitely do," she said, grinning even wider. "You notice how the FOOT of the boots is plain black? And I made sure—I ran it by Fox, to BE sure—that the colors don't start until well up the shaft, near the top. You pull your trousers down over the shaft, and nobody will know the difference from a regular pair of shoes or boots, even if you sit down. You got those dress boots you sometimes wear in the winter anyway, when it snows."

"Yeah," Echo said, picking one up and turning it about. "That's good quality leather, and the workmanship..."

"Ooo, I love that leather smell," Omega murmured, inhaling.

"Yup, me too. But baby, these must have cost a mint."

"They're nice boots," Omega admitted. "I made sure everything was done right on 'em."

"You spent too much."

"No, I did not," she declared, a spark kindling in the sapphire gaze. "You're my partner, you're my family, and you're my best friend. You're the guy who flew across the galaxy to save my fried tail just a few months ago, and the guy who kept me going when we crashed on the protoplanet and I klonked my noggin. By comparison with that stuff, having a nice pair of boots made for you is peanuts. Now," she said, waving at the back door, then tapping the boot box, "go get dressed."

* * *

When they arrived at the Alpha Line Room, properly attired in their Suits—with a certain pair of special footgear on Echo's feet—Romeo and India had everything under control.

"Yup, m' man, we took care o' the morning department meeting, done got th' shift reports collated, combined, and sent on to Fox, an' we printed out the latest couple of applications for ya," Romeo declared, pointing at the small sheaf of papers.

"AND we have a little something for you," India said, handing Echo a small wrapped present, red paper with a blue bow.

It turned out to be a black leather belt, well-matched to the boots; the buckle was Western-style engraved silver, but very simple and understated; the leather was delicately tooled, though largely around the back and sides. Beneath Echo's Suit jacket, run through the loops of his trousers, at first glance it would resemble a typical dress belt.

"Still coordinating, I see," Echo noted with a chuckle, as he stripped out his old belt and threaded the new gift through his trousers belt loops.

"Just wait'll this Christmas, man," Romeo laughed.

"Oh boy," Echo mock-groaned. "I can't wait."

"Well, let's see 'em," came a voice from the door of the room. They all spun to see Fox standing there, grinning. "The boots, Echo. I want to see the boots. You damn well better have worn 'em today."

Omega grinned hugely, proud as punch, and Echo sat on

the corner of his desk, held out one foot, and hiked his trouser leg up to the top of the boot. Ooos and aahs went around the small group as the bright design became apparent.

"Omega, tekhter, you did good," Fox decided. "Those are handsome boots, yet the design is high enough that it would take a deliberate effort on Echo's part for anyone else to see it. And the foot part doesn't draw attention, by itself."

"That was the idea, Fox," Omega said. "You approve?"

"I do."

"Good," Echo decided, "'cause I don't think I'm gonna be takin' 'em off any time soon. These things are damn comfortable."

"Great!" a happy Omega exclaimed, clapping once. "I meant to ask."

"Nice belt, by the way, too," Fox observed. "Had to look three times to tell it's not a regular standard-issue belt."

"As Meg just said, that was the idea, Fox," India said with a smile.

Just then, Zebra entered and skidded to a stop beside Fox, a large shopping bag in hand.

"I'm here," she panted, breathless. "Sorry I'm late; Zarnix and I have a little, uh, project going on, and I lost track of time."

"You're fine," Echo noted, then shot a sharp look at his partner. "I didn't THINK there was supposed to be anything to be late FOR."

"There isn't," Fox noted. "That bit was addressed to me; I'd made arrangements this morning to meet her here about this time."

"What, you were afraid we were gonna spring a surprise party on you?" India wondered.

"Naw, Echo," Romeo murmured. "We, um, Fox told us 'bout y'r mom an' all, an' we kinda figured it wasn't a good time f'r, I dunno, a big celebration. We ain't told nobody nothin', outside th' fam'ly, if ya get me."

"Oh, okay."

Are those the boots? Oh wow!" Zebra exclaimed.

"Aren't they great?" India enthused.

"Yeah, I like 'em," Echo admitted. "An' the belt is pretty cool, too. Flat black an' white does get kinda old for a wardrobe, after a while."

"It does," Fox agreed. "A pop of color now and then can be a nice thing. Bubeleh? Is this it?"

"Yeah," Zebra said, handing the shopping bag to her soon-to-be mate. Fox took it and extracted another largeish wrapped gift box, similar in size and shape to the one the boots had occupied, but in green paper with purple ribbon.

"Here, zun," Fox said, handing him the package.

When Echo got it open, it was a black felt Stetson with a classic cattleman-creased crown, and a gorgeous woven-horsehair band in a Southwestern stairstep-mountain pattern in shades of black, white, and gray, studded with silver conchos.

"I think I've got a theme goin', here," Echo decided, lifting out the hat and settling it on his head. A quick, instinctive adjustment, and it set perfectly on the dark hair, casting a shadow across the handsome face. Echo cocked his head and glanced at Omega; the gesture and expression conveyed, *Well? What do you think?*

"Damn, Ace," Omega said, both eyebrows as high as they would climb. "You make a helluva cowboy."

"What she said, dude," Romeo agreed.

"Whoa," India mumbled, impressed.

"Alla that," Zebra averred.

"Yep," Fox said, succinct.

"Thanks, guys," Echo murmured, dropping his gaze to the floor. "I appreciate the opportunity to...remember. Especially in the circumstances."

"Echo?" Omega said, and he looked up, into her earnest, concerned face. "Hon, I swear to you, this didn't have anything to do with your mom. I had this in process for weeks, now—it took that long to have the boots made. The others keyed off me."

"She's right, Echo," Fox agreed, and the others nodded. "We wanted to respect the man you were, and the man you've become. The timing was just...unexpected."

Echo considered for a moment, then nodded his head.

"Okay, guys, thanks," he said in a quiet voice. "Shall we get back to work?"

"That is a plan," Fox said, turning and escorting Zebra out of the Alpha Line Room, as Alpha Two handed over to Alpha One.

* * *

Omega took Echo out to dinner that night, commandeering the Corvette and heading for their most recent discovery, their new favorite Italian restaurant, which was run by an off-worlder, a Gurguv from Dekken named Gianna Ricci. Omega had already given Ricci a heads-up about the day, so the alien restaurateur had reserved their favorite table in the back corner, complete with a couple of lit pillar candles in the centerpiece, and all of Echo's favorite dishes were prepared for the meal.

"Baby, are you trying to tell me something?" Echo wondered, as he dug in to the chicken marsala entrée. "You've sure pulled out all the stops for my birthday."

"Well," Omega said, feeling her face heat, "let's just say... okay, look. Breakfast this morning, and the boots, an' all that? Yeah, I had that kinda planned for a while. I figured to take you out to dinner, too; probably just to the deli or something, but...after your mom an' all, I decided to make dinner more of a big deal, too. Not because I feel bad for you or anything," she added hastily, seeing the expression on his face. "But because it made me think. About how short life can be, and how you never know what's gonna happen tomorrow. Especially in our job. Which has already nearly taken us both out a couple times over, now. I just," she tried, "I wanted you to know that you were appreciated, Ace. To know that...that you're special to me, and I care about you, and all. All that gushy stuff. While I still could."

Her face grew red-hot, and she kept her gaze on her plate,

until the silence on the other end of the little table made her glance in Echo's direction. He watched her with a gentle, warm expression that told her the feelings were reciprocated. *Maybe not quite how I'd like 'em to be,* she thought. *But he cares about me, too.* She offered him a shy smile, then tucked her head.

* * *

That, Echo decided, watching her embarrassed but obviously heartfelt reaction, *was the closest she's ever come to telling me she loves me. And I still don't know if she meant it like I would or not, though that blush was kinda significant, if you ask me. And that might have been the best birthday present of the lot.*

In any event, I guess that hare-brained notion about her and Fox was just that—hare-brained. And evidently, she's been running around on errands for Fox, just like she said.

He saw the shy smile, and smiled back.

"That's...pretty cool, baby," he told her, voice low. "I appreciate it. And I hope you know...I feel the same way."

"I kinda figured," came the soft response, barely audible. "Hoped so, anyway. Nice to know it's true."

"Good. Feel like dessert?"

"Oh, THAT is ALL taken care of!"

He laughed, delighted.

* * *

"Hey Meg?" Echo said the next afternoon, as she came into the Alpha Line Room from the break room with a couple of pastries, one for him, one for her.

"Yeah?" she said, handing over a pastry and going to the department's pod brewer to make fresh coffee.

"You think you might be ready to run by Fox's office when we're done with the afternoon snacks, and see about getting him to make those reservations at the Ranch?"

"Huh? I figured you'd already have done that."

"No, I..." Echo broke off, feeling ashamed at his letting the matter slide. "You're right; I should've done it already. I'm

70

afraid I've kinda...had other things on my mind, baby."

Omega glanced up from her steaming coffee mug, gazing at him with soft blue eyes; he had to blink, and nearly averted his own gaze, knowing that she could see the pain he was trying hard to hide, despite his best efforts.

"Yeah, okay," she said, voice gentle, without protest. "That'll work."

"All right. I'll pop him a message that we're coming."

"Okeydoke."

* * *

"So," Fox asked, as Alpha One entered his office and closed the door, "have the two of you decided where you want to go on your vacation? You've only got a couple days left before it starts, you know."

"We've had that worked out for a while, Fox," Omega said. "We've just been...too busy to act on it." She shot her partner a sidelong glance, letting Fox see it, so he would understand. Fox responded by blinking at Omega, acknowledging the message. Astute enough to catch the subtle exchange, Echo rolled his eyes, as Omega added, "Echo said he'd handle it with you, but it worked out for us both to stop by, so here we are."

"Yeah, yeah," Echo grumbled. "What she's tryin' to tell you is, I been too worried about Ma to get around to it. And I know it, and I screwed up. An' I know that, too."

"NO, Ace!" Omega exclaimed, upset by his self-recriminations. "I didn't mean it like THAT at all! You HAVE had stuff on your mind, and it's legitimate worries, and I hurt for you and I understand, and I don't have a problem with it. I was just lettin' Fox know you were...preoccupied."

"All right," Echo accepted the explanation. "I'm still sorry I let it slip through the cracks until now."

"No big deal, hon. I swear it's not."

* * *

"Where are you going, then?" Fox pretended to ignore the interjected conversation while he activated his virtual key-

71

board and woke the small screen on the corner of the desk, preparatory to entering the information and beginning the process of issuing travel orders for his top team of Agents.

"The Ranch," Echo said.

"The Ranch?" Fox wondered, surprised. "Are you sure about that, zun?"

"Yeah, Fox, I'm sure," Echo replied, subdued. "I...I kinda think I gotta, you know? I need to...close some stuff."

Omega listened to the oblique conversation with some obvious concern, one eyebrow raised, but said nothing. Fox glanced at her briefly, realizing she was taking it all in with that sharp mind of hers, then dropped into a private code he had developed with his protégé and successor, for those times when he needed to pass on important information that only Echo could know.

Does Omega know? Fox asked. *About the Ranch, I mean.*

...No. Not yet. I mean, she knows where I'm from. But I don't know if she's realized THAT yet. I kinda think she hasn't, because she hasn't said anything.

Echo, are you truly sure this is what you want to do?

Yeah, Fox. It isn't like I haven't been there a bunch of times before.

Think hard, zun. I know that, what with your mother and all, it will be far more painful this time. Is it really going to be a vacation for you, if you're haunted by memories and 'might have beens'?

I know. But I need to do this, Fox. I need the closure. But, if I'm honest, I don't really wanna do it by myself. So this times out right, if anything about losing a parent can be said to be right. Anyway, if Meg's there, it'll...help.

All right, then. I understand. And yes, in that case, this is a good plan.

"Do I need to step out and give you two a chance to talk in private?" Omega asked, uncertain, and seeming reluctant.

"No, Omega," Fox said, offering her a slight smile as he recognized the private conversation had hurt her, in that her father figure and her best friend—*not to mention the man I'm 99% certain she loves,* Fox added mentally but did not say— had just deliberately excluded her from the conversation. And she was observant enough to see that signals were passing back and forth between the two men, so she knew there WAS a conversation. "No, I merely need to..." he broke off, thinking of wording, then finished, "I needed to have what you would term a 'private medical conference' of sorts with your partner, here. After all, as the two of you discussed earlier, he received some very bad news recently." Fox shrugged. "And I could see that he didn't want to worry you with his...feelings about things."

"Oh. True," Omega agreed instantly. "Okay. I can still step out, though." She rose and headed for the door. "Just throw something at the door when you're done talking, and I'll come back in."

"Thanks, baby," Echo murmured. She shot him a slight smile—though both men could see the anxiety in her eyes— and was gone, closing the door behind herself. Fox's office was silent for several moments.

"She's worried about you," Fox noted then.

"I know," Echo acknowledged with a sigh. "I couldn't want for a better partner than that lady. She has been staunch at my side through all of this. I'm...shocked at how much it... helps."

"I'm not surprised," Fox agreed. "You mean a lot to her."

"The feeling's more than mutual, believe me."

They fell silent again.

"So you need one last time to look around, while your mother is still alive, to...say goodbye to the memories of the area?" Fox wondered at last.

"Something like, yeah, I guess," Echo agreed. "Like I said, I know I need some closure on a few things that, way back when, we deliberately left open, just in case."

"All right. Do you need me to tell Omega, or can you handle that yourself? Forgive my prying into your private matters, Echo," Fox apologized. "I'm simply still trying to get a read on how you are dealing with your mother's illness. I want to help, to be there for you, but I'm uncertain how I can. Or even IF I can."

"Aw, I dunno, Fox," Echo sighed, slumping in his seat. "You'd think, as long as I've been gone from that whole thing—my life on the family ranch and all—it wouldn't be such a big deal."

"No. I remember when your grandfather died. You took it hard. You didn't let on much, but X-ray and I knew. For all you're so strong and tough, with a reputation for same, you are still a sensitive man, mayn khaver, with a big heart. When you choose to allow feelings, they run deep. And this...is your mother we're talking about. Your last remaining close relative."

"Yeah." Echo paused. "I guess...yeah. It did hit me pretty damn hard. And I wasn't expecting it—either the news, or how hard it hit."

"Right. I understand. So should I tell Omega for you? To ensure that she knows, and you don't have to try to say things you feel so deeply? To force them out?"

"Nah. I'll tell her, somehow," Echo decided. "I sorta feel like it oughta come from me, anyway."

"Well, but I'm certain she would understand if you needed me to do it. And there is the matter of security— I can ensure she understands the need for secrecy."

"Yeah, I know, but..." He shook his head. "I'll find a way. And she'll understand. Everything. She always does."

"And speaking of such matters, how is that relationship progressing?"

"Damned if I know." Echo gave him a rueful half-grin. "Sometimes I think she gets that I'm trying to get us closer in THAT kinda way, and sometimes it looks as if it goes flying past her like a kite in a tornado. It seems to depend on her mood. Like, if she's feeling bad about what got done to her, maybe 'cause somebody said something without thinking or whatever, she gets in a kind of funk—sometimes nobody else would even have a clue she was IN a funk, but I can see it—and then it seems to all kind of turn into, 'I'm a thing, I'm a monster, nobody could ever want me.' And then at other times, she almost—ALMOST—flirts with me."

"So you're still not sure of her affections."

"Depends what kind of affections." This time Echo gave Fox a full smile. "I don't think I'm exaggerating if I say that each of us is the best friend the other has ever had, or ever likely to have. So in that respect, I'm completely confident of her affections. It's whether or not we could ever have a romantic relationship that I'm still nosin' around."

"Well, that's better than it was last February, when you weren't sure of much of anything at all, where she was concerned."

"True," Echo admitted. "I'm workin' on it, best I can around missions and administrative work and shit like that. She's turned into a damn fine assistant chief for Alpha Line, by the way, just in case you haven't noticed. She can make 'em toe the mark as well as I can, and the whole damn department—well, except for Yankee, who's still holding a grudge from back at Christmas—adores her. And even Yankee has to respect her, even if he's not sure if he likes her very much."

"I had noticed," Fox said with a smile. "All of that. It has proven to be an excellent choice, Omega as your second."

"Yup. And if I ever do end up moving into this office, I expect one of my first acts will be to promote her to department chief, to fill my shoes."

"I rather expected as much. I think it a fine notion. Especially if the two of you are life partners by then. A finer power couple I can't imagine."

Echo laughed.

"Yeah, I've already thought about that. I hope, by that point, we will be, too."

"That's better," Fox decided, listening to the laugh. "One thing I DO plan to tell Omega, is to try to keep you laughing as much as she can, while the two of you are vacationing. I've noticed she's already trying to do just that." He didn't mention that he had already had such a discussion with her.

"Yeah, she has been, and it helps, I suppose. As long as she gives me some space to grieve a bit, I guess that'll work," Echo admitted.

"I think she will," Fox concluded after a moment to consider. "She's sensitive, too, and she already understands your mindset—possibly better than I do, and I've known you your whole adult life."

"I dunno," Echo said with a shrug. "I just know that it's a pain in the ass tryin' to hide anything from either one of ya, and if the two of you gang up on me, I'm a goner."

"Good! That's as it should be. Then let me call her back in." A smiling Fox caught up a disposable pen, rose partway from his desk chair, and flung it with considerable force at the office door. It smacked into the door, then fell to the floor in a clattering cascade. Within seconds, the door opened.

"You rang?" Omega asked with a smile.

Chapter 3

Two Division days later, about mid-morning, the unmarked ebony helicopter dropped the black-denim-clad Alpha One team off at the Ranch in west central Texas. Echo—who wore a certain cowboy hat and belt he had recently been gifted, but who had chosen NOT to wear the boots, preferring to save them for special occasions, instead wearing an older, more battered pair—grabbed two bags and set them on the ground as Omega followed suit, then together they carefully maneuvered out the large trunk containing her fragile telescope equipment.

Ranch hands met them and caught up their luggage, carrying it into the guest house nearby. Omega and Echo got clear of the rotor blades, and Echo gave the Agency pilot a thumbs-up. The specialized aircraft lifted off and disappeared into the distance.

"Well, we're here," Echo remarked.

"Yep," Omega replied with satisfaction, looking around. "I was beginning to forget what air without auto exhaust smelled like."

"It...doesn't smell like anything, much," he looked at her, puzzled.

"Exactly." She grinned. "Although..." Omega sniffed the air, "something's blooming..."

"Wildflowers." Echo casually waved at the surrounding fields and pastures as his partner sighed in appreciation. He glanced at the main house and watched as a man emerged and headed their way. "Here comes Joe."

The imposing Haepergen rancher approached; other than his size, he looked like an ordinary human and was taken as such by civilian visitors, but he was somewhat taller, being nearly seven feet tall, and considerably broader and more muscular. Concurrently, he was a good deal stronger, as well— which was a useful thing to have in the ranch hand he had been, and the ranch foreman he was now. Most of the civilian visitors just called him the manager, and most thought he owned the ranch, as well.

"Hi, Echo," Joe greeted the Agent warmly as he walked up, offering a big right hand in welcome. "Good to see you. It's been a while."

"Sure has, Joe," Echo replied, shaking hands. "I'd like for you to meet my partner, Omega. Meg, this is Joe Beck, our... host."

"Hi, ma'am." Joe touched his hat brim in a courteous, almost courtly, fashion. "Your partner an' I go back a ways. You're the second of Echo's—what? three?—partners I've been privileged to meet. And in all honesty, I haveta say Echo's partners are definitely gettin' prettier."

Joe, Echo, and Omega all grinned, and Omega responded, "Thanks, Joe. I can already tell we're gonna get along just great, you an' me!"

All at once, Joe did a double-take, and stood for long moments, staring at Omega in something like bewilderment. Disconcerted, Omega blinked, and glanced at Echo, uncertain.

"What's wrong, Joe?" Echo wondered. "You keep staring at my partner."

"Yeah, I'm sorry, ma'am," Joe excused himself, flushing and dropping his gaze to the toes of his boots. "You, uh, you just look like somebody I usedta know, is all. An' I'm tryin' 'a figger out where I know ya from."

"Well, back before I joined the Agency, from time to time I would bring my telescope and equipment out from Houston and observe not too far from here," Omega explained. "I had an arrangement with a local rancher to use a little plot of land on the weekends, sometimes. It was way on down near the county line, just a little isolated piece of land that they didn't use for a lot, 'cause it was mostly a dry playa, and there wasn't any forage for the cattle. So you might have seen me in town, getting camping supplies or the like."

"Which town?" Echo wondered.

"Oh, I used to head down to that grocery over on Highway 90 in Langtry," Omega said. "It was the closest. If I was desperate for supplies, sometimes I'd run over to that convenience store in Flatrock by the river."

"THAT'S where I know ya from!" Joe said, slapping his forehead with his hand. "Pardon me, ma'am; I just didn't recognize ya in the standard all-black now."

"That's okay," Omega said, shooting him a smile as she looked about the place. Echo and Joe exchanged glances; Omega was so busy looking around at the rugged landscape that she missed seeing them. "Wow. I'd forgotten just how many hills and mountains and canyons this area had. And how beautiful it is."

"Hey, lissen, Omega. That rancher's name wouldn't have been Roberto Gonzales, would it?" Joe wondered.

"Yeah!" Omega exclaimed, returning her attention to Joe for a moment. "That was him. Small world, huh? Oh wow, that view is pretty..." She waved a hand at a ridge in the distance.

Joe met Echo's eyes, and they both grinned. But somehow there wasn't as much humor in either man's expression as Omega might have expected, had she seen them. Echo eased around until his back was to his partner, trying to ensure she couldn't hear, before he commented.

"Smaller than she knows," Echo murmured.

"Ain't it the truth," Joe agreed in similar fashion, then he raised his voice. "C'mon, you two, let's get outta the sun."

* * *

"Now, Omega, th' first thing ya need to know is, we don't operate here on Division One days," Joe explained. "'At's 'cause cows don't operate on Division One days, an' we got a-plenty o' them around. An' if we have reg'lar human guests, come ta vacation at a dude ranch, well, they ain't gonna be on Division One days, neither."

"So we go on a standard Earth 24-hour day, while we're here," Omega verified.

"Right, Meg," Echo confirmed. "Chances are, we'll get in

enough outdoor activity—the fresh air and sunshine you want-ed—to sleep awful damn well, even though the days aren't as long as what we're used to."

"Sounds okay to me, Ace. And it makes good sense. I just wanted to make sure I was understanding," Omega agreed, with a nod.

"An' ya did fine, ma'am. Now, I put y'all up in the guest house," Joe told the two Agents, with a quick glance at Echo. "There's just the two of ya here right now, so you'll have plenty of room that way. Unless you'd rather be in the main house...?"

"No, that sounds fine," a subdued Echo remarked.

"You wanna look around the place? Maybe show your partner around?"

"Not...right now," Echo murmured. "Maybe later. What about horses?"

"I already got Spirit all ready for ya anytime you want 'im, Echo, and I thought we'd wait an' see what yer partner c'n handle."

"All right. Meg, whatcha gonna want to do first?"

Omega glanced at the sky, considering, checking the sun's position. It was still early afternoon, so after a moment's thought, she said, "Let's get settled in a bit, then meet at the stable."

* * *

An atmospheric distortion moved through the atmosphere over central Texas as the sun fell toward the horizon, headed against the wind, moving west toward the Pecos River. As it approached the river, it slowed, then began to move in a spiral search pattern. Finally it hovered over a small impact feature, a recent—geologically speaking—oblong meteor crater that had thrown up a low hill at one end. The bottom of the crater was flat and fairly smooth, partly filled in with the silt and salt deposits of the playa it had become. The feature was a known geomagnetic and gravimetric anomaly area, and it was to this flat surface that the distortion now settled.

As it did, two circular depressions and one elliptical de-

80

pression crunched softly into the silt...

...As the cloaking fields dropped, revealing three alien spacecraft.

* * *

There were two saucers and one bullet-shaped ship. After nearly an hour of apparent inactivity—not that anyone was watching—a hatch on one saucer levered open. It was followed by hatches on the other two spaceships opening.

Eight beings, of five different alien races, emerged.

"Anything?" one of the two Glu'gu'ik asked the other. The second Glu'g'ik waved around a scanner of some sort.

"Nothing," he said.

"Then let's go," said a squat, dark gray Zargothian female. "I'm tired of being cooped up in a little spaceship."

"You'll go when I say go," the first Glu'g'ik snarled. "Remember, Zzs, I can make things very hard for you." He turned to the Aves, a male avian, purple with black crest feathers. "Do you get anything, Birdy?"

Birdy put a plumed hand to his temple and closed his large eyes. After a few moments of silence, he opened his eyes and looked at the lead Glu'g'ik.

"Nothing," he reported. "I detect no sentients anywhere near."

"Tiln?" the Glu'g'ik asked the Botanoid.

"One moment, Eb'vuv," the shambling plant-being murmured. "I must first find some local flora and merge with it."

Tiln rustled across the crater floor to a clump of button snakeroot near the rim. He grasped one of the fronds...and promptly morphed into a much larger clump of snakeroot, next to the original plant.

The odd, mixed group of extraterrestrials waited for fully five minutes before Tiln morphed back into his normal, semi-bipedal form and shuffled back to his companions.

"There are some of the indigenous cattle in a field a few klicks that way," Tiln told them, waving a frond to the southeast. "The nearest sentients are more than twice as far, near the main structures of the...what is it called...? Ah. The Ranch."

"Take note, Lu'vin'du'v," Eb'vuv told the other Glu'g'ik, who recorded the information on his instrumentation. "We want to avoid those structures."

"I still don't understand why you chose to land on a Division One ground station," Zzs complained. "It's about the worst possible place we could land!" At that, her fellow Zargothians nodded, then started to add their own grumblings to the mix.

"Zzs, tell Zzu and Zzt to be quiet, if you know what is good for you," Eb'vuv threatened, and Zzs scowled, but gestured to the other two Zargothians, who silenced. "We are here because this place provides some of the best natural cloaking on this Creator-forsaken planet. Kelto, is the equipment ready?" he addressed the short, green Delzantian.

"Yeah," Kelto replied, laconic almost to the point of insolence. "Everything's loaded on the antigrav sleds."

"Lu'vin'du'v, where is the ravine we are to follow?"

Lu'vin'du'v studied the readouts on his device, then turned to face due south.

"This way," he said. "We have to bypass the main buildings a good distance to the west, then once we're well south of the station, strike the main route, headed roughly east."

"Everyone grab your gear," Eb'vuv ordered, "and follow Lu'vin'du'v."

The group gathered up various packs and antigrav sleds, and headed south, disappearing into the lengthening shadows.

Behind them, the hatches on the three spacecraft slowly closed, and their portals went dark.

* * *

Echo was already tacking Spirit—in a Western saddle and Texas hackamore, complete with lead line—when Omega walked up behind him.

"Okay, looks like you're set. Now I need a horse," she remarked.

"Nice, quiet one over there, if you want to try 'im." Echo

gestured to a nearby stall. Omega shot him an amused glance.

"Lemme take a look." She wandered among the stalls while Echo finished tacking up. As Echo led his horse out, he saw what Omega had picked.

"Celeste?! Are you sure you can handle 'er, Meg? She used to be a racehorse! She can be pretty hot."

"Celeste an' me have already made friends." She scratched the flea-bit-gray horse affectionately behind one ear. "We're gonna be just fine together, aren't we, girl?" Celeste whickered softly in response.

"Need a leg up?" Echo offered. He noticed with considerable interest that the saddle and bridle Omega had chosen was English, not Western like his own. As he watched, she tacked the already-groomed horse with swift skill, and he raised an eyebrow. He also noted that she had placed a halter and lead rope over the bridle, to allow for dismounting and tying the horse. *Hmmm...*he thought. *I'm seeing experience here, I think...or bad overconfidence, one; I'm not sure which, yet. Knowing Meg, though, it's probably experience. At least, I sure hope so. The tacking sure leans toward experience. I'll know as soon as she gets in the saddle.*

"Nah, I'm good," Omega replied to his offer, placing her booted foot in the stirrup and swinging smoothly up into the saddle. Once seated, she began calmly adjusting the girth and stirrups. "There. That's about right."

That would definitely be experience, Echo amended, and raised an eyebrow. "...No, I guess I won't be teaching you to ride," he declared.

"Told you." She grinned.

"English?"

"Yeah. Somewhere in between English an' Western, really. 'S the way I mostly used to ride. I can ride Western style no problem, but I used to do...well, most anywhere else it would've been a foxhunt, I guess, but back home we hunted coyotes."

"You used to ride hunts??" Echo, caught slightly off-guard, mounted up as they talked. "I didn't know they even had coyotes in Alabama."

"Yeah, they do. A bunch, actually. Way too many, given the terrain, population, kids, pets, livestock, all that. And they tended to go after the livestock. I even heard a couple tales of coyotes stalking kids on the walking trails, too. And they really didn't have anything that predated on them. That's why we were allowed to hunt 'em—to keep 'em thinned out some. We did it humanely, though—the hunt wore 'em down, and then one of the hunt leaders dispatched 'em with a rifle."

"Well, that's good, I guess. What other kind of riding have you done?"

"Lessee; there's trail riding, of course, over pretty much any terrain, 'cause remember, we had mountains in the area. I've played the odd chukker of polo, too. But I wasn't that good. Strictly low-goal. You look surprised."

"A little, I guess. You don't look the type."

"Well, you've hardly ever seen me in anything other than the black Suit. Don't feel alone, though; like I've told you a couple times, most people tend to think of me as city folk for some reason. No idea why. I guess I project that kind of image. And they really don't think of me in horse terms. Go figure." She looked around. "You've been here before, so you know the area, Ace..."

"Mmm...you might say that," Echo hedged.

"Where d' you wanna head?"

"Let's head southeast...we can scout out a good location for you to observe."

"Southeast it is." Omega and Echo lightly spurred their mounts and headed off.

* * *

The two off-duty Division One Agents rode companionably for some time without even speaking. Echo was content to relax and observe his surroundings, while Omega was obviously reveling in the opportunity to let go. As they topped a slight rise, she turned to Echo.

"Is this fairly level?" She gestured at the expanse before them.

"Yeah, it's flat and even once you get past that ravine over there, if we just keep to the left. And Joe's pretty good about taking care of the..."

"Hyeeah!" And Celeste was off, Omega low over her neck, racing across the field. Echo reined in his mount and simply enjoyed watching as his partner blew off months of steam, her hair coming loose from its accustomed braid and flying behind her like a silver pennant. Carried down the breeze, he heard, "Echooo!! Come ooonn! You're fallin' behind, Ace!"

And with that urging, Echo, too, joined the race with the wind.

* * *

As Echo and Spirit gradually caught up with Omega and Celeste, who had slowed somewhat to allow it, Echo could hear Omega's laughter and playful, exuberant whoops, and he grinned.

"Havin' fun, Meg?" he called.

"You know it, Echo!" she yelled. "I feel like I'm back in the first flight of a hunt back home!"

"Careful up here, Meg," Echo warned her. "There's an earthen berm comin' up ahead. It's 'bout 3 or 4 feet high. But it's flat on the other side."

"Jump it?"

"Sure, why not? Follow me, I'll show you the best place."

"Right behind ya."

Echo urged Spirit ahead, turning slightly to the left, and Omega followed on Celeste, dropping back so she could watch Echo take the jump first.

Echo and Spirit soared easily over the earthen berm, and Omega urged Celeste onward, judging speed and distance as she adjusted her seat. Echo pulled up and turned Spirit to watch his partner take the jump. *Yeah, Meg knows exactly what she's doing. She's got really good form. I shoulda known. Here she goes...*

At the last possible moment, however, Celeste balked, refusing the jump, and with too much forward momentum to counter, Omega came out of the saddle and over her mount's head, as Echo gaped in horror. She somersaulted in mid-air, twisting her body and managing to land on her feet; a temporarily-immobile Echo recognized a maneuver they had worked on last week in the gym. But Omega's forward momentum was still too great to remain standing, and before she could even take a step to try to counter it, she pitched forward and went face down, sliding across the ground on her stomach.

"Oh, shit!" Echo exclaimed then, dismounting swiftly and hurrying to catch Celeste. Tethering both animals to opposite sides of a nearby tree along the berm with their respective leads, he ran to Omega, who still lay face-down on the ground.

"Meg?!"

No answer. Echo knelt and began quickly, gently, checking his partner for injuries, palpating down the length of her body.

"Meg? You okay? Baby? Answer me, Meg..."

"Yeh," finally came the panting, breathless response. "Got...got the wind knocked outta me, 's all..." Omega rolled over and sat up, brushing off the dirt and grass.

"Slow down," Echo cautioned, holding her back with a hand on her shoulder. "That was quite a spill you took."

"Yeah, but I couldn't stick the dismount," she pointed out with a grin. "That'll cost me on the technical score. But I'd give it about a nine-point-five on artistic merit, don'tcha think?"

"Mmm. You can't be hurt too bad, I guess," Echo deadpanned, still checking her out. "Ow. You lost some hide on your chin, Meg. Are the teeth okay?"

* * *

Omega dragged the back of her hand across her chin; it came away blood-smeared.

"Uh-oh. Uhhh. Dunno, Echo," she muttered, running her tongue around to try to explore inside her mouth. "'T be honest, everything's kinda numb at the moment..."

"Open up and let me see, then." Omega opened her mouth, and Echo checked for broken teeth. "Nope, you look fine. I'll get the medic at the main house to have a look when we get back, just to make sure. You coulda cracked a couple or something. I hope not—helluva way to start a vacation, if you did—but you never know. Here." Echo pulled a black kerchief out of his hip pocket and reached for her. "Let's get that chin cleaned up a bit." Gently, he brushed debris out of the scrape, then gave her the kerchief. "There. Ooo, that did it—you're bleedin' like a stuck pig. Hold it to your chin 'til the bleeding stops."

"Dammit. Any cut or scrape on the head or face is just the worst."

"Yeah, I know. It doesn't have to be bad to bleed like crazy. Good; that's better. Now just sit there and catch your breath a minute. I'll bring Celeste over."

"No, wait a minute. Did you see what happened?"

"Yeah."

"What did I do wrong?"

"Nothing, that I could see. Looked to me like Celeste just refused the jump."

"She knows how to jump, though, right?"

"Yeah, she's been taught. Gotta be able to do that from time to time on a ranch, anyway."

"Any reason she couldn't make the jump?"

"No. I'd have stopped you in the first place if there were. She just gets...temperamental sometimes."

"Am I 'bout done bleedin'?" she wondered, pulling away the kerchief for Echo to check her chin.

"Yeah, that looks better. I think it's stopped. Just try not to bump it or scratch it or anything."

"Okay. Wait here."

Omega got up and finished dusting off, cramming the bloody kerchief into her hip pocket.

"All right, Celeste," she said, striding toward the horse with purpose, "you and me have got a little understanding to come to. Come on." She climbed over the berm, mounted the horse, and trotted him away from Echo, who stood looking on. "Now, Celeste," she turned the horse back and spurred her on, "we ARE goin' over this jump—together!"

* * *

Echo watched as Celeste tried to run out to the right, but Omega kept her horse firmly in line this time, using her legs and the reins as cues. Her form was perfect, with a low half-seat, body slightly forward, reins firm but not tight. The horse finally acknowledged her rider's commands, and launched herself over the barrier. Omega rode smoothly through the jump with her, and Echo smiled in admiration as he watched.

"Okay, Ace," Omega said to Echo, as she turned Celeste back to give Echo time to mount Spirit, "where were we?"

"Headed yonder way, I think," Echo drawled laconically, with a nod and a grin.

"All right then, let's go!"

* * *

"So how long have you been riding, Meg?" Echo asked his partner when the pressure had finally been vented, and they'd settled into a slightly more-sedate slow lope.

"Oh, quite a while, Echo, Ah guess. Daddy taught me back on the farm when Ah was a girl."

Echo smiled to himself over his partner's paternal reference: As Omega relaxed, her native Southern was growing more and more pronounced, and the word had emerged as "Da-yudeh."

"Actually, Ah remember my riding lessons really well," she continued after a thoughtful moment. "One of my early lessons was pretty much a disaster..."

"How so?" Echo asked, curious. "And how old were you?"

"Oh, I was—what? Maybe eight? Ten? And it all started out okay. The day was a gorgeous early spring day—I think it was March, or maybe April—the temperature was unusually warm, with a nice soft breeze. Daddy said we should have a lesson, so I put on my riding jeans an' boots, and we went out to get ol' Bob, Daddy's quarterhorse. But when we got to the field, there was Bob with his hoof thoroughly hung in the fence wire. He 'uz prone to kinda pawin' at the fence for some reason we never figured out, and it got him into trouble like that every once in a while. And this time was worse than most. Somehow, he'd managed to get the wire so wedged between his hoof and the horseshoe that Dad and I together couldn't get it loose, and Bob was one unhappy horsie. If Dad and I had tried any harder, we were afraid we might rip the shoe off and damage his hoof in the process. Dad told me to hold Bob's hoof still, an' he'd run back to the tool shed for the wire-cutters. So I stuck my boot in the fence and leaned into it to hold the wire still, and reached through the fence to hold Bob's hoof still, so he wouldn't hurt himself—'cause he kept tryin' to yank it free, which was only making things worse, 'cause he was yanking the wrong direction. Daddy took off runnin' for the shed."

"And?" Echo prodded. Omega grinned.

"Well, needless to say, ol' Bob wasn't the happiest of campers about havin' to balance on three legs for an extended period of time, an' he'd already been doin' it a while by that point, so the fence and I got to know each other real well while Daddy was gone. I hated to tell it I wasn't near old enough to date yet."

Echo let out a laugh, then said, "Since it was corralling a horse, I assume the fence was not barbed wire."

"You assume correctly. Good thing, too. I'd 'a been a bloody mess, 'stead of just a black an' blue mess. As it was, when the bruises started showin' up against this pale skin of mine, I looked like somethin' from a horror movie. Felt like it, too, come to think of it."

"Ouch."

"Uh-huh. That's about the time I decided the Theory of General Relativity needed an addendum."

"Oh? Waitaminit. You'd studied General Relativity by then?"

"Yup. On my own, I'll admit, but I'd studied it. An' believe me, it needed that addendum."

"Which would be...?"

"The distance between the site of an emergency and the location of help dilates with increasing urgency..."

Another chuckle from Echo.

"I take it your dad took his time getting back with the wire-cutters."

"No. He sprinted the whole way, goin' an' comin'. But it seemed like it, anyway."

"So when he got back, what did you do? Cut Bob out of the fence?"

"Yeah, and used some pliers to pull the piece of wire out from under the shoe. Then we fed him to try to settle him down. Nearest thing to an equine vacuum cleaner I've ever seen."

Echo nodded with a knowing grin.

"So, did things settle down after that?"

"I wish..."

"Uh-oh. Go on, then."

"Ol' Bob decided, after slurping up all the feed Dad would give 'im, that he was still hungry from fightin' the nasty fence monster—I dunno, maybe the Japanese shoulda made a movie about it. Been right up there with Mothra. Anyway, he starts on the grass under the trees beside the feed bin like he was a lawn mower. Problem is, I want him to follow me back to the barn so I can saddle an' tack up. Imagine this eight-year-old, gawky kid with two long blonde braids, yankin' on the lead for all she's worth, fat lotta good it does, as the dang horse works his way further an' further back up under the trees."

"Dragging you along for the trip?" Echo was grinning hugely at the mental image conjured up of a very young Omega, blue eyes narrowed in annoyance, blonde pigtails flying, tussling valiantly with her horse, and losing badly.

"Yup."

"What was your dad doing?"

"Oh, he was busy—first he kinda braided the fence wire back together—you know what I mean...patchin' it up..."

"Yeah. I've had to do that a few times, myself."

"Then he started feedin' the other horses, so they wouldn't get jealous of Bob."

"What happened with you and Bob?"

"Well, I learned several things about horses that day. Did you know that long hair, horses, and low-hanging tree limbs are not a good combination?"

"Uh, no, can't say as I've ever had occasion to find out," Echo deadpanned. "But I think I get that picture. How bad did it get tangled in the limbs?"

"I'm not sure. It didn't feel too good at the time, I know that. But I finally managed to get pulled loose. Momma pitched a fit later about the state of my braids, an' we had to undo it all for her to pick the leaves an' tree bark an' crap out of it, then she combed out the tangles—while I howled—and re-braided it."

"Ouch!"

"Yeah. I tried to explain to her that Bob wouldn't behave for me, but she didn't listen, and Daddy just grinned and winked at Momma, who rolled her eyes and waved the comb at him." Omega paused, thinking. "Huh. Now that I remember it, I believe she did issue some sorta threat that if he didn't keep a better eye on his only daughter next time, she'd be usin' the comb on him, an' it wouldn't be on his hair. Then she made a swatting motion with it."

"Uh-oh!"

"Yup."

"What did your dad do to that?"

"I'm afraid I don't really know, Ace. I think he sorta winced an' nodded, but I'm not sure; I wasn't payin' much attention at the time. Well, to be honest, I was crying, 'cause it hurt to untangle my hair."

"Aw. What else did you learn that day?"

"Let's see...how 'bout, 'In a dispute with a horse over which of you has the right to occupy a given square foot of ground, the horse will always win...'"

"Oops. What else?" Echo's eyes gleamed as he suspected

what was coming.

"Umm...I derived another General Relativity corollary." Omega looked sheepish.

"And it was?" Echo was completely entertained.

"Time dilates during an exceptionally stupid and painful event, with the limit on delta-t approaching infinity as the levels of pain and stupidity increase."

"In other words, time slows down when you do something dumb that hurts like hell. And you derived that because...?" Echo pressed, determined to get the complete, unabridged version of events out of her. Meanwhile, he fought to keep a straight face.

"Uh...shall we just say that letting a tree scalp you is much preferable to estimating the weight of the horse with your foot?" she offered, even more sheepish. "And if the horse is standing on you, and you aren't big enough to push him off, you are NOT gonna go anywhere, no matter how much you want to—and you will want to, very, very much!" she told him, highly emphatic. Just then, Spirit snorted, whether in annoyance, approval or general laughing humor, neither Agent could tell.

By this time, Echo had to bring Spirit to a halt until he could stop laughing; he was doubled over in the saddle, fairly guffawing.

"Sorry, Meg. I'm not laughin' at you, I swear. It musta really hurt, I know, 'cause I've had horses step on me, too. But it's funny as hell the way you tell it, baby. Only an astrophysicist would connect it to relativity. Did your dad eventually come to your rescue?" he finally asked.

"Yeah. Finally." Even Omega was grinning now. Echo suddenly remembered Fox's injunction about laughter, and realized with considerable gratitude that that had been her plan all along. "Worst pain I'd ever experienced to that point in my short young life."

"So that was the end of that lesson." He still chuckled, warmed by her efforts to ensure his mood was lightened.

"Nope."

"What?!" Echo was shocked; he had seriously thought that was the coda of the story.

"Well, my foot wasn't broken—at least, we didn't think so at that point; we found out later one of the small bones in the instep, the fourth metatarsal I think it was, had a hairline crack, and I spent a couple months in a boot, never mind losin' a few toenails—and Daddy wanted me to be tough enough to handle an injury if I was out in the middle of nowhere and needed to get myself to help. Which was reasonable. So he led Bob over to an old stump, and I used that as a mounting block. Then I learned another lesson."

"Yeah?"

"Gettin' oneself into the saddle when the foot you're s'posed to mount with has been smushed can get real interesting. The saddle gave my ribcage an enthusiastic greeting when I aborted the first launch attempt due to main engine failure." She shrugged. "The fact that, as I came down off the side of the horse in something less than a controlled descent, my face smacked into the pommel...well, it didn't help. At least I managed to avoid hitting the ground."

"Ow," Echo said in sympathy. "Did you break anything? Like, a rib or something?"

"Nah, nothing broke on THAT one. Guess I was tougher than I look, even before the 'improvements'...but you should've seen me the next day. Or...maybe not."

"Black eye?"

"Among other things."

"Did you finally make it into the saddle?"

"Eventually. It took about three more tries, though, and a little help from Daddy. I think, when it was all said and done, he ended up just picking me up and setting me on the horse, if I remember right. But by that time, neither Bob nor I was too happy about ridin' that day—Bob was gettin' real fidgety—so Daddy cut it short. I think the whole lesson ran a scant twenty minutes, after I finally managed getting into the saddle."

"For which curtailing you were glad, I'll bet," Echo remarked, sobering as he realized just how beat-up her young self must have been after that.

"You got that right!"

"How'd your training go after that?"

"Oh, Daddy gave me a couple of days to heal up. Actually, it was prob'ly closer to a week. I looked like I'd been in a fight with an Aurigan were-bear. Felt like it, too. Between Bob yankin' me into the fence over an' over, steppin' on me, tangling my hair in the tree limbs, smackin' myself on the saddle, an' Momma detanglin' my hair, it was NOT a good day."

"I bet. Poor baby."

"Anyhow, after alla that, I was so mad at the dang horse for trompin' all over me an' gen'rally disrespecting me, I was determined to show him who was boss. The end result was that I pretty much got to where I could handle anything with four legs and a saddle."

"So you rode hunts and...played polo, you said?"

"Yeah."

"Steeplechase?"

"No. Too...artificial for my taste."

"You prefer the 'real outside,' huh?"

* * *

"I'm a farm girl, Echo. This is great." Omega waved her right hand around at the Texas countryside. "This Ranch is gorgeous. The hills, and the canyons, the flat stretches and the streams. I'm really comfortable here already. In some ways, it reminds me a whole lot of...of home. Not the terrain, particularly, just...the feel. If I didn't have other obligations, it'd be... real easy to stay..." Her voice trailed off as she gazed around her. Echo's eyes flashed for a moment in response to her comments before she continued. "Which makes me think. There's something I've been meaning to ask you..."

"What's that?"

"Oh, I was just wondering...what happened to the—to my—farm when...I joined the Division One Agency. I'd kind

94

of like to buzz by there some time, maybe every once in a while, just to check on the place. I did once when I was on...sabbatical...after...well, after that whole mess with Slug went down, but I was afraid to stay too long, and risk getting seen. I didn't even go to the house. I just..." She broke off and sighed.

"Your old home is fine, Meg," Echo told her gently. "It's...held in trust...by the Agency. If the day ever comes when you decide to, you know...retire from the Agency, Megan McAllister can reappear—or her cousin, or whatever—and move back home to Huntsville...if that's what you want."

"Oh..."

"Are you homesick, Meg?" Echo's voice was now quiet, subdued.

"No. Just...got a little nostalgic, I guess. Remembering when I was a kid and all."

* * *

"Since there's really...no one left there to see you, just Agency personnel maintaining it, we can go back any time you want to," Echo offered. "If you want to. Or you can go alone, if you'd rather."

"Okay. We might drop by there sometime if we're in the area, you an' me. I...think I'd rather not go alone."

"Nosy neighbors?"

Omega shook her head.

"Ghosts..." Her voice was sad, distant.

Echo glanced at her, just for a moment, but Omega's eyes were hidden behind her goggle-glasses as she gazed at the trail ahead, and her windblown hair partially obscured her face. *Well,* he decided, *I can sure understand that. Especially these days. Like I couldn't, before. Damn.* Finally he looked away, back to the trail in front of them.

After a few moments, Omega said, "What about you? Do you ever go home? You know, just run by to see the place?"

* * *

"Mm-hmm," Echo answered without looking. "Now and again. I even took my closest pal there just recently."

"But I thought I was..." Omega broke off and looked sharply at Echo's profile, taking in the faint curve at the corner of his mouth, contrasting with the hint of pain in his dark eyes, just before he glanced to the other side.

Her eyes widened behind her goggle-glasses, and she surveyed the rugged, beautiful landscape around her thoughtfully, viewing it with a fresh perspective.

* * *

"This is where you were gonna take me, wasn't it?" she asked, after a long silence, during which she seemed to consider his comments.

"Huh?" Echo looked at her, confused by the apparent non-sequitur.

"After we crashed, back in the spring, when I had the head injury and it looked like I might not be able to do Alpha Line stuff any more. You said you were taking me to the Ranch. This is where we were gonna come, isn't it?" Omega jabbed a finger downward. "Here, to this place."

"Yeah, it was. I thought it might be a good place for both of us to kind of retire. Not completely, because it's still an Agency field station, so we could still do the cool stuff you like, once in a while. Even go off-planet from time to time."

"But what about Joe? Wouldn't we have taken his job? Um, you, rather?"

"Nah. I actually had a couple of conversations with him and with Fox about that, while I was still in the medlab and working out the details. It turns out he stays busy enough that he figured we could split the work between us and still have plenty for everybody. He was also thinking about the possibility of training me on the guest-ranch end of things—the hotelier stuff, you know—and then leaving us to it, going home to some girl there and seeing about maybe starting a family."

"Aw. I didn't know he had a girlfriend back home."

"Yeah. I gather they talk a lot on interstellar calls—the bunkhouse, where he stays, is off a piece from the other buildings, and has all of the high-tech stuff. She might come here eventually. Anyway, back to the plan—meanwhile, see, I'd have been teaching you all about ranching. Given what I know now, and probably woulda found out about pretty quick after arriving, I expect we'd have just given over the remuda and the barn to you, to manage."

"Well, I probably could have done, at that. Even as mentally impaired as I was. I've had a thing for horses since I was real little, and it's partly instinctive, sorta."

"We can always keep it in our hip pockets for the future, Meg," Echo offered. "After all, accidents happen, and maybe one of these days one or both of us can't do field work any more, but the Ranch is always still here. Or maybe we just get older and tired, but we like the work and don't wanna leave the Agency; we come here and keep working for the Agency, but it isn't quite as dangerous, or whatever."

"But...you mean, even after you retired...and you'd still want me to...?"

"Of course, baby," Echo said, voice quiet. "Bestest buddies an' all that shit. An' you're the one that called me family, just a few days ago; turn about, an' all that. At this point," the phrasing went through his mind, and he decided to risk it and see how she reacted, "I'm not sure I can really imagine doing it without you beside me, anyway."

"Aw," Omega said again, and dropped her gaze, flushing a bit.

But Echo saw the wobbly grin on her lips.

YES! he thought, elated. *She liked it! Score!*

"You good with that, then?" he said aloud.

"Yeah, Ace, I think I am," she said, seeming thoughtful. "Maybe we can even manage to do something similar with my farm, and then we got two places to bebop between or something, I dunno."

"Sure, we can look at that."

"Then we got a backup plan, you and me."

"Good."

* * *

97

Well over an hour later, Omega glanced at the low sun. "Blast an' damnation. It's gettin' late. We better start headin' back."

Echo shot her a grin as he realized her Southern accent had now deepened significantly.

"Don't sound so disappointed. We've got two whole weeks—Division weeks, at that. Besides, we probably need to get you back anyway, paleface. Looks as if somebody forgot the sunblock."

"Uh-oh. I sure did." Her free right hand flew to her face. "How bad?"

"Take off the goggle-glasses a minute, and let me see." He waited until she complied, then surveyed her face. "Ooo. Well...let's just say Bozo has nothing on you right now."

"Heap big lotta red skin, huh?" She broke off. "Eh. I meant it as a joke. It didn't come out right. Sorry."

"No, it's fine. I took it the way you meant it. And I'm the half-Apache. After all, I called you 'paleface' first, so I kinda figured we'd start into the old Western movie jokes right quick."

"So I'm pretty sunburned?"

"Yup. Like you said, red skin. Looks like we got a definite Wild West theme goin' here, too. But you're gonna feel that later." He gestured at her face.

"Aw, crud. It's bad enough, I'm gonna be sore tomorrow. I hadda go pull a stupid like this."

"Sore from what?"

"Echo, I haven't been in the saddle since before I joined Division One, almost a year and a half ago, now."

"Uh-oh. Ow. Yup—you're not gonna get out of bed tomorrow. Especially after the spill you took. I'd better go ahead and call in that crane now," he deadpanned. She gave him a tolerant look as she replaced the goggle-glasses.

"To tell the truth," she said, "I wasn't plannin' on going to bed until tomorrow. Tomorrow morning, anyway."

"Breakin' out the 'scope when we get back?" he asked,

and she nodded. "Need help?"

"No. But if you're offerin', I sure won't turn you down."

"Good. I think I'd like to learn a little more hands-on astronomy from you."

"Okay. Maybe you can even help me start brainstorming that next Division One University course."

"I could do that, sure."

* * *

When Celeste and Spirit had been groomed and fed, the two companions headed into the guest house. Echo fished out the Agency medikit from the luggage neatly stacked in a corner of the guest house's den and handed it to Omega.

"Here. Go take care of that sunburn, and your chin, now, before they get too painful. When you're done, I'll see about getting hold of the Ranch medic. Oh, while I'm thinking about it, heads up, 'cause combing your hair out may get fun, too. Right now it looks like Celeste's mane did. If you need help, yell. I swear I'll be gentler than your mom was!"

Omega grimaced.

"Urgh. Looks like maybe a hat or a helmet with a visor is in order tomorrow," she decided. "Maybe I'll just whack the stuff off like the mane on a polo pony, rather than try detangling it every day. I wonder..."

"Wonder what?"

"I can't remember if I brought any scissors."

Echo raised a mildly-alarmed eyebrow.

"Uh, no. I'll go see if Joe's got a hat lying around that you can borrow."

"What? You don't think I'd look good in a crew cut?" she grinned at him. "It's not Agency dress code?"

Echo just folded his arms and looked at her, eyebrow still elevated.

"Okay. I get that message. When is dinner? And where?" She began hunting through her luggage for a wide-toothed comb, as Echo headed for the door in search of a hat.

"In about an hour, up at the main house. You've got just

time enough to get cleaned up, doctor the boo-boos, and meet me there."

"Good. I'm starved!"

* * *

"I'm sorry, Echo, we don't have a medic here at the Ranch, at the moment," Joe said, as the Alpha One team stood in his little office in the main house. "Angamar had a fam'ly situation come up, and she got called back to th' homeworld to take care of her sire, after 'e got 'imself hurt on th' job."

"Oh," Echo said, blank. "Well, damn. We sure could stand to have Meg's teeth checked, after that spill she took this afternoon. I wanna make sure there aren't any, you know, hairline cracks or something, that'll come back to haunt her later."

"I'd have figured you'd have done a field scan on 'er," Joe pointed out.

"That would be my fault," Omega sighed. "I was supposed to pack the field medical stuff for our trip. And I got here with the medikit itself, but I evidently went off and left the medscanner sitting on the dining room table."

"Oh, well then, I kin fix that," Joe said, going to the cabinet in the corner and opening it up. "Top shelf here is our emergency kit. Angamar had a bigger one, but she took it with 'er when she left to go home. I guess she figgered her pa might need it."

He pulled out a medscanner and handed it to Echo.

"All right, baby, now we can at least verify if you're okay or not," Echo said, flipping the on-switch. "Hold still for a minute."

Omega stood silent and unmoving, while Echo did a thorough scan of her neck, face, jaws, and chin, studying the readout on the device as he did so.

"Terrific," Echo said with a smile. "Meg, looks like you're good to go. I don't see any signs of damage to teeth or bone. It's all soft tissue bruising and abrasion. And what we've already done should take care of the worst of that by tomorrow."

"Great!" Omega declared. "Then let's eat!"

100

* * *

Dinner was in the big dining room at the main ranch house. With Echo and Omega the only guests, they chose to sit together at one end of the big parquet-inlaid mesquite dining table. At their request, Joe joined them, and the small kitchen staff brought out the meal family-style, in large serving bowls and platters, for each person to help themselves.

And while the guest list might have been short, the menu was not—the first course was a mixed greens salad with cinnamon/cayenne-candied pecans and fresh strawberries, drizzled with balsamic vinaigrette. The entrée was a hearty beefalo stew, the meat a lean, delicious hybrid of buffalo and cow, the stock rich and thick, loaded with carrots, potatoes, yucca root, mushrooms, and a smoky, spicy hint of diced chipotle; this was accompanied by German potato salad, barbecue baked beans, fresh-picked green beans, sweet onion relish, and jalapeño cornbread. Dessert was an American Indian-style sweet corn pudding. It was all accompanied by tall glasses of iced sweet tea.

"Oh. My. Gosh," Omega sighed, patting her belly at the end of the huge meal. "That was DELICIOUS! The corn pudding reminded me of yours, Echo! Joe, is there any chance I can get hold of the recipes? Or are they kinda, like, proprietary?"

Joe glanced at Echo, who gave the slightest nod; Omega saw, but said nothing, and didn't change expression.

"Sure, ma'am," Joe said then. "I reckon as how that won't be a problem. You just let me know what dishes you want, an' I'll have Cook make copies o' the recipes. They're all from th' recipe list of the fam'ly what lived here before, ah, th' Agency took over runnin' the establishment."

"Mmm," Omega murmured. "Echo, you want the last of the beefalo stew? If not, I call dibs..."

* * *

"...You want that look around the main house now, Echo?" Joe wondered as the male Agent and his partner rose from the dinner table.

"That...might be good, Joe," Echo decided. "I'm not gonna put anybody out, am I?"

"Nah, we ain't got any other guests here at the moment," Joe noted. "Just you and Omega, there. And y'all don't quite count, ya know? You're 'home folks.'"

"Yeah, I know. Meg, you wanna look around the ranch house with me? You've never been here before..." Echo offered. His partner's blue eyes were gentle as she answered.

"Sure, Ace, that sounds good."

* * *

Joe led the pair around the main ranch house. Whereas the guest house was relatively new, built to add more visitors' rooms to what was essentially a functioning guest ranch, the main house was very different, having housed the original family that had owned the ranch.

The main house was in no wise 'new'; it was an historic building, the core of the original house having been constructed in 1873, according to the engraving on the limestone cornerstone. The house still bore strong Spanish and American Indian influences in architecture, furnishings, and landscaping.

The area around the house was landscaped with desert and semi-arid plants using xeriscape principles and indigenous plants; though the area was considered the extreme western part of the Hill Country on the edge of the Edwards Plateau, its position so near the lower Pecos River—the other bank of which began the Trans-Pecos region—meant it had a blend of foliage from the two regions, and rather less rainfall than the rest of the Hill Country. This also meant that the area was more rugged than lands either farther east or west, as the Pecos and its tributary streams carved into the edge of the hard limestone strata of the plateau, resulting in a savannah-like plateau 'floor' laced with many dendritic ravines and canyons, all of which eventually drained into the Pecos, thence to the Rio Grande. The whole of the region was interspersed with thousands of flat-topped hills, buttes, and ridges, remnants of the plateau isolated by canyon erosional growth.

Consequently, mesquite, live oak, piñon pine, several species of yucca, juniper, prickly pear, and cholla comprised the landscaping around the main house, with evidence that the edible fruits and seeds of each had been harvested regularly. Along the eastern side of the house was an old herb garden, surrounded by a low stone border and comprised largely of osha, sarsaparilla, several varieties of yucca, passionflower, sweetgrass, chaparral, and white, purple, and blue sages. In addition, the garden had a small but substantial plot of more Celtic plants, such as burdock, nettle, and comfrey, in one corner. It was overhung and shaded from harsh southern sun by two ancient and venerable pecan trees.

The exterior of the house itself was comprised of native stone and stucco, with a flat roof intended to collect the often-scant rainwater of the region and funnel it into a cistern—though these days, it was furnished with an excellent well, drilled down into the aquifer; now the cistern largely functioned to water the herb garden. The house itself was framed with big timbers and possessed tall, narrow windows, mostly on the north and south sides, though all were equipped inside with insulated blinds.

The front of the house faced roughly north, where a long, winding gravel drive led off toward the main road, which was invisible to the house due to being over a mile distant, as well as the fact that it ran along the floor of a wide canyon. A small gravel parking lot, sufficient to hold some six or eight vehicles, had been installed to the west of the entrance. The front entrance itself was equipped with a single huge, heavy, carved-wood-and-wrought-iron door in the mission style, the mesquite wood dark with age, and shaded by a small, hewn-beam mesquite pergola over pieced limestone flagstones.

The rear of the house faced the barn, stable, and guest house to the south and west, and had a full, verandah-style porch, albeit in a more southwestern style than was typical of the verandahs Omega was used to seeing.

Though they had long since been filled in to accommodate the central heating and air with which the house was now equipped, the gun slots built into the walls of the house in case of Indian or bandit attack were still there, and made a fascinating historical sidebar. Omega asked lots of questions about the tactic of using such openings, as well as the historical events surrounding the house. To her delight, Echo answered at least as many of her questions as Joe did, seeming quite knowledgeable of the ranch's history, and of the original owning family—though she noticed that neither male ever mentioned a surname for the clan.

* * *

The interior had been modernized some three decades earlier, with lovely mesquite cabinetry and trim, and sheet rock walls painted in various pale desert hues, and it had been well and subtly maintained and enhanced ever since. The single-floor dwelling was divided into wings, with the west wing housing the kitchen, a breakfast nook, a laundry—though not of the hotel variety; guest linens were handled in a special outbuilding elsewhere on the ranch, constructed for the purpose—and a roomy mud room. The east wing contained five bedrooms and three baths—a large master suite, and two pairs of smaller bedrooms connected by jack-and-jill bathrooms—while the central portion of the house held the commons areas: a dining room that seated up to twelve; a large, comfortable den with delightfully overstuffed leather furniture into which one could sink, with a large flat-screen television—an Agency satellite dish nestled discreetly in a corner of the roof—and entertainment center. One end of the den held a huge fireplace and hearth of native stone, with a thick, wide mantel comprised of one solid piece of mesquite; the antique iron hangers and supports for cooking were still embedded in the firebox. There was also a spacious study, a tiny ranch manager's office, a powder room half-bath, and a small sitting room or parlor.

The flooring was mushroom-toned tile throughout, and plush throw rugs in muted colors and soft yarns graced the bedroom floors, as well as helping to delineate areas throughout the rest of the structure.

The furnishings were largely of leather and mesquite, with parquet inlaid tabletops, decorative accents in wrought iron, and the occasional antler piece. Quite a few of the furniture pieces were antique, as were numerous other items, such as vases, bowls, and many of the copious books lining the study shelves.

In addition to landscape paintings—including a couple by Georgia O'Keeffe; actual paintings, not prints—and photos as décor, several utterly beautiful, vintage Native American rugs and blankets in bright colors served as tapestries adorning the walls.

Echo tended to gravitate to the den and the study, hovering near certain items of furniture or perusing this or that book from the shelves. Omega watched him, thoughtful, but said nothing.

* * *

"This is just a gorgeous house," Omega enthused by the time they had reached the bedroom wing. Echo missed the meaningful look she gave him; he was busy peering wistfully into one of the smaller bedrooms, which was painted a light cornflower blue, with a rustic-style bedroom suite. "I'm loving the design, and the décor, and...well, just everything about it."

"We can put y'all in here if you'd rather, ma'am," Joe noted. "The room Echo usually stays in is over here—this 'un he's lookin' at now, in fact—an' there's a nice room right next to it that I can put you in. Real comfortable. You'd share the bathroom, though. Or I could put ya on opposite sides of the hall, and you could have your own bathrooms, since nobody else is stayin' here." He shot a glance at Echo, who shrugged.

"It's up to Meg," he said. "It isn't like either of us has really gotten unpacked yet, although I'm afraid we've already messed up the showers in our rooms in the guest house, after that horseback ride this afternoon."

"Ah, that ain't no big deal," Joe waved away the concern.

105

"I kin have maid service clean the bathrooms, sweep the tile, smooth th' quilts, an' be done. How 'bout it, Omega? You wanna stay in the guest house, or move inta the main house? We ain't got no other guests scheduled to arrive. We're gettin' inta the hot time o' year around here, see..."

"Getting into?" Echo wondered, raising a querying eyebrow.

"All right, Mr. Smart Ass," Joe chuckled. "We're already there. Anyhow, we don't usually get that many visitors this time o' year, so you got your pick, and no problems."

"Would you mind?" Omega looked at Echo. "The guest house is lovely, don't get me wrong. But there's just...something about this house. It has character, history. I adore it. I'd love to stay here at least a few days." She shot him a sidelong glance that said, *I bet you would, too. C'mon Ace. Let's do it.*

"All right. We can do that," Echo agreed, capitulating with little resistance. "How much did you spread out already in the guest house?"

"Oh, nothing but my bathroom. I was gonna unpack properly later tonight, before we head out for stargazing. I'll have to go gather some stuff up and shove it back in my overnight kit, though."

"Okay. I didn't even unpack my shaving kit yet, so I can just—"

"I'll have Juan run over there an' get your things an' fetch 'em to your, uh, usual room, Echo," Joe said. "No trouble."

"All right," Omega decided. "As for which bedroom, I don't mind sharing a bathroom with Echo, if he doesn't mind. It isn't like we haven't done that before, on missions. Hell, we've zonked in the same room before a couple times, when we only had a few hours to catch some shut-eye; sometimes we had beds, and sometimes we had the floor. A shared bathroom is fine by me if he's good with it."

"I'm good," Echo said. He shrugged, then offered her a slight, one-sided grin. She ran a gentle hand over his near shoulder; it communicated, *Are you all right?* and he nodded.

"Okay. In that case, let me run throw stuff back into my overnight bag," she told them, "and I'll have everything ready for Juan to trundle over here on a cart or something."

"'At works," Joe agreed, as a delighted Omega scampered off.

* * *

As soon as Omega was out of sight, Joe moved closer to the Alpha Line chief.

"So she don't know? I mean, about this place?"

"No," Echo answered with a sigh. "At least, I don't think so. I delivered a pretty strong hint this afternoon, but she didn't seem to catch on. Which isn't like her, so maybe she did, and just chose not to risk...ripping off the bloody bandage, as it were." He shrugged. "Or maybe she was just so exuberant about being out of the big city that she missed it. I'm not sure."

"You gonna tell 'er?"

"Yeah, eventually. I...just need to find the right time and place. And be in the right mood," Echo confessed. "At least, about the place. I'm still not sure what it says about your predecessor, that arrangement she had."

"You mean Gonzales?"

"Yeah. I'm wondering if that was just coincidence, or if Gonzo wasn't the Wintourn we thought he was."

"Well, he went home last year, finally retired an' all, but he didn't seem in no rush," Joe pointed out. "Nor like anybody was breathin' down 'is back, either. I always thought he was a right straight-shooter."

"And he probably was," Echo admitted. "But after everything that went down with Slug..." He shook his head. "That damn gastropoid had layers upon layers of planning and schemes, and sometimes it's hard to know who was in on it, and who was just being manipulated. And damn, could that telepath manipulate." Then he shrugged. "Maybe it's better that Gonzo retired and went home right before Slug's end game went down. Otherwise he mighta ended up one of the casualties."

"Yeah, I hear ya. Lissen, I heard some scuttlebutt a while back—it 'uz around Christmas, I think—'bout you and Omega. If, uh, if you want, I can put y'all in th' master bedroom together..."

"No!" Echo exclaimed, flushing despite himself. "I, uh, I dunno what you heard, but...we don't...we're not...sleeping together. Never have. Don't even let on that you heard anything LIKE that to Meg, or she'll be twenty shades of embarrassed red."

"You've got some impressive color goin' there yourself, pal," Joe noted, a slight, teasing grin on his face. "So I take it, you'd like it to go there, but it ain't anywheres close just yet?"

Echo smeared a hand over his face.

"Can everybody see it BUT Meg?" he wondered, morose.

"Nah. But I got privileged info just now that let me figger it."

"How's that?"

"One—you brought her along with ya to look around the house. That says you're hurtin', but havin' her around helps. An' speakin' o' hurtin', I'm here for ya, too, pal. Fox gave me a heads-up 'bout yer mom, under th' circumstances. I sure was sorry ta hear. Ain't like I ever met 'er, but I know YOU. An' that says a bunch about her, all of it good."

Echo nodded his thanks, then waved a hand for Joe to continue, as they meandered toward the door of the master suite.

"Okay. Two—you shot a glance at the master bedroom afore ya answered me, which tells me you liked the idea and wish ya could, but ya can't, so you ain't even goin' there."

Echo raised an eyebrow in surprise; he hadn't even realized he had done that.

"An' three—you an' me go back a ways, hombre. I know you. I been watchin' you two all afternoon, leastways when you was in sight. An' I can see when a human male has found his female. There's a way you human guys treat 'em, leastways the ones of ya that was raised right, what says they mean somethin' to ya. An' you treat her like that. I ain't never seen you treat anybody else the way you treat her. You two are close, real close, an' you want it even closer."

***

Echo sighed, but didn't deny it. Instead, he shoved his hands into his jeans pockets, and stared at the tile of the floor for a time. Joe, knowing there were emotions inside the other male that he was trying to handle, remained silent, letting Echo collect himself.

Meanwhile, Echo looked around the master bedroom, noting this piece of furniture and that detail, most of which had been left as they were by the original owners...who were all too familiar to the male Agent. He sighed, temporarily losing himself in memory, before very deliberately letting it all go.

Finally the head of Alpha Line spoke.

"I dunno, Joe. It just seems so...ironic, so, so, almost ludicrous, somehow, like the universe itself is mocking me. Here I bring Meg to west Texas, to introduce her to the kind of life I once knew, just as Ma...is leaving it." His voice cracked in spite of his best efforts. "And there's not one damn thing I can do about it. I had," he confessed to the ranch manager, whom he'd known since Joe was only a junior ranch hand, "hopes of maybe, somehow, introducing Meg to Mom one of these days. I wanted to bring her here, and show her my life, and find a way to have her meet Mom, and all that; dreamed of it for months now. And I finally got her here, but it looks like..." He broke off, tried to clear his throat, and choked. Eventually he ground out, "Maybe I can take her to the funeral. We'll have to stay way in the back, and hope nobody recognizes me..."

Joe laid a light hand on Echo's shoulder.

They simply stood like that until Omega returned with Juan and the luggage.

***

After the huge, hearty ranch-hand dinner and the exploration of the main house, not to mention settling into their rooms in the main house, Echo wandered out onto the porch, to find a relaxed Omega sitting alone, her legs stretched across the top step and leaning against a column, watching the sun go down, and bathed in its rosy golden glow.

Damn, he thought, captivated. *That's just gorgeous. The sunset, AND my partner. I've never seen her look so...beautiful. I wonder if she'd object to my company.*

"Mind if I join you?" Echo asked softly, leaning one hand against the column and looking down at her, "...or am I interrupting?"

"Oh," Omega said, glancing up, "no, it's okay. C'mon, I'll make room," she said, drawing her legs up.

"No, stay put; you look comfortable there," Echo told her, as he stepped over her and sat down on the second step, resting his elbows on his knees. Omega stretched back out, sliding down into a comfortable slouch as Echo added, "Nice sunset." The two gazed at the horizon as they talked in low tones.

"Yeah. This has always been my favorite time of day."

"A chance to be quiet and thoughtful," Echo stated. Omega glanced at him, seeming a little surprised.

"Exactly."

"Ever get the urge to...follow it?" Echo pointed at the sunset.

"You mean literally ride off into the sunset? Wanderlust?" she asked, and he nodded. "Every time." She sighed, wistful. "But then the sun goes down, and the colors fade, and it's twilight. And the mood changes."

"Like it's doing now." The last sliver of the sun's disk disappeared behind the horizon as Echo spoke.

"Uh-huh. I start thinkin' about what I've done, what I have. And I get this deep sense of...of..."

"Contentment?" Echo suggested.

"That's it."

"Yeah."

The two companions were silent for a while, watching the bright colors fade into blue and purple.

"Mmm...this is nice," Omega murmured as the deepening twilight was slowly underscored by the myriad chirps of crickets, cicadas, and the odd katydid, and the heat of the day cooled. An intermittent breeze sprang up, cool and soothing. "Just like a summer evening on the farm, when I was little. The only thing missing is a whippoorwill."

"Well, let's see what we can do about that..." Echo pursed his lips and emitted a loud whistle: *whip...whip...whip-poor-WILL, whip-poor-WILL...*

Omega straightened up and looked at her partner with a delighted smile.

"That was good, Echo! I never got the hang of a whippoorwill. I can do a passable bob-white quail, but—"

"Shhh," Echo whispered. "Listen."

Floating in on the soft evening breeze came a faint, "Whip...whip...whip-poor-WILL, whip-poor-WILL, whip-poor-WILL..."

"Ohhh," Omega sighed, leaning back with a dreamy smile, as the bird continued to call, "perfect."

"Meg," Echo asked gently, turning to look at her, "are you happy?"

"Right this moment, or in general?"

"Both."

"Yes, Echo, I am. On both counts. What, are you worried I regret running into you a year and a half ago? Or," she added, teasing, "maybe that oughta be you and your perp running into me?"

"A little, yeah." He glanced away for a moment, as a wave of remorse washed over him for all that he had brought upon her, inadvertent though it had been. *At least, on my part,* he added mentally.

"Don't, then. I'm enjoying myself hugely," she told him. "My world, my UNIVERSE, my...life. Granted, my life isn't what I expected it to be, and I suppose there are things I'll never have now..."

"Such as?"

"...Children, for example."

"Why not? You're not that old."

"Echo, think about it—with my genetics? I wouldn't dare. Never mind the issue of where the other set of chromosomes would come from."

Echo nodded then, understanding her point of view. *After all,* he realized, *we don't have a 'thing' going yet, as Romeo would say. So it isn't like she can—*

"Just as well it's a subject that isn't gonna come up, I guess," Omega added softly. Echo blinked, startled.

"Huh? What do you mean?"

"It can't be a problem if there isn't a man on the planet who'd look twice at me." She shrugged.

"What gives you that idea?" Echo asked, mildly shocked, watching her. Omega gazed fixedly at the flaming sky along the horizon where the sun had gone down, avoiding his eyes as she replied.

"Echo...we're really close friends, so I'm gonna be blunt here and say what I'd never tell anyone else. I don't know what I am, but whatever I am, it isn't human. I...can't imagine any man seriously considering me for a mate."

Echo stared at her silently, astounded, trying to decide how to answer. *She still hasn't caught on,* he grasped. *That, or she's trying to hint that I'm not under consideration, and do it without hurting my feelings. What do I...? How do I say...?* But before he could formulate a response, Omega dismissed the issue with a slight wave of her hand.

"It's not important. Like I said, it saves me the trouble of worrying about the offspring issue."

"It IS important, baby. I can see it in your eyes."

She blinked, and looked away.

"Sometimes, Ace," Omega murmured, voice husky, "you're a little too perceptive for my own good. All right, try this instead—it doesn't matter. I am whatever I am, and I've accepted that. I just don't expect anyone else to."

"But—"

"'Nuff said, Echo. Please."

Echo paused briefly, disappointed at the curtailing of the

conversation when there was so much he wanted to say, wanted to tell her. *Only the subject hurts her,* he recognized. So for the time being, he continued the original line of inquiry, as he turned to stare out over the Ranch.

"But you're still happy with your life, baby?"

* * *

"Sure," Omega answered, confident. "I was an astronaut, Echo. I dreamed of going into space, of exploring it. Of discovering life on other worlds. And now I work with aliens every day, and flying around the galaxy is routine—well, as routine as it gets for us, anyway! I don't think ANYTHING we do is really routine! But I get to play with the coolest toys," she said with a grin, then her voice softened as she added, "and I do have a pretty terrific—if a little unorthodox—'family.' Name of Echo. And Romeo, and India. And Fox, as well. And I guess Zebra is joining it now, too. Not to mention a 'friend of the family' who runs the whole damn galaxy." Omega laid a light hand on Echo's back, rubbing his shoulder blade affectionately for a moment before dropping her hand. "Why shouldn't I be happy?"

Echo said nothing, still gazing thoughtfully into the distance, and after a couple of minutes Omega asked, "How about you? Are you happy, Echo?"

He was silent for a bit, then said simply, "Yeah."

"Had to think about it?" she asked, noting the hesitation.

"Not really." Echo shrugged.

"Is it...your mom?" she wondered, trying to get him to open up to her.

"...No." He shook his head. "I'm...coming to terms with that."

"Echo...do you still miss Chase?" Omega asked then, very, very gently.

Echo glanced over his shoulder at Omega with an odd expression on his face, one she couldn't interpret...but which somehow looked hurt, as he leaned back and rested his elbows on the top step, tucking them against her side, before gently leaning into her.

"...No," he told her quietly as she inched over slightly to give him room, while allowing the familiar contact to remain. Echo stretched his long legs out in front of him, resting then on a limestone flag, tilted his head back to look upward, then pointed. "First star."

Omega studied Echo's profile, trying to interpret his expression, then gave up and glanced upward, following his gaze.

"Yup. It's a star. As opposed to a planet, that is. It's off to the south a bit, and it's red. Want to take a guess?"

"Mmm..." He glanced around the sky, considering, then took a look at his wrist chronometer. "I'm thinkin' Antares."

"Ooo! Good job." She grinned and applauded.

"Good schoolmarm." Echo grinned back. "Shouldn't we be getting out your equipment here, pretty quick?"

"Soon." Omega glanced at her own wrist chronometer. "But we're in no rush."

* * *

"Hey, y'all," Joe said moments later as he walked past the back of the house, then paused. "Wow, y'all look really comfortable there."

"Yeah," Echo replied, laconic, as he leaned lightly against his partner's side. "Pretty spot, good company, good conversation. Nothin' breathing down our necks."

"Makes for a relaxing evening," Omega added. "And that means yeah, we're comfortable."

"I s'pose so. I don't reckon I've ever seen Echo look this relaxed." Joe's eyebrows were as far up his forehead as they could get.

"Then that's...good," Omega decided, and Echo offered them both a slight smile.

"Yeah, baby, it's good," he agreed.

"No offense, but why do ya call 'er 'baby,' Echo?"

"Baby agent," Alpha One said in unison, and laughed. "See, it's a nickname from my rookie days," Omega explained. "Only it stuck, and I kinda like it. It reminds me of livin' in

114

Alabama around my family an' old friends, callin' me honey an' stuff."

"I think it makes her feel more at home in the Big Apple," Echo concluded. "She calls me 'Ace' the same way."

"Well, I won't bother y'all any more, then," Joe said with a smile. "You two are like peas in a pod. Ya belong together, I think. I just wanted to tell ya, me an' some o' the boys an' girls are gonna build a bonfire out behind th' guest house, make coffee, mebbe roast marshmallows an' some other stuff. There'll be beer, too, if you'd rather. Pete said he 'uz makin' his special chili an' bringin' a pot; some 'a th' others gonna throw on some beef."

"A barbacoa?" Echo wondered, enthused.

"Sure. Not big, though. Mostly it's an excuse ta build a bonfire an' have a few beers. I'd'a told ya afore dinner, if I'd known. But they kinda threw it together at th' last minute."

Just then, a spiral of smoke ascended behind the guest house, the thin dark column silhouetted against the sunset sky. A shower of sparks went up, then died away.

"Looks like the fire's started," Omega observed.

"Yup. I suppose we could maybe do a little more dessert," Echo decided. "We got some chocolate bars, cookies, food bars and the like, that we brought for snacks on trail rides; we could contribute some of that to the cause. Meg? Whatcha think?"

"I believe I could be talked into it, Ace," Omega said with a grin. "Sittin' around a campfire in west Texas on a late June evenin', tellin' stories on each other with a beer and some s'mores? It's a plan."

* * *

They did indeed contribute most of their chocolate bars, and some graham-cracker-like snack bars, toward making s'mores, and the pair enjoyed sitting around on hunks of log and large rocks, swapping stories around the bonfire with the ranch hands. Echo ensured Omega got samples of the various other foodstuffs, as well, especially Pete's chili and Joe's barbecued ribs.

115

"No more," Omega said, holding up a staying hand when Joe made to bring her yet another steak. "I'm gonna 'splode! Oh, this stuff is good!"

"I kinda figured you'd like it, baby," Echo said with a grin.

"Agent!" the ranch hands promptly chorused, almost before Echo could finish speaking, then they all started laughing in delight. Omega and Echo both blinked.

"I told 'em about your nickname, Omega, just so some 'a these wags wouldn't go misunderstandin'," Joe explained. "See, um, some scuttlebutt got back here last Christmas..."

"...Oh. That stuff," Omega said, all pretense at levity dropping away. Her gaze went distant, and fell to the ground. Echo winced.

"No, no, no ma'am," Pete—one of the ranch hands, from Kufthuria—said, kneeling in front of her. "'At won't do. Don't you go reactin' like that, now. Most of us, we know Echo from a long time back, an' we knew it wadn't like we heard, ennyhow. Couldn't be, an' be th' Echo we know an' respect. B'sides, we got eyes in our heads. We seen you two today. Echo treats you like a proper lady, so we know ya are one, an' you treat him like the gennelman we already know he is. Y'all's good folks. It's all right. Joe 'uz just lookin' out fer y'all. That's all."

"Yas'm," and, "'At's eezackly right," came the affirmations.

"Aw," Omega said, as Pete coaxed a shy smile from her. "All right, y'all. Thanks. I 'preciate it."

"Near as we kin tell," Joe added, "your mama an' daddy raised you right, ma'am. An' the two of y'all, well, you just kinda fit, never mind your team reputation. We don't wanna do nothin' to screw that up for ya."

"And I agree with my partner," Echo said, quiet. "Thanks, y'all."

"No problem, Echo," Joe said. "Speakin' of, you doin' all right, in the circumstances?"

"You mean Ma?"

"Yup."

"I suppose so. In the circumstances."

"All right. You let us know if you need anything. We're here for ya, pal, all of us."

"Okay."

"How 'bout another round o' beer, ever'body?"

A cheer went up.

* * *

When the barbacoa finally died down, somewhat later into the night than they had expected—it was already well past eleven in the evening—Echo and Omega decided to postpone any serious observing until the next night. But they did choose to go ahead and break out the telescope, just so Echo could begin to get some experience handling the equipment.

"Now, you're sure it won't hurt not to do any real observing tonight?" he asked, concerned. "You won't, I dunno, miss something? Have it set and go behind the Sun or anything like that?"

"Nah, it won't be a problem," Omega told him, confident. "My regular observing program is designed to be pretty flexible."

"Okay, that's good," Echo concluded. "What if we go off in one of the pastures nearby, and set up there, then? That way, we don't have so much to do before we get there, loading stuff on horses an' all that. It's already pretty late."

"That sounds like a good idea," Omega agreed. "Let's do it. You know the area already; where should we go?"

* * *

Less than fifteen minutes later, they were setting up in a field to the north of the main house, with Omega teaching Echo how to handle and unpack the equipment, as well as how to return it to its various cases when they were finished.

Then they spent another hour as Omega took him on a telescopic tour of the solar system, and they discussed the differences in appearance of the various planets in the telescope versus from orbit, and what factors made the differences.

Finally, around a quarter to one, they called it a night,

packed the equipment, and lugged it back to the main house, where they both collapsed in their respective beds, tired but content.

* * *

Omega slept hard but well, and woke up surprisingly early—the sky was just beginning to lighten in the east—ready to explore the Ranch even farther afield. She rose and tiptoed through showering and getting ready, trying not to wake up Echo in the next bedroom, then dressed and headed for the kitchen.

But Echo was already there, with a pot of coffee waiting. As soon as she walked into the kitchen, he poured coffee into the mug he had nearby, adding cream as she liked it, then handed it to her.

"Here," he said, picking up his own mug. "Let's go out on the back porch and watch the sunrise. Grab a throw blanket. We may be going into the hot season, but it'll still be chilly and damp this time of the morning."

* * *

"Which do you like best? Sunrises, or sunsets?" Omega asked, as they sat together in the porch swing, blankets wrapped about the pair, and sipped their coffee. In the east, the black sky had already lightened to dark blue, becoming striated with deep purples and reds. Several distant clouds, low on the horizon, began to turn a bright, neon pink.

"Mm, kinda depends on my mood, I guess," Echo considered, leaning into her lightly. "They mean different things to me. A sunrise? That's a new start, a fresh day. Starting over, if necessary. A sunset, like we talked about last night, tends to activate the wanderlust in me. I wanna follow it, somehow."

"Me too. On both."

"Kinda figured. We're too much alike not to see 'em the same way."

"I really hope..." Omega began, then broke off.

"Hope what?"

Omega drew a deep breath, let it out slowly, then answered.

"I really hope we truly ARE that much alike, as opposed to...my having been made like you."

"I doubt that's possible, at this point," Echo said, offering comfort. "There's only so much that can be done to things like that by genetic manipulation, and the programming has been broken. So what's left is your real personality, Meg. And as Dad used to say, and Joe still does, we 'get along like two peas in a pod.'" He cocked his head and looked at her. "Do you get what I mean?"

"Yeah, I do."

"Do you agree with it?"

"I...think so," she decided. "It's just...now and then, I...worry."

"I understand. But I've seen enough of you, of your behavior, of the way you acted under the programming, to be able to easily tell the difference, I think. So if you won't trust yourself, trust me, baby: we're alike because we're alike, not because you were made to be alike."

Their eyes met, and they looked at each other for long moments, then Omega nodded affirmation. Satisfied, Echo also nodded in response, and they returned their attention to the sunrise. The pair were content to sit together, sipping coffee and watching the sky as its colors brightened from purple to red, to orange, yellow, then white as the Sun itself rose, and gradually the sky became turquoise once more.

"What do you wanna do today, Ace?" Omega finally broke the congenial silence.

"I want breakfast, for starters," he said, giving her a grin. "Although you may not be hungry yet, after all the barbecue you ate last night. On top of a mammoth ranch supper."

"Well, embarrassingly enough, I'm starved," she said, sheepish. "Lots of fresh air, sunshine, and activity have a tendency to do that to me."

"Yeah, me too." Echo sipped his coffee for a moment, thinking. "Have you ever actually been on a functional ranch before? I mean, not just for astronomical observing, but to watch the activity? The business of running a ranch?"

"No, I haven't."

"Are you curious about it?"

"Yeah, I am, to tell the truth; I just never had an opportunity to even ask, before. Daddy raised some row crops—cotton and soybeans, for the most part, but he always had a field of feed corn, too—'cause mostly we worked with horses. I'm curious to know how a cattle ranch would be different from a horse farm. ARE they different?"

"Yeah, they are. Oh, there's similarities, because they're both herd animals. But the end purpose for the animals is different, and they behave different—especially the longhorns we raise here. You interested in finding out more?"

"Yeah, I am. A lot."

"Then what say we find out if Joe will let us tag along with him today, so you can see? I can always play extra ranch hand, to make it worth his while. I'm betting he'll say yes, and between him and me, I'm sure we can explain how it all works, and answer any questions you come up with."

"I like that idea." Omega gave him a smile. "Let's do it."

"Okay. And then tomorrow, we can go into some of the canyons, and you can look at the geology. I saw you studying the rocks yesterday."

"I like that idea, too."

"Kinda figured. Just do me a favor?"

"What?"

"Don't forget your sunblock or hat this time."

"Right."

* * *

It was time to 'doctor' the cattle, deworming and providing vaccinations—the Ranch tended to deworm their cattle at least three times a year, instead of the usual two, to keep them as healthy as possible, using galactic veterinary medicine and techniques—so Echo and Omega rode along with Joe as he and a specific group of hands rode from pasture to pasture, round-ing up the longhorn cattle before cutting out one or two at a time and administering the medications. Riding Spirit, Echo joined the ranch hands working to gather the cattle and cut them out for Joe to medicate.

"No, Meg, you stay close to Joe," Echo instructed, when she started to follow him out into the pasture on Celeste. "Longhorns can be dangerous, and you aren't used to working cattle."

"But hasn't it been years since...?" Omega wondered.

"Nope," Joe noted. "He's down here often enough on assignment an' junk, he rides with us a couple times a year. He keeps his hand in. He's a cowboy, sure enough, ma'am. Don't you worry 'bout him none. You just stick close to me, and I'll explain what we're doin' an' why. I kin even show ya how to administer some of the vaccinations, an' then you kin help me shoot 'em up, if you like. It'll go faster, thataways, too."

"Okay," Omega said, agreeable. "I'm always game to help out."

She and Echo spent all morning helping ensure the herds of the Ranch would stay healthy.

* * *

"How is she coming?" Zarnix asked Zebra, as they met in his office. "I have seen your reports, but..."

"Echo's mom, you mean?" Zebra clarified. "Mrs. Bryant?"

"Yes."

"She's doing okay, I suppose," Zebra decided, thinking for a moment. "Unlike Meg did, I don't think she's gonna wake up while she's in there."

"I don't think anyone but Omega has done so," Zarnix noted. "Not even Echo, during the short time he was in, to jumpstart the repair to his broken legs."

"Yeah, I think that was probably just a function of Omega's unique physiology," Zebra agreed. "But Mrs. Bryant, while strong and determined—I think I see where Echo gets it, at least in part; some probably came from his dad—doesn't

121

have the 'enhancements' Omega has...and she was weak and tired to begin with, when we put her in the regen pod..."

"And so she does not have the strength to overcome the fact that all her energies have been diverted to healing," Zarnix finished for her.

"Exactly."

"Well, it is good to know that it is going well, I suppose."

"Yeah," Zebra agreed. "I might actually start relaxing here in another day or two."

* * *

By the time Alpha One had taken a quick shower and dressed in clean jeans and shirts, Joe had seen to it that the kitchen staff had prepared a picnic lunch for the pair, and he sent them off to enjoy it. Echo chose to stay relatively close to the house so that they didn't have to ride horseback; he realized, just from watching her, that Omega had become a bit stiff from her fall the day before, and he wanted to keep her flexible, providing a break from riding—more so as she'd already spent almost the entire morning in the saddle. They wound up on the bank of a creek, under a small copse of live oak.

"There's a nicer place to picnic, a ways on down, near what we used to call the Pool, 'cause there's a good swimming hole there," Echo noted as they unpacked the picnic basket onto a blanket, "but it's kinda too far to walk. And I really don't wanna walk a long way along the creek in the heat of the day, because the snakes will all be out sunning."

"Good point. What, a couple different kinds of rattlers, copperheads, and cottonmouth? Or do y'all call cottonmouth 'water moccasins' around here?"

"Closer to around half a dozen different species of rattlesnakes, but that's about right. And I know 'em by both names. Dad usually called 'em water moccasins, though. And yeah, we do have 'em around here."

"Yeah, let's not, then," Omega agreed. "The meanest, foulest-tempered snake I ever did see was a pissed-off cottonmouth. I was playin' in the creek that cut across the corner of the property at home when I was real little, an' Daddy was nearby, when we accidentally stirred up a cottonmouth. That thing chased me clear across the creek and up the bank, with Daddy chunkin' rocks at it as big as his head, the whole way, trying to divert its attention, but it just kept coming. It had focused on me, and it was mad that I woke it up from sunning—never mind that I hadn't disturbed it. I don't really know WHAT woke it up. I hadn't even known it was there, until it came after me. An' me bare-footed, tryin' to run across the rocks in the stream bed."

"Wow. I guess your dad finally nailed it?"

"Yeah. With the biggest rock he could pitch. Exit one cottonmouth."

"Okay, no, we're not walking all the way down there, Ms. Trouble Magnet. Maybe we can ride down there in a couple days and I can show you."

"That sounds good, but this is really nice, too," Omega declared, as they ate cold fried chicken, fresh biscuits, and sliced brisket sandwiches, accompanied by fresh tortilla chips and salsa, and finished with homemade pecan pie.

"Are you enjoying yourself, Meg? Is this the kind of break, the kind of vacay, you wanted?"

"It's bang-on, Ace," she told him with a happy smile. "And I'm having a great time. Are you...doing okay? I know this is kinda...the home area for you, and with your mom..."

Echo waved off the inquiry.

"I'm doing okay, baby," he said. His voice was quiet, and ever so slightly hoarse, but even and steady. "Thanks for asking, though. I guess I...kinda needed to come down here, after y'all told me about Ma. It's why I didn't suggest we change our destination after that. Closure an' all."

"Yeah, that's sorta what I figured. Does..." She broke off. "Does what?"

"Aw, it's gonna sound egotistical. I didn't mean it like that, but it'll still sound wrong."

"Say it anyway. I know you better than that."

"Okay. Well...I was kinda hopin', maybe...does having me around help, a little bit?"

"Yeah, it does. It takes my mind off of internalizing things, and gets me thinking about other stuff."

"Good. I'm glad."

"When we get done eating, there's a little cave up here near the headwaters of the creek," Echo told her, deliberately changing the subject before it could get maudlin. "It's where the spring comes out, and it's got some cool rock layers, AND some Native pictographs, though I'm not sure which tribe did 'em, or even if they're from one of the current tribes of the area. They might be a lot older. I remember they brought in some archaeology types from one of the universities at some point, but I don't think they ever figured it out, either. You wanna take a look?"

"That sounds cool!"

"Yeah, and speaking of cool, it gets us outta the sun, too."

* * *

"Oh, man. This. Is. Great!" Omega enthused, that evening after dark had fallen at last on a companionable, cheerful day of vacation explorations. "Look at that sky! Fantastic seeing!!"

"I take it this is a good night for observing?" Echo deadpanned as he watched Omega efficiently set up and align the telescopic equipment. Earlier, he had helped her unload it from the packs on the horses, then extract the various pieces at her instruction, but they had decided that this time, he should sit back and watch as she performed the setup, because she had a specific way she wanted the equipment assembled for the observing session. Now, the soft sound of loosely-hobbled horses grazing rose nearby—there was neither fence post nor tree nor bush sturdy enough, or close enough, to tether them in that location.

"That, Echo, is an absolute understatement," she told him. "Not only are we way out from any city and the light pollution from 'em, the air is dead calm, clear, and there's no moon tonight, 'cause it's in new phase. And there's almost no scintillation."

"Say what?" Echo had started spreading out a blanket, intending to lie down and relax while Omega worked at the 'scope, but he paused to look at her in intense curiosity. "Scintillation? Dammit, I should remember that from your class..."

"Twinkling," she answered. "If the air along the line of sight is really still, the star won't twinkle much at all. That's good, because a twinkling star jumps all over the place in the telescope focus. And no, I didn't cover that in class, because the class didn't focus on observational astronomy. Well, I guess celestial navigation from space is a kind of observational astronomy, but it's different from this." She waved a hand at the telescope. "I wanted to make the class something that would be of use to Division One agents, and ground-based observational astronomy of this sort really isn't in y'all's purview. I already got the comments at the end of class, but if I get more interest in it from serious hobbyists in the Agency, I'll look at putting together a 200-level class in it."

"Oh, okay. That makes sense. And yeah, I might just wanna consider taking a class like that; I have to admit, hanging out with you has kinda got me a little curious about it. Okay, more than a little curious, if I'm honest. I'd like to be able to actually work WITH you on some of your observing—to know and understand what you're doing, and to help out."

"Aw! That'd be fun, Ace, and I'd love to have you do that."

"Okay, it's a deal. What are you gonna look at tonight? Anything you can show me?" Echo asked as he stretched out and settled down on the blanket, folding his arms behind his head and gazing skyward.

"I'm picking up where I left off a year and a half ago—before you, and Cartman the big purple bulldozer, came crashing into my world, trashed my setup, and made life interesting," she teased as she worked. "I finally managed to reconstruct my observation schedule and most of my data. I was studying compact-object binaries—regular stars circling black holes, neutron stars, or white dwarfs...or compact objects circling each other, for that matter. Photopolarimetric analysis. I was trying to help identify events that the gravitational-wave observatories detect; I've managed to gin up a cover story to keep doing it, because the folks in the Sciences department said it would still be useful, on account of celestial navigation. They even helped me with the cover story—I'm now a colleague of 'the late Dr. McAllister,' who is picking up where she left off."

"That's way cool, baby."

"Yeah, it is. But it's not much to look at, I'm afraid. Most astronomical research isn't very spectacular to see. When I'm done, I'll try to pull up some more fun stuff for us to look at." Omega flipped a couple of switches, then booted up the laptop and inserted a data chip. "All right, let's see...yeah, my old observing order will still work...there. Let 'er rip." After entering some commands, Omega came over and sat down beside Echo on the blanket, stretching sore muscles. "Mmh; I'm still stiff. And gonna be stiffer, I expect. Anyway, that's got it. I'll check it in a while and make sure everything's okay."

"You're not gonna stay with it?"

"Nah. I got it all automated now. What did you do with the snackies?"

"In the right-hand saddlebag on Spirit."

"Spirit. Wasn't that your old horse's name, Ace? The one you were riding when you came upon the First Contact?"

"Yeah, it was."

"This isn't the same horse, is it? I mean, did you have the Agency acquire him, like they did my farm?"

"No, he's not the same horse," Echo said, quiet. "But I did have the Agency acquire him, yeah. The original Spirit died, oh, ten or twelve years ago. When this one was foaled, I was... notified...and they let me name him." He shrugged. "His full name is...lessee...Spirit Echo, I think it was. He's a registered quarter horse, just like the original Spirit was, so the name had to be a little bit different. He looks a good bit like him, though."

He deliberately failed to mention that Spirit had sired Spirit Echo—if sophisticated extraterrestrial genetics technology were factored into the siring. Spirit had been gelded, and when the decision was made to do *in vitro*, then implant the fetus in the donor mare, they'd had to reconstruct Spirit's genetic contribution from a tissue sample. However, Echo had a suspicion that might not be a good topic to discuss with his partner at the moment, given certain conversations the previous evening about her own genetics. So he conveniently neglected to bring up the subject, to avoid spoiling her cheerful mood.

"I actually came down here a couple times during his training and helped out with it," he continued. "It...helped. Me, I mean; I dunno that it made any real difference in his training. But I kinda feel like he's more or less my horse."

"Should I have maybe not brought it up?"

"Nah, it's okay. I actually meant to tell you earlier, but I forgot."

"Okay. Listen, I got some serious munchies goin' now..."

"You're kidding," Echo teased with a grin. "You mean after another huge ranch-hand dinner, you're hungry again?"

"Aw, shuddup. That's why we brought the snackies, silly. Want anything?" Omega asked as she got back up to track down Spirit, and the all-important right-hand saddlebag.

"No, thanks. Not yet. Probably later, though."

"Okay."

Echo lay silently on the blanket, looking up into the jewel-encrusted heavens, trying to identify the stars and constellations his partner had taught him. Out here, away from the lights of the city, there were many more stars visible to the naked eye, as well as other things like nebulae and galaxies, and he found it more challenging, as well as more interesting. After a while, it occurred to him that Omega hadn't returned. He glanced at his wrist chronometer, then sat up and looked around.

There were Spirit and Celeste, still contentedly grazing, complete with saddlebags, but Omega was nowhere to be seen.

"Meg?" Echo called into the warm Texas night.

"...Ssshhh..." came faintly through the dark.

Uh-oh, he thought, straining his eyes to pierce the darkness in the direction from which the sound had come. *That ain't good.*

After a few moments, he spotted Omega creeping along, low to the ground, between the two horses. Every instinct in Echo screamed a warning as she worked her way silently back to him. He opened his mouth to speak, but she put a finger to his lips and leaned forward.

"Follow me," she breathed in his ear, "but stay low, and be dead quiet."

Omega started back the way she had come, and Echo followed closely, imitating her actions. A short distance past the horses was a slight rise they had ridden past on the previous afternoon, just before racing across the field beyond, and she headed up it, dropping onto her belly as she neared the edge of the ravine on the other side. At the edge, she carefully parted some low scrub, and motioned him close to look through.

At the bottom of the ravine was a small group of beings, maybe eight or ten, only a couple of which appeared human. They sat clustered in a circle, discussing in low tones the map which one of them held. Blonde head and brown bent together in the darkness for long moments, watching and listening, then Echo touched his partner's shoulder lightly and began worming his way back the way they had come. Omega followed suit. Once back at their own 'campsite,' he turned to her.

"Pack up your telescope, Meg," Echo said quietly. "Our vacation just ended."

Chapter 4

"What do you think we've got, Echo?" Omega whispered in the dark as she hastily packed her astronomical equipment.

"Judging from what I picked up listening to that galactic polyglot, we've got ourselves an illegal alien smuggling ring—and I don't mean Mexicans without papers," Echo answered in a low tone as he assisted her. "How'd you know they were there?"

"I heard voices when I went to chase down Spirit. When I realized I wasn't hearing English or Spanish, I was puzzled, so I decided to go check it out."

"You always did have sharp ears."

"Thanks, though I expect Mom an' Dad had little or nothing to do with it, if you get my drift. But what are we gonna do? I don't know about you, but I didn't bring much work equipment with me on vacation, and most of what I did bring is back in my room at the main house."

"Well..." Echo walked over to Spirit and opened one of the saddlebags, "I'm in a little better shape." He pulled out his principal proto-cyclotron blaster, slung in a modified Western-style holster, and belted it on his hip.

"I swear, if he pulls out a star and pins it on his shirt, I'm gonna lose it, stealth or no stealth," Omega muttered under her breath, stifling a laugh with a desperate effort. "What else have you got stowed in there, Ace? A cell phone to call for backup, I hope?"

"No. It wouldn't do any good. We're way the hell out of range here."

"I didn't know we could get out of range of an Agency cell phone."

"You wanted to get away." Echo shrugged. "But it's 'cause there's an anomaly in the area, produced by some odd ores. Not to mention, remember the name of my family's ranch?"

"Meteor Mountain, yeah."

"Well, apparently the meteor was part of said ore—probably the origin of it—and part of it shattered, either just before hitting atmosphere, or right after. It's like scattershot over a good chunk of the county. Natural cloaking, comm interference, you name it. It isn't just 'cause the cell phone towers are way apart, out here."

"Ohhh, I get it; it created a strewnfield," Omega murmured, understanding, just before an idea hit. "Uh-oh. Then that brings up a whole 'nother consideration of why those guys are HERE, specifically. An' I bet their transportation is parked in a certain crater you're familiar with."

"Huh. Good point. Got your Winchester & Tesla?"

"That," she said softly, reaching into her jeans pocket, "is always on me."

"Good girl."

"Echo...I'm not a 'girl'. I'm only a few years younger 'n you, if that much. You know that." Her remonstration was gentle, but firm.

"I...know." Echo looked disconcerted for a moment. "I don't mean it like that. It's...you know...like 'baby.'"

"All right. I guess 'good woman' has a whole different connotation, anyway." Omega accepted his statement. "Let's go. What's the plan?"

Echo stood for a moment, thinking, then said, "Okay, here's what we're gonna do for now. I'll stay here, and keep an eye or three on things. I want you to take your telescope back hom— back to the house..."

"I know it is. You can say it in front of me. I won't tell anybody."

"Huh?"

"This is home. This is YOUR home. I know." A calm Omega met his startled eyes, trying to get him to relax. "I've been watching you ever since we arrived. It's like you're saying goodbye to memories, on every square foot of the place. I'm more honored than I can say that you brought me along, and I hope I really am helping you get through it. And I get that, because of the Agency, its connection to you has to be kept secret...but you don't have to hide it from ME any more. The Ranch...its original name was Meteor Mountain Ranch. This is your family's ranch."

Echo said nothing in response to her statement, but he offered her a slight grin—somewhere between sheepish, pleased, and relieved, she adjudged—as he continued the contingency planning. But he also gave her the slightest indication of what might have been an acknowledgement of her deduction, tucked into the mix as a lead-off.

"Okay, baby. Take your telescope back, get whatever work gear you brought, along with the medikit, and stow it in some saddlebags. Then wake Joe up and get a couple of sleeping bag bedrolls and some more food and water. And don't forget your hat and sunblock. We're gonna trail these guys, and we may be out here a few days. If you get sunburned bad tomorrow, you're gonna be miserable."

"Wilco. Should I tell Joe what's going down? He could call Fox on the land line. That's satellite tight beam, right? It oughta get through."

"Yeah. Go ahead and tell him, but tell him not to call Fox just yet. We need to check this out first. It could be innocent, although I doubt it. Tell Joe if we're not back in...three Earth days, call Fox. And tell him to keep EVERYBODY away from the crater, until we know more. I don't want somebody stumbling over these guys' pit crew and getting killed."

"All right." Omega began counting off fingers as Echo removed the hobbles from the horses. "Work gear, medikit, food, water, sleeping bags, sun gear. Stay away from the meteor crater. Three days, then contact Fox. Anything else?"

"Anything you might need, you know, personal stuff. But don't take long. If these guys move out while you're gone, I'm after 'em. You can wilderness-track, right? Like, animal shit and prints? Scat?"

"Oh yeah. Daddy taught me that, too. And the galactic

polymer shoes our horsies use ought to be pretty easy to follow."

"Good. We got a plan, then. Have at it."

Omega nodded by way of response. She was about to mount up when Echo stopped her.

"No. It'll be quieter if you lead Celeste away, out of earshot, then mount."

"Good point. Oh, do you want me to bring you a change of clothes?"

"Don't take time for that, Meg. We're gonna rough it a couple days."

"Whatever you say, Ace. I'm game. Or I sure will be in 'a couple days,' I guess. Back soon."

"If I'm not here, track me."

"Roger that."

* * *

When she arrived at the Ranch and woke up Joe and half the hands to explain what was going down, the place turned into a beehive of activity, with most of them fetching things for her and efficiently stowing them in multiple saddle bags, which they then strapped on Celeste—after gingerly removing the telescope equipment and carrying it to the main house to stow for her. As a result, Omega only had to fetch her few personal items, and matters proceeded apace.

A little over an hour later, Omega was back at the grassy knoll.

Echo, unfortunately, was not.

"Oh boy," she remarked to herself, as she dismounted and surveyed the area, "trackin' in the dark. What fun. And me without my infrared vision. For all the dinkin' with my senses that that bastard Slug did, why he didn't think to throw that in the mix, I don't know, dammit. It's one thing I coulda really used! Next time I go on vacation, I'm bringin' a whole dang suitcase fulla Agency gear. Blaster, tachyon splitter rifle, IR goggles, spectral analyzer, basic flashlight...the works. Oh wait! Echo showed me one time..."

Omega extracted her goggle-glasses from her gear, studied them for a moment, then tapped a sequence along one temple, and donned them.

"Ooo," she murmured. "Instant night vision. Nice. That'll sure help. Now lessee." She began sweeping a small search pattern across the area. "Aha," she finally said with satisfaction, spotting Spirit's tracks, "they went thataway—to coin a phrase."

Omega mounted back up and, leaning well off to one side, painstakingly tracked Spirit's hoofprints by starlight. Horse and rider headed roughly east, meandering around the various ravines and canyons, and she realized she would have to be careful to avoid riding off a cliff in the dark, even with the goggle-glasses in night vision mode.

Boy, am I glad I'm dark-adapted already, into the bargain, she thought as she progressed. *Not to mention knowing how to ride practically hangin' off the horse. Now if I only had my old polo mallet...but then I might be tempted to use it when I catch up to the perps. And that'd be a waste of a good mallet. Because I would surely crack it over some skulls, just for interrupting our nice vacation.* She shifted position slightly, then glanced at her wrist chronometer. *Man, is this gonna hurt tomorrow...no, make that today.*

* * *

Several hours later, Omega finally caught up to Echo. By this time, dawn was just breaking—the sun was not even up yet—and Echo had dismounted, to crawl to the edge of the slight ravine the aliens had been using as cover, and check the smugglers' activities. Omega spotted Spirit tied to a bush in the dim light, and reined in, surveying the area for Echo. He was nowhere to be seen.

He's good, she thought with a smile of admiration. *Really, really damn good. Plus, he knows the area, too. I don't see a single sign of...wait, there he is, hidden in the brush. Wow. I almost missed him. Well, I did miss him, three times. An' I'm the one with the enhanced vision, that HE trained. He is DAMN good.* She dismounted with slight difficulty, having grown stiff during the ride; she secured Celeste near Spirit with the halter and lead, and slipped over to the edge of the bank.

"Incoming," Omega breathed when she was within a few yards of Echo, warning him of her approach. Without looking, he raised his left hand slightly and motioned her forward. She eased into position beside him as he pointed down the slope into the canyon.

The smuggling ring had made camp, and appeared to be bedding down.

Traveling by night, then. Looks like they're on foot, too—which makes sense. As rugged as this terrain is, it'd be hard on mechanized ground transport. And using hoverpods or the like, going airborne...that makes 'em too easily visible. But they don't have access to horses, and we do. Easier for us, woo-hoo, she thought. Omega glanced meaningfully at Echo, and dropped into their unspoken codes.

She raised both eyebrows and extended a hand. *Find out anything while I was gone?*

He nodded decidedly. *Oh, yeah.*

She raised a lone eyebrow. *So tell me.*

He made a circle of his right index finger and thumb, sliding it around his bare left ring finger.

She looked puzzled. *A...ring?* Her eyes widened in understanding, and her lips formed a circle of their own. *OH. Smuggling ring.*

Echo nodded. *Yep. Like we thought.*

She shrugged thoughtfully. *All right...now what?*

Echo glanced back at their horses, then at his partner. He nodded at her, jerked his head back over his shoulder, and closed his eyes, letting his head droop. *Go get some sleep.*

Omega cocked an eyebrow and nodded toward him. *What about you?*

Echo tapped his wrist chronometer, then jerked his thumb away. *Later.* Then he pointed several times in rapid succession between them. *We'll take turns.*

She nodded and began working her way back toward the horses.

* * *

Omega hadn't been asleep long; the sun was barely risen when Echo came and woke her.

"C'mon, Meg, wake up," he murmured. "I need your help, here."

"What's wrong?" Omega sat up, then with some surprise, pushed aside a small tumbleweed. "Do the perps know we're here?"

"No, and I don't intend they'll find out," Echo said, as a tumbleweed rolled up and struck him in the side. He grabbed it and tossed it away. "It's a different problem we've got, and I'll need your help to negate it."

"Where did all these tumbleweeds come from?" Omega wondered, shoving away another that hit her in the back. "Waitaminit. That's not an *amaranthus*, or even a *Kali tragus*. And the wind is barely blowing."

"No, it isn't; no, it's not; and these aren't from around here," Echo said, standing as Omega extracted herself from her sleeping bag.

"Oh, no. You don't mean...?"

"Yup. They're called 'Shrubs,' they're from Dryad in the Embelu system—which is where the Botanoid race hails from, and there's a Botanoid in our group of perps, so I can't think this is a coincidence—and they've never been seen on Earth before."

"Uh-oh."

"Right. They're semi-sentient, as it turns out, and they're pains in the ass. Not really harmful, they're just the vegetation version of a cat—they get under foot a lot, and want attention. They travel in small herds, and they're capable of independent movement, though they like to use wind to travel long distances, especially the winds around storm systems, which might mean we've got something moving in."

"Double uh-oh." Omega looked around their sparse camp,

and fairly gaped. There was a three-foot-high bank of the things piled upwind of where her body had been in the sleeping bag, and the horses were snorting, stomping and shifting position in an effort to avoid more that tried to pile up around them. Already a five-foot-high mound stood upwind of the horses. And Echo kept having to shove them away, as they practically leapt at his tall, muscular form. "What the hell?!"

"Like I said, baby, they're the vegetation version of a cat. The sun isn't up good yet, so it's cool; we're warm, they wanna snuggle. During the day they travel, at night they round up and bed down. They're awake but not warm yet, so they want to use us as heat sources. If I hadn't woken you up when I did, you'd have found yourself completely buried under a pile of 'em, when you did wake up. Not in danger, but believe me, it'll really do a number on your head, waking up like that."

"Do you think the Botanoid sicced 'em on us?" Omega asked as she and Echo waded into the huge pile around the horses, tossing the shrubs this way and that.

"No. And I don't think they're that intelligent. In as far as I could tell, they came in from BEHIND us. Which probably means that they came from wherever our bunch of perps landed."

"Which makes sense," Omega decided, hauling several Shrubs off Celeste's back before the horse could panic. "Ace, I got an idea."

"What?"

"Let's pitch these things over toward the edge of the ravine," Omega suggested. "Some of those guys in the gang have gotta be warm-blooded, right?"

"Yeah, several are. The Glu'gu'ik and the Zargothians in particular. Oh," Echo said, as Omega's plan, by way of her sudden, wicked grin, hit him. "That's an idea, all right. And it might even help us out in several ways."

"Exactly. And these things aren't heavy."

"Nope. All right, baby, let's form a bucket brigade, here. You grab 'em and pitch 'em to me; I'll move a little closer to the ravine, and pitch 'em close to the edge. I don't want to heave-ho over the lip of the gully, in case they've got somebody watching."

"Right." Omega grabbed as many Shrubs in reach as she could get into her hands—feeling the slight vibration as they emitted what she could only describe as a soft 'purr'—while Echo moved roughly a third of the way toward the edge of the gully. Then she began flinging them at him, one at a time. "Alley-oop!"

"I didn't play much basketball," Echo said with a grin, "but okay." He caught the first Shrub and tossed it, discus-style, toward the lip of the ravine. The Shrub promptly rolled, then apparently cheerfully pitched itself off the edge, into the gully. "This'll work! Keep 'em comin', Meg!"

It took nearly half an hour to do it, since for a while more kept coming into the camp, but eventually, one by one, Alpha One managed to clear their campsite of Shrubs, much to the relief of poor Spirit and Celeste, who snorted their thanks. All of the Shrubs ended up in the ravine, and when they were finished clearing their camp, Echo crept over to the lip of the scarp, parted some foliage, and peeped down. Then he pulled back, turned to Omega with a wide grin, and motioned for her to come over to him. She slunk over, dropping to all-fours, then to her belly as she got close, and wormed her way in beside him. Echo parted the bushes for her to peer into the gully.

The group of illegal extraterrestrials was evidently quite confident of being unobserved, and had posted no sentry. They had also lit no campfire, and instead huddled together in their bedrolls for warmth. Said huddle was now nearly entirely obscured by a mammoth pile of tumbleweeds. The Shrubs quivered once, en masse, and settled down; Omega could have sworn she could hear them cooing.

Echo tapped her shoulder, and they pulled back, well away from the edge, before standing and returning to their campsite.

"That oughta be good to watch in another couple hours," Echo decided, jerking his thumb over his shoulder at the ravine, with a grin. "Thanks for the help, Meg. If you wanna go crawl back in your sleeping bag and get some more shut-eye, go for it. I doubt you'd been asleep half an hour."

"Okay," Omega agreed, ambling toward her own bedroll.

* * *

A couple of hours later, as Echo sat on a fallen log near the horses—he was using a tiny Agency-provided device called a Field-Issue InstaCaf to make a single hot cup of coffee, hoping to combat the early-morning chill and unusual dampness and humidity, while still far enough away from the ravine that the scent wouldn't carry—a slight commotion arose from the vicinity of the ravine. Setting the InstaCaf aside to finish its cycle, he glanced at his partner, who never stirred.

Sacked out, he realized. *She's tired. It stands to reason. I'll see what's going on, then. I bet I already know, anyhow. If it's as funny as I expect, I might even wake her up to watch.*

So he crept over to the lip of the gully, parted a few branches of scrub, and peered into the aliens' campsite. Then he grinned.

Below, the campsite was in a state of confusion bordering on pandemonium, as the various members woke up to find themselves completely buried in a deep pile of what appeared to be tumbleweeds. Several voices rose in panicked cries; at least one rose in anger. The pile of Shrubs started to shift, then to churn, as the beings underneath it fought to get free.

Abruptly the shrill crack of a weapon reverberated in the quiet early-morning air. The pile of Shrubs began to squirm, and a soft, almost-mewling sound rose from the ravine. The weapon cracked again; several Shrubs disappeared, apparently disintegrated, as a hole opened up in the pile, and the mewling grew louder as the Shrubs now moved faster, trying to get away from the vicinity of the hole.

Smile vanishing instantly, Echo looked on in something akin to horror. *They're not harmful!* he thought, incensed. *Lots of Botanoid kids have 'em as pets. What the hell?!*

An angry Glu'g'ik, temporarily abandoning his human

quantum disguise, rose from the midst of the pile of animated foliage through the hole he had carved, a sleek gold-plated beam pistol in hand; Echo recognized it as a gluon suppressor pistol.

Whoa, Echo realized, *those are RARE. And dangerous as hell. That's only the second one I've ever seen; how the hell did he get hold of one of THOSE?!*

The Glu'g'ik began targeting the Shrubs, picking them off by twos and threes, as the semi-sentient creatures shrieked in pain and fear and tried to roll away.

Moments later, he was joined by the three Zargothians, who drew their own beam weapons—variants on Echo's own blasters—and began gleefully killing the creatures. A soft, kitten-like wailing sounded from the wounded Shrubs, as parts of their bodies disintegrated. The rest of the band of aliens crawled out of the mound of fleeing Shrubs, running to get behind their leader...to safety; in his fury, he had only narrowly missed the Delzantian and the Aves with his weapon's beam.

"No! STOP!" the Botanoid cried, flinging out his appendages. "Eb'vuv! STOP! They meant no harm! They only wanted to get warm! Aahh! I can FEEL them, Eb'vuv! It hurts! It is hurting them! STOP!"

"I TOLD you not to bring them, Tiln!" Eb'vuv shouted, continuing to fire. "Did I not? Did I not specifically instruct you to bring no other plants?"

"You know I must have a connection! I had to!"

"Then why did you not keep them confined to your quarters aboard the ship?! What are they doing here?? Did it never occur to you that any Division One agent who saw them—and we crossed directly across one of their stations—would REC-OGNIZE them?! You imbecile!"

"Stop! Please stop!" Tiln pleaded, but Eb'vuv and the Zargothians ignored him. The Zargothians, Echo noted, true to their nature, seemed to delight in the slaughter, laughing with each Shrub hit.

A few more minutes and it was all over. Every Shrub lay

dead or dying; many simply no longer existed. Moments later, even the soft mewling ceased, as the last Shrub died.

"Burn them," a cold Eb'vuv declared, stepping over a weeping Tiln, sprawled on the ground.

"NO," Tiln said, abruptly rising to the root balls that passed for his feet. "Bring them to me."

"What in the name of perdition do you think you're going to do with them?" Eb'vuv scoffed.

"This," Tiln said, as he laid a gentle frond on the Shrub body that an apparently-human male brought him. Within moments, the plant matter had been absorbed into Tiln's body.

"You ATE it?!" the Delzantian asked, seeming mildly perturbed. "That's, like...cannibalism!"

"No. I made it part of myself," Tiln said with a kind of shrug. "Now I will hold its memories, its genetics, along with my own."

"There aren't too many left," the human man noted. "Do you want them all, Tiln?"

"Yes, Lu'vin'du'v. I will merge them with my own being, and they shall not be forgotten."

"Hmph. Very well," Eb'vuv grumbled, walking past Tiln to a nearby rock, where he sat. Behind his back, Tiln glared at the Glu'g'ik. "Lu'vin'du'v, you and Kelto feed the damned things to Tiln. The rest of you, clear off your bedding and return to sleep. We will not move until later in the day."

* * *

Thoughtful and mildly sickened, as well as somewhat incensed by the scene, Echo very carefully eased away from the lip of the ravine, then crawled a good fifty feet away before standing and heading back to his waiting mug of coffee. As he sat and sipped its fragrant warmth, he considered what he had just seen.

Well, at least it takes care of a potentially invasive species, I suppose, he decided, rueful. *It wasn't the way I'd planned to do it, which would have been a bit more...humane. Okay, a lot more humane, compared to that little scene. Now I kinda wish*

Meg and I hadn't done it. I mean, I know what she was thinking; it was only a couple days before we left Headquarters that we watched that classic Trek episode. But that dude...Eb'vuv... damn, he means business. And doesn't care what he has to do to achieve it. Whatever we do to stop 'em, we'll have to be careful, with that fruitcake as part of the show. Especially if they've got gluon suppressors. Though I'm betting that's his personal weapon, and intended to be for show as much as anything, given the gold plating.

On the other hand, it looks like the group is anything but harmonious. And that little incident didn't do a damn thing to help the harmony. Hm. I wonder if we can exploit that somehow, Meg and me.

He sat, nursing his coffee, lost in thought, until the sun rose high into the sky.

* * *

Later in the day, Omega felt a hand shake her lightly, and she stirred in the sleeping bag with a soft moan.

"Ssh, Meg. Wake up." Echo's voice was low but urgent. Immediately she was awake, her eyes snapping open at his tone. "C'mon," he told her. "They're gettin' ready to move out. Sooner than I expected; it's not even near dark yet. I've got the horses ready. Where are your boots?"

"Inside the sleeping bag, by my feet. Keeps the critters out of 'em, that way," she whispered.

"Good. Let's go." Echo turned and headed for Spirit.

Omega made a single spasmodic move within the sleeping bag, grimaced, and lay still. *Oh no,* she thought, intensely annoyed with herself. *Not this. Not now.* She tried again, and only succeeded in emitting a small grunt of pain.

"Echo..." she called softly.

* * *

He turned at her faint call, and his eyebrows went up when he saw her still in the sleeping bag.

"Meg! Move it!" he hissed, urgent.

"I can't."

141

"What do you mean, you can't? Just get it in gear."

"I mean I'm STIFF, Echo. Bad. Like, I can hardly move, bad."

Echo's eyes widened in shock and understanding.

"Uh-oh..." he murmured, grasping exactly what was wrong. He turned and came back to her side, crouching down by the bag.

"Look, Echo," she told him. "Take the gear I brought and go on. I'll get myself back to the ranch house as soon as I can and call Fox for a replacement and backup."

"What hurts?"

"About what you'd expect—my back and thighs. Feels like I got some nasty bruises on my chest and stomach, too, from where I went Texas body surfing. But it's my back, mostly."

"Can you turn over?" Echo unzipped the sleeping bag.

* * *

"Yeah, I think so..." With some difficulty and a little help from Echo, Omega managed to roll onto her stomach. "Oooh. My back is just killin' me." She bumped her bruised hipbone. "Ouch."

"Easy, baby. Don't bang yourself up worse," he told her. She felt Echo quickly probe the musculature of her back through the chambray shirt she wore. "Ooo. Knotted muscle. You probably wrenched it when you backflipped off Celeste, just like you did on your first ice skating session. That means you're doin' something consistently, when you get in an emergency sitch, that's throwing off the move. One of these days we need to analyze that, figure out what's off, and re-train your kinesthetics. Otherwise you're gonna end up with a chronic injury, here. For now, try to relax, as much as you can. I'm gonna see if I can work it out for you." He began massaging the offended area, evidently attempting to work out the tension in the affected muscles.

"Ooo...ooo...easy! Take it easy!" she gasped, and he lightened the pressure. "Aah...yeah, that's it. Mmm. That feels a lot

142

better. But Echo, listen, don't worry about me, just grab the gear and go after the perps. If you stay here until I get flexible again, you'll lose 'em."

"No."

"Why??"

* * *

"Because I'm not leaving you alone out here," he murmured as he worked, stroking firmly but gently into her injured muscles. "Not in this condition. I let you ride way too long your first day back in the saddle, 'specially after you came OUT of the saddle. I stuck you back in the saddle all morning yesterday and most of last night, and I didn't get you loosened up enough yesterday afternoon, then I went and had you out here sleeping on the ground today—and the second day after the exertion is always the worst. And that's today. And I'm supposed to be the trained massage therapist. Not to mention the senior partner. I should've taken better care of you, baby."

"Aw, hush that. It wasn't like I was fussin' about it or nothin'. You had no way of knowing. Besides, it wasn't all that bad until just now. An' I'll finish the therapist training in a few more weeks, my own self. By now, I know how it works—an' I didn't think about it, either, an' it's my back."

Echo ignored her interjection and continued his rationale.

"...Plus, you don't know the territory, it's too far to walk back to the house, and you're in no condition to ride until I get you loosened up. Anyway, I don't want a replacement—I want my partner. My best bud. The woman who can glance at me and know what I'm gonna do next. And vice versa." Echo squinted at the sky momentarily even as his hands continued to massage her back, the touch intimate, familiar, and soothing in a way that only the two of them understood. "The weather looks like it'll hold a while yet. We can track 'em. Now quit worrying, baby. You're tensing up and making my job that much harder. Listen, while I'm thinking about it, how are the inner thighs? You got any chafing or anything?"

"No, that's all good. I made sure to bring jeans with flat

inseams, so nothing would rub. An' I wore bike shorts underneath, at least the first two days."

"Well, that's something, at least. Meaning, I suppose, that you don't have 'em on now? The bike shorts, I mean?"

"No. When we showered after deworming and vaccinating the cattle yesterday, I didn't put 'em back on."

"Okay."

"Can I ask something?"

"Of course."

"Why aren't you the least bit sore?"

"Because I ride every week or so."

"How the hell do you manage that??" she wanted to know.

"The Agency has a riding club in the upstate area. Those mornings I go off on my own for a couple hours, on our days off? That's where I go. If I'd known you rode, I'd have brought you along, and glad of the company."

"That figures," Omega sighed.

"Okay, the knot's worked out, Meg," Echo told her as he switched to a soothing rubbing motion. "How does that feel? Any better?"

Omega moved about slightly, then attempted a slow, cat-like push-up into a kneeling position. "Mmh. Yeah, much better. I can actually bend again."

"All right, good; now the legs." He gently pushed her back down and started on her right thigh, kneading into the muscle through her jeans.

"Mmph. I don't...don't think that's a good...mmmh...good idea, Echo...hunh..."

"Why not?" Curious at her odd reaction, he leaned back slightly and looked at her as he worked, wondering what to make of her broken statement.

"Mph...Because...heh...it tickles! Ha-ha-ha!"

"You're kidding." Echo's jaw went slack in disbelief. He lightly dug his fingers into her hamstring, testing.

"No! Haa! Cut it out!"

"You ARE ticklish. A lot." A grinning Echo was thoroughly entertained...while he ignored her protests and continued massaging her sore legs.

"I said I was ticklish! Hmph! Hee! Now stop it! Agh!"

"Ticklish or not, Meg, if I stop before your legs are loosened up, are you gonna be able to ride?" Echo got serious.

"Heh! Yeah, I'll manage. Better than giggling myself to death, anyway, let alone giving ourselves away to the smuggling ring. I'd prefer a little more dignified exit when the time comes, than gettin' killed by a perp who heard me giggling 'cause I was bein' tickled crazy by my partner."

Echo stood, and helped his partner up after she put on her boots and jammed on her hat. Together they rolled her bedroll and strapped it onto Celeste, then Echo turned to Omega.

"Come on, Meg. I'll give you a leg up."

"I'll take it this time."

* * *

Echo and Omega silently tracked the alien-smuggling ring through the late afternoon and into the evening, following behind and slightly north of their quarry as they moved roughly eastward. A concerned Echo periodically reined his horse back, in order to eye his partner in the saddle, checking on her, and he sent her frequent querying glances: *You okay?* The answer was always the same—Omega nodded, and they kept going.

From time to time, shadowing the perps became difficult when the terrain provided little cover. But the Alpha One team wasn't designated Alpha One for nothing, and their game never knew they were being hunted.

As the day became night, Omega found she was somewhat more comfortable in the saddle, her muscles slowly growing accustomed to the activity. *'Bout damn time,* she thought, disgusted with herself. *I expected I would have done better than all this, as often and as hard as Echo an' I train in the gym. Training specificity, I guess...nothin' trains you for ridin' better than ridin'.*

* * *

Along about midnight, Omega, who was taking her turn

145

on point, reined in her mount and held up her right hand. By this time, they were well off Ranch property, and nearing the county line, the alien smuggling ring having managed to avoid all homesteads and population centers, and stay out of sight of the local inhabitants by dint of moving along the bottoms of the various canyons and ravines, moving from one to another as needed. Consequently, Alpha One had had little difficulty in maintaining a low profile, either.

Echo immediately halted Spirit, and watched closely as Omega sat completely still, obviously intent on something. After a few moments, she began trying to dismount, but she was still stiff, and struggled a bit. Echo quickly got down from Spirit and ran to help her ease to the ground.

"It's okay, baby. I've gotcha," he whispered as he caught her by the waist. "Just hang on to the reins. I'll get you down."

"Thanks, Echo," Omega murmured as her booted feet touched the ground. "Gimme a minute to walk it out, and I'll be all right."

"What are we stopping for?" he asked as he tethered the horses to a nearby oak.

"They've stopped. Meal break, I think."

"How do you know?"

"Feetstoops."

"What??"

Omega smiled slightly, dismissing the remark with a wave of the hand.

"James Joyce. Never mind."

"Oh. Duh. I'd forgotten about that passage in *Ulysses*."

"I kinda figured," she grinned. "Anyway, I could hear 'em. They're down in that gully." She pointed to a ravine about twenty-five or thirty yards south.

"Damn, Meg. That's some hearing, baby."

* * *

Omega shrugged, continuing to stretch.

"Quit tryin' to make me out as human, Echo."

A light hand touched her shoulder, and she looked up into

her partner's dark brown eyes.

"Meg...just because some alien perp spliced some DNA onto your genes doesn't make YOU an alien." He squeezed her shoulder gently and added, "You're human, Meg. In every possible way that counts."

She smiled up at him in gratitude, and instinctively covered the hand on her shoulder with her own. The smile faded slowly, and the two Alpha Line Agents stood there for a long moment, eyes locked, transfixed. Echo opened his mouth to speak. His voice was low, uncharacteristically hesitant.

"Meg...I..."

* * *

But before Echo could continue, Omega's attention was forcefully diverted. Her head cocked to one side, then jerked around to glance behind, as her breath caught in surprise and her blue eyes widened in stunned amazement. The spell was broken, and both Agents were instantly watchful. Omega began making her swift, silent way toward the bank of the ravine, motioning for Echo to stay put.

Echo watched, tense, as Omega crawled closer to the edge, stopping just before reaching it, and lying perfectly still, flat on her stomach in the bushes. She stayed there for long minutes, until Echo began to get impatient.

About the time he was starting to think of how to get her attention and find out what was up, Omega held up one hand behind her. The gesture was clear: *I haven't forgotten you. Hold on a minute.* Echo settled back down to wait.

After another few moments, Omega returned, making her cautious way back to her partner. As she got some distance from the gully, she stood and walked toward Echo, a strange expression on her face.

"What's up, Meg?" he whispered as she neared. "Those super-ears of yours catch something?"

"Yeah," Omega breathed, then suddenly sat down on the ground. Surprised, Echo moved to crouch in front of her, waiting expectantly. Finally, she continued. "We got a way bigger problem than illegal aliens, Echo."

"What do you mean?"

"This is the original JFK hit squad being smuggled in. They're headed back to Dallas...to meet the current President on his re-election campaign junket."

"What the hell?!"

* * *

As they grabbed a hasty, cold meal from the supplies in the saddlebags, Echo and Omega tried to make sense of what was going on, and formulate a plan.

"Are you sure this is the JFK hit squad?" Echo verified. "I mean, absolutely sure? Most of what they've been speaking is a hodgepodge of languages."

"Yeah, I know. And you can understand it a lot better than I can; I just haven't learned all the languages yet. But evidently, they're only using it as a code in case they're overheard. And one of the humans may not be human."

"What do you mean?"

"He was speaking pure Glu'gu'ik. And he's NOT one of the original members of the team...but he's leading them now."

"That guy. Huh. And you've boned up on your Glu'gu'ik since last fall. Okay. So it's just using a quantum manip of its appearance so it LOOKS human. All right. Well, I mean, I knew one of 'em was a Glu'g'ik since this morning, 'cause I saw him—remember, I told you about him killing all the Shrubs?"

"Oh yeah, I remember. So—what? He lost his cool when the Shrubs made him angry, and dropped the disguise?"

"Probably."

"But the other apparent human?"

"Now that I think about it, the leader Glu'g'ik did call him Lu'vin'du'v..."

"That's a Glu'gu'ik name!"

"Yep. So I guess they're all off-worlders."

"Right. And so you'll never guess WHY the Glu'gu'ik are here."

"Uh-oh. Lemme guess," Echo anticipated her. "They're really members of one of the factions trying to bring back the monarchy on Va'du'sha'ā."

"You're really good, Echo." Omega nodded, a grim smile on her face. "First try. The leader dude...well, one of the others called him, 'Lord Eb'vuv' or something like that. It sounded like maybe he's claiming to be in line for the monarchy."

"Damn. So it's real personal for him."

"Yeah. But I don't get it. Why here? Cutting across the the Ranch, of all places, a Division One facility?"

"If I had to guess, I bet it's because of the impact crater," Echo said.

"Impact crater? What impact crater?" Omega wondered, trying to shift gears.

"The one that threw up Meteor Mountain, remember? According to what my grandfather a few generations back—the one who founded the ranch—was able to get from the local Indians, a fairly large meteor hit in the corner of the ranch," Echo reminded her. "Or what became the ranch. It left a largish crater and pushed up a mound of dirt and rock. Over the years, the crater has partly filled in with silt and sand from flash flooding, but there's evidently something under there that naturally screens incoming spacecraft. And a partial breakup near atmospheric interface peppered the whole area with the stuff. That's why the First Contact occurred in it, and why any meetings with the pre-Agency tended to happen there...and why it's a pain in the ass to try to get lightweight comm in or out of the Ranch."

"Oh, duh." Omega smacked her forehead. "The strewnfield; that's right. But so why didn't they just go straight to Dallas?" she wondered. "Woulda been a lot faster and a WHOLE lot easier."

"Several reasons," Echo explained. "For one thing, Dallas is bigger now, with a helluva lot more traffic of all sorts. Second, it's an aviation hub—a busy one, with lots of aircraft. Third, cloaking technology doesn't work nearly as well in real life as it does on TV shows, at least in atmosphere. Remember how easy we were able to track Houdini's cousin back at Halloween, once we knew to look?" He grinned, but his expression was tight. "So getting in and out of the DFW area via spacecraft wouldn't be nearly as easy as it was over half a century ago, not any more. Plus, in the current political environment, if they play their cards right, as they travel, they'll get mistaken for illegal aliens of the human sort, and a fair number of the regular authorities—and a certain percentage of the civilians—will just ignore 'em."

"And then they hike cross-country, straight to Dallas," Omega realized.

"Right."

"Shit."

"'Bout like," Echo agreed. "Damn. This complicates things." Echo studied his partner carefully, eyeing her from head to toe. "How are the back and legs doing?"

"Pretty good now. Still a little sore and stiff, but I can manage."

"All right." He considered a moment. "Meg, I'm gonna have to go back to the Ranch. The trip needs to be fast, and I can ride faster right now, or I'd send you instead. I don't like leaving you out here in less than perfect shape, alone, with a strike team literally just over the hill..."

"Echo, I'll be fine," she reassured him. "I just wish I had my blaster. A Winchester & Tesla's beam hum kinda tends to give away my position. But I didn't even bring one; I figured with a vacation at an Agency facility, I wouldn't need it. I'll never do THAT again."

"Here." Echo began unbuckling his holster. "Take this." He handed her the holster with his blaster.

"No way!" Omega refused to accept it. "That leaves you defenseless if something happens on the ride."

"Well...not exactly," he said with a raised eyebrow. "But if it makes you feel better, swap with me."

The two Agents exchanged weapons, and Omega buckled

the holster's belt around her waist, cinching it as tight as it would go. Echo grinned.

"You're some smaller than me," he remarked, as he observed the blaster's final position, riding low on his partner's thigh.

"Yeah, a little. At least it isn't gonna fall off. I feel like one 'a those movie gunslingers, with mah holster halfway down mah hip." Omega nudged her cowboy hat into a rakish position, put her hands on her hips, and affected an exaggerated Western twang, patterned—very loosely—after John Wayne. "Whaddaya think there, pardner?"

"I think I better get goin' before I accidentally encourage any more of that fake cowboy nonsense." Echo turned toward Spirit.

"That's cowperson ta you, mister. An' who said Ah needed any encouragement?" she grinned up at her partner in the saddle as he brought his horse back around the way they'd come. Echo grinned back, then sobered.

"I'll be back as soon as I can, Meg."

"I'll be a-waitin' somewhere down the trail." Omega gave him a thumbs-up.

"I'm countin' on it, 'pilgrim'. Don't go walking into trouble, now." Echo nudged Spirit forward slowly, quietly, for some distance, before urging him first into a lope, then a full-out gallop, and Omega watched as the darkness swallowed horse and rider.

* * *

Echo pressed Spirit as hard as he dared in the darkness. The horse was not his original quarterhorse from his teen days— the shorter lives of horses meant that THAT Spirit had died, quite some few years prior. He was 'sired' by Echo's old horse, however, and had been trained well—partly BY Echo—and could move at speed when required. But the terrain was decidedly uneven, and even this equine lineage was not indomitable.

So I have to be careful, he thought. *I don't want to give the poor guy a heart attack. He wouldn't survive, and having him fall out from under me at speed wouldn't do me any favors, either.*

At some point the assassin squad would undoubtedly switch modes of transportation in order to pick up speed and enter the Dallas-Fort Worth area less conspicuously. Interstate 10 was not that terribly far to the north of their present position, and it ran into San Antonio; from there it was a quick jaunt north, up I-35 to DFW—or an even shorter trek to cut off the angle and use secondary roads from near Junction up to Temple or Waco. And the ring appeared to be roughly paralleling the interstate for the time being, so Echo fully expected that to be the mode of entry into the metropolitan complex. When the switch happened, he and Omega—both—needed to be there and ready. *And Fox and Company need to be in Dallas waiting,* he decided, mulling the scenario.

The thing Echo was most concerned over was the possibility that the switch would occur while he was gone, and Omega would be forced to go it alone to keep up. *Meg is good, damn good, but the Agency never sends a lone agent in, cold, unmonitored, no backup, to infiltrate a criminal group of any kind,* he thought. But that would almost certainly be what she'd have to try if Echo wasn't there. *And with next to nothing in the way of equipment. Not to mention simply being stiff and sore. Hell, I let her get way too banged up. On a damn VACATION.*

So Echo was raising a lather on his equine companion, in order to ensure that his Alpha Line companion—his partner, his best friend, and the woman for whom he'd fallen hard—wasn't placed in a hot spot. He'd have to pace Spirit; it was some little distance back to the Ranch house at this point, and Spirit couldn't go flat out the whole way. But he could go hell-bent for now, and Echo could get a fresh horse for the trip back. *Maybe,* he thought, *just maybe Fox can manage something mechanized...if he can get it to me fast.*

* * *

By the time the sun had risen decently, a hard-pressed Spirit had gotten Echo reasonably near the Ranch main house.

152

On recognizing the horse and rider rapidly approaching in the near distance, and the urgency with which Echo rode, Joe hurried out to meet them. Several hands followed, and he summoned more as he went.

"Echo?!" Joe exclaimed, as Echo brought Spirit to a sliding stop in a cloud of dust. "What's happenin'? Where'd ya go? Where's your partner?"

"I left her guarding the perps, Joe. I need—"

"Ya left her? That little lady? Alone out there with a buncha illegal offworld-alien smugglers? Echo! I thought you 'uz a gentleman!"

"'That little lady'—and she is—can still outrun, outshoot, and outfight any ranch hand on the place, Joe," Echo told him drily. "I oughta know; I trained her, too. But she IS outnumbered, and I need to get back to her as fast as I can, so—no offense, buddy—shut up and do what I tell you, okay?" A confounded Joe nodded, subdued. "All right." Echo began to tick off fingers. "I need a team to go scope out Meteor Mountain and the crater on the sly; chances are, this bunch picked it as a landing site for the same reason the First Contact did, and they may have backup or crewed transportation still there, so whoever is on that team needs to be awful damn careful, and STAY OUTTA SIGHT. I also need a fresh horse tacked up, the fastest we've got, in a Western saddle and Texas hackamore with lead, an' I need a case I've got in the main house strapped on 'im. I'll bring it out in a minute. Transfer the saddlebags from Spirit to whatever horse you give me. If you can gin up some nonperishable food for the saddlebags, it'd be great, but if you don't have something immediately available, don't spare the time to fetch the kitchen staff."

"Got it," Joe said, as he flipped his index fingers at various ranch hands, issuing nonverbal orders regarding who got what task. "What else?"

"Okay, then I need Spirit properly taken care of, after I 'bout rode the poor fella into the ground. Put an extra scoop of feed in the feed box in his stall for the poor guy's trouble, too.

Brush him down—bathe him if he needs it—and make him comfortable. He did mighty good for me tonight. And THEN I need Fox on the secured land line—now. Go."

Joe and the other ranch hands moved out as Echo dismounted, tossing Spirit's reins to a waiting hand and giving the horse a final, affectionate pat.

"You've been a good boy, there, Spirit Junior," he murmured affectionately to the equine, rubbing Spirit's upper lip. The horse responded with a nuzzle. "I hate to leave you behind, but you did really good, and you need to rest now. You've earned it, and then some. I'll see you when I get back, okay?"

Spirit whickered a soft response, hooked his head over Echo's shoulder, and pulled the Agent into the horse's chest— the equine equivalent of a hug, as nearly as the male Agent had ever been able to figure based on a lifetime of experience. Echo smiled and wrapped his arms around Spirit's neck, returning the affection, before slapping the horse lightly on the shoulder.

He turned and headed into the main house, emerging only a few minutes later with a black, high-tech, hard-sided suitcase, which he handed to another ranch hand to strap onto the fresh horse, then he headed back into the main house to find Joe.

* * *

Omega crept back to the ravine's edge to survey the terrorist group's activities. She listened carefully, trying to pull out as much of their polyglot conversation as she could understand.

(We are getting...to the rendezvous.)

(Yes. The slow part of...is...over.)

(How far away are we?)

(About one and a half planetary rotations from the rendezvous point, perhaps two. From there, it is not long.)

(...is it?)

(Near the local......Junction. South of the...crossroad, near the...stream.)

(What...now?)

(Rest. We must be...before sunrise.)

Blast an' damnation, a worried Omega thought. *Looks like I may be wingin' this one all alone. I sure hope Echo gets back before they reach the rendezvous, but I'd better have a plan just in case.*

* * *

"Fox?"

"Go ahead, Echo. The line's secure. And you're coming in five by five."

"I read you loud and clear as well. We've got a real situation here, developing fast. I need you to get Romeo and India, and maybe a couple other Alpha teams, to Dallas on the next maglev, as quick as possible. Get 'em as close to the President as you can, and try to steer the motorcade away from the school book depository, Dealey Plaza, and the grassy knoll."

"Oh, no. You're kidding."

"No, Fox; I only wish I were. Meg and I have been trailing the core of the original JFK hit squad for the last couple of days. This time they're being led by a renegade Glu'g'ik, out to pay us back for capturing the Hou'd'ni medium and locating and reassembling the F'al...and NOT sending it back to the Zeta Reticuli system, so he could become emperor."

"Great. A rabid monarchist on a revenge kick, complete with delusions of grandeur."

"Exactly. And a president on a campaign junket makes a damn good target."

"Some vacation."

"Yeah. Meg really knows how to come up with a fun time. So much for quiet. We're gonna need a vacation from our vacation. Listen, any chance you can get me some mechanized covert transportation here to the Ranch in the next ten or fifteen minutes? Meg's alone out in the middle of nowhere doing surveillance on these guys, on horseback for the first time in nearly two years, so she's twenty-five kinds of stiff and sore, never mind that the horse threw her on our first day here, and banged her up good. So I really need to get back there to her

ASAP, before they do something to force her hand."

"Not inside a couple hours, Echo. Sorry."

"Well, it was worth a shot. All right." Echo sighed. "Horseback it is, then. Oh, and be prepared for Joe to request backup; I suspect they landed at Meteor Mountain like y'all did at the First Contact, and they may have spacecraft with crew still there."

"Got it. I'll have a good-sized force ready. A brokh, we've got Glu'gu'ik involvement; we'll need aluminum foil, a crap-ton of aluminum foil. Ech. Oy vey. Where am I gonna get...?"

"Can't help you there, Boss."

"I know, zun. I'm on it. But Supplies is gonna have a harts bafaln."

"Yeah, I bet. Okay. Gotta go, Fox."

"We're on it from this end, Echo. Stay in touch if you can."

"You know the comm around here. I'll do the best I can, when I can."

"That'll have to do, then. Fox out."

"Echo way the hell out."

* * *

Echo was headed back down the trail toward his partner by the time the sun was well into the sky. Ditok, Joe's horse, was making good time. Echo still thought it was an odd name for a horse, but Joe had explained it was Haepergen for 'swift,' and Ditok was certainly that; he might be the fastest horse Echo had ever seen—and that included racehorses. The big thoroughbred was also strong and untiring, exactly what one of the huge Haepergens would need in a mount, and Echo suspected that Joe had seen to it that some genetic manipulation had occurred, not unlike that to which Omega had once been forcibly subjected, except unlike Meg, more than likely it had occurred prior to the horse's conception—and compassionately, at that.

The thought returned his attention to his partner. *Backup's coming, Meg. We'll stop those bastards.*

He glanced back to make sure that the case he'd taken

such pains to bring was secure. *Good. It's fine. Aw, damn. I got a storm front headed in on my ass; just what we need. I guess that's one thing that was driving that herd of Shrubs. Let's make tracks, then.*

Echo leaned well forward, over the horse's neck, as he brought his heels into Ditok's flanks, and the horse all but sprouted wings as it strove to become a pegasus.

* * *

It was early afternoon when the storm caught him. Echo was forced to slow Ditok as the leaden skies opened overhead, and a heavy summer squall line moved through. He pulled his rain gear from a saddlebag and donned it while still moving.

"Damn," he murmured as the deluge grew heavier and the wind began to whip about, "I sure hope Meg is still close behind the perps. This'll wash everything away if we have to trail 'em." *Not to mention slowing me down,* he thought. *I really hope Meg brought her rain gear.*

* * *

As the summer storm increased in ferocity, Echo tensed, and watched the roiling skies cautiously as he and Ditok progressed across open terrain, occasionally having to jump gullies or clamber down into a canyon and back out again. Had the situation been less urgent, he would have sought shelter and waited out the storm. But that would have meant a significant detour and delay, and Echo begrudged every minute lost, knowing his cherished partner was within shouting distance of a gang of interstellar murderers.

And with the way the leader treated those Shrubs, he realized, *if any one of 'em spotted Meg, they're apt to shoot first, and to hell with questions. I'd kinda like my partner around a little longer than that. Like, long enough to have a future together, preferably.*

So he pressed on, despite the impending storm.

* * *

It hit all at once. Suddenly Echo and his mount were being pelted in the face by hailstones, blown by a powerful headwind, as the swirling sky overhead turned an ominous, indescribable shade of purple-green-grey. A roar, sounding like a combination of the T-bird on afterburners and a Haepergen transport ship, came from behind, and Echo twisted in the saddle to look back. He knew what he would see; he just wanted to know where he'd see it.

"Aw, shit!" Echo exclaimed, as his eyes followed the funnel up into the clouds almost overhead; a churning, spinning debris cloud rose in the near distance behind him. Echo reined in Ditok just long enough to verify the twister's most probable direction of motion—northeast. Then Echo turned Ditok hard to the right, and laid into the horse's flanks with his disc spurs, shouting urges to his mount as horse and rider galloped flatout, heedless of mud or terrain, headed southeast.

Echo's one chance lay in heading at right angles to the tornado's track, and getting far enough away to be out of danger by the time the base of the funnel drew even with him. Even so, he found the time to send his partner a warning thought: *Meg! Forget the perps! Take cover!!*

* * *

Omega abruptly turned in the saddle and looked back, as if impelled, seeing the approaching storm on the horizon.

Oh man, she thought as she watched the rotating supercell, like a giant greenish-purple spaceship low on the horizon, *that looks bad. I really hope Echo isn't in the middle of that. I better keep an eye on it. If it gets too close, I might want to forget the perps and take cover.*

* * *

As Echo sought to outrace the storm, he heard a secondary rumbling begin, and he glanced back, over his right shoulder.

"Aw, hell. You gotta be kiddin' me."

The panicked, stampeding cattle, fleeing the twister, were approaching swiftly from behind and to the right, evidently having emerged from a ravine leading into a canyon. Already the leading animals were almost on top of him, and a solid mass of beef was within a hundred yards, by Echo's estimate.

158

He realized that his path had converged on the stampede from the side; if he and Ditok maintained a steady course, and if the herd wasn't too wide, he could be past it before it was on him. *Maybe. Gotta try, anyway.*

Echo leaned even lower over Ditok's neck, taking up the slack in the reins and seating himself deep in the saddle, and Ditok's ears swiveled around to listen as Echo coaxed the animal to even greater speed, maneuvering him around the outlying cattle. Echo glanced back momentarily and saw horns, hoofs, and wild, rolling bovine eyes; one slip, and horse and rider would be trampled to death.

As he turned back around, Echo spotted a narrow, steep-sided creek gully ahead, and made for it. Ditok could jump it; the cattle would be diverted, or at least slowed, by it. Gathering his mount, Echo urged Ditok over the creek and forward. Behind them, the bawling cattle turned eastward. He was clear of the stampede.

But there was still the little matter of the tornado.

* * *

Horse and rider together moved like a centaur in their attempt to outrace the storm. Behind them, the funnel had grown, spreading into a giant wedge tornado, covering a frightening amount of land. The big, powerful Ditok leaped over gully and stream and fence, carrying his rider away from danger as fast as he could gallop, and Echo kept his seat low and streamlined, as the gale shifted into a strong headwind again.

Echo knew the twister was almost abreast of him then, and he guided Ditok down into the next ravine they came to, rather than jumping him over it, hoping he was far enough to the southeast to escape the huge wedge. Quickly he dismounted, into the shallow water of the almost-dry creek bed, and ran underneath an overhang in the stream bank, leading Ditok, just as the rain became torrential. After a few moments, the heavy rain stopped, as the rain core moved on, along with the storm. They were safe...

...From the tornado.

With that, Echo led Ditok out and remounted. He needed to get out of this creek gully fast; he didn't want to be in a stream bed when the runoff from all that rain came through. Echo headed Ditok downstream at speed, looking for a good place to take the horse up the bank. Upstream, in the distance, a rushing sound began. Echo spotted a gentler slope in the bank and spurred Ditok up it, just as the wall of water rounded a bend of the stream.

Echo sat his horse atop the high bank, looking down at the muddy, debris-filled floodwaters as they spilled over the lower banks on the far side, and into the surrounding fields.

"Aw, damn it. Now I've got this between me and Meg." He sighed. "C'mon, boy. We've gotta find a way across, somewhere."

Echo turned Ditok and slowly retraced his path upstream, looking for a good place to either ford, or jump, the flood.

* * *

The heavy rain swept in from the southwest, and Omega pulled her rain gear out of her saddlebag and donned it. After a few moments, she reined in Celeste, dismounted, and crept toward the ravine to see what the hit squad was doing. Before she got more than ten feet, however, she turned and ran back to Celeste, mounting and frantically urging the horse back in the direction she'd come, galloping hard until she got to the other side of a stand of trees. There, she halted Celeste and dismounted rapidly, tethering the horse to a tree, then crept through the undergrowth to get a better look.

Whoa, that was close, she thought in relief, watching the assassins emerge from the gully. *I should have thought about that. Of course, the gully's gonna flood with this rain. And if they're smart enough to have outfoxed the pre-Agency once, they're smart enough to get out of a flash-flood-prone gully in a downpour.* She crept back to Celeste, and began rummaging through her scant supplies, hoping for something to make the time pass a bit more pleasantly...without giving away her presence.

A bit of improvisation resulted in decent shelter for both woman and horse; Omega found a medium-sized tarp, a small roll of twine, and a large Bowie knife in her saddlebags. Moving as quietly as she could, and making small moves in case any part of what she was doing could be seen through the trees, she proceeded to string up the tarp to various tree branches, providing shelter from the rain; in despite of perceiving a circulation in the storm cloud earlier, the part of the storm where she was had no winds to speak of...at least, not yet. A grateful Celeste moved under one end of the tarp, nosing down to graze on what foliage she could find.

Finding a low-forking tree in the thicket, and thankful that the trees were live oaks and not mesquite, Omega cut several branches, then stripped them of foliage and sliced them into thick cane-like slats. Some quick weaving, followed by wedging the resulting slabs into the tree fork, resulted in a reasonably satisfactory seat under her rain shelter. It wasn't cozy, but at least it provided some comfort, out of the weather.

Of course, she thought, *if the center of the circulation heads this way, this tarp turns into a big ol' sail, and we go flyin' right into the middle of the perps. Which would be very bad. So I better be ready to cut it loose and pull it down in a hurry. Not to mention finding sturdier cover.*

Omega continued to watch the perps to her east, and the skies to her west. To her relief, the hit team settled down beside the ravine to wait out the rain, and she was able to concentrate on the storm as it continued to intensify. Night fell early with the overcast sky, and Omega continued to watch with some trepidation, until she decided that the worst of the storm would pass northwest of her position. Then she began worrying about Echo.

Blast it. There's no way I can find out if Echo was caught in that. By the looks of the cloud as it came up, that thing had a STRONG circulation. If it wasn't a supercell, I'll eat my hat, horsehair hatband an' all. And the lightning was somethin' fierce, too. Ace, please be okay, partner-buddy mine. Don't be...not that. Not you, too. And if I lose you now, I get to go home and tell your mom that you died on my watch. Before she could see you again. She shook her head. *Then the two women grieving you the most probably won't even be speaking to each other. Not that I'd blame her. And then...I dunno what I'd do. But I expect busting up crockery would be the least of it.*

The rain slackened as the storm moved on, and Omega heard the aliens striking camp. She returned to Celeste, removed and stowed her rain gear and the tarp, mounted, then paused in thought. Omega dismounted again, and pulled her shirt out of her jeans, tearing a strip off the bottom of her shirttail as quietly as she could. She tied it high on a bush, in as near plain sight as she could judge in the dark, hoping Echo would come by during daylight hours. Then she remounted, and resumed surreptitiously following the sinister group through the pitch-black night.

* * *

Meanwhile, Echo was searching diligently for a place to cross the swollen stream in the dark.

Hell, at this rate I could've waited for Fox to get me that mechanized transport. Damn El Niño, he thought. *I'd just go ahead and have Ditok swim across if I didn't have this case. It should be waterproof, but I'd rather not risk it, especially at night. And the last thing I need to do at this point is to lose it in the flood waters. In the dark, no less.*

Echo turned and headed Ditok back downstream.

* * *

Early the next morning, shortly after sunrise, Omega was mounting back up, preparing to follow the departing perps after a rest break, when it happened: The sound of a rattle, close in the brush. A panicky Celeste shied, knocking into Omega just as she placed a foot in the stirrup. Sore muscles gave way, and she fell backward to the ground, landing partway under the foliage—where a sharp, burning pain suddenly lanced through her left thigh.

"AAaah!" She instinctively grabbed the rattlesnake be-

162

hind the head with adrenaline-enhanced reflexes, yanking up and around to dislodge the fangs, then she crushed the snake's neck in her strong fingers, flinging the carcass away before clutching her burning thigh.

"Ohhh. Not good...not good," Omega groaned, rocking back and forth on the ground, holding her leg tightly. Finally, she gained control of the pain response and pulled out her Swiss Army knife, cutting open the leg of her jeans to get a look at the bite wound. Two small puncture holes welled tiny ruby droplets. The area was already swelling and discoloring.

"Well...I'm gonna be sick," she muttered, as she got to shaky feet and caught Celeste, who was busy stomping the remains of the rattler into the dirt.

Next, she went over to the rattler's carcass and studied it with a knowledgeable eye; back in the days when she had spent weekends camped out, observing in the area, she had had to become familiar with the less-welcome denizens.

"Huh," she murmured. "About three feet long, greenish skin, diamondback—but the diamonds fade out about halfway, two-thirds of the way, to the tail..." She shook her head, dismayed. "Shit. It's a Mojave green. So I'm gonna get the hemotoxic AND the neurotoxic effects. Lovely. Things just keep getting better and better."

With a quick slash of her knife, she neatly cut off the rattle—which miraculously remained intact after Celeste's murderous and completely unnecessary dance—before dropping it into her shirt pocket, then wiping the knife blade on her shirt to remove the blood smears.

Next, Omega dug around in the saddlebags and retrieved the medikit. Opening it, she surveyed its contents.

No snakebite kit. At all. Serious omission, that. I'll have to remember to tell Fox about it, assuming I last that long. Then again, I don't suppose the Agency expects us to be skulking around in the brush. At least I can keep it from getting infected, she decided. And remaining completely calm, she began treating the bite as if it were a simple puncture wound, disinfecting it and swabbing it with antipathogenics. When she was done, she got out a couple of analgesic capsules and washed them down with a swallow from her canteen, augmenting that with a micropore syringe injection of a galactic pharmaceutical intended to help counter nerve agents. *There. That oughta help...a little. Good thing Daddy—and Echo—taught me to be tough. I'm sure gonna need it now.*

Omega spent a few precious moments searching the foliage very carefully for a particular plant.

"Where is it, where is it," she murmured. "There's gotta be some around here someplace."

Finally she located several clumps of the plant she wanted: delicate, almost fernlike leaves with tall lavender-purple flower spikes.

"Bingo," she said in relief. "Dotted blazing star!" Then she grabbed the base of one of the plants and pulled. In the sandy, wet soil, it came up relatively easily. Extracting her knife once more, she shook the root free of soil, then whacked off the trailing roots from the main tap root, followed by the foliage. Then she rolled the thick, almost tuber-like root between her hands, crushing it as best she could.

Next, with the help of the knife, she tore another strip off the bottom of her shirt and spread it out.

She slit the root open and extracted the pulp, laying it carefully on the strip of chambray. Omega wiped her knife clean on her jeans again, then commenced binding the herbal poultice on her left thigh, positioning the mashed root pulp directly over the snakebite. A quick entry on the alarm function of her cell phone—one of its few uses in the area, thanks to the lack of any decent signal—would remind her to remove it later, and she carefully set the alert to <vibrate only> mode, to avoid attracting unwanted attention.

I'm really glad I talked to that old Apache elder, back when I first started observing around here, she decided. *His herbal info has proven useful more than once, now. This ought to at least help draw out a little of the venom.*

Omega paused for a few minutes and looked around, taking stock, and trying to gather her thoughts sufficient to decide what to do next; the snakebite had temporarily rendered everything else of lesser priority.

Oh, she realized, as she mentally reviewed the big picture. *I need to leave a clue for Echo to find.*

So she tore yet another strip from her shirttail, and tied it to a bush as she'd done several times during the night, then tied her ragged shirt around her torso, since it was not long enough to tuck properly into her jeans any more.

Omega moved around to Celeste's off side then, and mounted with some awkwardness; the entire left leg was already starting to swell, and had become slightly numb—except for the pain, which was intense and growing worse.

"All right, Celeste, you're gonna have to pay close attention to the reins today, girl; this leg isn't gonna be much use. Let's go."

* * *

At last Echo found a ford in the flood-swollen creek, by the pre-dawn light. He nudged Ditok down the gentle slope to the water's edge, allowed him a moment to drink, and eased the big horse into the stream, on guard for water moccasins and floating mats of fire ants as he went.

Ditok obediently stepped forth, and as the giant animal crossed the current, the water rose around him until Echo's boot soles just touched the water's surface. Then the water began to fall again as horse and rider exited the stream on the other side.

Echo took his mount up the gentle grade of the riverbank, and then started searching for landmarks to locate Omega's trail.

* * *

A slightly soggy clump of horse apples was his first clue. Echo rode Ditok over near the pile of horse manure and studied it from the saddle briefly, noting how it had been 'sculpted' around its periphery by flowing water. Then he dismounted.

Time for Shiitsooyee's lessons, he thought. *Lipan warrior, don't fail me now.*

A quick swipe with his knife removed a small branch from a nearby cedar tree, which he immediately stripped of needles. Then he crouched beside the mound of manure and, using the tip of the stick, began to dissect the scat.

"Mm," he murmured, studying the interior of the droppings. "That's bits of the special feed Joe mixes for our horses—that offworld grain he throws in sure packs a nutritional punch. Yep. It's Celeste, all right. It's been a while, though, 'cause it's pretty dried out inside. So they're nowhere close now. Let's see what direction they were going."

Echo stood and looked around, studying the ground initially.

"Aha," he said, walking a couple of paces to his right. Another, smaller scat lay there, and he could see additional deposits, fewer and farther between, trailing off in the same direction, finally vanishing. "Here's the rest of it. Celeste must have taken a dump while Meg was riding her."

Abruptly he crouched again, and reached down to finger a rain-washed depression in the wet, sandy soil. *And here's Celeste's hoofprint,* he realized. *There's not much left of it, but it's U-shaped, with the bottom of the U pointing the same way as the droppings. I'm on the trail. Aheeiyeh, Shiitsooyee.*

Echo returned to Ditok, mounted swiftly, and followed the faint marks that told of his partner's passage.

* * *

The area Echo now traversed was somewhat scrubby, with a lot of low brush and the occasional mesquite or cedar; now and then a piñon pine found its place. It appeared to his knowledgeable eye—his Shiitsooyee had trained him well in tracking, and he used his skills not infrequently in trailing a perp, though never before with such urgency or concern—that Celeste was choosing to follow an animal track; deer by the spoor, he adjudged.

But horses were larger than the deer of the region, and it

was easy to see the signs of the horse's passage, if one knew what to look for. There were broken twigs and nearly-detached leaves hanging from the brush, as well as broken bits lying along the trail. Caught in some of the broken twigs could be seen pale gray horsehair, and he even found a black cotton thread, likely from Omega's jeans, in the bark of one tree.

He pushed Ditok ahead, going as fast as he dared without losing the trail.

* * *

A dogged Omega followed the hit squad, still managing to maintain a reasonable semblance of stealth despite her condition, partly by dint of allowing a bit more distance between herself and those she followed. Her leg had swollen nastily, and she sliced open her jeans leg and lengthened the stirrup to accommodate it. She was hesitant to begin cutting open the shaft of her riding boot, but that might come next if the leg continued to swell.

Twice already she had had to halt Celeste in order to retch. The horse had been patient, not caring for the sound or the smell of its rider vomiting from its back, but enduring it without swaying or shying. Her mount seemed to understand that its rider was in some difficulty, and the mare took obvious care as she walked, smoothing the ride for Omega as much as the animal could manage.

Once she finished purging her belly, Omega pulled Echo's grass-stained, woolen, Southwest-style blanket—on which they had picnicked, and on which they had stargazed—out of her gear, slinging it around her cold, sweaty form as she went into shock.

In determined defiance of her circumstances, however, Omega was able to keep up with the alien task force without their knowledge, and she was beginning to formulate a plan for how to infiltrate the hit squad if the need arose. It wasn't a pleasant thought, and stood as much likelihood of getting her killed, maimed, or abandoned in the middle of nowhere as into the group—especially if Echo's estimate of their leader was anything close to accurate. *And, knowing Echo,* she considered, *it's probably dead-bang-on.* But if she were the only thing between the squad and the President's assassination, she would have to try.

Echo, hurry up there, big guy, she thought. *I could REALLY use your help at this point.*

* * *

Dawn became morning, morning became high noon, and still Omega followed the perps.

And still no Echo in sight.

Omega sighed in misery as she glanced over her shoulder, hoping to see a familiar tall form on horseback headed her way.

The rear field of view remained stubbornly empty.

Double vision, damn the snake, but still...empty. Am I really on my own? Is Echo...? No. Not Echo. But if...if the tornado did get him...oh damn. I guess I better get with it...just in case.

She sighed again, and set herself to brainstorming as best she could, given the multiple distractions of intense pain, decreased coordination, and difficult respiration, all caused by the potent neurotoxin that was the rattlesnake venom. Likewise, the hemotoxic effects caused localized internal hemorrhage, dropping her blood pressure and leaving her cold and light-headed. *In general, miserable,* she thought, as she slipped in the saddle and had to adjust her seat.

All right, then, let's see about this plan...oh, I feel rotten... so...my story's gonna be...I got snakebit—THAT'S no lie—and Echo found out I wasn't really human when he went to treat me, so the truth came out about me bein' Slug's agent to assassinate him, and disgusted and repelled, he left me to die. But I'm not dead quite just yet; I'm slowly getting better. Don't I wish. Now I'm mad as blazes...maybe...yeah, maybe in both senses of the word...and want to...want to...to what?? Ah! To draw Echo in for a face-off! Heh. A shoot-out. That sure seems appropriate! I already feel like I'm in a damn B-western flick as it is. So anyway...I'll do whatever it takes to get Echo's attention, anything to pull him in for that face-off. Go on a ram-

page, shoot up some people, kill the President...whatever. Rave a little bit. That oughta do it. That, and this leg. That's assuming, I suppose, Echo's...still around to have attention to get. But then, I guess, the perps won't know, one way or the other.

Celeste had to adjust her stride for a rough patch of ground; as a result, Omega slipped in the saddle again, and only caught herself from falling off the horse by grabbing on to the pommel. The sudden, hard movement sent lightning bolts of pain searing through her body.

Ow. Ow, ow, ow. DAMN, that hurt! Times like this I really wish I was in a Western saddle, she thought then, grimacing in pain. *They got a little more to grab onto. Like a saddle horn, for starters. My left leg is pretty much useless at the moment. And boy, does THAT show. It would help,* she decided, *if I couldn't feel it any more than I can use it, but oh well.*

She reined in Celeste and listened intently as she scanned her surroundings: The perps were still moving eastward, and the westward horizon was still stubbornly empty.

Omega sighed again, and urged Celeste onward.

* * *

"So how is she doing?" Fox wondered, meeting with Zebra in her office. "Is the regeneration coming along like it should?"

"Well, I thought so," Zebra said, biting her lip, "but now I'm not sure. And I've talked with Zarnix, and he isn't, either."

"What's wrong?"

"Fox, the cancer was a LOT farther along than we thought," a worried Zebra explained. "It's gotten into her liver, her stomach, her intestines, her colon..."

"Oh damn," Fox murmured, sobering. "Did we get to her too late?"

"I don't know," Zebra said, unhappy. "Zarnix has an interstellar call in to try to reach Doron for advice and consultation..."

"That's a good plan, bubeleh," he said. "Is there anything I can do to expedite matters?"

"No, not really," Zebra sighed. "Doron is off handling a viral outbreak; it's not serious, but he's awful busy. We have word that he should be able to return our call in a few hours; he knows this is Echo's mom, and he's making a special effort to break away long enough to help us."

"You're using a secure transmission, right? After all, this is the mother of our top Agent; I'm sure there are those out there who would love to strike at his heart through those he loves."

"All over that one, hon. Zarnix and I both thought about that, independently."

"That's good," Fox decided. "Anything else?"

"No. Well, yeah. Pray," Zebra said, blunt. "We could use it. I don't want to have to tell Omega we let her down, let alone admit what happened to Echo. Besides, I...kind of already like Mrs. Bryant."

"I understand," Fox said, keeping his voice soft. "Keep me posted?"

"When do I not?"

"Never," Fox chuckled. "I'm just saying."

"I know. I will."

"Then I'll get out of your hair, bubeleh."

"You were never in it. It always feels...good...to be able to talk to you when I have a problem like this."

"Good," Fox said, rising. "That's what life mates are all about, I suppose."

* * *

Echo found where Omega's trail apparently entered a shallow ravine, but the water was still up, and while if the water had been low, he would have looked for disturbances on the moss and algae at the bottom of the stream bed, all that was largely invisible now, thanks to the heavy load of silt still flowing in the water.

"Okay," he grumbled, nudging Ditok across the shallow stream, "let's see if I can pick up the trail on the other side."

Just then he spotted a clear hoof print, high up on the muddy bank.

"Here we go," he declared, and pushed onward.

* * *

"...And you haven't heard from either member of Alpha One since the tornado?" Fox wondered, on a high-priority, emergency vidcall he had placed to the Ranch, upon receipt of the tornado information from an agitated Lima. On the other end, Joe sat at the desk in his tiny office in the main house. "It has been all over the news up here: a huge, wedge tornado ripping through that part of Texas."

"No, Fox, we ain't heard nothin'," Joe averred. "I'm powerful worried, but there ain't much I kin do. We can't reach 'em on account o' th' comm interference in the area, an' other than the gen'ral direction they both went when they left the Ranch, we don't know where they are, or how far off they are."

"Did they have Echo's big black case with them?"

"That 'uz what Echo came back to get, so yeah."

"Good. Then, unless something VERY bad has happened, I will just have to wait to hear from them, I suppose." Fox shook his head, impatient and concerned, then settled. "How is the Ranch? Did it affect you? Was there any damage?"

"No sir. Th' twister clipped th' southeast corner of th' property, but it hadn't no more than touched down when it did. So it wasn't near as big or strong as it got, later on. I done sent some o' the hands out to ride the fences through there, an' they's all fine. Hadda get some trash outta th' fence wire, an' the way I heard it, that 'uz a real mess 'cuz it 'uz all kinda woven through the wire, but we didn't have no damage. I sent some fellas over to th' neighbors to make sure they didn't need help either, but I think ever'body's fine."

"And the cattle?"

"The cattle all had enough sense t' git the hell outta Dodge when they saw it comin'. We done a head count, an' nobody's missin' that we see."

"Right. Well, should you hear anything out of Echo or Omega, notify me at once, please."

"I'll be sure ta do it, Boss."

"Fox out."

"The Ranch out."

* * *

"And you say this is Echo's bearer you are treating?" the little red-skinned Edeptan physician verified on the vid call. "His...how do you call it...mother?"

"That's right, Doron, and she's got pancreatic cancer," Zebra explained. "You remember that aspect of human anatomy, I hope?"

"Yes, I do," Doron averred. "If memory serves, that is a particularly virulent form, yes?"

"Yes. And it is well advanced," Zarnix added. "It has essentially taken over a goodly part of the upper central abdominal cavity."

"Ooo," Doron murmured, yellow eyes going wide. "That is...unpleasant. But I have seen worse."

"And healed it?" Zebra asked, worried.

"Oh yes," Doron averred, serene. "Much worse. And healed. But you will have to 'stay on top of it,' as you say, and adjust the fluid formulation daily, if not hourly."

"I'm all over it," Zebra volunteered. "I'll get it done, if I have to sleep in the room with the regen pod. Just tell us what to do."

"All right." Doron's image on the screen nodded. "Tell me what the chemistry looks like currently, and I will explain to you, step by step, what you must do..."

* * *

The next couple of shifts were hectic in the medlab. Zebra, with Zarnix and as many of the rest of the medical staff as could find time, worked tirelessly over the unconscious Nalin Bryant in the regeneration pod. Samples of the fluid were drawn off and tested every hour on the hour; as soon as the test results returned, Zebra and Zarnix adjusted the composition of the fluid.

Several additional interstellar calls went back and forth

between Earth and Edeptis, and consultations and reminders occurred frequently, sometimes several times in a day.

Eventually the chemistry of the regeneration fluid stabilized, as Nalin Bryant's cancer finally relented and allowed itself to be controlled. An entire staff of physicians, on-and off-world, drew a collective breath.

Zebra kept close tabs on her much-beloved patient.

Chapter 5

Echo pulled the strip of black chambray from the branch of one tree in a small copse, and studied it in the morning light. He laid it against his own shirt; the material was a dead match. Echo raised the cloth to eye-level then to examine it, and spotted the telltale clues confirming its source of origin. A few silver-blonde strands still adhered to the material, and his nose caught the faintest whiff of his partner's unique scent.

One of these days I gotta ask her what it is—wait, she told me back in Australia last fall. What was it again? 'Heavenly Bodies' or some such drivel—something she has custom-made. Cutesy-sweet name, but damn it smells great, at least on her. And I don't know of anyone else that wears it. It sure makes identifying her easy for me, though. Not that she wears a whole lot; she gets the concept of 'subtle.' Which in this job, you gotta be, or you don't live long. But she wears juuust enough. For me, anyhow. As Romeo would say, whoa baby.

He smiled to himself, a mischievous, slightly sensual expression, and scanned the still-damp ground. Finding a rather large pile of horse manure under one of the trees, he repeated his earlier process, dissecting the fecal matter with a stick and finding that the exterior was dry and crusty but the interior was still somewhat moist; it was layered, as well—indication that the horse had likely stood there for some time—and also contained little to no evidence of feed, but plenty of shrubbery and some grass. *Getting closer,* he decided, and looked around.

Whoa, waitaminit, he noted. *This area isn't nearly wet enough, even despite the clump of trees here. I wonder what...*

He stopped and looked around the copse, then saw some bits and threads of twine still wrapped around several low-hanging branches, as well as a lattice of crudely-hewn wooden slats wedged horizontally in the fork of a tree. Another, similar lattice was wedged vertically about a foot above the horizontal lattice.

Sonuvabitch, he thought with a delighted grin. *Meg musta had a tarp or something, and rigged a nice comfy shelter and a chair of sorts, to get outta the rain. But why the hell did she do that? Was it an overnight camp, while the perps stopped for the night? Why didn't she get some shut-eye? Well, I guess she might not have wanted to, in case she slept through the perps leaving or something. Let alone the risk of being found, while asleep. But I need to investigate a little more and see what went on here.*

He walked away from the copse of trees under which his partner had sheltered—confident that, if Omega had stayed dry, then Celeste, along with the tack and equipment, would have been protected as well; his partner was nothing if not thorough—and commenced looking for any evidence of what else went on in this area.

As he drew near to the ravine in which he knew the alien assassin team would have slunk, Echo abruptly saw the signs he was looking for: a company of some ten beings had made camp along the top of the ravine's bank.

They knew what they were doing, Echo realized, glancing over the edge of the ravine. *Looks like a flash flood came through, and they cleared out before it got to 'em. Here's the signs of their camp, and there's...look at this. It's a 'hatful of fire.' Or it was. I can still smell the smoke—but not until I get right on top of it.*

He crouched and poked around in the small patch of disturbed soil, not more than eight inches or so in diameter, eventually uncovering cold ash and charred twigs, some six inches below the surface of the ground.

They made a fire in a hole, so the light wouldn't be visible. Probably they were cold and wet; I doubt they had a lot in the way of rain gear or the like. So that's why Meg paused and took cover behind...and under...the trees back there. She had to get out of sight, and took the opportunity to get out of the rain while she waited.

He returned to Ditok and mounted, moving forward. As he crossed the ravine, which still had flowing water in it—though it had decreased to little more than a trickle in this area—he watched for evidence that others had crossed it. So he spotted several shiny rocks with moss on their undersides, evidence they'd been overturned, as well as several patches of dislodged moss and algae. But as Ditok surmounted the far bank, the indications of the alien passage faded, and he began looking for signs of a heavier, galactic-polymer-shod animal—Celeste, with Omega on her back. Finally he noticed something.

There; Celeste's hoof prints. Clear and sharp, with dribbles of water in the bottom. I'm gettin' close, Meg. Hang on, baby. I'll be there soon.

Echo spurred Ditok on in haste.

* * *

"And how is Echo's mother progressing now?" Fox wondered over dinner. "I gathered from Zarnix's department reports that you have finally managed to get things stabilized?"

"Yeah, we think so," Zebra confirmed, but Fox noted she stopped eating, and laid down her silverware. "I was pretty worried there for a bit."

"And you still are, judging by your reaction just now," Fox observed.

"Well, yeah," Zebra sighed. "I just...can't seem to help it. I mean, it LOOKS like things have leveled out, but..."

"Bubeleh, you have been—uncharacteristically—highly anxious since Omega and I presented the situation to you, with our request," Fox pointed out. "You are a better physician than this. And your confidence in your abilities is as it should be, at least normally. You shouldn't have any cause for such concern. What is wrong, my dear girl? Why does it trouble you so?"

Zebra gazed at him for long moments, her countenance worried. Eventually, she spoke.

"Okay, honey, it's like this. Completely aside from my oath, and my responsibility to heal whenever it's in my ability, this patient isn't like any of the others I normally treat.

This is Echo's MOM. There's only two women in the universe who mean the world to Echo: his partner...and his mother. And because Echo means the world to OMEGA, she's wrapped up in this—she wants Mrs. Bryant healed about as much as Echo would, I think. Maybe the fact her own mom is gone factors into that; I dunno."

"Probably," Fox agreed. "Keep going, meyn gelibte."

"Well, and then there's the fact that you think of Echo as your son...and to a lesser extent," she shrugged, "only SLIGHTLY lesser, Omega as your daughter. And so somehow or other, this big ol' extended family we got, which I love too," she threw him a wobbly smile, "is all tied up right now in the idea of 'we gotta keep Echo's mom alive.' And all of that... lands on my shoulders." Zebra put her face in her hands; her next words emerged muffled. "And I don't want to disappoint any of you by failing."

"Oh, meyn teyere gelibte," Fox murmured, pushing back from the table and rising, "no, no, no. We never meant...*I* never meant...to put such weight on your shoulders." He moved around the table and knelt beside her. "All I ever ask is that you try. I already know you will do your best. And if you cannot succeed, then I know that chances are, no one in the galaxy could."

He scooped her up in his arms and stood, carrying her to the couch, where he sat, eased her into his lap, and simply held her for long moments, stroking her glossy dark hair. She clung to him, trembling lightly, as emotions that she had kept tightly bottled for many days finally surfaced.

"Just relax, Zoë," he whispered into her ear. "Just relax, my love. It is all going to be all right. You are doing wonderful things. Even if we cannot save Mrs. Bryant; even if we save her life, but cannot return her to full health...you have done your best. You have even brought Doron in remotely to virtually assist. And he is the expert, the inventor of the procedure. You can do no more. And I would ask no more."

"That's...that's not all I'm scared of, Franz," she confessed in a low voice.

"What, then?"

"It's stupid."

"So?"

"I mean, I know it's stupid, I just can't...stop thinking about it."

"Tell me anyway. I swear I won't laugh, bubeleh."

"Promise? It's...I think I know what you're gonna say, I... just need to hear you say it."

"I understand. Tell me."

"O-okay. It's like this. If...if Echo is, for all intents and purposes your son, and Mrs. Bryant is his mother...I mean..." She sniffled, but did not cry, although Fox could see the tears standing in her eyes. "Does that mean you...and she...?" She shrugged and looked away. "Where does that leave me?"

"Right here," Fox said, tightening his arms around her. "Where you've been for the last year. Where I hope you'll always be, if you want to be. In my heart, in my soul, by my side."

Zebra raised her head and gazed into his warm hazel eyes, her own blue-gray eyes wide and still glimmering wetly.

"There," Fox murmured. "Was that what you needed to hear?"

"Oh, honey! And then some!"

She flung her arms around his neck and hugged him tightly.

* * *

Echo was following his partner's trail when a strong, sour, spoiled smell assailed his nostrils. He sat back in the saddle, cocking his wrist to produce a light tug on the reins, and the obedient Ditok immediately slowed to a halt. Echo dismounted and, holding the reins, looked around.

Whoa, he thought, spotting the source of the odor. *Somebody got seriously sick. There's barf all over, right here. And,* he realized, growing grim, *the distribution, spread, and general splatter is about what I'd expect if somebody threw up from horseback. Either someone else is out here on a horse and got sick, or Meg got into something. Maybe something in the food supplies spoiled? I didn't think we brought along anything that COULD spoil, but there's a first time for everything, I guess. Wow. Looks like my poor baby was sick as a dog.*

Or maybe...something bad happened to upset her. Like... being detected by the perps? Lord God, not that. That damn bloodthirsty Glu'g'ik would kill her as soon as look at her. But... He paused and looked around. *There's no sign of blood, or really of any other beings close. Not that I'm seeing here.*

He mounted Ditok and eased the big horse farther on, watching the landscape around him for any unusual sign. Gradually they left the vomit stench behind, and Echo saw no more sign that Omega had been ill. Nor did he see any indication that she had been detected or captured...or seriously injured. Or killed.

Well, that's good, he decided. *Maybe she just needed to purge something that disagreed with her, and she's okay now. I hope so. It's a pain in the ass, trying to track a perp when you feel bad.*

He clucked to Ditok, and they picked up the pace.

* * *

Having verified the direction of travel, and now able to clearly see and follow the hoofprints of Omega's horse, Echo was racing across relatively open range on Ditok when he heard the shout.

"Dammit! Who the hell d' you think you are, trespassin' on my property?! Who give you permission??" And then there was the ominous sound of a shotgun being pumped. "SLOW DOWN! Who the hell 're you runnin' from? You followin' 'long behind the twister, stealin' from people, boy?"

'Boy'?! The hell you say! Sorry, Meg, now I know how it feels, Echo thought.

He looked around to see an armed and irate elderly rancher on horseback off to his left, shotgun up but not yet aimed, and he reined Ditok back to a slow lope, turning aside to meet the man.

Damn, it's old Billy, Echo realized, recognizing the man as he got closer. *I didn't even know he was still alive. I do NOT need this complication. I gotta get to Meg.*

Echo pulled his hat down low, lest the old rancher recognize a vaguely-familiar face, years ago though it had been. Carefully, nonthreateningly, reaching into his hip pocket, Echo retrieved his *carte noir* and held it out. By the time the rancher was close enough to see it properly, a shiny silver star inscribed in a circle had appeared—the traditional 'star in a wheel' of the famed Texas Rangers. And Echo planned to make full use of that organization's well-deserved reputation.

"Texas Ranger, sir," Echo replied to the elderly man, dropping his voice as low as it would go, which was considerable. "Undercover operation. Tracking a smuggling operation cross-country. Had to leave my partner trailin' 'em alone and double back to warn the others. Now I'm tryin' to catch back up to 'em." He replaced the *carte noir*.

"Smugglin', eh?" the suspicious rancher followed up. "Smugglin' what?"

"Illegal aliens, sir," Echo said with a straight face. "Known criminals at that."

"Damn may-hee-canos!" the rancher spat in a knee-jerk response, misunderstanding as Echo had intended. He immediately lowered his shotgun. "Comin' in here thinkin' they own th' place. Go git 'em, son. You give 'em one fer ol' Billy, y' hear? You an' your boys c'n ride across my ranch any day! Git on, now, 'fore they get away!"

Echo touched his hat in thanks and turned Ditok, speeding away. As he went, he kept reminding himself, *It takes all kinds...*

* * *

As Omega traveled steadily eastward, the landscape and foliage gradually changed from the dry, rugged canyonland terrain and grasslands of the western Edwards Plateau near the Pecos River in west Texas, to the green, rolling hills and wooded slopes of the eastern Plateau and the Texas Hill Country. The increased ability to find both cover and shade from the hot sun was of some small relief to the injured and very ill Agent as a tenacious but severely-weakened Omega continued trailing the would-be assassins.

It was midafternoon when Omega heard the hoof beats in the distance, but by that time, she was struggling just to remain upright in the saddle. A quick glance over her shoulder served to demonstrate that the approaching rider was in fact Echo and not another assassin, but it also nearly unseated her—between the snake-bitten leg's uselessness and a bit of vertigo produced by badly-blurred vision, the movement seriously challenged her equilibrium. Relief surged through her—Echo was alive and apparently unhurt. Which was, she realized, more than could be said for her.

He probably just got held up by the storm, she grasped. *I mean, even the perps had to come outta the ravine because of the flash flood, and it was dying down by the time it got to us. I bet he was on the wrong side of a stream or something.*

By this time, the venom had worked its way throughout her system, and she was deathly ill. She was, however, still determined, still on the trail, and very aware that they were only a few hours away from the rendezvous site she had overheard the assassin squad mentioning earlier.

But the only knowledge she had of her left leg any longer was a fierce burning pain, and she could not have dismounted if she had wanted to do so.

* * *

Echo spotted her as he rode up, and slowed Ditok to a walk for the sake of secrecy. He wondered that Omega made no reaction to his approach; with her acutely-sensitive ears, she had to have heard him coming.

"Incoming!" he called in a low tone, and he saw her nod, but she still did not turn or motion to him. As Echo brought Ditok alongside Celeste, he noticed the blanket wrapped around Omega, and raised a curious eyebrow, not a little puzzled; it was an unusually hot late-June afternoon in west central Texas, and his own shirt was almost plastered to his back in the heat. "Meg? What's up?" he asked her quietly. "Aren't you about to melt down, in that blanket?"

Without answering verbally, Omega reached under the blanket, into her shirt pocket; she retrieved an object and held it out to him. Echo looked down at the snake rattle in her hand, and he felt his face blanch as the blood drained away. The color of the rattle told the tale to the knowledgeable Agent.

"A Mojave green?! Where?!" he exclaimed, and she hushed him, then flipped the blanket back to expose the swollen leg.

"Oh, dear God," Echo breathed fervently, and leaped off Ditok, ran to Celeste, and pulled Omega down off her horse; relieved of their riders' weights, both horses came to a halt. The bitten leg buckled under Omega, and Echo clamped her tight against his torso to keep her from falling. "When??"

"Uhn. Long enough."

"WHEN?"

"Um...this morning, a little after sunrise, I think. Before? After. I dunno. Sometime around sunrise. Ish."

"Damn! Can you feel your leg?"

"Aside from the pain? No."

Echo studied his partner, trying to determine how serious matters were. Omega's face was very pale, and the freckles forming beneath the sunburn-turning-tan stood out in stark relief; her eyelids drooped in a fashion that indicated something other than weariness, and her breathing was labored. *And the vomiting, up the trail,* he remembered. *Not because of anything she ate. Because a rattler bit her. It was the venom that made her throw up. Shit. This is NOT good.*

"Um, Echo? Can I maybe...sit down now? I'm...kinda... kinda woozy inna head..."

With infinite care, Echo sat Omega on the ground, swiftly unpacked her sleeping bag and bedroll, and placed her in it, blanket and all, laying her in the shade of a nearby tree. Then he began feverishly going through her saddlebags, eventually coming up with the medikit.

"It's no good, Echo," Omega told him, watching from where she lay. "There's no snakebite kit in it. No antivenin. Nothing."

"Shit! That's a major oversight," he observed, shocked. "This 'stocking of the field medical supplies' stuff is getting old."

"Yep."

"I guess nobody thinks about an Agent having to bushwhack."

Omega did not answer; she sighed instead.

"Damn," he whispered then, dropping the medikit and coming back to kneel at her side, as the seriousness of the situation, and its probable outcome, struck home. *No no no,* he thought, despairing. *After all we've been through, side by side—Antarctica, Hatterats, dire beets, Veelsii, Slug, the Cortians—and a damn stupid RATTLER is gonna take her away from me! NO! It can't end like THIS!* He shook his head, near desperation. "Meg—what do you want me to do, honey? I can take you to help—"

"Listen to me, Ace. I'll be okay—"

"Meg, you were bit by a rattler, baby. A particularly nasty species, at that. Trust me: you are NOT okay."

"Hush. That's not important...right now. What you need... to know is that...ohh..."

Omega stopped for a moment, weak and shivering uncontrollably, and it hit Echo that she was suffering from shock as the hemotoxic effects of the venom, and the resulting internal hemorrhaging, had caused her blood pressure to drop. *And that explains the blanket,* he realized.

Echo lifted her upper body, wrapping the sleeping bag tighter around her shoulders before unzipping it, slipping his arms inside, and pulling her against him, offering his body heat to combat her chills. Grateful, she nestled into the warmth of his body and rested her head against his chest, her trembling quieting a bit as she did, and continued.

"Mmh...'at's better. Thanks. All right, lessee. You need to know that...that they've got a rendezvous point...'bout four hours away from here. Near...Junction, I think. Isn't there a town called Junction, east of here? Something Junction, anyway. They're meeting somebody...in some vehicle, I guess. South of a crossroads, near a river." Omega paused to pant for a few moments, struggling to get her breath. "From there, they'll hit Interstate 10, then cut across to I-35 on back roads. So...the rest of the trip will be quick. They'll be in...in Dallas by late tonight. You need to...to go...after them."

"Don't worry about it, baby. I've notified Fox. He's on it. Romeo and India, and several more Alpha teams, will be ready and waiting in Dallas. They can take care of it. I'm not leaving you here alone, to die."

"Echo, it's all right, honey," Omega sighed, lapsing into her most Southern voice as she finally relaxed and succumbed to the snake venom now that she had delivered her message. "Ah'm not gonna die. Ah got bit 'bout...mmm...what time is it?"

Echo automatically glanced at his wrist chronometer, seriously concerned at Omega's apparent detachment from reality. "It's a little past two in the afternoon."

"Ah got bit over eight hours ago. More or less." Her weary voice was low.

"What?! Eight... How did you—?" The bottom seemed to drop out of his stomach, even as the center fell out of his world. *She's dying,* he thought, horrified. *My baby's dying. Right here, right now, right in front of me. In my arms. Any minute. While I get to watch, and can't do a damn thing to stop it. Not this time. First Ma, now Meg. From a damn, stupid RATTLESNAKE.*

Echo shifted out of his kneeling position and sat back down on the ground beside the sleeping bag, where he gently gathered his partner back into his arms, sleeping bag and all, and cradled her against his chest, expecting her to quietly give up the ghost any moment.

"Then I'm not going anywhere," he swore to her. "I promised you once I'd be here when..."

"Echo, Ah'm okay, hon, Ah swear Ah am. Ah've been bit before."

Echo stared down at Omega, confused.

"You're doin' it again. Forgettin' Ah'm...forgettin' Ah've got recombinant DNA. Ev'dently Slug...wanted t' make sure...I survived long 'nuff to, to do his dirty work." Her head drooped onto his shoulder. "Mmh...it hurts. So bad. Everything jus' hurts. Tired...'m so tired..."

Echo's eyebrows rose as he realized what she was trying to tell him, and he quickly put his fingers to her throat to check her pulse. It was rapid and slightly weak, but steady, and her skin, while cold, was not clammy. Then it all suddenly hit him.

She's not sweating abnormally; she's not drooling, and while I can tell her vision sucks by the way she's looking at me, she's focusing and tracking fine. He breathing's a little ragged, but fairly steady, especially given the pain she's probably in. Coordination is decent, if not quite up to her usual levels. And fully eight hours in, and she's still functional? To a fairly high degree, 'cause she's been tracking and surveilling our assassin ring this whole time. And getting—and remembering—detailed info, too. Damn, baby. 'Tough' doesn't begin to cut it. Your picture is beside the word in the dictionary.

"Then you're poisoned, but not fatally so?" he asked quietly, and she nodded slightly against his chest. Relief surged through him great enough to make him temporarily light-headed.

"Ah'm gonna be sick...for a few more hours, but then Ah'll get better," she told him. "Ah 'uz never in any...real danger, not from th' snake bite. Ah jus' feel awful rough. Least Ah've quit hurlin' mah guts out."

And that confirms the source of the vomiting, he thought, then added aloud, "How long before you're able to...?"

"Should be back with ya—if Ah ride hard—before the perps...reach the rendezvous..."

"Okay. That sounds...damn good, really. At least over what I thought was gonna happen."

Echo eased her back to the ground, double-checked the immediate area for 'critters,' as Omega tended to call them—the last thing they needed was another snake bite, or adding a spider bite or scorpion sting into the mix—then he returned to Ditok. But instead of mounting the horse, he unstrapped the black suitcase, then grabbed the medikit where it had fallen near Celeste, and brought them both over beside Omega. Opening the medikit, he got out a micropore noninvasive syringe.

"Here, Meg. Give me your arm, honey. I'm gonna give you something heavy-duty for the pain. Now that I'm here to watch out for you, we can afford to do that." Echo administered the medication, and tucked her arm carefully back inside the bag to keep it warm. "There. That should help. Just relax, baby. You'll get sleepy in a few seconds."

Then he turned to the black case and entered the codes on the combination locks.

"Wha's that?" she murmured, still watching, but already sounding drowsy to his knowledgeable, familiar ear.

"A little something I brought along just in case."

Echo opened up the suitcase to expose a small Alpha Line command center, customized especially for the Alpha One team, and outfitted with small warp sections—the inside really was bigger than the outside, at least to a limited extent. There were extra blasters, collapsible-stock tachyon-splitter rifles, a long-range audio/video comm set, spare brain bleachers, spectral analyzers, and other equipment, including basic IR goggles and flashlights, all carefully cushioned in foam padding. Omega started laughing as soon as she got a good look at it.

"What?" Echo asked, glancing up at her.

"You were a Boy Scout when you were a kid, weren't ya?" she asked him then, grinning from ear to ear.

"What about it?"

"Nothin', it's just that Ah'd decided to put together almost the identical kit once we got back from this little jaunt. Ah didn' know ya already had it. Is it standard issue?"

"No. I had this made up, special, to carry on vacay years ago, after X-ray and I had what we took to calling The Vacation That Wasn't. An' it looks like this trip is shaping up to be The Vacation That Wasn't, Part II: The Sequel. Anyway, I try to keep the equipment in it up to date."

"Is that what ya went back for?"

"Yeah."

"What are we gonna do...?"

"You are going to rest. I am going to call Fox and check in, pull up a satellite view and locate the rendezvous site, and see if we can get a team there in time to surprise the whole lot. If there's time, I'll catch a nap, too. Then, when you're able, we're headed for the rendezvous. Together, hopefully." He met her gaze, keeping his own soft and understanding, then added, "Feeling any better, baby?"

"Yeah, I am. I'm still awful cold. But it doesn't hurt near as much. Thanks, Ace." She nodded and gave him a weary smile. "I'm glad you're back."

"You're welcome, Meg. Always. And I'm glad I'm back, too, and I'm really glad it's not hurting so bad. Now hush, quit fighting the stuff I just gave you, and go on to sleep, baby. You need to rest if you're gonna let your system do its thing and throw off the venom."

"Hokay," she sighed, as weary blue eyes slid closed.

* * *

"What is it?" Fox said, coming into the medlab at speed. Zarnix and Zebra awaited him, but it was Zebra who answered.

"Come on in here, honey," she said, leading the way into her office. "Grab a seat."

Zebra took her desk chair; Fox and Zarnix took visitor chairs.

"Okay, what's this all about?" Fox wondered.

"We've got one last problem with Mrs. Bryant," Zebra said, frowning and worried. "Zarnix noticed it first."

"What?"

187

"She has a heart arrhythmia," Zarnix declared. "And it's getting worse."

"Can you fix it?"

"We're working on it," Zebra noted, tight, "but I thought you'd want to know."

"Right." Fox nodded. "I see that look, bubeleh. Remember what I told you the other evening, now. All I ever asked was the best you could do; I never asked for a miracle. Nor would Omega, and Echo would not expect it, either."

"I know. I just...thought we were almost home-free."

"Stay calm, liebchen. It cannot be any harder than the cancer."

"No, you're right, it's not...but it's not any easier, either."

"Why not? Just modify the fluid to heal the heart."

"It does not work like that." Zarnix shook his head. "You cannot just throw in a hodgepodge of chemicals to the regen fluid, or it is not much better than putting your patient in a mud bath. And it can actually make things worse, if the components react badly together."

"Then...how...?"

"You have to take each thing you're treating, and do it one at a time," Zebra explained, tag-teaming with her department lead. "Evidently she had an underlying, and previously undetected, weakness in her heart—no, don't look like that; I've already gone through all of Echo's records, and I'm ninety-nine point nine-nine-five percent sure he didn't inherit it. In fact, we went back and looked at all of the tests we ran on her before we put her in the pod, and we're pretty sure that at some point in her life, she developed mild, asymptomatic endocarditis from some infection she had, and that's what damaged her heart. It isn't inherited at all."

"That can happen?!" Fox asked, shocked.

"Yes, it can, Director, and in surprisingly simple fashion," Zarnix noted. "Something as seemingly insignificant as a diseased gum, or a cut that got infected with certain bacteria."

"Oy vey. So there's no telling when it was, or what caused

it."

"Exactly," Zebra agreed. Just then, a medtech knocked, then stuck his head into the door.

"Excuse me, Doctors, Director. Zarnix, he's on the line."

"Ah. Excuse me," Zarnix said, rising and following the medtech out of the office at something just shy of a sprint.

"Anyway, she has this heart weakness now," Zebra continued, "and the pancreatic cancer tended to create diabetic-like conditions, which exacerbated it with crazy blood sugar levels all over the map, and subsequent inflammation. Unfortunately, the way this whole regen system works for pancreatic cancer, the hormonal components are some of the last to respond to the treatment, which means that the heart problem is continuing to worsen."

"Then pause the cancer treatment, and fix the heart weakness."

"We can't," Zebra told him, stifling a groan. "We're at a critical point. If we stop treating the cancer right now, it'll run wild and kill her before we can even begin to heal the heart." She shook her head. "No, what we're having to do is to try to support the heart as much as we can, while we also try to rush the cancer treatment through to the end. THEN we'll reset the fluid to heal the heart tissue. It's a race, Fox—can we heal the cancer in time to fix the heart before it kills her, or not? I swear," she raked a hand through the hair over her ear, "I don't know how Doron stays so cool. The more I get into working with this whole regen thing, the more amazed I am at his..." she shrugged, looking for the word, then tried, "...zen."

"Speaking of whom, have you consulted him about this new challenge?"

"Yeah, Zarnix is already consulting with Doron, right this minute, on the best way to handle it—that's what the medtech came in for, to tell him Doron was finally on the vid call. I'm hoping it's going to be a similar technique to what we've already done. I had an idea about how to do it, but this is so important, I wanted Doron to verify it first."

"I understand. But then why are you not in there with Zarnix, instead of calling me down here?" Fox wondered, puzzled.

"I will be, in just a minute. But for one, you wanted to be kept in the loop, so I thought I'd tell you while Zarnix tried to reach Doron, only Zarnix couldn't reach Doron initially, so he came in with us..."

"Very well. I appreciate that. And 'one' presupposes a 'two'..."

"And two..." Zebra rose and came to stand beside his chair, slightly shamefaced. "This is off the clock, Fox. Swear to me."

"Of course, if you need it to be. Just us?"

"Just us. I'm so stressed, honey. I...could really use a hug right now. Only...I didn't want to admit it to Zarnix; I mean after all, he's my department chief, so I'm kinda glad he left already..."

"Aw."

And Fox immediately stood, wrapped his arms around his mate, and held her until she settled.

* * *

By the time Zebra reached Zarnix's office door a few minutes later, that worthy was already emerging, electronic tablet in hand. He smiled at his second.

"Doron said to tell you that your instincts are very good," Zarnix said. "He only had a few modifications to the protocol you designed. Here." He handed her the tablet, and she studied it.

"Oy, as Fox says," Zebra said after a moment. "This next shift is gonna be 'all hands on deck.' What else have we got going on in the medlab?"

"Not a lot at the moment," Zarnix said. "The tornado did no damage, and India is on the comm as we speak, handling Omega's rattlesnake bite..."

"WHAT?!" Zebra nearly screamed the word. "Tornado? RATTLESNAKE?!"

"No, no, it's all right," Zarnix soothed, holding out his hands in a placating gesture. "That amazing Agent of ours is already recovering, using nothing but a standard medikit, a couple of indigenous herbals, some help from Echo, and her own incredible, unusual genetics and willpower."

Zebra put a trembling hand to her eyes. She drew in a deep breath, and let it out in a shaky sigh.

"All right. So the damn psychopath that tortured her wanted to make sure she was alive for the end game, no matter what."

"Evidently. But by the time anyone with full-on medical training heard about it, she was already through the worst of it."

"What? But... Why didn't she call in?!"

"Because apparently wherever they are has..." Zarnix broke off and shrugged. "Not even Agency cell phones can get a signal through whatever it is in that area. Have you read the reports of the First Contact?"

"Oh. It's in that area? Yeah, Fox told me they selected it because of a natural cloaking ability of something in the area. He and Echo have always suspected it was because of that meteor crater."

"Yes, I have heard them say as much, on the few times they talk about it. At any rate, she could not call in, because she could not get a signal out."

"So have they gotten out of that area?"

"More or less, I gather; perhaps not fully out of the cloaked area, but Echo brought along some sort of special kit with a larger, more powerful communications set, according to the word I had from India a bit ago. Oh, and we will need to be prepared for injuries, some possibly severe, when Alpha One leads Alpha Line against the JFK assassination team, which has returned to Earth under the direction and sponsorship of an imperialist Glu'gu'ik faction, to try to kill the current president."

"Oh SHIT!"

"Not to worry. It is still a couple of days before the U.S. President arrives in Dallas. We have time. I'm surprised Fox didn't tell you all this, when you briefed him."

"Aw, double shit," Zebra grumbled, then blushed. "No, that's my fault. I filled him in on the situation with Mrs. Bryant...and then I...I went off-record with him, because I'm so worried..."

"Hush," Zarnix murmured. "And he is your beloved, and you needed to lean on him for a moment. I understand entirely, and I do not fault you. I think, in the circumstances, you made a wise decision in that. We all need such things from time to time."

"You don't have a mate. How...?"

"But I have family," Zarnix pointed out. "Even some which are here on Earth. AND dear friends. I have my support group, Zebra, just as you do. Do not make me out as some sort of super-being. You are every bit as strong as I." He laid a hand on her shoulder. "Now come. India is monitoring the situation with Omega, we have several days before the medlab needs to be ready for additional injured, and we now have the rest of the medlab at our beck and call. Let us go see to Mrs. Bryant."

* * *

Zebra, Zarnix, Whiskey, Rglfrz, and the rest of the medlab staff pitched in. None but Zebra and Zarnix knew who their patient really was, or why she was so important, but they knew she was about to become one of them, and they knew she was in need, and that was all that truly mattered.

Together, Zebra and Zarnix adjusted the regeneration fluid in Nalin Bryant's chamber, accelerating the elimination of the cancer and the healing and regeneration of the organs it had affected, while supporting her weakened heart as much as possible.

Meanwhile, the other physicians and medtechs monitored her condition in any of a hundred ways, providing constant feedback and analysis, so that the department's chief and assistant chief could continue adjusting the fluid's composition on the fly, according to the protocol Doron had given them.

* * *

When Omega awoke a couple of hours later, she found she was cocooned under Echo's sleeping bag, as well as inside her own bag, still wrapped in the blanket. She currently lay comfortably, her back resting against Echo's chest, belly, and groin, as he made like a recliner for her.

Echo sat slouched behind her, leaning against the tree trunk, legs spread, knees drawn up on either side of her torso to help keep her in position, his inner ankles pressed lightly against her upper thighs well above the snakebite, so it wouldn't hurt her. His arms were folded across his knees above her head, and his head nodded forward almost to his arms as he rested, eyes closed. A trickle of sweat made its way slowly down his right temple.

The portable command center lay open nearby. The horses had been tethered to another tree and given feed bags.

Omega looked up into the handsome face of her sleeping companion for several long moments, studying the relaxed features with a gentle smile, in which was more than a hint of deep affection, even love.

Then, much too warm, she began trying to worm her way out of the wrappings without disturbing him or making any noise.

The slight movement, however, woke her lightly-dozing partner. Echo opened his eyes and looked down at her.

* * *

"Well, hey. You're awake. How do you feel?" he asked in a quiet voice, reaching down with a gentle touch and checking the pulse in her throat again, as he'd done periodically while she slept. It was a steady sixty-five. *And her skin is warm,* he realized with relief.

"Hot," she answered, and he grinned.

"Me too. Good. I thought you were going to freeze to death on me, there for a while. Eventually I had to resort to becoming a heater myself, just to try to keep you from going deeper into shock. I'm still not sure if that was from the venom, or from the pain meds ramping you down, or both, or if it's just how your body throws off poison, or...what." Echo helped his partner extricate herself from all the coverings. "Do you still feel sick?"

"No. I feel reasonably decent now, if still a little bit weak, maybe. But my mouth feels like Death Valley," Omega replied, sitting up on the grass and starting to roll the sleeping bags. "Tastes like it, too," she observed, smacking with distaste. Echo stood and walked over to the horses.

"That much is actually normal after a rattler bite, from all I've heard of people who survived the damn things. Here." Echo brought one of the full canteens over and gave it to her. "Knock it all back. As much as you want, plus at least eight ounces past that. It oughta help flush out the last of the venom. Drain it dry if you want to; I got several more fresh ones. You're probably dehydrated anyway."

"I wouldn't doubt it."

* * *

Omega stood with her partner's help—she was still a little wobbly on the bad leg—took the canteen, and guzzled the water in it, as Echo went to the command center. He brought her the Winchester & Tesla she had given him, as well as a blaster and belt holster sized to her frame, and she returned his holstered weapon. He donned it, then closed the case and started strapping it to Ditok. The sleeping bags went on Celeste, as did most, but not all, of the remaining food and water. Then he got out all of Omega's equipment from her saddlebags and put it in his own.

"What are you doing that for?" Omega asked as she watched, still killing off the canteen, preparatory to ducking into the bushes to relieve herself...and hopefully flush out the last of the venom in the process.

"We're gonna take Ditok and ride tandem."

"Echo, I can ride now. The swelling's even gone down." Omega pointed to her thigh.

* * *

Echo came over and knelt beside her, tearing the sliced

denim of her jeans open further in order to thoroughly examine the bite. He lightly and deliberately fingered the soft, smooth skin around the bruised and discolored wound, watching her face with concern for a particular reaction. He got it. Omega smothered a giggle.

"Good. Much better. Now give me your hand." Omega laid her hand in Echo's extended palm. "Squeeze," he commanded. She gripped his hand tightly. "Harder."

She bore down, as his fingertips reddened. He nodded, and took the empty canteen.

"Yeah. You're strong enough. You can ride now. But we're still taking Ditok; Celeste wouldn't be able to keep up. Don't worry, Joe will be along to pick up Celeste soon. Now go duck behind that bush and take a leak if you need to; I already checked for critters for you."

Omega promptly headed for the indicated foliage.

"Echo, you're gonna overload that poor horse." Her voice floated out from the thicket.

"Not Ditok."

"Why not?"

"Because I'm pretty sure he's...kinda like you." He scrunched his mouth.

* * *

"You're comparing me to a horse..." Omega's head popped up over the foliage and she rolled her eyes.

"I like horses."

"Thanks...I think. So how is Ditok like me?"

"Ditok's a horse, but he's not an...ordinary horse. He's got a few surprises—like somebody else I know."

"Oh."

Echo untied Ditok and mounted, as Omega emerged from the brush.

"Meg, is that leg strong enough, or do you want to come around to the other side to mount?"

Omega took a moment to consider, studying the big horse.

"No, I can get up there, I think," she decided. "It's probably gonna be better if I do it on the near side now, anyway; if I was to try mounting from the off side, I'd have all my weight standing on the bad leg while I got my foot into the stirrup, and I'm not sure it's that steady yet. I'm getting better fast, though. I just gotta be careful. But I'll definitely need your help in mounting, because I don't think the leg is strong enough to push up anywhere near that far, quite yet. Ditok is a big ol' horsie."

"Right, then. Here. Grab on."

Echo slipped his left boot out of the stirrup and extended his arm down toward his partner. Omega placed the ball of her foot firmly in the stirrup, took Echo's arm, and he pulled hard as she swung up behind him, settling in between the saddle cantle and the command case. Echo retrieved the stirrup, and Omega eased her hands underneath his arms. She felt a soft exhalation in his chest as her arms wrapped around Echo's waist.

"Echo? Are you all right, Ace?"

"...I'm fine. Ready?"

"Yep. Let's go."

"Hang on tight," he told her, and they were off.

* * *

"Are you doin' okay back there, Meg?" Echo asked his partner over his shoulder as Ditok carried them swiftly toward the rendezvous site. "You've got a death grip on me."

"Too tight?" Omega asked.

"No, you're fine." *I don't think it could ever be too tight, you holding me,* he thought...but did not say. "I just wanted to make sure you weren't still dizzy or something."

"No, I'm feeling fairly decent now; I think I'm pretty much over the snake bite."

"Good."

"I'll still try to loosen up my hold some. It's just adrenaline, and I don't want to interfere with your riding," Omega said.

"You're not. Do whatever you have to do, just stay on."

"Copy that." Omega leaned closer into Echo where he

rode low over Ditok's neck, as she attempted to streamline and stabilize her body. Echo felt the position change, understood it, and glanced back, in an instinctive response.

Omega's face was just behind his shoulder; the blue eyes beneath the hat brim sparkled with exhilaration, and the full lips smiled broadly as she glanced at him.

"If I didn't know better, Meg," Echo told her, trying unsuccessfully to stifle an answering grin, "I'd think you were enjoying this."

"Good-lookin' horse, good-lookin' companion, and speed...what's not to enjoy?" She grinned at him, a mischievous twinkle in her eye. Echo nodded, an answering glint in the brown eyes.

"Yeah, sure enough. The ex-rocket jockey's found a new way to be fast. Rephrase that—go fast."

A silver-blonde eyebrow rose.

"Careful, Echo—my fingers are awfully close to poking in somebody's ribs." Omega gave a meaningful squeeze to Echo's waist with her arms.

"Go ahead. Try it. But you'll only get one chance. I'm not ticklish." It was a brazen, bold-faced lie, and Echo knew it. *But,* he thought, rationalizing the lie to the being to whom he was closest in the universe, *what she doesn't know won't hurt her. It's nobody's business but mine, anyway. If we ever become lovers, I'll 'fess up, I guess; I'll almost have to, knowing her. And then just hope it doesn't disillusion her, or dispel my 'hero' image, in her eyes.*

Omega snapped her fingers in front of his belly, and Echo felt the chuckle against his back as she responded.

"Drat! That's no fun!"

* * *

Oho, Omega thought, carefully controlling her expression, maintaining the grin without giving away her thoughts. *Wow. THAT was a HUGE fib, Ace! And to me, no less! Well, I'll let you off on this one, 'cause you don't know that I know. Besides, I can see why Mr. Badass Tough Guy Alpha Line Chief*

197

Agent doesn't want it to get out that he's ticklish. I think it's adorable—my special hero is secretly sensitive enough to be ticklish—but not everybody would see it that way.

But you owe me one, Echo! You just don't know it yet! Some time, when you're not expecting it, I'll get ya for that big ol' fib!

* * *

Good, Echo decided in satisfaction. *She bought it. I don't have time to explain, let alone deal with a laughing fit just now. Or the ensuing embarrassment and humiliation, when the woman I want more than anything else in life discovers I'm not the Mr. Tough Guy Hero she thinks I am. I wonder if that would put paid to any hopes I've got, or if she could get past it.* He shook himself mentally, and shoved all the emotion—about Omega, about his mother, about the Ranch—deep down inside and closed and locked a mental door on it; he needed to stay focused or they could end up dead. *Get with it, Echo. We've got far more important things to do in the short run.*

"Time to get serious, Meg," he told her then. "We've gotta start putting together a plan."

"I figured you'd already have one," she said, surprised. "I thought you'd do that while I was asleep."

"No. By the time I got off the horn to everybody, then got you all snug and warm, I decided I needed some down time, too, or I wouldn't be alert enough for this leg of the trip."

"Smart move, I expect."

"Yep. That's what I figured, too. So. Do you have any ideas?"

"Well, now that you mention it, I was developing this plan in case you didn't get back in time..."

* * *

The medlab stayed hard on Nalin Bryant's case for hours. Those few personnel who could be spared were set to the task of preparing the department for any injuries resulting from Alpha Line's attempt to abort the presidential assassination.

Fox, getting periodic reports on the status of the medlab's

efforts, saw to it that hot meals were delivered regularly and often, since none of the medical personnel had time to go get it themselves, or even make or heat anything in the department's break room, given everything that was going on in that department. They barely had time to eat what he sent—and that was usually on the fly, sandwich or pastry in hand. Fortunately, Fox also had a 'hot table'—a specially-outfitted table with an infra-red stasis field—set up in a corner of the break room. Everything stayed piping hot and fresh, and there was no chance of spoilage.

"I don't care how busy you are! The lot of you need to keep up your own blood sugar levels," Fox told Zebra on the internal vid call, "or you're going to go all fuzzy-headed, and that won't be good for any of you. Let alone Mrs. Bryant. If I have to, I WILL make it an order. And I WILL set ordered meal times, during which every last blessed one of you will have to stop everything else to eat. Now, do you want that?"

"No; and you're right, of course," Zebra agreed. "And thank you. Everyone appreciates it. And we ARE doing our best to shovel food in, I promise, hon; we're starved. It's just that sometimes we gotta grab something as we go by the hot food table, and stuff it in our faces on the go. Thank the good Lord for galactic medical sanitation methods."

"Well, that's better than nothing, I suppose. And amein on the sanitation, otherwise you'd probably all be sick already. Do you know what time you're getting off duty tonight? Shall I have something nice for dinner all ready, when you get home? I'm fairly busy myself, what with preparing to block an assassination, but I can always send Lima or Bravo for take-out, if I have to, in lieu of cooking something myself. That way, all you have to do is collapse at the dinner table and eat..."

"I...may not get off duty. Not tonight."

"Uh-oh. That wasn't what I'd hoped to hear."

"Tell me about it."

"How is it going?"

"Not great," Zebra admitted. "We're skirting the thin edge

of losing her. In order to get to the heart treatment before the heart gives out, we've had to rather rush the cancer treatment a lot. So much so that, if we pull this off, I plan to keep her in the pod a little longer, so I can go back and do a quick revisit to the cancer treatment."

"But I thought if you stopped the cancer treatment too early..."

"We won't," Zebra said, offering him a slight smile. "It's hard to explain if you haven't had Doron's training. The cancer will be gone. The PREDISPOSITION to the cancer may not be—the causative factors, the genetic drift or mutation in the particular cells, all of that sort of thing, may not be fully eliminated. I don't want to do this, only to have it come back in six months or a year."

"Oh, I see," Fox said, nodding. "So you take her to the point where the cancer is gone, then heal the heart, THEN ensure you've fixed any genetic predispositions and environmentally-induced factors."

"Right."

"Which may already be fixed; you just want to make sure."

"Bingo."

"Well, you're thorough, bubeleh; I'll give you that, no question."

"Thanks, hon," she said with a wry laugh, just as an alert on her cell phone went off. "Woops, that's the alarm for me to go. It's time to make some adjustments to the regen fluid."

"Off with you, then."

"I love you."

"As Romeo would say, 'Back atcha,' meyn teyere."

They both laughed, and the vid screens went dark.

* * *

Five minutes later, Zebra met Zarnix outside Lab B.

"Judging by those dark circles under your eyes, you could do with some sleep," Zarnix observed.

"You're not much better, pal," she shot back. "C'mon, let's go play biochemist."

"This should be the next-to-last adjustment for the cancer, should it not? This evening, we start on her heart?"

"That's the plan, yeah."

"After you, Zebra."

"Oh gee, thanks so much..."

* * *

"No, Echo. Absolutely not." Omega was firmer than her partner had ever heard her.

"Meg—" Echo tried to protest, but he didn't get far.

"NO, Echo. I will not deliberately injure you in order to provide you with a cover story. End of discussion."

"You got any better ideas? We don't have a lot of time or resources here, baby," he pointed out.

"So we should eliminate one of our few resources by wounding our most experienced team member? Besides, I don't think I could intentionally shoot you in cold blood."

"Then you need to toughen up, Meg." Echo frowned. "Division One agents—including, but especially, those of us in Alpha Line—have to be ready to do whatever it takes to get the job done." *I can't believe I just said that,* he suddenly thought. *After all that shit with the snake she just went through—still pulling out of it—and idiot that I am, I went and told her to toughen up.*

"Now there's an interesting change in philosophy. According to what you and Fox taught me, I always thought that statement had a qualifier phrase on it: 'Within rational, reasonable, and moral limits.' Stop the horse, Echo."

"What?"

"WHOA."

* * *

Echo sat back in the saddle and brought Ditok to a halt. Immediately Omega swung her right leg over the horse's hindquarters—negotiating the command center case in the process—and slid to the ground. She removed her hat and tucked it in one of the saddlebags, then walked about fifteen paces in front of the horse and rider. Then she turned and faced them.

"Meg, what the hell do you think you're doing?" Echo protested. "We're nearly there. We don't have time for..."

"Shoot me." She spread her legs, holding her arms out, making the best and biggest target she knew how to make.

"What?!"

"We'll play it your way, Echo," she explained. "Use your scenario. But let's turn it around and go with my original version. I'm the one with the alien DNA. I'm the logical fugitive; you caught me in the act. Shoot me. In cold blood. Now. Go ahead. Do it." Omega pressed hard.

Echo stared at her for a moment, then his eyes narrowed and his brows knit almost as if in physical pain, and he slowly drew his blaster, bringing it up and aiming it at his partner's left shoulder. Omega looked calmly at the weapon, rock-steady in Echo's grip, waiting for him to shoot. As his finger moved toward the trigger, she spoke once more, her voice and expression impassive, even if her roiling emotions—of which, deep hurt and disappointment loomed largest—were not.

"You might want to know one thing before you pull the trigger. I will ask Fox for a reassignment when this is over."

Echo stiffened momentarily, incredulous, his dark eyes widening in disbelief. Staring him in the eyes, her silver-blonde brows furrowed in something that was intended to look like anger but which was really intense mental and emotional pain, Omega answered his unspoken question without hesitation.

"Because I refuse to work with a partner who has the capacity to premeditatedly shoot me with so little emotion. That's cold, and cold-blooded. If you do pull that trigger, Echo, you're not the man I thought I knew for the last year and a half. The man I trusted with my life."

* * *

Echo noted the past tense in the statement with a considerable amount of hidden pain of his own. This was the scenario he had dreaded for so long, the reason he had not yet pushed the notion of a romantic relationship—only this had nothing to do with romance. It had everything to do with trust, with knowing each other so well that they didn't have to talk...normally.

He sat watching her with narrowed gaze, analyzing her expression—seeing the anger AND the pain; his blaster was still pointed in her general direction. But his finger was not on the trigger; even before she had made her threat, he had realized it was not in him to do it. More, he knew it had been a bad idea, and he should have known that Omega wouldn't do it, either—especially given their history together. *Especially given the programming,* he added to himself.

"You want a reason to do it, Echo? Here."

Omega suddenly drew her own blaster, and Echo's eyes went wide, then narrowed again as she leveled her weapon at him. He brought up his own...but again, refused to put his finger on the trigger. *She isn't gonna shoot,* he realized. *BECAUSE OF the programming. As much as it traumatized her to see her own hands aiming at me, out of her control? No way she would ever do it deliberately...no matter what. She's bluffing, and I know it, and she knows I know it. And she's right...I'd betray everything I am, everything I've worked so hard to become, if I shoot.*

They stared each other down for long seconds, blasters aimed, though neither had a finger anywhere near the trigger; then, unexpectedly, she tossed her weapon aside.

"There. I pulled on you. Now do it. We're wasting time. We've got a job to do, remember?" she goaded.

* * *

Her beloved companion of many missions sat for long moments in the saddle with his blaster still trained on her, though she noted with some small gratification that he had yet to even place his finger through the trigger guard; so she waited, watching his face, seeing—as no other being could, in that moment—the fleeting hints of expression that told her of his churning thoughts.

So she saw when he came to a conclusion, though she had no idea what that conclusion might be. She only knew that his finger was still not in the trigger guard.

"Can you run?" Echo spoke at last, gesturing to the snake-bitten leg with his weapon. Omega raised a silver eyebrow, uncertain what the question indicated he had in mind.

"Yes."

"Get your gun."

"All right." She retrieved her blaster and replaced it in its holster. "There. I've got it."

"Start running."

Omega shot Echo a puzzled look and met his eyes. In his chocolate gaze, she read pain, concern, and something that looked rather like sorrow or grief, as well as a kind of urging, a desire for her to understand. Suddenly, she knew what he wanted her to do, and why.

"I said...RUN." He leveled his blaster, putting his finger on the trigger at last.

Omega spun and ran. Her long legs covered distance rapidly, and within moments she was well ahead of her stationary, mounted partner.

A blaster discharge sounded behind her, precisely destroying a small mesquite sapling she had just passed. Seconds later, she heard the sound of hoof beats.

Omega picked up the pace, and ran as if her life depended on it.

Chapter 6

Lord Eb'vuv Ub'he'tae'la, Ha'ar'ec of Clan Ab'ra'kud'un, House Bi't'ir, was a Glu'g'ik from Va'du'sha'ā, and a member of the extended royal family of that planet—though other members of that family were far less amenable to his claims to the throne. Even those who had no particular interest in it for themselves were disinclined to support his claim; he was known to be headstrong and merciless in his pursuit of whatever he considered the correct path. There were those who called him heartless and cruel, even megalomaniacal...though never to his face; Glu'gu'ik who did that tended not to live long, one way or another.

His current path was intended to apply pressure to Earth to return the F'al and its current presumed-Hou'd'ni caretaker to Va'du'sha'ā, in order to facilitate his rise to the throne—there was no doubt in his mind that the F'al would select him as the next ruler. Not that he intended to allow it a choice; methods of 'gaming' the F'al were well known among the royals, after so many millennia.

After some study, he had concluded that the American President was among the planet's most powerful leaders, if not THE most powerful, and he intended to take out the holders of power on the planet, one by one, until Earth capitulated—and this included the current Director of Division One, if necessity so drove. Then he would take the Division One headquarters to Va'du'sha'ā, where it ought to have been in the first place, and consolidate power in the Division on his homeworld.

Unafraid to lead from the front—because, it was rumored on his homeworld, he believed he could not be killed until he had accomplished his task of reviving the monarchy, with himself at its head—he had taken command of the first mission in his plan, fully expecting that success would bring flocks of followers to his feet, and he would be able to break up this current assassination squad to train and lead many other such squadrons against the Earth leaders.

Taking out the Agency Director would likely be hardest, and he kept his plans for that event carefully under wraps. Where matters went from there would depend upon the Ennead's response to his ascension to power. But galactic rule was a definite option for his endgame, should Ennead capitulation not follow immediately.

The fact that the majority of Earth's population was unaware of an extant galactic civilization as anything more than science fiction did not enter into his planning in the least; the innocence of the current American President—who had never even been read in on the Agency's existence—was beneath his consideration. Nor did the fact that the Agency's confiscation of the F'al had been approved by the Ennead, nor the greater Council's sanction of the location of the Division One Headquarters on Earth, affect his plans. Never mind the fact that the current Director—and his successor—were old and dear friends of the current chairbeing of the Ennead, and assassinations of these beings would likely mean swift and certain wrath descending. As it happened, Eb'vuv was not even aware that a successor for the Director had been named, let alone approved; he had simply not bothered to look into the possibility of a chain of command or line of succession for what amounted to a bureaucratic extension of the galactic government. His plan was perfect because he, Lord Eb'vuv Ub'he'tae'la, had deemed it so.

A psychiatrist in the Medical department at Agency Headquarters would have diagnosed him with the Glu'gu'ik version of Nyssen-Van Bogaert syndrome, including irritability, violent behaviors, probable hallucinations, megalomania, and possibly the onset of dementia.

Alpha Line would have simply called him crazy.

* * *

At the moment, Eb'vuv was quantum-disguised as a human male to address his team of assassins, now assembled at the rendezvous point on the riverbank. He was pleased; the opening salvo of his grand plan was proceeding apace.

"We are precisely on schedule," he noted with undisguised satisfaction. "The van should arrive at the rendezvous point within the hour. And we are a scant ten minutes away from it."

"What is the plan when we reach the city?" Tiln the shambling, chlorophyll-based Botanoid, asked in a voice like wind in the leaves.

"The American President's aircraft lands in Dallas in two more Earth days," Eb'vuv answered. "He—"

Unexpectedly, a shriek resounded from somewhere close by, and a disheveled blonde female human clad in ragged black denim, French-braided hair coming loose, tumbled breathlessly over the embankment above, rolling headlong down into their midst. She jumped up with a scream, and would have run on, but the two burly male Zargothians jumped up, grabbing and restraining her.

"No! No! Let me go! He's gonna kill me!!" the blonde cried.

"Human female, what are you doing here?" Eb'vuv demanded, threatening.

"No, I'm not! Don't you see, I tricked him! And now he knows! He almost killed me already!" She clutched at the torn denim on her left leg, trying—ineffectively—to hide the bruises, as she babbled. "Please, let me go! I've got to get away!" She lunged forward desperately, but the hit squad members held her tight by the arms, and she struggled in vain to get free. The sound of hoof beats rose in the distance.

"He's COMING!" she wailed then, and fell to her knees at the feet of a tall purple alien with black crest feathers. "Help me! Please! I'm one of you! Check my DNA! I had human DNA spliced in so I could pass as one of them!!"

"She's telling the truth, Eb'vuv," a short green Delzantian, wielding a small scanner, replied. "The gizmo shows human AND alien genetic structure."

"She's got an instinctive telepathic block up, too," the purple Aves before whom she knelt added. "No human I've ever met can do that."

"I told you! And now he hates me, because I deceived him! Hide me! Quick!"

"Too late." The deep voice sounded from overhead, at the top of the embankment. "Much too late, Meg. Way the hell too late. Emphasis on hell."

"NO!" she cried.

"I'm not interested in the rest of you." The tall, powerful horseman was starkly silhouetted against the sun, nearing the horizon. "Give me the woman and the rest of you can go." He pointed at Omega.

The aliens glanced at each other. The Zargothians released Omega's arms.

"Why do you want her? What has she done?" the Delzantian asked, curious.

"He's an agent! He's Division One!" the mildly-telepathic Aves cried.

"WAS Division One," Echo replied, grim. "By the time I get done with her, Division One sure won't have me. Hell, nobody in PGLEIA will. And I'm not waitin' around to get brain-bleached. Or worse."

"Once again," Eb'vuv pressed, "what has she done?"

"I was sent to infiltrate the Division One Agency and assassinate him," Omega sobbed. "We were on vacation—I was supposed to catch him off-guard..."

"And if it hadn't been for the damn rattlesnake, you'd have succeeded," Echo spat. He dismounted, looping Ditok's lead around an overhanging tree limb. Drawing his blaster, he made his way down the bank. "Now hand the little bitch over."

Omega winced at the epithet, flinching away instinctively. Then suddenly she ran to him, clutching his free arm and clinging to it. Eb'vuv noticed her bare midriff, the torn denim shirt tied high on the ribcage exposing plenty of skin, and his eyebrow rose.

"Echo—honey—Ah wouldn't really have done it! Ah

swear! Ah was plannin' on double-crossin' Slug anyway! Ah figured you an' Ah could go someplace...quiet...together. You know, just the two of us..." Her voice dropped into a sultry tone as she pressed suggestively against him.

"You expect me to believe that?" Echo snarled, backhanding her and knocking her to the ground. Omega's cheek reddened where Echo's hand had struck, and before she could do more than sit up, he drew back his fist again and clocked her on the chin; she flew backward into the muddy dirt as he brought up another fist. She raised her left arm to ward off another blow, but he grabbed the wrist in an iron grip instead. "Now come on." He began dragging the struggling woman back up the embankment as the aliens watched. He was not gentle.

"Do you intend to kill her?" Eb'vuv asked, calm and cool, completely detached. Echo glanced back over his shoulder as Omega whimpered at his feet.

"...Eventually." He continued dragging her up the steep slope as she fought in vain to get free. "I've got...other things in mind first."

"When you are finished, return here," Eb'vuv said. "We will wait. I believe I have a proposal that will be...mutually beneficial." Echo paused and considered the statement, then nodded without turning.

Suddenly Omega went for her own blaster, but Echo easily kicked it out of her hand. One hand twining in the loose platinum-blonde mane, and viciously yanking her the rest of the way up the bank, Echo proceeded to bind Omega's hands with her own belt and roughly lifted her, laying her across Di-tok's withers, face down. She tried to kick him in the head, and he dodged, then spanked her hard on the buttock with a resounding slap.

"The more you fight, the worse it's gonna be," he growled. "Behave, and I might just take you out fast, instead of prolonging it."

Then he retrieved her fallen blaster, threw it into the saddlebag, mounted, and rode away into the deepening twilight.

* * *

"Well, that worked rather nicely," Omega remarked, from the cover of a depression some hundred yards distant, as Echo freed her hands.

"Yeah, it did," Echo replied. "Are you okay, though? I tried to pull all my blows, and what you showed me about cupping my hand a little when I smacked you on the ass worked great for making noise without hurting you...but I'm afraid that backhand got kinda tricky." He gingerly rubbed a red welt on her right cheekbone with his fingertips, worried that he had caused her an injury. "I think one of us zagged when we shoulda zigged. And it mighta been me."

"Well, it wasn't like we had a lotta time to rehearse! No, I'm fine, Ace; don't worry," she told him. "And the cheek is okay. To be honest, I'd completely forgotten about it until you said something—I can't even feel it, so it's not hurting me. You grabbed my hair just right, too. You got enough of it to pull hard and look really savage, yet still have the force distributed so it didn't hurt." She paused, then added with reluctance, "The, uh...the 'bitch' remark hurt more than any of the manhandling. I'm...not really used to being called that, at least to my face. I mean, I know some people THINK it, but...you know."

Omega busied herself with threading her belt back through the loops in her jeans as she spoke. A concerned Echo glanced at her through the dusk as she fastened the buckle.

"Meg, you know I was only...I mean, it was an act—" a disturbed Echo broke off the statement, spreading his hands in a placating gesture, his brow creasing, and she looked up.

"I know." She looked away again. "I think it was just... hearing it come from your lips that made it sting."

"Aw. If I'd realized it was going to hurt, I'd have..."

"Nah. Don't worry. Gotta toughen up, remember? Besides, it was effective as hell. Maybe even more so, because it DID sting, and I reacted to the fact."

Dismissing the incident, Omega took the blaster that Echo returned and holstered it. Then Echo handed her Ditok's reins.

"Here," he told her. "After we've gone, take Ditok to the road and wait for Fox. He's already in position, waiting. Once we're gone, he plans to block off the road, so the only vehicles on it will be Agency vehicles. That means you don't have to worry about staying out of sight at that point."

"Okay, that's good. Are YOU ready?"

"Yeah. I'm all bugged now, and you've got the monitor equipment in the case, so you'll be informed about the plans."

"Any chance of them finding the bug on you?"

"No." He took her hand in his, pulled aside his shirt collar with his other hand, and ran her index finger lightly along the skin underneath his left collarbone. "Feel that?" With sensitive fingertips, Omega delicately probed the small, invisible lump beneath Echo's skin.

"Ooo, cool. Subcutaneous transponder?"

"Yep. New toy. Organo-tech, so it won't scan. And hyper-dimensional signal, so it's undetectable—unless you already know the right frequency. R&D based it on that stuff you derived for 'em 'bout two-three months ago, when you were goin' stir-crazy after our little crash landing adventure." Echo pulled his blaster. "Almost time for me to get back. You ready?"

"Not...quite yet."

"Why?"

"Echo..." Omega laid her fingers lightly on the hand that held the blaster, "...you'd really shoot me?" A pair of blue eyes intently searched brown ones.

Echo met Omega's gaze wordlessly, and she nodded in understanding as she read his answer in his eyes. She sighed.

"All right, I'm ready. Let's get this over and done with. Just...be careful, Echo..."

Echo raised his blaster.

* * *

In the distance, the hit squad listened as the sounds of a savage attack were punctuated by shrieks, screams, and cries.

"Echo! No! NO!! Please, Echo—don't! STOP!! Aaaahh!" The sounds of a fist striking home again and again resonated in

211

the air. "Ungh! St-stop! Uh!"

"Damn you, you will—"

"Aaaaiii!! No! Echoooo! It hurts, it hurts. AAAAA!! You're hurting me!!"

"Hurts, huh? How 'bout this?!" Another blow.

"AAAIIII!! Echo, no, please! Echo, I'm begging you! Don't! Don't take—AAAA!!"

"You're begging?? Damn, Meg, that's a good one. Mmm. What's wrong, baby? You used to really like this..."

"Echo...oh, no...put the switchblade away, Echo...I'll do anything you want...anything...no... no...NOOOOO!! No! No, not that! AAAA!! My EYE!!"

"Hmm...I wonder if I can cut away the alien parts..."

"Oh, no. Please, Echo, don't do that...DON'T DO THAT! AAHHhggh...oh, dear Maker, it hurts, it hurts..."

"Well, shit. It didn't work. Guess I'll have to try something else..."

"No! NO!! AAAAIIIII—"

The high-pitched scream was abruptly terminated by the ululating sound of a proto-cyclotron blaster discharge on high power. The night became silent.

After a few moments, the crickets began chirping once again.

* * *

About ten minutes later, a grim Echo strode down the river bank and over to Eb'vuv. He pulled a long, platinum-blonde lock of hair, singed and stained with now-dull crimson, partway out of his shirt, then tucked it back in, out of sight.

"All right. What have you got in mind?" Echo asked.

* * *

"Well, Fox is off," Zebra said, as she met Zarnix in front of the door to Lab B.

"To Dallas?"

"And surrounds, yeah. We have until he gets back with Alpha One, presumably in about two days' time, maybe three, to get Mrs. Bryant all done and decanted."

"Have you seen the latest lab reports?"

"No." Zebra exhaled in exhausted annoyance. "What's wrong now? Lemme see."

Zarnix handed over a sheaf of papers on a clipboard—hallmark of active patient records everywhere—and Zebra scanned down through them, then paused, flipped back to the beginning, and began reading in detail. Finally, she looked up at her department supervisor.

"You're kidding," she said, voice flat. "Really?"

"Really," Zarnix said, grinning.

"Come on," Zebra demanded. "Let's go see. I'm not gonna believe anything until the fat lady sings."

"No fat ladies in here," Zarnix said, as they both pushed through the door of Lab B.

* * *

A very much alive and intact Omega watched the lights of the dilapidated burgundy van drive down the dark road from her position hidden in the brush southwest of the highway, knowing the decrepit old vehicle held the one being in the universe she treasured above all others.

Oh, be careful, Ace, she tried to send to him. *Come back to me in one piece, please.*

Once the van was well out of sight, she ducked back into the hollow—where Echo had abused and 'killed' a tree in her stead while Omega sat on a rock and screamed bloody murder, mugged at him for all she was worth, and they both tried to keep from laughing—and led Ditok up onto the road shoulder.

Unstrapping the command center from the horse's rump, she sat it, and herself, on the ground and opened it, activating the surveillance monitor as she waited for Fox. Echo's voice sounded in mid-sentence.

* * *

"...So I help you take out the President, and in return, you get me off-planet?"

"That is the deal, yes. " Eb'vuv's voice.

"Hired gunslinger."

"Something like that. But do not cross me; if you try, rest assured, your...indiscretions... back at the river will be reported to the appropriate authorities in an anonymous tip."

A pause.

"I...see. What exactly is it that you want me to do?" Echo pressed.

"Are you in, or not?" Eb'vuv hedged.

"I'm here, aren't I? You think I want to be planetside once the Agency finds what's left of my... 'partner'?"

* * *

Just then, a certain familiar black 1996 Chevy Corvette pulled up, an armored black hovertruck right behind. Behind that was a black diesel dually pickup truck towing a gooseneck horse trailer.

Omega looked up, and gestured urgently for silence. The drivers of all three vehicles shut off the engines at once, as Fox and a couple of other agents emerged. Omega pointed at the monitor without looking up, and Fox crouched beside her, listening intently.

* * *

"You make an excellent point. Very well," Eb'vuv agreed. *"The President arrives in Dallas during the morning hours, two Earth days from now. Later that same day, his motorcade will take him to the campaign headquarters for a speech to his supporters. Along the way, he will pass near the very same grassy knoll that President Kennedy passed so...terminally... in 1963. We will be waiting."* Eb'vuv's voice was calm and satisfied.

"Well...I see several problems with your plan," Echo volunteered. *"First off, Presidential limos are enclosed now, in bulletproof materials. Partly because of that assassination."*

"That is why we are not using bullets."

"Mmm. Nice piece. What is that, a Mark VII Mosin-Dobrovolsk trans-warp flux rifle? You don't see those on Earth too much."

* * *

Omega and Fox, bent over the monitor, glanced at each other; Fox signaled one of the attending agents, who quickly ran to the armored hovertruck to put out the word.

Meanwhile, the Agency ranch hands from the dually pickup were loading Ditok into the horse trailer. Joe checked in all the saddlebags, then eased one off the big horse and bore it to Omega, since it contained her personal gear; its attached mate contained Echo's. She patted the ground beside herself; Joe laid it there, and she nodded, then shook his hand and smiled. He smiled back and tipped his hat, then headed for the dually, just as the speaker resumed function.

* * *

"You have a good eye for weaponry, Agent Echo." Eb'vuv's voice sounded again from the comm set.

"Let's drop that 'agent' shit, all right?" Echo growled. *"The Division One Agency's been nothing but a pain in the ass to me since I first encountered 'em. If we run into any of 'em on this little gig, I'll be happy to give it a...personal touch."*

"Is there a reason you suspect we might?"

"Yeah—the other problem I mentioned. It's a case of 'been there—done that.' The Division One guys may be a manipulative buncha bastards, but they're not stupid. You've got the U.S. President, Dallas, and the grassy knoll, all together in one package. You can bet we won't get close."

"That is why I am here," a third voice rustled.

"I don't get it," Echo's voice answered. *"No offense to attendant parties, but how the hell is a Botanoid gonna help us assassinate the President?"*

"Tiln is a MUTANT Botanoid, a...shape-changer, ag-er, Echo," Eb'vuv explained, correcting his mode of address in mid-word. *"You might say he IS the grassy knoll. Or will become it."*

* * *

Well, that sure explains a lot, Omega decided. *Like what happened to all the carcasses of the Shrubs, for one thing.* She could practically see Echo's eyebrows climb his forehead,

215

right through the comm link, as he took in that information and its ramifications. The monitor fell silent, and Fox signaled the dually and horse trailer to move out, carrying Ditok back to the Ranch. Then Fox laid a hand on Omega's shoulder where she knelt, pointing to the command center case. He himself grabbed the saddlebag with Alpha One's gear.

"Omega, bring it into the warp seat in the back. I've got your bag. We need to get to Dallas."

She nodded, and carefully maneuvered the large, awkward case through the door of the Corvette and into the warp seat, then climbed in beside it, continuing to listen to the still-silent speaker. Fox got into the front passenger seat, and Tare drove.

"Hi, Tare. How ya doin'?" Omega asked.

"Fine, Omega. How was the vacation?" Tare grinned.

"Great. All—what?—forty-eight hours of it. Thanks for bringin' the 'Vette down, too. Where's Yankee?"

"In Dallas already, waiting for us, along with a couple-three or four other Alpha Line teams, and some other Agency peeps for backup."

"Y'all get the Dallas Office involved?"

"I contacted them at soon as I got the word, Omega," Fox informed her.

"Good. Then let's get there in a hurry. We got a gang ridin' into town."

* * *

As they headed northeast in the 'Vette, Fox twisted in the passenger seat to look back and survey his Alpha Line assistant chief.

"Omega?"

"Yeah, Boss?" She looked up from the command center.

"Echo gave me a heads-up about your condition earlier, shortly after he caught back up to you. He told me about your rattlesnake bite."

"Oh, that. Yeah."

"Was it actually a Mojave green, as he said?"

"What's a Mojave green?" Tare asked.

"Oh, it's a particularly nasty type of rattlesnake," Omega explained, pulling out the rattle to hand to Fox. The Director looked it over with a discerning gaze, then held it out for Tare to glance at as he drove, before returning it to Omega. Omega took the thing and dropped it back into her shirt pocket. "*Crotalus scutulatus*, if memory serves. Most rattlers have venom that's only hemotoxic, see—that means it breaks down tissue, kills red blood cells, and prevents blood from clotting right. I guess it's intended to start kind of 'pre-digesting' the snake's meal or something. Anyway, it tends to result in internal hemorrhage; if it gets into the body systems good, the person bitten can die from shock as his circulatory system tries to crash."

"It can also result in loss of limb, even if the victim survives," Fox pointed out, gazing pointedly at Omega's leg; he had already spotted the tear in her jeans, and Echo had informed him earlier which thigh had received the bite, so he had no doubt the reason for the large tear.

"Yeah, it can," Omega agreed. "Mojave greens are a little different kinda rattler, though, Tare; their venom is also neurotoxic, meaning it damages or even kills nerve tissue. The danger with a neurotoxin is asphyxiation and the like, when the nervous system fails. Or in the case of a Mojave green, it can be both—when, say, the cardiovascular system collapses to the point where the nerve-impaired respiration can't provide enough oxygen to the brain or heart, and stuff like that."

"And you took a bite from one 'a those?!" Tare exclaimed, watching her in the rear-view mirror.

"Um, yeah," Omega said, pulling open the torn jeans leg to expose the wound on her thigh. The twin puncture marks were still visible, red dots of coagulated blood surrounded by residual bruising that had already diminished significantly from the time Echo had first seen it.

"Omega, do you need medical treatment?" Fox asked, concerned.

"Nah, not really, not now."

"No offense, Omega, but WHY are you still ALIVE?!" an

appalled—and not a little flabbergasted—Tare wanted to know. Omega drew a deep breath and let it out in a slow, pained sigh.

"Because of Slug," Omega noted, seeming incredibly tired all at once. "It's not the first time I've survived a snake bite. Nor even the second. That's the second Mojave green bite, though. Those are awful rough to get through, and this one was no exception. I spent the first half of the day barfing my guts out, and the second just trying not to tumble out of the saddle...and feeling like my whole body was gonna fall apart at the seams, the whole time, not to mention wishing my damn leg really WOULD fall off, 'cause it woulda felt better. But it's like I told Echo—apparently Slug didn't want anything taking me out by accident before my programming triggered."

"Damn the gastropoid," Fox snarled, the curse heartfelt, as Tare looked horrified. "But I AM glad you are still with us, tekhter. I gather your body knows how to counter the venom on its own, then?"

"Apparently so," Omega concluded. "It's not a pleasant process, by any stretch of the imagination, but it seems to be fairly efficient. Echo had me down a whole canteen of water before we set back out after the perps, and that helped flush the worst of it out, what was left, anyhow. I'm gonna need a nice big meal pretty soon, though, to help offset the process."

"Right," Fox said. "Tare, let's hit the first fast-food drive-thru we come across. A bag of burgers with all the trimmings should provide enough calories and nutrients for her."

"Yeah, that oughta work," Omega agreed.

"Damn," Tare barely breathed. "She really ISN'T human."

Fox shot him a sharp glance, having just caught the remark, then he threw a quick look at Omega. If she heard, she gave no sign. But Fox was almost as aware as Echo of how acute her hearing was, and he suspected she had indeed heard. When she tugged the gap in her torn jeans closed, covering the wound and hiding the exposed skin, then averting her face, his suspicions were confirmed.

Oh, meyn tekhter, he thought, saddened. *My poor girl.*

He glared at Tare, pondering repercussions, for the next ten miles of road.

* * *

"Listen close to the monitor, y'all," Omega told Tare and Yankee, as they bent over the monitoring equipment in the hotel suite near the Dallas-Fort Worth airport. "If anything happens to my partner and our department chief because you missed something, I'll take it outta y'all's hide."

All three agents grinned, but the blue eyes of Alpha Line's assistant chief were grim, and the Alpha Seven team sobered rapidly. A brisk Omega turned to Fox.

"Were you able to find everything I asked for, Fox? Or do I need to hit up a local drugstore?"

"Yes, Omega, I arranged to get all of it, no problem. It's waiting for you in the master suite bathroom."

"Good. Thanks, Fox. I appreciate it."

"Are you sure you really want to do that?"

"I'm sure. Oh—Alpha Two?"

"Romeo and India are on their way here now. They've been setting up the situation with the Secret Service."

"Great." Omega sighed. "Everything's in shape. In that case, I'm for a long-overdue hot shower. I hope I was bearable for you two, cooped up with me in the 'Vette. But I sure feel sorry for Echo..."

* * *

Echo, meanwhile, also having arrived in Dallas, was gradually getting to know the hit squad, learning personalities, hidden foibles, weaknesses and strengths, as they set up in an abandoned warehouse within a few miles of the old school book depository. He had put all thought of his mother into the box in his mind, closing and locking it, and now he focused exclusively on the task at hand—one mistake, with this group, meant sure, swift, and certain death. *And probably damn painful, into the bargain,* he added to himself.

"So there's—what?—ten of us, to get this job done?" Echo asked the second Glu'g'ik, whose name was Lu'vin'du'v.

"Yes," Lu'vin'du'v said quietly, volunteering no more.

"I've gotta admit," Echo said, shaking his head, "I don't get it. What are a couple of Glu'gu'ik doing involved in this? I thought Va'du'sha'ā and Earth were on pretty good terms, all things considered."

Lu'vin'du'v glanced around, then moved closer.

"You Terrans located a certain Glu'gu'ik device almost an Earth year ago, and confiscated it," he told Echo. "Something the Imperialists wanted in order to bring back the monarchy of Va'du'sha'ā. We...are from a political faction demanding... retribution. And Eb'vuv...well, let us just say he...leads us all."

Mm-hmm. Just what Meg and I thought, Echo realized. "You sound a little...unsure," he murmured then.

"Oh—no!" Lu'vin'du'v responded hastily, glancing around again. "I would follow Eb'vuv anywhere."

Interesting choice of wording. Hmm... Echo pressed further. "He's the head of this outfit. So I guess that makes you second in command."

"Well...yes, I suppose so," Lu'vin'du'v said, seeming hesitant. "Yes, of course."

Hope you're getting all this, Meg. "Well, then. I'll make sure I report in to you, too, before I off the Prez." Echo nodded at the diffident Glu'g'ik, and moved on.

"Hi, guys," Echo greeted the three short, stocky, dark gray Zargothians—looking like nothing so much as squat Frankenstein's monsters, sans sutures—as he wandered by.

"Hiya, Echo," Zzt responded in a friendly fashion, with the typical rasping Zargothian voice. "You get set up here yet? Caught some sleep?"

"Not really. Since I'm kind of an add-on to the team, I don't have a place to bunk. Meh." Echo shrugged. "I'll figure it out."

Zzs sidled up to Echo at that remark. The alien female was, like most Zargothians, relatively short, being a scant five feet, and rather dumpy and thick; Zargoth was a hyper-Earth, and the inhabitants tended to be heavy and muscular and, relative to humans, extremely powerful. Their typical build, Echo sometimes thought, would have been useful to a stevedore from a century past. Any one of them could easily have lifted all 180 pounds of Echo's tall, muscular frame over his—or her—head, without batting an eye.

More, the women were not much different in build than the men, save for the particular physical characteristics of their respective sexes—their women did nurse their young, so were possessed of breasts, though rather more than the normal human pair. But the means of sexual intercourse was quite different: it was the female whose genitalia entered the male's body, to fetch the gamete, rather than receiving or ejaculating it. To say that Zargothians and humans—or most humanoids—were not sexually compatible was putting it mildly; there were really only one or two possible combinations in which it could work, and the humanoid never survived the experience.

Consequently, Zzs's next words were reason for alarm bells to sound in Echo's head.

"I'll share," she murmured, close to his shoulder. "I like Agents—official or not." Zzt and Zzu sat up abruptly, scowling, and Echo went on high alert, thinking fast.

"I'm used to roughing it." The brown eyes grew hard, and Echo gave them a grim smile. "'Preciate it, but it's an offer you might not make if you'd seen what I left behind, back outside Junction."

"That little thing you had? I could've broken her in half with two of my fingers."

You could try, I suppose, Echo thought with a hidden smile. "I'm sure you're...twice the woman Meg...was..." *You'd make at least two of her,* he thought, "—but I'm sure you'll understand when I say that I'm not inclined to...replace her, at the moment."

"I don't do 'no', Echo."

"You will this time." Echo turned on his heel and walked away from the frowning female and the glaring males.

* * *

Tare and Yankee looked at each other in the corner of the hotel room, as Fox unobtrusively listened across the room.

"Uh-oh. That's bad," Tare remarked. "Real bad."

"Yeah," Yankee agreed. "Should we tell Omega, or wait and see what happens?"

"After that look she gave us, about making sure nothing happened to him? I'm not sittin' on this."

* * *

Kelto the Delzantian was happily engaged in tinkering with his gadgets when Echo sauntered up.

"Hey, Kelto, how's it goin'?" *Stereotypical Delzantian electronics nerd,* Echo thought, watching him work. *They're the electrical engineers of the galaxy, and brilliant at it, but damn. If it wasn't for the green skin, he'd fit right into a certain comic strip, all the way down to the eyeglasses. 'Cept I guess those are magnifiers for the detailed work.*

"Pretty well," Kelto said brusquely, without looking up. "Getting ready to calibrate the trans-warp flux rifles." He gestured to the four weapons at the end of the table.

"One o' those mine, I hope?" Echo asked.

"Nah. You're anti-security. Birdy's our sharpshooter—"

"Eagle-eyes, huh?" Echo interjected with a grin.

"...And the snores are the other guns."

"'Snores'?"

"Yeah, you know, the Zargothians. Zzt, Zzs, and Zzu. The snores."

Echo nodded with another grin.

"I like it. What's your job?"

"Equipment. Only."

"You goin' on the actual junket?"

"Yeah, just in case we have a malfunction. I'd rather stay here. But at least I'll be in the back of things."

"You don't like firefights?"

"I don't like people." He glared at Echo, in a pointed fashion.

Echo took the hint.

* * *

Birdy saw Echo coming, and quickly turned, heading up the piping to a perch in the rafters of the empty warehouse.

Echo looked up at the purple Aves, who gazed back down at him with hostile black eyes.

Echo just shrugged and wandered on, murmuring under his breath for Omega's benefit, "The Aves is a potential problem..."

* * *

"Hey, Tiln," Echo addressed the Botanoid, who looked like nothing so much as a giant, animated chia pet—though the Agent had noticed the alien was distinctly withdrawn, unsurprising after the incident with the Shrubs. "Where's the other human? I thought I'd like to chat with a fellow Terran—no offense."

"Robert is merely the driver. He will be back when we need him. He knows nothing of our plans; you would be wise not to befriend him. As did the human we took into our plans in 1963, he will not live beyond our need for him."

A chill went through Echo.

"A UFOnut, then, I presume. Scapegoat?"

"Yes."

"Right. Changing the subject...what does 'Tiln' mean, anyway, if you don't mind my asking? Just wondering. I got a thing for languages."

The Botanoid let out a longsuffering sigh before answering.

"In your tongue, it would translate as...'Sod'."

Echo absorbed that—as well as all the potential puns associated with it—while somehow managing to maintain a straight face, all the time completely convinced he could hear Omega's melodic laughter in his head.

"So...you're our camouflage, huh?"

"Yes."

"How does that work, exactly?" Echo asked, curious.

"I will...merge...with the indigenous plant material, shaping it...and myself...to our needs." He shrugged. "It is...difficult to explain. You will see when the time comes."

* * *

Omega emerged from the bedroom of the hotel suite the Division One Agents were using as a command post, and the gathered Alpha teams gasped.

"Meg—what have you DONE??" India exclaimed, shocked.

"What I had to do, India," the close-cropped, brown-eyed brunette in the black Suit replied. "The hit squad has seen me as a long-haired blonde. If I need to get close, I've gotta look like someone else entirely."

"Echo's gonna hate it," Romeo remarked.

"Oh, I doubt he'll even notice," Omega began with a rueful grin, then paused, suddenly recalling her partner expending some effort to track down a hat for her at the Ranch, upon the threat of a pair of scissors taken to her platinum locks. "Anyway, it doesn't much matter whether he likes it or not. I've got a job to do, and this is what it takes to do it. Let me assure you, he'd be the first to tell you that."

"So you're ready to become a Secret Service agent?" Fox asked, raising an eyebrow.

"Just point me at the Commander in Chief," Omega said with a grin.

* * *

Tare motioned her over to the monitor table just then, and Omega headed over immediately.

"What's up?" she asked.

"Echo's got a situation," Yankee said quietly. Omega stiffened.

"Tell me." It was a command.

"Two separate scenarios. The Aves evidently doesn't trust him. And that's the marksman."

"That's bad. Aves are low-level telepaths. I really wish Echo would've let me go in, but after the rattler bite, he was worried I wasn't strong enough yet."

Alpha Seven exchanged glances. Yankee raised a shocked eyebrow: *Rattler bite?! And she's walking around??* Tare nodded confirmation, having observed Fox's concerned queries in the Corvette on the way in to Dallas.

"What's the other sitch?" Omega asked, noting the silent exchange, but choosing not to remark on it.

"One of the Zargothians is coming on to him."

"Is that all?" Omega responded, rolling her eyes. "Echo's a big boy. He can handle an aggressive woman. Or is it one of the males...?"

"The female." Tare nodded.

"Omega," Fox's voice sounded quietly just behind her as he walked up, "I know you haven't encountered them before, but Zargothians are several times stronger than humans. If you think about their build for a minute, you'll realize they come from a planet much larger than Earth, with stronger gravity. And they're not...designed...like humans, anatomically-speaking. So...if this woman decides to put a serious move on your partner, and she catches him off-guard, not even Echo may prove able to stop her."

Omega simply stared in disbelief at the three men.

"This is a joke, right?" she finally said. The others shook their heads. "You're seriously talking about...rape?! Echo?!"

"For starters," Fox said, grim. There was a silence as she absorbed the information.

"Shit. I guess I better download the file on Zargoth, like yesterday or something. What's happening now?" Omega demanded.

"Nothing, at the moment," Yankee said, after listening carefully to the headset. "Echo's been getting acquainted with the members of the hit squad. He seems to understand the danger, and he's keeping his distance. But he doesn't dare let his guard down."

"Aw, damn. I don't guess Echo's gonna be getting any sleep, poor Ace, until this whole mess is over," Omega murmured to herself. "All right, y'all, here are your instructions.

You will monitor Echo continually until we extract him. Set up shifts if you need to, but I want him monitored around the clock. That is now your primary—your only—task, until further notice. Understood?" Alpha Seven nodded. "Good. Now, listen up, guys, 'cause this is important: Echo and I set up a code word before he went in, in case he needed backup fast. That code word is 'pilgrim.' If at ANY TIME you hear Echo use that word, determine his exact coordinates, and immediately relay them to me, and to Fox. Preferably simultaneously, if possible. Fox and I will then pull our extraction plans from our respective and metaphorical hip pockets and get Echo out, as near to immediately as practical. Possibly with Alpha Seven's help. Got it?"

"Got it," Tare and Yankee told her, as Fox nodded his approval.

"I already have a dozen different extraction plans, Omega," Fox told her, "designed to fit as many different scenarios. All you have to do is give the word."

"All right, Fox. That's great, and a big relief, 'cause you're more experienced at that than I am, quite yet. I got some ideas, though, and I'll pass 'em on to you to evaluate."

"You do that, tekhter. I'll be happy to see what you've come up with, and give you my opinions on their veracity; it's a good teaching opportunity, into the bargain. I figure it's about time I paid you back in kind for your fascinating astronomy course! Now, go take care of the President."

"Right. Romeo, India," Omega called across the room, "fill me in, y'all. We need to get moving."

* * *

"Meg, you've got a nasty black eye developing there, girlfriend," India remarked as she and Romeo finished briefing Omega on Presidential security around the table in the Agents' suite. Across the room, Tare, Yankee, and Fox huddled over the monitoring equipment.

"Oh, thanks for reminding me, India. Is there anything you can do with it? It's a little more than makeup will hide, and it'll probably look better if I'm not too banged up when I go in to meet the Service," Omega responded, as India gently grasped Omega's chin—which was now healed after the horseback-riding fall, thanks to swabbing with Rejuvic after she got to her room in the guest house—and began examining the bruise. "Be patient, Romeo. We'll head out in a minute, I swear."

"I'm wit' it, pretty lady," Romeo said as India pulled out her personal medikit and began treating Omega's bruised cheek. "I'm jus' worried 'bout Echo, 'at's all."

"Me, too, Romeo, me too. Think you can do something about this, India?"

"Yes, I believe I can take care of it," India replied, swabbing the cheekbone with a certain familiar lavender solution. "How did it happen?"

"Oh, that's where Echo hit me."

Alpha Two, Alpha Seven, and the Director of Division One all stopped what they were doing to gape at Omega.

"Omega—it was an accident...?" Fox said, awaiting confirmation.

"No. He hit me right where he intended to. At least he didn't shoot me." Omega suddenly noticed her colleagues' expressions. "Oh. OH! No, no, no, y'all. Echo would never do that! This happened when we were getting Echo into the hit squad. They had to think Echo killed me, that he's a renegade Agent, see; otherwise they'd never trust him to get within rock-chunkin' distance of 'em. So we made it look as real as possible. Only thing is, it wasn't like we had much of a chance to rehearse, so when he 'backhanded' me," she quirked her fingers around the word, "one of us zigged when we shoulda zagged, and he didn't pull it quite fast enough. He says it was him that goofed, but I think it was my fault. Maybe it was both of us, and we just crossed wires; I dunno. Anyway, his knuckle caught me right there. It looked great, and it didn't hurt, but it did bruise a bit. I kinda figure it was the aftermath of the hemotoxic snake venom, maybe—I remember bruising easier for a couple days, the last time that happened. Don't tell Echo it bruised, though; none of y'all will be able to see it, but he'll get upset and self-flagellate for a week if he thinks he hurt me bad enough to leave a mark."

"But...shooting you?" Fox wondered.

"Oh, that. No, his original idea was that one of us should shoot the other one with one of our blasters, just a slight graze, you know, to create a mild wound as proof that we'd been fighting. Only I wasn't willing to shoot HIM, and I guess he figured the snake bite was enough for me, already. After all, 'mild' is relative, when it comes to blaster injuries—there's nasty, and there's worse nasty, and then there's dead. Nah. It was only a brainstorming thing, and we came up with a much better idea, in the end, and ran with it—pretty much literally."

The others nodded, satisfied, and resumed activities.

"So how IS that snakebite, Meg?" India wondered, as she continued to work. "Is there anything else I need to treat? Like that? I heard you took a header off the horse, too, at one point, at least according to Echo."

"Not now, no," Omega said, holding her head very still to allow India to complete treatment of the facial bruising. "Even the residual bruising on the snakebite is almost all gone; Echo told me he hit it with some Rejuvic after he dosed me with pain meds and I went to sleep. And that's on top of my normal fast healing, and Fox saw to it I had plenty of fuel for the healing, on our way here—I stuffed down, like, three double cheeseburgers with the works, plus two bottles of orange juice! I was starved. An' yeah, I came off the horse, my first day at the Ranch, 'cause she stopped at speed an' I was rusty; but other than a little leftover stiffness, that's all gone by now. And I already popped a dolocet for that. So...no, I'm good."

"All right, Meg," India told Omega, as she spread a thin film of ointment over the wounded cheek, "that combo should take care of it in a few minutes."

"Thanks, India. Are we ready to go, then?"

"Yes," Fox told them. "Alpha Line Agents should blend in

pretty well, considering. The lot of you are government agents, after all—just from different governments. Be careful, though."

"You know it, Fox," Romeo answered. "Meg, you on things with Echo?"

Omega put on a small wireless headset, tapped the tiny microphone, and looked at Tare and Yankee. They nodded. She removed the headset, folded it up, and pocketed it.

"Yep. Round 'em up, and let's move 'em out."

* * *

Echo volunteered to stand guard that night; it kept him well away from the 'snores,' in more ways than one. Kelto was assigned to help him, but the short green creature did little more than tinker with the equipment. After a while, Kelto wandered back inside to his worktable on the pretext of getting another tool, and simply never came back.

Huh, Echo thought, not sure whether to be annoyed or not. *Eb'vuv's orders or no, he's gonna do whatever he damn well pleases, I guess. Oh well. It only makes things easier for me. No façade to keep up.*

A cautious Echo patrolled the warehouse, keeping a wary eye out for police and stray people; it wouldn't do to have innocent civilians wandering into the middle of this. *At least I've got a brain bleacher tucked away inside my shirt,* he thought. He reached into his shirt to check on the device, and found the bloodstained strands of Omega's hair tucked away. He removed the pale lock, nearly white in the moonlight, and stared at it, fingering it with unconscious affection.

Good idea Meg had, providing 'evidence' of her murder, he decided. *Even sliced open her finger with my knife to get it bloody, cool as the proverbial cucumber...then hit her finger with some Rejuvic. And it completely convinced 'em. Except maybe the Aves...but he isn't certain. Wow, the hair from the nape of her neck is so soft.*

Damn, I thought I'd laugh my head off while we were 'killing' that tree. Who'd have thought Meg could come up with such a sick torture scenario...and then make jokes about it??

229

Every other scream, I think, she muttered a one-liner at me. And the faces she made!

But I guess it kept her from getting too intense over it, though. I wonder if...maybe it hit a little too close to home. Maybe that's WHY she had to joke about it. He shook his head. *I never have gotten her to tell me very much about exactly what happened when Slug kidnapped her and enhanced her as a kid. Even if she and I ever become an item, I bet she still won't tell me. I think she's actually trying to protect me...which probably means it was really, really...bad.*

I just wish I knew how to get it across to her that I'm serious, and that I don't care about all of that. She's special, and I want her to know it, dammit.

Echo started to toss the strands of spun platinum aside, then hesitated, finding himself unable to throw the lock away— it was, after all, effectively a piece of the woman he loved. Instead, he got out his ID holder, took the pale platinum curl and twisted it down into a tight coil, knotted the strands about themselves, then secreted the coil carefully behind his *carte noir*, thinking, *Who knows? It might...come in handy later,* as he replaced the wallet.

Then he pulled the brain bleacher out just far enough to check its condition, and quickly returned it to its hiding place.

Good, he considered. *It's just as well Kelto wandered off, I guess. If anything does come up, I can probably handle it with no casualties. Maybe Meg was right: This is much easier if I'm in one piece. Especially with the Zargothians around. It's all turning out to be way more complex than I'd have expected— there's a lot of different personalities involved. They've got carefully specialized team members for every task in the job.*

I dunno if this is as well-organized as the original JFK assassination or not. Might be even better. Of course, the original JFK thing was way before my time, let alone the official Agency.

There's schisms there, though, if I can just figure out how to make use of 'em. Neither Zzs nor Tiln are especially fond of the lead Glu'g'ik, this Eb'vuv dude, though I think the original assassin team is loyal to each other...except there's something going on where Zzs is concerned, maybe, like they're tired of whatever proclivities she has, or something. Damn. I wonder if I've got TIME to scope all this out, let alone make use of it.

His train of thought was derailed as a harsh feminine voice sounded behind him.

"Hello, Division One man."

"Hello, Zzs," Echo said without turning, all the while thinking, *Speak of the devil.* "What brings you outside the warehouse at this time of night?"

"You do." The alien woman moved to his side.

"I'm doing just fine. Everything's quiet."

"Then let me liven it up for you." Zzs laid a taloned, ham-like hand on Echo's arm in a caricature of seduction. It rested heavily. Echo was powerfully reminded of a similar gesture on Omega's part earlier, during her 'capture'—her touch had been light and gentle, almost a caress, and it had taken a great deal of effort on Echo's part to avoid responding to it. There was no doubt in Echo's mind which of the two was more...effective.

"Somehow I don't think Zzt or Zzu would like that." Echo stood his ground.

"Perhaps not. But I would."

"I'm flattered." Echo's voice was flat, expressionless.

"But not interested."

"No."

"I told you, Echo—I don't do 'no'." Zzs's tone had grown angry and more than a little belligerent. The hand on Echo's arm tightened its grip until his fingers started to go numb. The implied threat was blatant and anything but subtle...like every-thing else about this female.

"Look, Zzs, it's...like this," Echo turned to her, acting his role to the hilt. "Maybe you and I could've...had something, if things had been...different." *Maybe if I'd been blind, deaf, and generally insensate.* "But we've got a job to do, one that's bigger than both of us." *What movie did that line come from...?*

Something like that, anyway. Oh, yeah. Sorry, Bogie. "And you wouldn't want to be the cause of a fight breaking out on the team, would you? We've all got to work together for this mission to succeed."

"No, that's true..." The Zargothian woman paused, thoughtful, evidently considering Echo's point of view.

"Besides...I know a noble lady like you can't have experienced this, Zzs, but..." Echo laid the pathos on with a putty knife, trying not to gag, "if you'd ever had someone you...cared about, someone you trusted, betray you...the way Meg betrayed me, dammit...I thought we were...I mean, I thought we had something, Meg and me...and then it turned out...oh, hell..."

A memory of Omega's response to a similar, but real-life situation—her reaction to the memory of her programming trying to kill him—floated to mind, and he did his best to recreate it. Echo twisted his face and he turned away, running what would look like a distracted hand over his jaw, into his hair. Then he added a paraphrase of what Omega had told him.

"I keep...seeing her face in the sights of my gun, just before I...oh, dear God..."

There was a pause, as Zzs watched Echo's back; he let his shoulders slump, and bowed his head, as if in pain.

"...I just...need some time, Zzs." He kept his voice low, slightly rough.

The hand still resting on his arm vanished, as Zzs responded, as gently as she could with her grating voice.

"I understand, Echo. I'll be waiting...when you're ready."

* * *

At the command center in the hotel, Tare and Yankee breathed sighs of relief.

"Smooth job, boss-man," Tare told the monitor equipment.

"Whoa. I didn't know Echo had it in him," Yankee grinned. "He played her like the proverbial violin."

"Give the man some credit," Tare said, returning the grin.

"There's a reason why he's the department chief. Let alone the youngest of the Originals."

"Yeah, but I bet having Omega as his partner probably helped on this sitch."

"What, you figure he polished his technique on Omega?"

"Well, I'd think he'd need to know how to convince a hard-headed woman to do things his way from time to time."

Fox, across the room working on his tablet, was paying attention to the conversation without appearing to do so, and now he prepared to interject. Tare, however, spoke up first.

"Aw, c'mon, Yank, man. Ditch the chip on your shoulder, where she's concerned! I think you're just biased because Omega turned down the pass you made at her during her Christmas party last year. You're damn lucky she understood. That taught you to go mixing flu medicine with champagne!" Tare chuckled, and his partner grinned, rueful.

"Yeah," Yankee said quietly, "that was before I knew she was a—"

"Uh-huh," Tare interrupted in a low voice, throwing a surreptitious glance Fox's way. "Before most of the regular field agents knew that much. I mean, we all knew about Slug's programming, we just didn't know about...the rest of it. Kind of a pity, really. Romeo calls her 'pretty lady,' and she is. Kinda makes her...exotic, you know? But I can't imagine any man who knew about it actually going there...not for a long-term thing..."

Fox frowned.

"Yeah. Especially when she's so hard-headed on top of being inhuman."

Fox scowled, but said nothing—for the moment. But he filed the exchange away in memory; one more black mark against the Alpha Seven team.

"Oh, open your eyes, Yankee. She's not hard-headed. Just because Omega's a strong woman doesn't make her partnership with Echo so different from any of the rest of the teams. In fact, it looks to me like they're at least as good buddies as any of the same-gender teams. Echo's as close to Omega as he was to X-ray, I think; maybe more. There's no manipulation on the Alpha One team that I can see. But there IS respect and trust. Just stop and think about that whole Cortian mess—what she did to save him, and what he turned around and did for her. That wasn't hard-headedness, that was caring and trust...on BOTH sides. Never mind the Cortians stranding them on the protoplanet, either. The condition they were in after the crash? That took working together, in concert, to survive! No, man. If they disagree, they say so, they figure it out. Neither one of 'em would put up with that kinda bullshit anyway."

Fox raised a thoughtful eyebrow.

* * *

Bullshit was exactly what Omega was encountering as she attempted to integrate herself into the Secret Service detail preparing for the President's arrival, around a conference table elsewhere in the hotel.

"I'm sorry, it's just not protocol," the head of the detail, an agent named Murphy, told her. "We can't change the route now. It's far too late in the game. Besides, the JFK analogy is essential to the President's campaign, and security is already set up. There's no way anyone can get to the President, so there's no call to change anything."

"And I'm telling you, you're wrong."

"I don't know what Secret Service office you're from, but you report to me now, and I'll determine who's right and who's wrong around here," the chief huffed.

"Not any more." Omega glanced at Romeo and India. "Romeo, get Fox on the horn. Tell him we're gonna need a team over here with a new sequence of events when this is all over. We don't have time for this."

"All over it," Romeo said, pulling out his cell phone.

"Okay, Murphy," Omega told the detail head, "you and your boys and girls sit down and listen up." Jack Murphy and the other six Secret Service agents folded their arms tolerantly, and smiled maddeningly in a deprecating way, but did not sit down. Omega pulled her blaster; their eyes widened for a moment, then their smiles widened.

"Nice toy," Murphy condescended.

"Yeah, it is. I like this gun; it's a bit of a trophy. I won it from a perp on my first full-up mission, and it's been to hell and back with me, a couple times." Omega choked the beam focus down to a narrow column, replaced the weapon in its shoulder holster, then gestured to Murphy. "Toss those aviators about four feet straight up."

With a grin at the others, Murphy removed his sunglasses and complied.

In one smooth motion, Omega drew her blaster, fired off two shots, and holstered it, all while the sunglasses were still airborne. The Secret Service agents jumped, startled at the weapon's discharge: They had thought it really was a toy.

As Murphy caught the glasses, Omega said, "Hold them up for everyone to see."

Murphy's eyes almost popped out of his head as he held up his sunglasses: There was a neat, smooth, pencil-size hole in the center of each lens. All seven Secret Service agents sat down abruptly.

"Now that I have your attention, gentlemen and ladies, let me introduce myself and my colleagues. I am Agent Omega, and I'll be heading up this little operation beginning now. These are my friends, Agents Romeo and India. We're part of something called the Pan-Galactic Law Enforcement and Immigration Administration, Division One, Alpha Line department..."

* * *

Fox was on his personal ciphered comm headset, conducting a conversation with a colleague on Va'du'sha'ā, while Tare took his turn at the communications control.

"Mm-hm. Yes, that's right. No, he doesn't. No, we've had no reason to do so. Oh, REALLY? That's interesting, and not in the good way. You do? Excellent. I think we can oblige, then. Yes, I will. Yes, thank you. Fox out."

235

He cut the connection, then removed the headset, drawing a finger across his throat to indicate to Tare to cut the comm link.

"Good stuff, sir?" Tare wondered.

"Indeed," Fox replied absently, as he turned and headed for the bedroom. "I'm going to have to mull this one over..."

* * *

Echo was coming around the side of the warehouse when the squad car pulled up. *Oh, shit,* he thought. *Exactly what I was hoping to avoid. And I don't have time to program an appropriate memory into my brain bleacher. Dammit, I shoulda done that already, but no, I let myself get diverted by Zzs. I'm gonna have to wing it.*

Quickly he detached his holster, leaving it by the side of the building but around the corner and out of sight, and slipped his hand inside his shirt, removing his brain bleacher and goggle-glasses. He slipped on the goggle-glasses and held the brain bleacher low, down by his thigh, as he stepped around the corner. With a familiarity borne of long years of practice, Echo set the brain bleacher with one hand as he nonchalantly walked toward the police.

"Hello, officers," Echo said. "What can I do for you?"

"Who the hell are you?" one of them asked, blunt, eyeing the by-now slightly scruffy-looking man in dirty black denim, cowboy hat and sunglasses, with several days' growth of beard, who nevertheless still exuded an air of power. "What are you doing here? And why the hell are you wearing sunglasses at two in the morning?"

"It's all perfectly simple, officers," Echo said, straightforward. "I'm with a group of alien assassins out to kill the President tomorrow afternoon. Now look right here," and before they could even react with horror, a multicolored, holographic flash lit up the parking lot. "You encountered the caretaker, everything checks out fine, continue your patrol." Echo removed the goggle-glasses and tucked them, with the brain bleacher, back inside his shirt. The patrolmen blinked, as Echo continued, "...an' I just got done checkin' in the back, fellas. Everything's okay."

"All right. That checks out fine. Thanks there, buddy," the driver of the squad car said, as they got back in and started the ignition. "We'll continue our patrol, then. See you around."

"Not if I can help it..." Echo said under his breath, waving at the departing police.

* * *

As Echo watched the police car drive away, he stiffened with the sense of being watched himself.

"So. The heartless renegade who murdered his partner in cold blood chooses only to brain-bleach the local police," a soft voice said. "You don't even have your blaster on you."

Echo spun, to see Lu'vin'du'v standing at the edge of the weed-dotted asphalt, watching him.

"I figured a strategic brain-bleach was a helluva lot easier than trying to hide the bodies inside a city." Echo shrugged. "Out in the country in the middle of nowhere is one thing. Inside Dallas? Well, that gets difficult, even for me."

"Uh-huh," Lu'vin'du'v replied, unconvinced. "Considering that Birdy still doesn't trust you, I think I'm safe in taking a chance..."

"What chance?"

The Glu'g'ik in human form held out his hand.

"Agent Bi'hts'e Dh'u, Division One Ar'dug undercover operations, assigned to the Va'du'sha'ā High Council."

Echo studied the alien carefully, remembering their earlier conversation.

"Let me see you," he demanded.

Without hesitation or requesting clarification, Lu'vin'du'v's features blurred, as he used the Glu'gu'ik innate quantum foam manipulation on his own body. Moments later, a Zeta Reticulan Gray alien stood there, large black eyes solemnly gazing at him. He held out his identification badge; Echo scanned it briefly and nodded approval.

"Agent Echo, I should tell you that, per my pre-mission

briefing, the senior member of the Division's Alpha One team is known to me, by reputation at least. I should find it an honor to work with you. And your partner, about whom I know less, but what I do know is good. I assume she is still well, despite... appearances." The other male held out his hand again. Echo reached out and took his hand, shaking.

"Likewise. And yes."

"Do you have a plan?" Lu'vin'du'v asked as he morphed back into his human disguise.

"Let's go for a walk..."

* * *

"...So you've spent the time getting in good with the team?" Echo wondered.

"Indeed I have. Especially Birdy, as Eb'vuv plans to put me with him, to assist and as backup."

"And he trusts you?"

"Yes, he does. He is probably closer to me than anyone else on the team. I even know all about his family."

Echo raised an eyebrow.

"So the two of you are good buddies now."

"He thinks so, at any rate." Lu'vin'du'v all but smirked.

"How do you manage that?"

"What do you mean?" Lu'vin'du'v wondered, confused.

"He's an Aves. Aves are low-level telepaths. How can you fool him that completely?"

"Oh. Well, it is a function of my quantum manipulation ability, you see," Lu'vin'du'v explained. "I tell him a version of the truth, and manipulate both my and his brains, such that he thinks he is reading unvarnished truth."

"That...sounds complicated," Echo said, amazed despite himself.

"It is not simple," Lu'vin'du'v admitted. "It takes a great deal of concentration. How much experience do you have with Glu'gu'ik, Echo?"

"A fair amount," Echo decided. "I've caught several regular perps, plus that imperialist agent that was sent here last fall—well, Meg and I did that together. I'm not completely sure I could have handled her entirely on my own, to be honest—at least, not as easy as Meg and I handled her together. She was a hellcat."

"Hellcat I give you," Lu'vin'du'v said with a wry grin. "Exceptionally talented at quantum manipulation she was not, however. In fact, she washed out of our program."

"WHAT?! But...then you...?"

"Graduated at the top of the class," Lu'vin'du'v murmured. "Tied with another. That other is now dead in the line of duty, however, so that should tell you that it is by no means foolproof. But the Division One Office on Va'du'sha'ā only allows the most skillful at quantum manipulation to enter that program, to begin with."

"Shit," Echo said blankly. "I think maybe me an' Meg need to have some of y'all come here to Earth and train us in some techniques for negating highly-trained Glu'gu'ik." The transponder under Echo's collarbone buzzed lightly. "Yeah, I just got confirmation on that from my command center."

Lu'vin'du'v nodded.

"Yes, I can just barely detect the transponder under your skin. No, no, do not worry; it would take another Ar'dug Division One Agent from my world to detect it, and even then, they might not notice—especially if they are not at my level of training. I am, I suppose, the Glu'gu'ik equivalent to an Alpha Line Agent, you see. Eb'vuv will never notice it, and Kelto's instrumentation cannot possibly detect it," Lu'vin'du'v added, holding his hands up to calm Echo's concerns.

"Okay, good," Echo said, voice mildly gruff with relief. "Now, what about that training?"

"Very well. That can be arranged, fairly readily," Lu'vin'du'v noted. "I will tell my superiors of your request at our next check-in."

"Good. So what else do you know about these guys that might be useful...?" Echo wondered, as they returned to their patrol.

* * *

"LORD Eb'vuv? You're kidding," Echo murmured, dumbfounded. "I heard the reference once or twice, while we were trailing y'all, but I thought that was just ego talking."

"Unfortunately not, Echo," Lu'vin'du'v replied, shrugging. "There is some evidence of..." Lu'vin'du'v winced, "familial inbreeding...in certain of the branches of the royal house. Keeping the power within the clan and such, you know. I gather some of Earth's royal families have had similar practices, over the millennia, so you may know of what I speak, though I gather that ours is...somewhat worse than even...well. At any rate, Eb'vuv is...mentally...'off.' There have been several formal diagnoses of various mental illnesses, but in my mind, they all boil down to a crafty, intelligent, dangerous lunatic that it does not do well to underestimate."

"Well, damn," Echo said, concerned. "Tell me more."

"If what was in your dossier on Va'du'sha'ā is correct, you would be well advised not to bring up anything about your personal history with the Agency. He knows your code name, but apparently not your reputation or position, let alone your location in the chain of command..."

* * *

"...So the Division One chain of command may be threatened by him?" Echo confirmed.

"It is just possible, based on some things Eb'vuv has let slip," Lu'vin'du'v affirmed. "This is why it is best if you do not mention your history with the Agency, or your reputation. Should he find out that you are next in line for the Directorship, your life would be in immediate danger. No matter if he believes you have 'turned,' or not. He will not risk it."

"Shit."

"Exactly."

"What if one of the others recognizes me, though? Or looks me up online, or something?"

"I will endeavor to divert such inquiries," Lu'vin'du'v volunteered. "I will inform them that you are not THAT Agent

Echo, and that in recent years the Agency has been using dupli-
cate code names, or...or something of the sort. Perhaps agents
from different Offices can have overlapping code names? I
know it is not the actual truth, but what they do not know cannot hurt you."

"I guess that'll work," Echo decided.

* * *

As Echo and Lu'vin'du'v completed the circuit of the
warehouse, Echo paused to pick up his blaster, and stopped
dead as he spotted the dull red indicator light on the side.

"Aw, shit."

"What is wrong, Echo?"

"My blaster's dead." He picked up the weapon and exam-
ined it.

"Dead?!"

"Yeah; I've put it through a lot lately. The power pack
must have slipped loose. The contacts touched the metal of
the building and discharged. It's deader than Pluto in a snow-
storm." An annoyed, perturbed Echo spun and stared into the
dark. "DAMMIT."

"Is there any chance your partner can get a replacement
to you?"

"Maybe. Meg? Are you listening, baby? Zap my transponder once if you are."

* * *

"Ooo, shit. Get her patched in fast, Tare."

"As fast as I can, Yankee." Tare worked rapidly with the
comm set in the corner of the room. "There. Omega?"

"Yeah, Tare, it's Omega. What's wrong?"

"Echo's blaster is out, as in down for the count. Dead battery. Listen up; I'm patching you in."

"*...Maybe. Meg? You listening? Zap my transponder once
if you are.*"

"Zap the bug, Tare," Omega ordered over the comm set
speaker. Yankee hit a button on the comm set.

* * *

241

An intense Lu'vin'du'v watched the one-sided conversation, curious. Echo felt the tingle under his collarbone. *I'm listening.*

"Good girl, Meg—uh, sorry. Good goin'. Do you understand what's happened? One is yes, two no."

One tingle. *Yes.*

"Do you think you can get me a fresh battery pack?"

A long pause, during which the male Agent knew his colleagues were rapidly debating the matter, was followed by a single zap. *Yes.*

"All right, Meg, here's the plan, then. Around the corner from me, there's a coffee shop. I'll be there at eight o'clock local time for a breakfast of coffee and doughnuts—something more substantial if I can get it, but I'll take what I can get. And a nice big side of blaster pack. Got it?"

One tingle. *Yes.*

"See you there."

* * *

Echo was alone on guard duty when Zzt and Zzu came out to relieve him at daybreak.

"Hi, guys," Echo began in a friendly fashion, "good to see ya. It was a damn long night. Quiet, though; I didn't have any trouble. I think I'm goin' around the corner, and grab something to eat. You guys want any—?"

Abruptly Echo found himself pinned to the wall of the warehouse, as the two Zargothians leaned into him. They only came up to his chest, but given their weight and their muscle mass, that was plenty high enough. Echo eyed them warily; if they decided to rough him up, a single blow could rupture internal organs. He would be dead within minutes, from the internal hemorrhaging. *And Meg won't even have time to find me,* he realized.

"Uhnh. I take it y'all aren't too happy with me for some reason?" he drawled for the benefit of the hidden microphone.

"Stay away from our woman," Zzt growled, as Zzu shoved him back, hard into the wall. Echo all but felt his teeth rattle.

"If you touch Zzs, we'll kill you."

* * *

"Dammit, Echo, say it. Say it!" Yankee urged the monitor as Tare frantically called up Omega. "Say 'pilgrim', and we'll yank you before you can sneeze!"

"Put it on the speaker, boys," Fox said, removing his headset and walking across the room. "And calm down. Echo isn't in trouble yet. In danger, yes, but he's been through a helluva lot worse than a couple of big blowhards making threats. Be patient. And don't send his partner into 'call out the cavalry' mode. She's got a head of state to protect, and that's a handful in itself. Tell her to stand by."

* * *

"I think you boys have the wrong idea here," Echo told the jealous Zargothians. "There's nothing going on between me and her. I wouldn't do that to you, guys. I'm not even interested in Zzs."

These boys must not know too much about 'the birds and the bees,' at least where humans are concerned, he decided. *For that matter, neither does Zzs. Or she just doesn't care, and wants some sort of sick 'exotic' experience, at my expense. Hm. Actually, I think that probably fits her personality, pretty well. And wasn't there something in the galactic news, a couple years back, about a Zargothia—*

"You sayin' she's ugly?" Zzu scowled, interrupting his analysis. This time Echo's feet left the ground as he slammed into the building, and he let out a grunt despite himself, as the air was knocked from his lungs.

Shit, he thought, hiding a wince of pain. *I mighta lost a rib on that one. Damned if I do, damned if I don't. Some days, the rain just follows you around...*

"No, of course not," Echo panted, trying to think fast. "Zzs is a very...beautiful Zargothian woman. But if you'll recall, I...ended...a relationship only yesterday. And let's just say it wasn't an amicable parting. I'm not remotely interested in any other...companions...at the moment."

Zzt and Zzu glanced at each other.

"You believe him?" Zzt asked.

"Dunno," Zzu responded. "Maybe we should give him a reminder."

"And maybe I should quit being a team player and start using a little of my Agency training," Echo said, with glacial levels of cool.

"What the hell does that mean?" Zzu grumbled.

"Division One agents aren't solely black Suits and fancy weapons, you know," Echo pointed out. "They wouldn't send one of their agents into the field if I didn't have the capacity to take out anything in the galaxy—even bare-handed. And I've got a weapon." Echo fingered the hand grip of the useless blaster. The two Zargothians stared at him, trying to decide if he was bluffing or not.

"You're lying," Zzt said finally.

"Care to find out?" Echo casually planted his feet, firmly bracing himself against the wall, readying himself for hostilities if it came to that. "Look, guys. I'm not spoilin' for a fight among ourselves. I don't really want to fight at all—I wanna get along, an' lay low—but if I can go off-planet with y'all while getting my own back at Division One, I'm in. It's simple—I'm not trying to take your girlfriend, and that's it." Echo was dead calm and matter-of-fact. The Zargothians looked uncertain for a moment, then settled down. "That's better. Now y'all oughta get on patrol before Eb'vuv has all our hides."

* * *

Back at the hotel suite, Tare and Yankee relaxed, and Fox smiled in satisfaction.

"See, gentlemen?" he told Alpha Seven. "There was nothing to worry about. Echo knows what he's doing."

"That's one more Teflon-coated Agent," Tare grinned. "He slid right out from under."

"Yeah," Yankee agreed. "Nice bluff."

"Who was bluffing?" Fox said, turning away from the astonished faces to check the status on the command computer.

* * *

After deciding his ribs were intact, Echo was headed over the fence to get to the street unobtrusively, when Eb'vuv called his name.

"Echo? Where are you going?" The disguised Glu'g'ik stood by the side entrance of the warehouse, watching warily; Echo was already halfway up the chain link, and his intent to leave could not have been more obvious.

"Down to the coffeeshop in the next block to grab some breakfast. Haven't eaten in...uhh..." he mentally reckoned, "way over twenty Earth hours, at least. Mmm...couple days, maybe? Not since I found out about Meg's...well. Since I discovered my partner had betrayed me. So I'm hungry." His stomach, which really was empty, chose that fortuitous moment to let out a growl. A really loud growl. He glanced down at it, then gave Eb'vuv a wry smile, mingled with a shrug. "And I kinda didn't figure you guys brought along any Terran food."

"That is a correct assumption, but your meal will have to wait a bit longer. You, Tiln, and I need to go over the layout of the operation together. Your assistance in determining the most probable placement of Division One agents will be invaluable in planning how our strategy will differ from 1963. Come with me."

The statement was an obvious order, and did not brook contravening.

Hell, Echo thought as he turned and followed Eb'vuv back into the warehouse. *It looks like I AM gonna have to go this one bare-handed.*

* * *

"Omega? Fox."

"Hi, Fox. I'm en route to the coffeeshop in the 'Vette. What's up?"

"Turn around and head back. Echo won't be there."

"What?! What happened? Is he okay?"

"He's fine, but Eb'vuv just dragged him into a strategy session. He can't get away to meet you."

"Blast an' damn. It looks like Echo's gonna have to go this one bare-handed."

"Yes, he is. Or at least it looks that way, unless we can come up with another plan."

"Well, if anybody can go it without blasters, he can. Keep me posted."

"Will do, Omega. Fox out."

* * *

"According to media reports, the President will be arriving on his special aircraft at the Dallas-Fort Worth International Airport at about eight o'clock local time tomorrow morning," Eb'vuv told the others as they sat around a rickety old table in a corner of the musty warehouse.

The group of strategic planners was not large, and did not include the entire team; only Echo, Lu'vin'du'v, and Tiln were there, in addition to Eb'vuv. A basic road map, of the type handed out at gas stations, worn and tearing in the creases, was spread on the table to provide street reference, and Eb'vuv pointed to the various locations as he spoke.

"From there, he will proceed to an elite hotel at the airport and take the special suite reserved for him," Eb'vuv continued. "He and his entourage will spend the morning settling into the hotel. Then his motorcade will depart the hotel at eleven-forty-five, heading south along the International Parkway before turning east on the Airport Freeway, then merging onto this Interstate 35 road, following it into downtown Dallas. He will exit the Interstate 35 onto the Commerce Street headed east, pass through the center of the Dealey Plaza, and cross the Houston Street onto the Main Street. In so doing, he makes a point of passing close by the JFK assassination site, including the book depository and the grassy knoll. They will slow down substantially as they pass the assassination sites, in order to allow for publicity and photographic opportunities for the media, but, unlike 1963, they will not be semi-circumnavigating the Dealey Plaza, but passing straight through it."

"Hm. So they're coming at it almost 180° away from Kennedy's route," Echo mused. "'Cause he came west down Main Street, jogged north up Houston, then down along Elm Street around the Plaza. Didn't he?"

"Exactly, and yes, he did. This president is passing through the same area, but NOT along the exact same route," Eb'vuv confirmed. "Rather, it is somewhat reversed."

"That's probably deliberate," Echo decided. "They don't want to risk a copycat event by some home-grown nut job political extremist—which is what most people thought happened to JFK. Where do they go from Dealey Plaza?"

"The motorcade will then continue east on the Main Street approximately five blocks, until it reaches the Griffin Street, whence it will turn right and head south along the Griffin Street some four blocks, arriving at the convention center. It is all very...symbolic."

"Yeah, this guy is big on symbols," Echo agreed, pulling a face. "He'd have probably been a better leader if he was a little more into doing instead of showing. There are shorter, quicker routes he could have taken, but he wants to draw comparisons to what's sometimes called 'the American Camelot.' That might not make sense to you unless you've studied Earth history and legend, but politically, the symbolism is important."

"Mm," Lu'vin'du'v murmured, noncommittal. Eb'vuv continued.

"The motorcade will be timed to arrive at the headquarters at twelve-fifteen, with his speech slated to begin at half past twelve. He will, therefore, pass the schoolbook depository at precisely twelve o'clock."

"High noon," Echo remarked with a genuine grin. "Why am I not surprised?"

"This is humorous to you?" Eb'vuv asked, seeming puzzled. "Why?"

"Oh, there's a famous old movie western by that name about a gunfight at what some of us humans sometimes call 'high noon.' I think the term came from the sun being high in the sky at that time of day."

"Very well," Eb'vuv said tolerantly. "We shall dub this 'Operation: High Noon,' if it amuses you. Echo, do you still possess your Agency chronometer?"

Echo pulled back his left sleeve, revealing the rather large, unusual titanium-and-black timepiece—which, thanks to an extremely miniaturized space warp, had far more capabilities than a simple wrist watch, though it was unlikely that Eb'vuv knew that. *Not,* a glum Echo thought, *that anything I've got in there right now is gonna help me much at the moment. Damn, I wish I'd gotten the emergency power pack set up in that thing.*

"Good. PGLEIA-issued chronometers are renowned for their accuracy. Therefore you will make the precise timing call upon my order," Eb'vuv commanded.

"All right. Then as soon as I say, 'High Noon', we open fire." Echo nodded.

"Excellent. Birdy will be informed. In 1963, Birdy was on the roof of the schoolbook depository; in your opinion, is this still the best location, or should we choose another?"

"Do you have a more detailed map of the area?" Echo asked. "This old road map is okay for planning routes, but for determining a specific emplacement, we need something higher resolution."

"Yes." Eb'vuv pointed across the room, an imperious gesture, and Lu'vin'du'v rose and brought over a detailed orbital-view map of the city. Echo spread it open, located the historic area, and studied it carefully.

"You don't want to use the book depository," he said. "It's a historic site now. There'll be people swarming all over it—especially people in black Suits, if you catch my drift. But look here—right here, at the building directly across the street from the book depository. It's a little office complex kind of thing." He tapped the map.

"But is that not too close? And too busy?" Tiln wondered. "Satellite imagery indicates they have been performing construction work on the north side of the roof—perhaps repairing it?—so that side of the building will not be accessible to us as an escape route. And they may even have construction workers there, the day of our operation." He fingered a different location on the map with a frond. "What about here, across Houston Street from Dealey Plaza? Or here, across the street from the courthouse? Or even the courthouse itself?"

"You don't want the courthouse; it'll have security out your ass," Echo explained. "These days, they search you for weapons before you're even allowed in there, with metal detectors and x-rays and all kinds of shit. That building over across from Dealey Plaza houses a lot of the actual courtrooms, so it'll probably have the same kind of security. And the only flat-roofed building across from the courthouse is a military recruitment center. Do you really wanna try to infiltrate any of that?"

"Uh, no," Lu'vin'du'v murmured, and the others shook their heads.

"As for the construction, we've got nothing to worry about," Echo pointed out. "With a presidential motorcade coming through, the construction workers won't be allowed up on the roof that day, anyway. All we have to do is use some passive cloaking, waltz in, off the Prez, and waltz out. Besides, the southwest corner of that building is as tall as anything around there, and it's completely open TO the southwest, so it should give Birdy a good angle down into the Plaza, while the rest of us back him up from the knoll, to the west."

"Indeed. Well observed, all of it," Eb'vuv agreed. "So... back to the roof of this office building, across from the depository."

"Right. So you put Birdy over here, on the southwest corner of this rooftop, and he's got a clear shot. No agents in the way—boom. You've nailed the dude."

Eb'vuv, Tiln, and Lu'vin'du'v all looked at each other, surprised.

"It looks like a good idea to me," Lu'vin'du'v remarked. "It is unexpected."

"Yes," rustled Tiln. "It is the same as before, yet different."

* * *

Omega scanned the map of Dallas that Murphy handed her, listening intently to Echo on her headset, as Romeo and India looked on.

"Here," she tapped the map. "That's where the sharpshooter will be."

"We'll get a team over there right away," Murphy responded.

"Negative!!" Omega exclaimed. "You will place your team on the roof of the book depository. Division One's Alpha Line Agents will handle this; we need you as scouts and decoys. If you put your men there, it will jeopardize the entire operation."

Murphy scowled.

"Hey, ease up, there. We're on your side, Jack," India pointed out.

"Look," Omega said quietly, "we know what we're doing. We have numbers, names, species, skill set breakouts. We're working up a plan to handle every single member of the assassin squad. We've got a man on the inside this time, feeding us intel. That man is the person I trust more than anyone else on this planet—my partner. If they find you there, on that rooftop, Echo is dead. And so is the President. Is that what you want?"

Murphy scrutinized the golden-tan, lightly freckled face and sincere brown eyes. Then he shook his head.

"No," he said. "No, I don't want the President dead. Nor your partner either, for that matter. 'Brothers in blue,' and all that. Well," he amended, glancing down at himself, then looking over the Alpha Line Agents, "brothers and sisters in black, I guess." He gave a wry chuckle.

"Then work with us. Please."

Murphy drew a deep breath and let it out in a sigh.

"...All right," he agreed. "Tell me what you need us to do, or not do as the case may be, and I'll see to it that my people get it done the way you want it. The way it fits into your strat-

250

egy."

"Great!"

Alpha Line assistant chief Omega offered her hand, and Secret Service chief Murphy grasped it and shook.

* * *

"...And more than likely, they'll only station some agents around the periphery," Echo told the assassins, "just to be on the safe side. If they thought something was actually going down, they'd have agents in the motorcade itself—probably in the President's limo. But Division One has no reason to suspect a thing, and the last reports I saw before leaving on vacation didn't mention anything out of the ordinary. Oh, they planned on keeping a careful eye out on the campaign junket, just on principle, but they aren't expecting a damn thing. And that's all coming out of the Dallas Office. It barely got a mention in the regional reports at Headquarters."

"Excellent," Eb'vuv said, intensely satisfied. "That is valuable inside information. They will be caught completely off-guard. Where will Division One station its people, do you think?"

"Aside from the book depository, you mean?"

"Yes."

"Let's see..." Echo studied the map for long moments, systematically going over each quadrant around the plaza in his mind. "There'll be agents scattered through the crowd along the motorcade route, of course...up here all along the bridge... and around the infamous grassy knoll, you can bet."

"Tiln, are you able to handle that?" Eb'vuv turned to the Botanoid.

"How many agents do you expect to be there?" Tiln asked Echo. "On the knoll itself, I mean."

"Mmm...six or eight, maybe. Hard to say. But I doubt it would be more than that, and it might easily be only about half that."

"Yes, I believe I can handle it," Tiln replied. "It is simply a matter of reconfiguration."

"Very good," Eb'vuv decreed. "We will depart the warehouse not later than eleven o'clock local time, and be in position by eleven-thirty. Birdy will be across the street on the roof, as specified by Echo; Lu'vin'du'v will assist him. Robert will wait on the next block along North Record Street, with the van running. Kelto will stand by in the van in case of malfunction. Tiln will provide the rest of us clear access to the knoll; the Zargothians will supply additional backup firepower. Echo will be the lookout and master clock. Upon completion of our task, Robert will be eliminated, and Echo will take the driver's seat in the van, carrying us back to our waiting spacecraft. We will dispose of the body somewhere along the way. Is this understood?"

Echo, Tiln, and Lu'vin'du'v nodded.

"Where are the spacecraft?" Echo asked.

"I will tell you that when it becomes necessary for you to know," Eb'vuv informed him, raising an eyebrow.

"Okay, whatever," Echo said with a shrug. "Let's do this."

"Lu'vin'du'v, inform the others," Eb'vuv commanded.

* * *

"All right," Lu'vin'du'v said quietly as he walked up to Echo, "that's taken care of. Now let's go get you...'food'."

"Where's Zzs?" Echo asked.

"Standing guard with Birdy." Lu'vin'du'v pointed to the entrance.

"Damn." Echo glanced at his wrist chronometer. It was a little past noon. "Listen, Lu'vin'du'v. The thing I need most right now is some shut-eye. I've only gotten a couple hours' sleep in the last several days. Is there someplace around here I can afford to relax? I need to grab this chance, while Zzs is... otherwise occupied, if you get my drift."

"Ah, I see. And yes, I do understand." Lu'vin'du'v glanced around; no one was paying attention. "Wait a few moments, then casually follow," he whispered, and wandered toward a dark doorway.

After a bit, Echo nonchalantly sauntered in the same direction, the black-denim-clad agent rapidly vanishing into the shadows beyond the arch.

* * *

Lu'vin'du'v waited for him at a corridor junction, and led Echo down the side hallway.

"This is the office complex part of the warehouse," he whispered to Echo. "In here." He opened a door and waved Echo inside. The room was a small empty office with a couple of blankets folded in one corner.

"This is where I bedded down last night—I needed to report in, anyway. The door locks on the inside only. You will be safe here. I will watch and make certain you are left alone," Lu'vin'du'v told Echo, who nodded his deep gratitude.

"Thanks, Lu'vin'du'v. If I'm not already up, knock on the door and wake me around 5:00 local, okay? Maybe Meg and I can still rendezvous tonight for that blaster pack."

"I will do so."

Lu'vin'du'v left the room. Echo locked the door and checked for signs of rodents. Seeing none, he glommed one of the blankets and curled up on the carpeted floor in one corner. In moments, he was sound asleep.

* * *

"...So Echo's getting some rest, then?" Omega asked Tare, who babysat the monitor while Yankee took some downtime.

"Yeah, Omega, he is, and about damn time. The room is locked from the inside—I actually heard the lock click—and the Glu'g'ik agent is keeping watch over it on the outside," Tare responded.

"Good." Omega was relieved. "At least Echo will be rested for the big soirée."

"Yes, he will. You sound...really concerned about him."

"Echo's my partner, Tare," Omega said simply, as if that said all that needed saying; for Division One agents, that was pretty much true. Tare nodded in understanding.

"Oh yeah, before I forget," he added, "Echo also said something about trying to rendezvous with you tonight. He

253

wants that blaster pack. He NEEDS that blaster pack...though he probably wouldn't say it quite like that."

"Okay. That works. Did he say where or when?"

"No. Given the rest of the group he's embedded in, and the dynamics involved, I think a certain amount of winging it is gonna be necessary."

"All right. We can handle that. Keep me posted. I'm going to go get the Secret Service guys set up as 'Division One' now." She quirked her fingers around the term, and offered the other Agent a wry grin.

"Wilco, Omega."

* * *

"Wait a moment, Omega," Fox noted, coming out of the back bedroom, as she headed for the door once again.

"Yeah, Boss?" she wondered, turning back. "Whatcha need?"

"It isn't about what I need, it's about what you need to know in order to adequately run this operation, and safely extract your partner," Fox said, drawing her back into the bedroom and easing the door partway closed. "I got a communiqué from a colleague on Va'du'sha'ā a little while earlier. I'd have told you before now, but you were busy with the President's team."

"Right. What's up?"

"This Eb'vuv who is commanding the hit team is known to the government on Va'du'sha'ā. He's a member of the extended royal family, a royalist of one of the most extremist factions, and considers himself a contender—most likely, considers himself the LEADING contender—for the throne of Va'du'sha'ā. His full title is something along the lines of 'Lord Eb'vuv Ub'he'tae'la, Ha'ar'ec of Clan Ab'ra'kud'un, House Bi't'ir'...and he takes it all VERY seriously."

"Whoa," Omega murmured, staring at Fox with wide brown eyes, but listening carefully. "Keep talking, Fox."

"Well, as you and Echo might say, he's 'fruity as a nutcake,' and has been diagnosed with several different mental

254

disorders, including megalomania, and may possibly have the Glu'gu'ik version of Nyssen-Van Bogaert syndrome."

"Which means?"

"He's prone to violence and irritability, the aforesaid megalomania, narcissism and egomania, possible entheomania, probable theomania, and consequently he believes he can do no wrong—his plans are always right, always correct, always the proper way to do things."

"A real 'my way or the highway' sort, huh?"

"Yes. There's every reason to believe that he is already well into the onset of dementia, and that he's only going to get worse as time progresses."

"So...he's out to kill the President because...?"

"Our people on Va'du'sha'ā believe he's out to force Earth to hand over the F'al and its current Hou'd'ni keeper...you."

"Well, shit," Omega decided, frowning. "So I guess this assassination is an attempt at coercion?"

"Exactly. This is probably his opening salvo. We think that he would kill the President, then issue an ultimatum: Give me what I want, or I'll keep bumping off your world leaders. Which, incidentally, at some point would have to include me. And then likely maneuver to bring the leadership of Division One to his homeworld, whatever it took...including taking out as many in the division's chain of command as possible. And let me remind you, your partner is next in line for the Directorship."

Omega's eyes widened in horror.

"We think," Fox continued, before she could gather her temporarily-scattered wits, "that they don't realize he's my second, or Echo would likely be dead already. And speaking of Echo, I expect he'll be picking up on this whole ball of drek soon himself, if he hasn't by now."

"So...it might be worth making SURE Ace knows," Omega considered. "And we definitely need to keep you in the back of things, from here out. I don't want them getting to you, too."

"I thank you for that, tekhter, but I can likely handle matters," Fox said with a slight smile. "Still and all, as you say, it might be best if they are not in a position to find out that I am personally backing up this operation. It would unduly complicate things."

"Right. So I'm the figurehead, this go."

"They want you, too, meyn teyere."

"But they don't KNOW that they want me," Omega pointed out. "By the sound, he'll be looking for a member of Clan Hou'd'ni and a Glu'g'ik, and I'm neither. More, this guy has already met me and did NOT pick up on any Glu'gu'ik genetic material. Neither did the other guy...or if he did, he didn't say so, which might also be because he's on our side, from what I'm hearing out of Alpha Seven's reports on Echo. But none of the rest of the team did either, for that matter. And now I don't even look the same..."

"This is excellently observed," Fox decided. "All right, then. I'll see to it that the various groups working this report to you, and know that you speak with my authority. And I'll trust you to handle it as I might, and provide what advice and recommendations to you that I can, when I am able."

"And believe me, Fox, I'm gonna listen."

"I know you will, yung froy, just as your partner does. But I want you to keep me close in the loop, even if I AM in the background on this."

"Done."

* * *

A nigh-exhausted Echo slept deeply and well despite the lack of accommodations, and had drifted into that semiconscious state somewhere between sound asleep and wide awake, dreaming some strange, garbled dream about a young Omega's palomino pony changing into a chestnut bay as she struggled with it, when the light knock came on the door. Almost instantly he was awake, sitting up on the floor and folding the blanket which had been wrapped around him.

"Echo?" came the whispered call.

"Yeah, Lu'vin'du'v, I'm awake." Echo got up and opened

the door. "Is everything all right?"

"Yes. But the...'troops'...are restless. Eb'vuv has decided that you, and I, and the Zargothians, as well as himself, will go to the bar one street over. He says you can get something to eat there. And all of us are capable of consuming your ethanol products, so..."

"Ugh. Drunk Zargothians. What fun. I presume the Zargothians will be disguised?"

"Yes. They will have artificial skin suits."

"It's still awful damn dangerous..." Echo shook his head, questioning the wisdom of the move.

"Yes, it is. But so are restless Zargothians."

"That's true," Echo admitted. "When are we leaving?"

"In about twenty minutes."

"Meg? You got that?"

Echo's collarbone tingled once. *Yes.*

"You gonna meet me there?"

Another tingle. *Yes. I'll be there.* Echo knew her well enough to 'hear' the murmur.

"Okay. Don't come alone, Meg. It's way too risky, for both of us, if you were to be recognized."

Two tingles. *No, I won't come alone.*

"Good. Let's go, Lu'vin'du'v."

Chapter 7

The bar was, of all things, a country-western club, frequented by the local blue-collar workers. *This cowboy-western stuff seems to be a running theme this trip,* Echo thought, sardonic. He wondered, with no small amount of hidden humor, just what jokes Meg would make about it when she arrived; he hoped he would be near enough to hear them. *Hell, I hope she makes 'em to ME,* he decided. *Assuming she can get anywhere close enough to me without getting herself recognized.*

Five men and one short, dumpy woman entered the establishment in a very loose group; it would have been difficult for a casual observer to determine if they were a party or not.

Echo, the obvious loner, moved immediately to the bar proper and ordered a long-necked beer—a doppelbock from a local microbrewery, with the cutesy name *Ridin' Off Into The Sunset*, but he knew from experience, it was good—with a double cheeseburger and large French fries; he was seriously hungry.

A mug of the doppelbock was delivered by the bartender in moments, to his gratification. Then he waited impatiently for his meal to arrive, careful to sip the bock slowly, until he could get food in his belly; he couldn't afford to let the alcohol affect him, and he had no DeTox tabs.

Meanwhile, the others clustered around two small tables in the corner—the Zargothians at one, the Glu'gu'ik at the other—and ordered drinks. Predictably, the Zargothians ordered cheap beers, even Zzs, who was from one of the noble families on her planet. Lu'vin'du'v apparently watched Echo order, for he got the same doppelbock; upon its arrival, he tasted it, nodded, and raised the bottle in Echo's direction, in a subtle salute. Eb'vuv, upon being told that the bar did not carry wine, disdained ordering a beer, commenting that it was "a cheap drink for the masses"; he insisted upon seeing a drinks menu, and finally settled on a top-shelf, single malt whisky brewed in Texas. Echo turned away so the Glu'g'ik in question could not see his deprecating expression.

It isn't that it's whisky, Echo thought in disgust. *Meg likes the same stuff, and I gotta admit, it's good. If I'd had actual food recently, I might've ordered some, myself. It's his attitude, his pretension. The beer is 'beneath' him, even the good stuff like this doppelbock,* he paused and took a sip, *and he has to go for something that suits his presumed status. Qu'ils mangent de la brioche, I guess.*

When Echo's meal finally appeared, the burger was loaded with lettuce, tomato, onions, and dill pickles, as he had hoped; he added some more catsup and mayo for good measure from the tabletop dispensers, then smashed the whole thing down until it would fit in his mouth. Echo wolfed down the huge burger in record time, then reached for the tomato catsup bottle again and proceeded to dump it liberally over the greasy, but surprisingly good, fries. As he munched, a rasping voice by his shoulder said, "Hi, Echo. Wanna share?"

"Hello, Zzs," a longsuffering Echo sighed. "Have a French fry."

Zzs reached over Echo's shoulder with Dragon Lady red-tipped fingers and picked up a fry, dripping with catsup, as she'd seen Echo do, while she clambered onto the empty bar stool beside him. It was rather tall for her short, squat form, though, and she struggled a bit to gain the seat. Suddenly, with a hoarse cry, the alien woman in the human suit flung the French fry onto the bar, nearly falling off the stool in the process.

"Aie! N'dikat! It burns! The red substance burns!"

"What the hell?!" Echo caught up the glass of ice water that the waiter had brought with his meal, and shoved Zzs's hand into it, rinsing off the catsup. He pulled Zzs's hand out of the water, and studied her fingers as she whimpered. *Looks like...acid burns,* he thought in surprise. *Right through the sensory-permeable part of the human skin suit. Huh. I thought Zargothian skin was supposed to resemble rhino hide. But it didn't hurt me...what gives?*

The bartender came over in concern, and Echo told him, "It's okay. She's allergic. Wasn't thinking." The barkeep nodded and resumed making drinks for other patrons. Echo looked back at Zzs, who was still whimpering with unaccustomed pain, and said quietly, "Here, Zzs, take this glass and go sit back down with Zzt and Zzu. I know it hurts, but try not to draw too much attention to yourself. Keep rinsing your fingers in the water until you get all of the ketchup off. It'll be okay, I promise."

Zzs took the water glass from Echo, stuck her fingers in it, and sniffled her way back over to the table. Echo watched her explain the odd incident to her companions, who looked as puzzled as he felt.

Okay, let's see what's in this stuff, he thought, picking up the catsup bottle and studying it warily. *Looks okay. Tasted okay...* He removed the top and sniffed it. *Smells okay, too.* He replaced the top and scanned the label. *Hmm...tomato paste, water, corn syrup, vinegar...that all looks normal. Wait a minute—vinegar. That's, uh...acetic acid, isn't it? Whoa. Acetic ACID. Huh. That's interesting. It's an acid. And she said it burned. Wow. There must be something in Zargothian skin that reacts with it. Now THAT could be useful...*

Echo polished off the rest of his fries, thankful for the calories, then picked up the beer mug and turned to casually survey the room as he drank. A number of brassy bottle blondes were in evidence on the dance floor, but no familiar platinum blonde braid caught his eye. He sighed noiselessly. *Something probably came up. Maybe it's just as well,* he thought, glancing briefly over his shoulder at the two tables where the rest of his 'party' sat. *Zzs is watching me like a hawk now. I dunno if she thinks I did something to cause that, or what.*

Just then, a familiar voice murmured at his elbow, "Hi, there, cowboy. Do you dance?"

Echo turned to the brunette in black jeans and white western shirt who had appeared on the barstool beside him and replied quietly.

"I've been known to. Do you two-step?"

"I do now."

As the pair moved out onto the dance floor, Echo murmured to his dance partner.

"Good to see you, India. I didn't know you could two-step."

"I couldn't, an hour ago. Meg gave Romeo and me a crash course, just in case."

"Shoulda known." Echo grinned. "I swear, Meg's the Ginger Rogers of the Agency. I don't think there's a dance step she doesn't know. Maybe the lambada..."

"Nope. Romeo asked. She knows it."

Echo grinned again, slightly ruefully this time.

"I don't think I'll ask if she's ever actually danced it, let alone with who. It's probably better not to know." *Probably better that I don't know,* he added to himself.

"Actually," India interjected, amber eyes twinkling, "Romeo asked that, too."

Echo paused, wondering if that was a question he really wanted answered. Finally curiosity overcame reluctance, and he bit.

"...And?"

"Well, Meg got this funny look on her face. Then she said no, she hadn't, and it looked like she wouldn't ever, since she was a permanent wallflower. She...wouldn't talk much after that. I...don't get it," India said, and grew somber. "I thought you and Meg went out dancing from time to time now. You're terrific as dance partners."

Echo pulled back just enough to stare down at her.

"Is Alpha Seven working backup on this?" he wondered.

"Uh, yeah, now you mention it. They've got responsibility for communications—especially passing your, um, messages, to Meg, if she's with the Secret Service or something. But what does that have to do with you two dancing?"

That explains it, Echo realized, thirteen varieties of annoyed. *Especially if Yankee has been mouthing off around her. Tare is a little more subtle, but not a lot. They never did come around completely where she's concerned, after the whole ball of crap last Christmas—Yankee in particular. Dammit to hell. I'm gonna have to find a way to teach them to keep their big stupid mouths shut around Meg. Maybe I should just turn Monkey loose on 'em. HE sure came around.*

"Never mind, India." Echo's brow creased momentarily in frustration. "So where are Romeo and Meg?"

"Across the room. As far away from your companions as they can get. Omega was worried they'd recognize her and jeopardize the mission. Not to mention jeopardizing her partner."

"Right." Echo nodded. "And I appreciate that. A lot. What's the plan?"

"Well, I've got what you need right here in my pocket, if I can slip it to you without anyone noticing. I'm also supposed to make sure you know about LORD Eb'vuv, and his wacky ways."

"Oh, that. Yeah, I know, and I'm laying low on my personal, uh, 'achievements,' let's just say."

"Good. But Meg also wants me to maneuver you over to our table for a few minutes if I can, so she can go over tomorrow's details with you."

"All right. Sure, I'd like to have a drink with you, then, ma'am."

India smiled, getting back in character, and threw Echo a come-hither look, drawing him off the dance floor.

"C'mon this way, cowboy. My table's over here."

"Get your hands off him," a female voice grated behind them. "He's MINE."

"Aw, shit," Echo whispered to India. "Not now."

"Wait just a damn minute!" India was still in character. "I don't see him attached to you. He was alone. And I don't see either of you wearing rings. So he's fair game. And he's already said he'll have a drink with me."

"And I said...take your hands off him!" Zzs said, shoving India away from Echo, hard. Echo's eyes widened in concern, but India rolled with the force of the Zargothian woman's push, and although she knocked over several chairs and landed on the floor, India remained unhurt.

India sprang up, reaching for Echo, and Zzs dove for her. Echo managed to 'bump' the alien woman in the side—entirely by 'accident,' of course; it was a full-on hip check, delivered with all the force Echo could manage—and instead of hitting India, Zzs caromed into a nearby table, upsetting both drinks and inebriated patrons.

"Two short guys from your group on your six," an urgent India clutched Echo's arm and whispered. She spun to face Zzs's next charge.

"Dammit," Echo muttered, turning and holding up his hands. "Guys, ease up," he urged. "I'm doin' my damnedest to keep the peace here." *I have got to stop this, or innocent bystanders are gonna get killed,* he realized. *If any of these guys lands a blow on a human, somebody will be dying in a hurry. And that's someplace we don't need to be going, for a lotta different reasons.*

Behind him, he heard the cries of the more drunken patrons as they joined the mêlée, and Romeo's voice cried, "Look out, hon!" The Zargothians barreled on like juggernauts, heedless of Echo's protests.

Echo caught Zzu as he rammed forward, and quickly flipped the alien over his shoulder, using the Zargothian's own momentum against him. When Echo turned to take care of the other Zargothian male, Zzt was already lying across the room in the remains of a table, and Echo heard a loud crash from somewhere behind him. Just then, he felt someone press back-to-back against him, and he heard a quiet, familiar voice mutter over his shoulder.

"I've got your back, hon. Blast it! So much for this chair. Shit, Ace, she's goin' thermonuclear redneck on the whole damn bar! The guys go down easier than she does!"

Echo, struggling to keep a straight face at his partner's description, somewhat unsuccessfully stifled a snort and replied in a similar tone.

"That's why she has two mates, Meg," he said as he blocked the punch of a drunken human who was trying unsuccessfully to use Echo's face for a punching bag.

"Just be careful she doesn't wind up with three," the soft voice of his partner drifted over his shoulder, punctuated by the sound of blows, "unless, of course, you happen to like short, squat, and psychotic."

"No, thanks," Echo deadpanned. "Never mind certain, uh, survivability factors. Given a choice of...companions, partners, however you wanna put it, I think I'll stick with the tall, blonde human I've already got."

"I don't think I'm that flattered by the comparison. But thanks anyway. So how does it feel to have women fightin' over ya, Ace?"

"Huh," Echo grunted as he delivered another punch, careful not to actually injure the human on the receiving end. "I hadn't thought about it like that..."

"I'll have to watch out. I'll lose my partner if I'm not careful. And I would NOT be a happy camper."

Echo listened for the sound of a smile in Omega's voice, but didn't hear it. He nudged her lightly with an elbow.

"Like I said, Meg, I'll stick with the partner I've got..." he tried again. She didn't respond. *Uh-ohhh, somebody's worried,* he realized. The recognition sent a surge of conflicting emotions through the male Agent: warmth, caring, concern, gratitude, anxiety, apprehension. *I wasn't sure how much she knew about Zargothians, but evidently she's boned up, and knows the danger.* He sighed. *Well, at least she knows what we're up against.*

* * *

Meanwhile, on the other side of the bar, Romeo was doing his best to keep the human combatants at bay as India squared off with Zzs. Unfortunately, the undercover Division One

Agents could ill afford to use their specially-honed combat skills, lest they give away their identities to the alien hit squad, and they were hard pressed by sheer numbers.

Omega, loosely guarding Echo's back, faced India, and caught her compatriot's eye as an idea struck. After dispatching a would-be opponent into unconsciousness, Omega raised her index fingers to her head, bowed slightly at the waist, and briefly mimicked a charging bull. India's eyes narrowed, considering, and she immediately began maneuvering the fight across the room, just managing to avoid Zzs's murderous reach. Omega saw where India was headed, and nodded.

* * *

"Echo," that worthy heard from behind, "where are the Glu'gu'ik?"

"One grabbed Zzt, and the other grabbed Zzu, and they headed outside..."

"Good. Get ready to grab Zzs and follow 'em."

"She won't go, Meg."

"She will in a minute. Gotta go. Be careful, Ace. I want my bestest pal back in one piece."

* * *

Suddenly the contact against Echo's back vanished; he spun around to look, but his partner was nowhere to be seen. *Damn,* he thought, absently blocking a punch from an inebriated human, *it's like she vanished into thin air...OH SHIT!*

He watched in shock as a maddened Zzs lunged for India; he and Romeo both started forward to rescue her.

But India swiftly sidestepped the clumsier Zargothian, and Zzs slammed head-first into the steel support column India had been concealing. The column bent, and Zzs went down as if a semi truck had landed on her. *Damn,* Echo thought, appalled, and not sure whether to be worried or relieved. *Good thing their skulls are 'bout an inch an' a half thick. Literally. 'Course, that doesn't leave as much room for the gray matter... surprise, surprise.*

"Romeo!" Echo caught his ex-partner's arm. "Y'all got

the power pack?"

"Oh, hell!" India panted as she ran up, searching her pockets but coming up empty. "I musta lost it in the fight! Damn!"

"Try again later!" Echo caught up a red plastic, generic squeeze bottle of catsup from a nearby table—the kind with the pointy, capped top—and crammed it into his shirt, then grabbed Zzs, and with a grunt of serious effort, lifted the dense alien woman and staggered for the door as fast as he could go.

Which, he thought as he strained not to drop her, *given her weight, isn't near as fast as I'd like, dammit. Shit, she is heavy!*

* * *

As the door closed behind Echo, an attractive, short-haired brunette wearing sunglasses over golden-tan, lightly freckled skin climbed on top of the bar and held up a smart cell phone. Several bar patrons wearing black and white scrambled to extract sunglasses and put them on.

"Everybody, calm down!! That's it! Y'all give me your attention, please. If you'll all just have a look here at my cell phone, I have a special message about this whole mess, from a certain television producer whose name you might recognize. That's right! You've been Got!"

And the bar lit up with a multicolored, holographic flash.

* * *

Back at the warehouse, a profusely-sweating Echo dumped Zzs down unceremoniously on top of the still-unconscious pile of 'snores' with a loud gasp, then leaned on his knees and panted for several moments, trying to catch his breath.

"Sheeit!" he complained. "If I gotta do this very often, Zzs is gonna haveta go on a diet. I'd swear she outweighs me by twenty pounds, easy!"

"Probably closer to fifty," Lu'vin'du'v decided. "And at only two-thirds your height."

"Would you like to explain what happened?" Eb'vuv said with a quiet grimness that revealed the threat within the question.

"Aw, dammit, some pretty little Afro-Asian chick comes

up an' asks me to dance, then offers to buy me a drink. I'm thinkin' score, free beer...an' then Zzs goes ballistic. She seems to think I'm part of her harem, whether I wanna be or not. Meanwhile, the boys over there," Echo nodded at the insensate pile of gray flesh, "don't want me joinin' their ranks."

"And you? What do you want?"

"All I want is to get offa this damn planet. Preferably un-noticed. And un-brain-bleached. And ALIVE." He shrugged. "Intact and in one piece would be kinda nice, too. I already know about, uh, 'compatibility issues' between humans and Zargothians."

"So you had no intention of starting the altercation?"

"OH HELL, NO! The absolute LAST thing I want is to draw attention."

"Very well. That actually matches my observations, as well as those of Lu'vin'du'v. You and he will have to stand guard tonight. It is certain none of the Zargothians will be able to do so. I will...deal...with them later."

* * *

Meanwhile at the Division One hotel suite a little while later, Omega was sitting in front of a tablet, downloading files from Headquarters and studying them, when Romeo came over with a report.

"Update on Echo, Meg. Yankee asked me to hand it to you."

"Thanks, Romeo. What's the gist of it?"

"Echo's on guard duty tonight with the Glu'g'ik agent."

"Well, that's a good team-up. Any repercussions from the bar fight?"

"Nope. Not f'r Echo, anyway. Sounds like th' Zargothians 're in it pretty damn deep, though."

"That, I don't mind," Omega said, raising an eyebrow. "In. The. Least."

"Tell me about it. You shoulda heard India laugh when that came over th' comm. I thought she was gonna hurt herself. Whatcha doin'?"

"Learning a little more about 'snores'. I looked some stuff up right after I talked with Fox, but I didn't have long to research it at that point, so I decided to have another go."

"Huh? You havin' trouble sleeping, Meg? You been worryin' about Echo?" Romeo offered a concerned frown. "You want I should ask India f'r somethin' to help you sleep?"

"No, yes, and no."

"What??" Romeo responded, confused. "Damn! You been around Echo so long, you're startin' to sound just like 'im, Meg."

"Thanks," she grinned, and resumed studying the file on screen.

"Well?"

"Well what?"

"'No, yes and no' what?!" Romeo exclaimed, frustrated. "Do I need to go get India, or not?"

"Oh. No, I'm not having trouble sleeping; yes, I'm worried about Echo; and no, you don't need to get India."

"I...don't get it."

"What don'tcha get, hot shot?" Omega turned her desk chair to face Romeo.

"Damn, do you sound like 'im. First off, why are you studyin' snoring if you're not havin' sleep problems?"

"Oh, I see," Omega chuckled. "'Snores' is what the hit team calls the Zargothians. Think about it for a second: Their names are Zzt, Zzs, and Zzu."

* * *

"Oh. Aw, shit." Romeo snorted in amusement as he finally grasped the pun. "Yeah, that's bad. Funny as hell, but bad."

"Yeah, I know." Omega grinned. "Anyway. This is the file on Zargoth I'm looking at."

"Umm, okay. Lookin' for weaknesses?"

"Among other things. Research is what I've got the most experience at, so I thought I'd spend some of my down time seein' what I could dig up that might be useful. At least in this sitch."

"Whatcha learned so far?" Romeo asked, curious.

"Let's see..." Omega mused. "Of the three 'snores' on the assassin team, Zzs, the woman, is the 'alpha snore,' you might say—they're a matriarchal society. The women are far and away the stronger sex—though both sexes are stronger than humans, by a considerable amount—and consequently, they're polygamist; both of the males are Zzs's mates. No, Romeo," she said, as her friend started to say something, "don't go there. You don't even wanna know about the mechanics of that. They're nowhere close to built like we are. It's...not remotely sexy to a human. Or healthy, either. Let's just say...if she manages to get her...hands...on Echo? Well, I'm afraid his body won't be all we'll have to put back together. And we WILL have to put it back together...if he survives it." She shook her head. "I'm not sure even the regen procedure would fix THAT."

"Aw damn."

"Yeah."

The two Agents were silent for a while, studying each other earnestly.

"What else did ya find out?" a subdued Romeo asked then.

* * *

"Well, I'm not near done yet," Omega decided, "but it seems Zzs is actually a lesser member of one of the noble houses. That probably explains her insistence on having her own way, too. Eb'vuv must have something on her, to be able to stay in control. And judging by this," she electronically flipped through the last few pages of her research, "he probably does."

"Like what?"

"Like Echo isn't the first non-Zargothian she's taken a shine to. And the other guy...didn't survive. And she didn't much seem to care, though the noble house of which she's a member had to pay through the nose to hush THAT up. I haven't been able to determine for sure if the other guy was even interested, but it kinda sounds like he wasn't, so it was a rape/murder. Not to mention," she flipped back a couple of pages, "apparently if she likes something, she thinks it belongs to her, whether it does...or whether she's paid for it...or not."

"Uh-oh. And she's decided Echo is hers."

"Exactly."

"Oh man. All right. Keep goin', pretty lady."

"Okay. Lessee, where was I...? Rape, murder, theft, klepto...oh, yeah, the D&D's."

"D&D's?"

"Drunk and disorderlies. As for the number of drunk and disorderly charges, I flatly lost track. The term 'party animal' definitely seems to apply to this broad. As we found out the hard way, just a little bit ago."

"Ooo. Anythin' else?"

"I'd have to dig into the details to try to uncover whatever Eb'vuv has on her, but offhand," Omega decided, studying the files, "I wouldn't be surprised to find out that she made whoopee with still another offworlder, that nobody else knows about yet—she seems to get off on that. He may know where the body is hidden...literally."

"Shit."

"Yeah. After the bar fight, I guess it's no surprise by now that they're on average not as bright as humans, so it probably wouldn't be that hard to find out, anyhow—I don't expect she's very good at working out how to hide something, or even bothers that much about it, given the, ah, privileges of nobility. In this case, noblesse doesn't oblige."

"Ugh."

"Yeah. So...not that smart, as alien races go. As a species, they tend to be kinda one-track minded, too. And we pretty much have to use their own strength against 'em. No way we could generate enough force otherwise. Those two things are why India's tactic in the bar worked against Zzs."

"Okay. Judo-type stuff, huh?"

"Yeah. And don't be afraid of hurting 'em, 'cause I doubt you can, short of shooting 'em. On average, their bones are anywhere from four to six times as thick as a human's, way denser than a human's, and their skin is not only three or four times thicker, it's a lot tougher, too. Think...tanned, full-grain, belting leather. Not quite elephant hide, but not that far off. You'd need a helluva knife just to cut 'em."

"Damn!"

"Yeah. You MIGHT get their attention if you hit 'em with a two-by-four. Maybe. I'm thinking that's a factor in why they're not as intelligent overall, because they got roughly the same size heads as ours, but their skulls are so thick, it leaves less room for the brain. So that means, lessee..." Omega did a quick search, "so that gives a human skull volume of...but then we reduce those dimensions by an inch and a half, all the way around and...whoa."

"What?"

"Romeo, those guys have less than half the cranial volume of humans! Try a cranial volume that's only about 45% ours!"

"What, just on account 'a they got thick skulls, literally?"

"Exactly. So I'm not sure that two by four I mentioned would even work."

"You're saying we'd best not take 'em on?"

"No, not necessarily," Omega decided, leaning back to consider. "I mean, India did great in the bar. Echo and I did okay, too. You just gotta realize what you're dealing with. You got that belting leather over top of a thick layer of meat that's about four times as hard as the best muscle density you got in your whole body, all held up by bones that might as well be structural steel. Remember how Zzs's head bent the steel column in the bar?" she reminded him.

"Ooo. Yeah, I forgot 'bout that."

"Didja know our covert ops guys are still trying to get the column straight? That, around having to brain-bleach the staff and patrons." Omega shook her head and laughed, but it was a rueful sound, and she knew it. "Last I heard, they're thinking they're gonna have to just replace the post. But Zzs is only knocked out, not especially hurt...though I hope she has a concussion headache fit to make her see cross-eyed for a week." She scowled.

"Damn, girl. You sound like India, laughin' at the comm. Y'all are colder than I figured."

"It didn't make you mad, her trying to hurt India?"

"Well, yeah..."

"Okay, then. If you knew what Zzs wants to do to Echo, you'd know what we mean."

"So India knows?"

"She's a doctor; I'd expect her to know about the, ah, 'ins and outs' of that particular subject, yeah."

"Guess I'll just ask her, then."

"You really wanna know, hon?" Omega shrugged. "Okay, you asked for it, hot shot. Hang on and lemme show ya. And try not to have nightmares about it."

Omega pulled up the pertinent research, scrolled down to a diagram, enlarged it, then held up the electronic tablet, so Romeo could see the screen.

"SHIT!" he exclaimed, horrified. His eyes grew wide, and he couldn't seem to pull his gaze from the image on the screen. "That's...that's...just wrong, man."

"Not for them."

"But f'r US?! That'd kill Echo! Tear 'im to shreds!"

"Which is my point. And she KNOWS it would do this, and wants to do it to him anyway. And assuming he survived long enough for us to gather up the pieces and stick 'em in a re-gen pod, I'm still not sure he'd come out completely functional, despite everything the medics could do. Never mind what the rape would do to him mentally." She paused, then added in an almost-snarl, "And THAT is why I don't really give a rip if the bitch gets hurt or not."

"Damn. We got us a sitch, don't we, pretty lady?"

"We do, Romeo," Omega sighed, then drew a deep breath, trying to settle. "We seriously do."

"All right." He paused, in obvious concern, then added, "You got anything else?"

"No. That's all, so far."

"Okay, Meg, that's all good t' know. Well, it's not—some

of it's pretty damn disgusting—but you know what I mean. I'll tell India, and we'll start workin' out some kinda tactics to use, then pass 'em on to the other teams. Maybe even pass it on to the Secret Service guys while we're at it, you know, as a just-in-case kinda thang. Let us know if you come up with anything else we c'n use."

"Wilco, Romeo."

Omega turned back to the little tablet as Romeo went in search of India, and in seconds the scientist-turned-Agent was deep into the file again, even as Alpha Two began running through possible combination moves for dealing with Zargothians, in a corner of the hotel suite.

* * *

After about fifteen minutes, Omega chuckled. It was a rueful, borderline unpleasant sound, but there was subdued dark mirth in it.

"That's interesting," she murmured to herself. "I don't even wanna think how they found that out. Bleh." She paused for a few moments, considering. "Hmm...I better remember that, though. It just might prove useful."

* * *

Echo and Lu'vin'du'v circumnavigated the dark ware-house over and over, talking and planning in low, guarded tones, on the lookout for any other entity.

"So you expect the opposite of what you have told Eb'vuv?" Lu'vin'du'v asked, as they paused near the back of the building.

"More or less, yeah. If I know Meg, she'll either be sitting beside the President herself, or have Alpha Two sitting beside him while she helps Fox coordinate. Alpha Line Agents will probably totally replace all the Secret Service agents in the motorcade," Echo rejoined, seating himself on the edge of a concrete slab.

"But how will they protect the limousine from the trans-warp flux rifle?"

"Mmm...I can think of several ways they might handle it.

273

It all depends on what equipment Meg's got readily available to her. And I don't know what the Dallas Office has on hand, right off. Don't worry about it. My partner will take care of it. She's good, and she's hella inventive."

"How will you get out?" Lu'vin'du'v sat down beside Echo.

"You mean extraction?"

"Yes. My extraction has been planned and coordinated since before I was infiltrated. I gathered from our conversation last night that your infiltration, while skillful, was less... forewarned."

"That's true. And I don't know. But Meg's on it. I'll get out."

"You place much faith in your partner's ability."

"Yep."

"You trust her so much?"

"Completely."

"Why?" Lu'vin'du'v asked.

"Because she never lets me down," Echo replied, voice very quiet. "Ever."

"How so?"

"So...to the point of being willing to die, first."

"I see. Then what do you contribute?" Lu'vin'du'v asked, curious.

"In this operation, or to the partnership?" Echo asked.

"Both, I suppose."

"In this operation, I'm providing inside information to the Agency just by being here. I'm providing disinformation to the assassins. And I have to be ready to respond to whatever Meg and Fox come up with."

"And to the partnership?"

"Hell, I dunno," Echo said, leaning forward, elbows on knees. "I trained Meg as an Agent; together, we pretty much inaugurated Alpha Line, and I'm the department chief and still considered the senior partner—mostly because I've been in the Agency a lot longer. There's not that much difference in our ages. Experience, I guess."

The transponder in his chest tingled lightly, just once, and he knew she was listening and in agreement.

"I try to look out for her, be there for her, and she does the same for me," he continued. "We've saved each other's tails more than once."

Another tingle. *Yes.* His lips curved up for a moment, in response.

"And trust, and...friendship," he added. "Kind of extended family, I suppose."

The tingle lasted for a couple of seconds this time, leaving behind a sense of warmth, and Echo smiled to himself, glancing down.

"She is signaling you through the transponder, isn't she?" a shrewd Lu'vin'du'v deduced. "You are smiling. Yet I have said nothing."

"Yeah, she is. She apparently agrees with me."

The transponder tingled. *Yeah, I do.*

"That is...fortunate...that the two of you are so in rapport."

"Yeah, it is, in more ways than one. How 'bout you, Lu'vin'du'v? Have you got a partner back home, waiting for you? Backing you up, even?"

"Not...any more, Echo," Lu'vin'du'v said softly. "My partner Cho'f'en was the first to infiltrate Eb'vuv's damned 'political faction,' but...but was discovered. Cho'f'en was... eliminated. I will see to it that Eb'vuv is taken down if it is the last living act I perform."

"You sound as if it's real personal."

"It is personal, Echo. Very personal," Lu'vin'du'v told him, somber; unexpectedly, he quantum-shifted into his true form. The big black eyes blinked once, then gazed at him, steadfast, seeming incredibly sad. "Cho'f'en Dh'u was my wife."

A shocked Echo stared at the Glu'g'ik for a long moment.

"Aw, damn, Lu'vin'du'v," he said gently. "I'm sorry. I'm... really sorry." A gentle, tingling warmth surrounded Echo's collarbone, conveying a message, and he touched the place lightly with his fingertips, then extended that hand toward the bereaved alien, speaking for Omega. "We both are."

Lu'vin'du'v nodded in understanding, silent for the time. Then he spoke again.

"Echo, may I offer you and your partner some advice?"

Echo's chest prickled once, and he tapped the area and said, "Sure, Lu'vin'du'v. We're listening. Both of us."

"I do not know what kind of relationship the two of you have, nor is it really any of my business, but it is evident you have trust and caring. Enjoy it while you may. Your work—as mine—is hard, intense, and dangerous. See to it that it is also satisfying. And do not neglect the times of non-work, of recreation. Together and separately, but especially together. Savor those times while you can. For you do not know...what will happen tomorrow."

The disguised Glu'g'ik bowed his head as he fell silent again, quantum-shifting back to his human disguise, and Echo nodded as he felt the soft, vibrating warmth above his heart.

* * *

"Fox," Omega said quietly, still deeply moved by Echo's conversation with the grieving alien, "we need to contact the Glu'gu'ik High Council and the Division One Office on Va'du'sha'ā and make sure we coordinate. We don't want to throw a monkey wrench in their plans and get Lu'vin'du'v killed, too."

"Good point, Omega," Fox replied, voice ever so slightly gruff. "Don't worry about it. I'll handle it."

"Thanks, Fox."

"By the way, those extraction scenarios you pinged me were very good, yung froy. So good, given the focus on the specific races involved, that I've placed them all at the top of the priority list for extraction plans. Assuming all goes as planned, we'll probably go with the one you designated as Alpha-One-beta."

"Oh," Omega said with a tired smile, and eyes that

still sparkled more than they ought. "Thank you, Fox. I'm...
pleased."

Fox studied the Agent beside him, as she continued
to struggle with the sympathetic emotions produced by
Lu'vin'du'v's sorrow.

"Omega, how long have you been going?" he asked.

"What?"

"When was the last time you got some rest?"

"Umm...I got a couple hours' sleep the day I got bit by
the rattler, after Echo got there...'bout...let's see, it's 1:00
am...'bout thirty-three hours ago, I guess."

"And before that?"

"Uh, I dunno for sure. The first night at the Ranch, whenever that was. I've lost track of the days."

"Rest," Fox said simply.

"I will. This afternoon, it'll all be over with, and I'll—"

"NOW, Omega," Fox said in a firm tone, face grave as he
put out a hand and removed her headset, which currently hung
around her neck. "Echo got some sleep this afternoon. So did I.
Everyone else is working shifts, too. And none of us is recovering from poison. You're in charge of Presidential security, as
well as Echo's extraction. You're the front leader for this entire
operation. You need to be rested and alert."

"But, Fox—"

"Omega," Fox's stern tone had a gentle warning in it. "No
buts, tekhter; don't make me give you an order. I will, you
know. And see to it that it's enforced, if it means bringing in India to give you a prescription soporific, and every Alpha Line
team in the place to hold you down while she administers it."

"All right," Omega sighed. "You're entirely correct, of
course. Where can I crash?"

"The master bedroom is empty at the moment. I'll send
India back to wake you when you're needed. There should be
at least one change of clothing for you in there as well, though
you'll have to go through the closet and find yours among mine;
I'm afraid I mixed them earlier when I was getting dressed, be-

fore I figured out there were two sets in the closet. At least Alpha Two and Alpha Seven have other bedrooms for their use, otherwise sleep shifts would get awkward damn fast."

"Oh, okay. That'll work. All of it. Including...looking out for me. G'night, Fox. Thanks."

"Good night, meyn teyere, and you are very welcome. Sleep well."

* * *

"...So 'High Noon' is the code word for EVERYone to commence action," Lu'vin'du'v verified.

"Yep," Echo confirmed.

"Very well," Lu'vin'du'v said calmly. "I will handle Birdy."

"Are you sure? You don't have any weapons."

"I am hardly defenseless, Echo. Nothing is as it appears; you should know that by now. My current form is...'accessorized,' I believe you humans would say," Lu'vin'du'v said with a grim smile. "Birdy may get off one shot, but no more. And not that, if I can help it. He may not survive the encounter, however. He is not...a pleasant being."

"That works," Echo said, pleased. "Knowing Fox and Meg, you'll probably have backup on the roof in no time. Right, Meg?"

The region around Echo's collarbone remained quiet.

"Meg?" Echo grew concerned. "Hey. Is anybody monitoring?"

The transponder zapped. *Yes.*

"Okay, so there's an Agent monitoring, but it's not Meg?"

Another tingle. *Yes.*

"Is she okay?"

The bug prickled once. *Yes, she's all right.* Echo paused in thought; he glanced at his wrist chronometer. Sudden understanding dawned.

"Wait. She's asleep, isn't she?"

A zap. *Of course.* Echo smiled to himself in the dark.

"Is she pushing herself hard?"

An emphatic tingle wrapped around his collarbone, though how it could be emphatic, he wasn't sure. But it didn't take a fraction of his gray matter to translate it as, *Doesn't she always?*

"Did Fox have to twist her arm to get her to rest?"

Zap. *Oh, hell yes.*

"Damn, I feel like I'm playing Twenty Questions," a grinning Echo told an amused Lu'vin'du'v, aside. "How long was she up?"

Zap-zap-zap. Pause. Zap-zap-zap. Another pause, followed by one last zap, then another sequence began. Zap-zap-zap-zap-zap-zap-zap. Another pause. Zap-zap-zap-zap-zap. Then the implant was quiet.

"Wow—thirty-three hours plus seventy-five?! That's nearly five days! Well, I guess she's gone a lot longer than that before. Listen, y'all make sure Lu'vin'du'v has backup on the roof this afternoon, okay?"

Zap. Pause. Zap. Pause. Zap.

Echo raised an eyebrow, considering, as Lu'vin'du'v watched, curious. Finally he decided, "Does that mean it's already taken care of?"

Zap. *Yes.*

"Good. Thanks, guys," Echo told the transponder, then turned to his companion. "Your backup's all lined up, Lu'vin'du'v. Fox has probably also coordinated with your superiors, too." The transponder buzzed, and he added, "And there's the confirmation."

"Excellent. My thanks to you and your colleagues, Echo."

"No problem. Listen, we probably oughta split up for a while. You patrol back here, and I'll head around front."

"All right. Signal if you require my assistance," Lu'vin'du'v said.

"Wilco."

* * *

Echo was waving after the disappearing lights of the Dallas P.D. patrol car when he suddenly found himself airborne

279

without an engine, wings, or parachute. He tucked and rolled as he hit the ground, and came up in a crouched, combat-ready position.

"Aw, shit, not again," he muttered to himself, seeing who confronted him, truculent expressions on both faces. "The snores' attitudes are gettin' old." Echo raised his voice. "C'mon, guys, we're not gonna go through this again, are we?" The two Zargothians stood about fifteen yards away—where Echo had been standing moments before—and both were glowering angrily.

"We've had enough of you," Zzt growled. "You're not takin' Zzs away from us."

"Yeah, we don't need you anyway," Zzu added. "We did just fine on JFK without you. So we're gonna introduce you to him."

* * *

A sleepy Omega, jacketless, shoeless, collar undone, tie hanging loose down her chest, came wandering through the hotel suite, padding along in sock feet on her way to the kitchenette to get a glass of milk when her drowsy brain cued into the voices emanating from the monitor speaker.

"...We're not gonna go through this again, are we?"

"We've had enough of you. You're not takin' Zzs away from us."

"Yeah, we don't need you anyway. We did just fine on JFK without you. So we're gonna introduce you to him."

"What?!" an instantly-awake Omega exclaimed, running to the monitor. "Yankee, get his location! Fox, where's Alpha Two?"

Yankee pulled up Echo's position on a PGLEIA satellite view screen as Fox laid a hand on Omega's shoulder.

"Wait." Fox was calm.

"Fox—"

"He'll be fine. Don't worry. Trust him."

"But you're the one who said—"

"Omega, Echo is one of the Originals. Our top field agent,

the chief for our special forces department, and the senior partner of Alpha One. He's your partner. He's my successor. He's
ours, my dear, yours and mine. Part of our family. Part of the
Alpha Line family. And part of the overall Division One family, into the bargain. We take care of our own. I will not let harm
come to him if it is in my power to prevent it, nor will anyone
else here. But you know as well as I do what Echo is capable
of. I know you're worried, but don't underestimate him. Give
him a minute."

* * *

Predictably, the Zargothians charged the Alpha Line chief.
Echo remained in a low crouch and reached inside his shirt.

"Here ya go, boys," Echo said, aiming and compressing
his weapon, "want fries with that?"

A red beam shot from the weapon in Echo's hand, striking Zzt and Zzu in the face and neck. As the vinegar in the
catsup reacted with the Zargothians' bare skin, the alien males
began to howl in pain, collapsing to their knees and pawing
at their faces. When they managed to smear it into their eyes,
they screamed even worse. Lu'vin'du'v came running around
the side of the warehouse at the noise, and Eb'vuv appeared in
its entrance.

"What in the name of the Maker is going on?! Be quiet!
All of you, shut up! We shall have the police AND the agents
down on us!" Eb'vuv demanded, as Lu'vin'du'v ran to stand
between Echo and the Zargothians, who continued to bellow.
To Echo's knowledgeable ear, however, they sounded like coyotes howling in the night, and given that coyotes were not infrequently found in urban settings in that part of the country, as
a consequence he was not too worried about the possibility of
unwanted company.

"The boys here jumped me, and apparently figured on
getting rid of me—permanently," Echo informed Eb'vuv, one
eyebrow raised in displeasure bordering on ire. "I was just defending myself. Here," he continued, walking over and picking up a garden-type hose, wishing privately it was a fire hose.

"Hold still, guys." Echo turned on the water full-force, and aimed the spray at the Zargothians, rinsing away the condiment. "No—permanent—damage. I'd stay outta the sun for a few days, though, if I were you two." He tossed the hose down and walked over to the two short males, staring down at them as they lay on the now-muddy ground, as intimidating as he knew how to be, using his height to full advantage, well aware that the Zargothians were easily a couple of feet shorter than he was. "That was your third strike. Come after me again, boys, and you may be the ones renewing your acquaintance with President Kennedy. I don't put up with that shit." Echo walked over to Eb'vuv. "Unless you say otherwise, I just handed over guard duty to Zzt and Zzu."

Eb'vuv nodded, scowling at the Zargothians. "Yes, Echo, you and Lu'vin'du'v are relieved. Zzt and Zzu can finish off the shift until Birdy and Kelto come on at 9:00 local. And then I shall deal with them. AND Zzs."

Echo stalked into the building in high dudgeon, and Lu'vin'du'v followed. Eb'vuv stayed outside; Echo presumed he was 'having words' with the Zargothians, but did not particularly care. *At this point, if he takes 'em out the same way he took out the Shrubs, I wouldn't mind,* he grumbled to himself, then shook his head. *Nah. Nobody deserves that, just for a bout of jealousy. But those guys are comin' damn close. Never mind Zzs herself. And at least it would be three fewer assassins to deal with.*

After scanning the main floor and determining that all other occupants were in various stages and types of unconsciousness, the two undercover agents made their way to the office in the rear of the building. There, they reported in to their respective headquarters.

Lu'vin'du'v sat in one corner and went...inert, as his body transferred all of its resources into a covert, undetectable quantum-entangled signal. Echo took a seat in another corner and turned his attention to the transponder.

"Hi, guys. I guess you heard all the excitement."

A long, emphatic zap. *Oh yeah!*

Hm. I recognize that tingle, Echo thought. "Meg??" he tried.

A zap. *Yes, it's Meg.*

"I thought you were supposed to be asleep."

One zap, a pause, then two more. *"I was. I'm not now,"* Echo could almost hear Omega say.

"Things are okay now, baby, I swear. I'm locked into the old office in the back with Lu'vin'du'v now. So unlax. Tomato ketchup really does go with everything."

The bug remained inactive. Echo chuckled.

"Never mind. I'll explain later. Go back to bed, Meg."

Two tingles. *No.*

"It's all right. Things are gonna be quiet for a while now. Zzs is still out cold; Birdy, Kelto, and Tiln are asleep; and Eb'vuv's chewing the asses off the other snores outside. Lu'vin'du'v is even zoned, over here in the corner. I'm gonna study the map here in the back room for a bit, then catch a few myself."

One prickle. *Good.*

"Are you gonna go get some more sleep?" Echo pressed.

His chest remained quiet.

"Meg..."

Silence.

"Am I gonna have to pull rank?"

One zap. *Yes.*

"Dammit. Meg, just go get some sleep. Fox, help me out here."

A tingle. *Yes.*

"Fox? That you?"

Another zap. *Yes, it's me, zun.*

"Has Meg gone back to bed yet?"

Zap. *Yes, she has.*

"Good. Did you have to order her?"

Zap. *Of course.*

"Thanks. I don't think the male snores will be any more

trouble, at least until it all starts going down, and then who knows what they'll do. Everything else is going according to plan. I'm gonna look at the map for a little bit, and make sure I have everything laid out in my head, then I'm gonna crash. See you guys later on today."

* * *

"Fox, do you approve the plan?" an alert Omega, freshly showered and dressed in a clean Suit, asked the Director later that morning as both Alpha Line and Secret Service agents huddled over the monitor in the command suite.

"Yes, Omega, the plan is officially approved. I'll arrange the details."

"Don't forget the hoverpod."

"Already in the trunk."

"Thanks, Fox. The rest of you know what to do." All the agents nodded, and moved out. "Okay, Yankee, move over and let me talk to my partner."

Yankee moved aside, and Omega sat down at the equipment and began tapping the 'bug zapper.'

* * *

Echo was headed outside to find a remote corner, away from the off-duty Zargothians, to get a bit more rest—not sleep; he just found the back office area uncommonly cold, and the sunshine felt good, so he had the idea to kick back and relax in the sun for a few minutes—when he felt the tingling sensation under his collarbone.

"What—?" he murmured to himself; the zaps were coming in a series. He settled down in a sheltered recess of the building, bathed in the warm sunshine, and concentrated.

A short zap. A pause. A long zap, a short zap, a long zap, a short zap. Another pause. A short zap, a second short zap, a third, a fourth. A pause. Three consecutive long zaps.

The solution came to him suddenly. *Morse code*, he thought. *Dot—E. Dash, dot, dash, dot—C. Dot, dot, dot, dot—H. Dash, dash, dash—O. 'Echo'! Meg's signaling me!*

"Hi, Meg," Echo whispered, after glancing around to

make sure he was alone. "I read you. Go ahead."

There was a pause, then the tingling started again. Echo kept close track. *Dash, dot, dash, dot—C...Dash, dash, dash—O...*

After a couple of minutes, Echo had the entire message. "Verify message," he whispered. "'Coffee 9:30 A.M.' One if yes, two, no."

A tingle. *Yes.*

"Are you bringing me a present, I hope?"

A zap. *Yes.*

"It's a date, Meg—if I can get out of here for a few."

One zap. *Right.*

Good. She understands, he thought.

Echo glanced at his wrist chronometer. It read 9:12. He stood, glanced around to ensure no one was watching, then moved to the rusted chain link and slipped quietly over the fence, disappearing down the back street.

* * *

Within five minutes a tall brunette with short hair, a golden tan, and freckles, wearing a black Suit, slipped into a coffeeshop and took a table in the corner, facing the entrance.

When the waitress came over, she ordered a pot of coffee, two cups, and a couple of doughnuts, and waited.

* * *

Echo was halfway to the coffeeshop when he heard running footsteps behind him. Casually, he glanced over his shoulder to see Lu'vin'du'v coming up quickly on the Agent. Echo stopped and waited for the shorter Glu'g'ik agent to catch up to him.

"Echo, come back right away," an urgent Lu'vin'du'v told him. "Eb'vuv plans to move to another site after the hit—he has concluded we would do well to lay low briefly, before returning to our landing site—and everyone is required to help pack the equipment. He wants you especially, to use your specialized knowledge to help erase all signs we've been there."

"Damn," Echo grumbled. "Can you cover for me for a few

minutes?"

"No; we've both already been gone too long. I'll have to tell him you were headed to get more Terran food, and I had to chase you down. He already knows you haven't eaten well lately, and we all saw the size of the meal you tucked away last night without even slowing down, so he'll buy it."

"Shit. All right." Echo addressed his next remark to the transponder embedded in his chest. "Guys, tell Meg I'm sorry I had to stand her up."

* * *

The attractive brunette was halfway through one of the freshly-fried doughnuts and on her second cup of the excellent coffee when the cell phone in her pocket beeped. Casually she withdrew and activated it.

Omega listened for a few seconds, then murmured an acknowledgement, deactivated the phone and returned it to her pocket. She scowled for a moment, then made a motion as if to slam her fist on the tabletop, but she pulled up at the last second.

She downed the last of her coffee in one swallow, tossed a few bills on the table to cover the cost, and left the coffeeshop.

* * *

"I do not care if he 'checks out'," Birdy told Kelto, as Lu'vin'du'v entered with Echo. "I do not trust him."

"Is there anything definite you read off him?" Kelto asked the Aves, who shook his head as Lu'vin'du'v approached. The Delzantian and the Aves watched—one with suspicion; both with dislike—while Echo went to talk to Eb'vuv.

"No, nothing in particular. But he may have been with that woman long enough to subconsciously pick up blocking techniques," Birdy replied, and Lu'vin'du'v raised an eyebrow.

"Is there a problem?" Lu'vin'du'v asked.

"Birdy doesn't trust our black-dressed, homicidal recruit," Kelto offered with a smirk. "But he doesn't have a reason. And I've scanned Echo nine ways from RestDay, and he's clean. The Agency would never send 'im here on his own, so he's gotta be tellin' the truth."

"What is it you sense, then, Birdy?" Lu'vin'du'v asked, concerned, but not for the reason the two assassins thought.

"I sense hostility and dislike from him," Birdy said, "and distrust—all carefully disguised."

"Anything specific?"

"I already told Kelto—no."

Lu'vin'du'v thought rapidly.

"Perhaps I know what you are sensing," he told the Aves. "I made a point of talking with our new team member last night while we were both on guard duty, to feel him out. I found that he and his partner were...very close, shall we say?"

"Close? What do you mean?" a naïve Kelto asked, eyes wide.

"He means they were lovers, lackwit," Birdy growled. "Go on, Lu'vin'du'v."

"All right. When Echo discovered that she had been lying to him about everything, pretending to be human, and planning to betray him the whole time, I think all of that trust and...closeness...maybe even love...turned to anger and hate. It hurt him very badly, and he reacted in an extreme, negative fashion—we all heard THAT. But for all that, the torment and the killing, I think that it did not exorcise his partner from his mind, from his heart." Lu'vin'du'v shook his head. "It may have made it worse."

"How do you know all this?" Kelto wondered. "What he's feeling and shit."

"Because, to some extent, he has been there," Birdy noted.

"Huh?"

"Lu'vin'du'v has lost his mate," Birdy elaborated. "Didn't you tell me that a while back, Lu'vin'du'v?"

"I did," Lu'vin'du'v replied, sober. "A...virulent pathogen...attacked her system and overcame her. I...could do nothing."

"Oh," Kelto murmured, seeming—just slightly—sympathetic.

"Then what IS he feeling, Lu'vin'du'v?" Birdy wondered. "And why is it so different from your grief? He seems so... angry..."

"He IS angry," Lu'vin'du'v explained. "His partner, his lover, hurt him badly in her betrayal. He is angry with her, he is angry with himself—"

"Why with himself?" Kelto asked.

"Because he didn't see it coming?" Birdy suggested.

"Exactly," Lu'vin'du'v verified. "He berated himself for that over and over, last night. And he also berated himself for reacting immediately, and in anger. I think he may now wonder what might have been, had he taken her offer to double-cross her...sponsor, for want of a better word...and tried to work things out."

"But he killed her," Kelto pointed out. "Because she betrayed him."

"Yes," Lu'vin'du'v agreed. "And because of that, the image of her face, in those last seconds before he murdered her, is etched in his mind. He killed his mate. I had to stand back and watch while mine died. I love my mate still, and I am striving to be worthy of her memory. HE hates her...as much as he hates himself. And THAT is the difference between us."

The trio were silent for long moments, pondering that information. Finally Kelto spoke.

"Damn. That's a serious load of baggage."

"It is," Lu'vin'du'v said with a nod.

"Are you sure, Lu'vin'du'v?" Kelto continued.

"He's sure," Birdy murmured. "I see it in his mind."

"Yes," Lu'vin'du'v confirmed. "His emotions for his dead partner are very mixed; ask him yourself if you like. And now... in answer to your original question, as nearly as I can tell, he appears to have transferred those emotions to anything not human. But I am certain that he will not turn on us; he needs us to get off-planet without being caught. I do not think I would go out of my way to provoke him, as the Zargothians discovered to their detriment, but I think we need not fear for our mission."

The Aves and the Delzantian mulled over Lu'vin'du'v's explanation, watching as the subject of their conversation systematically wiped away all evidence of their presence, while the workhorse-like Zargothians—all three—docilely loaded equipment into the decrepit burgundy van, which had arrived a few minutes earlier. Kelto nodded finally.

"It makes sense, in an irrational, typical-Terran sort of way," he decided.

"Yes, it does," Birdy agreed. "But I do not have to like it—or him."

"No," Lu'vin'du'v agreed, "you don't. You only have to work with him."

"Very well. I suppose I can manage that."

* * *

"Echo," the Delzantian greeted the Agent as he approached, "how is it going?"

"Fine, Kelto," Echo said, looking up from his obliteration ops. "What can I do for you?" Echo casually glanced over Kelto's shoulder to see Birdy watching, typically eagle-eyed; Lu'vin'du'v stood just behind Birdy's shoulder, and gave the Agent a subtle nod, warning Echo that something was up, and to play along.

"Nothing. I'm fine," Kelto replied. "Mostly I wanted to find out how you're doing."

"Kinda out of character for somebody who doesn't like people, isn't it?" Echo asked, amused.

"Well," Kelto swayed his head from side to side, in the Delzantian equivalent of a shrug, "we got a job going down soon, and Lu'vin'du'v seems to think you've still got a hangup about your partner..."

"Ex-partner," Echo snarled, sending Lu'vin'du'v a dirty look before turning away; now he knew what was in the wind. "Damn betraying alien bi—"

Echo broke off abruptly, secretly wondering if Omega was monitoring; he didn't want to hurt her again if it could be avoided. Then he had an idea, and retrieved his ID holder from his hip pocket as he half-turned away, holding it casually where it could be seen 'accidentally,' over his shoulder. Reaching behind his *carte noir*, Echo pulled the blood-stained argent strands part way out, fingering them gently, affectionately. His touch was that of the lover he wanted, one day, to be.

"Damn, Meg, baby," he murmured just loudly enough to be overheard, "why'd you have to do that? Why'd you have to go and betray me? I trusted you, I—you an' me, we could've... we could...have...had..." Echo let his voice trail away, and allowed himself to feel the pain of possible rejection by his partner, coupled with the grief he felt over his mother's impending death, to enhance his performance; his face twisted with the combined anguish of it all, and instinctively he put one hand to his face for a moment. Then he suddenly shoved the lock of hair back into its hiding place.

"Damn it all to hell!" he exclaimed in a vicious tone as he crammed the wallet back in his pocket. He spun on Kelto, fist raised as if to strike, but he froze the arm at the top of its swing. "You happy now?" he growled at the Delzantian, who flinched. "You just had to remind me, didn't you? Now get the hell out of here and let me finish, so I can get off this shit pile of a planet."

An intensely nervous Kelto backed off from the blazing brown eyes, and as Echo turned to get back to work, he saw Birdy and Lu'vin'du'v exchange glances, and Birdy nodded.

* * *

As Echo looped the back of the warehouse to check for any accidentally-left items, Lu'vin'du'v casually approached.

"Hello, Echo," he called. "How is the erasure operation proceeding?"

"I'll be finished soon," Echo told him, brusque and cool, for the benefit of the Zargothians carrying the last of the equipment to the van; it did behoove him to do a good job, lest evidence of offworld involvement get left behind. "I gotta sweep the perimeter, then I'll be done." He dropped his voice as Lu'vin'du'v grew close enough to hear. "Is Birdy convinced now?"

"More or less," Lu'vin'du'v answered in kind. "They bought it, as you would say. But it has raised a point about which I am curious." The Zargothians went inside the building, leaving Lu'vin'du'v and Echo alone outside. He glanced around to verify that they were indeed alone, then nodded confirmation at Echo.

"And that is?" Echo offered then.

"Your partner, Omega. What is she?"

Echo stiffened, offended.

"What do you mean, 'WHAT is she'?"

"What species is she? I thought all actual Division One agents on Earth were Terran. Not necessarily human—I have met Klack, some years ago—but all from Earth. Oh, there is the odd exchange program here and there, but your agents should be well more than ninety-nine percent Terran."

"She is. She's Terran."

"Then how do you explain her genetics, and instinctive block of Birdy's telepathy?" Lu'vin'du'v gave Echo a skeptical look. Echo sighed.

"You heard the story she gave about being planted in the Agency to kill me?"

"Yes."

"It was true."

"What?!"

"Yeah, except she kinda reversed it—instead of being an alien with human genetic material added, she's human with... other stuff. An old enemy of mine kidnapped her, performed recombinant-DNA experiments—among other things—on her to enhance her abilities, and telepathically programmed her to kill me. Then he planted her in the Agency. God only knows what else he did to her; Meg doesn't like to talk about it. She couldn't even remember it until our Deltiri ambassador from Arcturus VII deprogrammed her and removed the memory blocks."

"You mean she really tried to kill you?"

"Yeah. 'Bout...oh, somewhere around a year ago, now, I guess it was, more or less. I couldn't tell you the exact date any more, though I bet she could, 'cause damn, was she upset. But she couldn't help it. She didn't want to, she just didn't know how to stop it once the program trigger had been set off. That telepathic block isn't really instinctive, by the way. The Arcturan ambassador taught her how, and she's practised it until it's automatic. And pretty damn solid, too, from what I gather. It's her way of defending herself against it ever happening again."

"So she is partly human."

"She's completely human, Lu'vin'du'v. She's just... unique."

"What do you mean?" Lu'vin'du'v asked, puzzled. "Either she is human or she is not."

"Mmm...are you familiar with the Agency's automobiles? Our cars?"

"Your mode of ground transport? Yes. What particular variety do you drive?"

"I drive a '96 Corvette. And you know they're specialized vehicles, relative to the standard Earth vehicles, right?" Echo pressed.

"Yes, of course. You do considerable retrofitting to bring them to Agency standard, and many of you—including Director Fox, I have heard—even take it past that."

"Right, and I'm one of 'em that does take it past the regulation specs. Well, specs or no, the Corvette is a car. It's got a lot of unusual equipment, and it can do lots of things a regular car can't do, but it's still a car. Meg is...kind of like the Corvette. She's human, she's just got some...extra equipment under the hood, you might say?" he tried.

The implant under Echo's collarbone began to tingle in a specific sequence, and Echo scanned the area to verify they were still alone, then held up his hand to Lu'vin'du'v as the Glu'g'ik opened his mouth to speak.

"Hang on a minute, Lu'vin'du'v. There's a message coming in..."

W.H.O.A. B.A.B.Y.

Echo smeared a hand down his face.

"Romeo, get your finger off the damn button and your mind outta the gutter, junior," Echo told the transponder with a wry grin. "Now what were you about to say, Lu'vin'du'v?"

"What is Agent Omega's expected lifespan, then?"

"I dunno...what's the average human lifespan? Seventy, eighty years?"

"But you have just said that she is not an average human. Do you not have to replace parts and refuel your Corvette more often than a 'regular car,' because its higher performance causes it to wear out faster?"

"Yes..." Echo murmured, feeling the blood drain from his face as he saw where the alien was going.

"So...do you not expect your partner to have a shorter lifespan?"

A badly-shaken Echo leaned heavily against the side of the building and slowly slid down to a seated position on the ground.

"I hadn't even thought about it," he whispered. "Meg?"

Two zaps. *No.*

"No. No what?"

N.O.T. M.E.G. R.O.M.E.O.

"Romeo? Where's Meg?"

N.E.X.T. R.O.O.M. W.I.T.H. I.N.D.I.A.

"Uh-oh. India's tending her? Did she hear?"

One tingle. *She heard.*

"Is she okay?"

Two tingles. *No.*

Oh, damn. Echo closed his eyes and leaned his head against the wall for a moment. "What happened?" he asked, as a worried Lu'vin'du'v crouched beside Echo and watched, deriving the other end of the conversation from Echo's questions and reactions.

T.H.A.T. S.U.R.P.R.I.S.E.D. U.S. A.L.L. M.E.G. T.U.R.N.E.D. S.H.I.R.T. C.O.L.O.R.

"She turned as white as her shirt," Echo murmured to Lu'vin'du'v. "Did she pass out?" he asked the transponder.

Two zaps. *No.* A pause, then three zaps. *It 'uz close, though.*

Echo looked up at Lu'vin'du'v and shook his head.

"She did not pass out, then?" the Glu'g'ik agent asked.

"No. But it was apparently a near thing."

There was a pause, then the tingles began again.

F.O.X. H.E.R.E., E.C.H.O. W.E. R. O.N. I.T. I.N.D.I.A. M.E.D.S.C.A.N. S.E.N.D. D.A.T.A. H.Q. M.E.D.L.A.B. Z.E.B.R.A. A.L.R.E.A.D.Y. S.T.A.N.D.I.N.G. B.Y.

"How long will it be before we know something?"

U.N.K.N.O.W.N. A pause. D.O.N.T. W.O.R.R.Y. S.H.E. B. F.I.N.E.

"Dammit, Fox! Meg may be burning the candle at both ends!"

E.C.H.O. S.H.E. O.U.R.S. W.E. T.A.K.E. C.A.R.E. O.U.R. O.W.N. Another pause.

H.I. A.C.E.

"Meg??"

One tingle. *Yes, it's me.*

"You okay?"

One tingle. *Yes. I'm fine.*

Echo wished he could actually hear her, or better yet, see her; he strongly suspected—knowing her as well as he did— that she was putting on a good front for him.

"Do you know...?"

Two zaps. *No, not yet.*

"Meg..."

N.O. M.A.T.T.E.R. J.O.B. T.O. D.O.

Echo closed his eyes for a brief moment, gathering him- self.

"All right, partner," he told her. "Then let's do it."

One long tingle. *Okay, let's go.*

Lu'vin'du'v watched the one-sided conversation come to an end, then made a single observation.

"You are fond of her?"

"Meg's my partner, Lu'vin'du'v," Echo looked up and replied, as if that said everything that needed saying.

"So you are close."

"Why this sudden interest in the specifics of our relationship?" Echo asked, somewhat annoyed...as well as trying to hide just what he felt for that partner, given that partner was listening and heretofore hadn't seemed to recognize how he felt. *The last thing I need to do is to throw a declaration of love into the works right now,* he thought, rueful. *She really might hit the floor if I did that, so soon after the shock about her possible lifespan.*

"Because Birdy believes his inability to accurately read you may be due to the possibility that you subconsciously learned at least some blocking techniques from her."

"Now there's an intriguing notion." Echo's eyebrows rose. "Is it a likely one?"

* * *

Omega stared at the monitor blankly.

"Well, blast an' damn," she said into the air, not sure whether to try for whimsical or deadly serious. "Bad enough that I don't know what's going down inside me. Now my own peculiar brand of weirdness may be rubbin' off on the folks closest to me." She looked up at Fox, Alpha Two and Alpha Seven. "Whaddaya think, guys?"

Romeo and India shrugged, nonchalant, attempting to encourage their friend and patently unworried about themselves, but Tare and Yankee edged away slightly. Fox noticed, and glared at them. They blinked, becoming aware of his ire, then offered him slight, surreptitious shrugs, uncertain what to do or say, but unable to hide their discomfort at the possibility.

Omega noticed, too, but ignored the reaction; it hurt, but there was little she could do about it. She had, quite some time back, learned the hard way that most people, even other Division One agents, were uncomfortable when forced to confront her...unusual nature. This was especially true when aspects of that nature, such as her latent telepathy and precognition, impinged upon others; those people who knew about it tended to be uncomfortable about the whole thing, especially if they were not close enough to her to recognize that she tried hard to avoid breaching others' privacy. Echo, Romeo, India, and Fox, as well as Fox's significant other, Zebra—her Agency 'family'—were really the only ones she could count on to consistently take it in stride. Echo in particular, once reticent and reserved about the matter, now tended to be accepting of the whole thing, and had been known to actually 'invite her in,' specifically asking her to attempt telepathic contact with him, trusting her to maintain his privacy.

And Echo, God bless him, defends my humanness with a vengeance, into the bargain, Omega thought with fond affection. *Like he just did. He acts like he believes it, too. He's either an awfully good actor, or he's...flat wrong, but...that level of trust and acceptance sure helps when I run up against...against the rejection. I really wish he felt about me the way I do about him...but it doesn't matter, I guess.*

Is Echo worried about all this? I sure am. I wonder if I AM affecting him. I suppose it's possible. We have made telepathic contact in the past, on several occasions, for various reasons. But Echo has completely human genetics. That argues that it shouldn't be possible...but he's also reached out to me, rather than me to him, and successfully connected before, so...huh.

"Hm. Beats the heck outta me," she murmured, shaking her head.

* * *

"No idea whatsoever," Echo answered Lu'vin'du'v. "I don't know the probability of a nontelepathic human learning a telepathic block from being in close, extended proximity to an enhanced human, 'cause it's never happened before, at least to my knowledge. Or anybody else in the Agency's knowledge, for that matter."

"How much time do you spend together?"

"A lot. Most of our waking time, I suppose. Closest...closest friend I've got. We enjoy doing the same things off-duty, and as partners, our quarters adjoin. Which means we hang out together, even when we're not actually working, pretty much all the time. Meg, are you listening, baby?"

A tingle. *Yes, I'm listening.*

"She's listening," Echo told Lu'vin'du'v. "Do you think it's possible, Meg?" Echo focused his attention on the area of his collarbone.

One zap. Two zaps. Three zaps.

Echo laughed.

"What is it?" Lu'vin'du'v asked, puzzled by his reaction.

"Remember: One zap to the transponder means yes, two means no," Echo reminded him. "Meg just gave me three zaps."

"Which means?"

"It means, to use Meg's words, 'Beats the heck outta me'." Echo's collarbone tingled once, and he chuckled as he stood. "She just said, 'Yep.' And probably smeared her hand over her face into the bargain." He addressed the bug. "Meg, I know you're wondering about this, and the answer is, 'No, I'm not.'"

"No, you're not—what?" Lu'vin'du'v asked.

"Worried about it. If Meg really is rubbing off on me, well...I can live with that. I don't have a problem with it at all. In fact, I can't think of anybody I'd rather have rub off on me." Echo put a hand on Lu'vin'du'v's shoulder. "C'mon. We can wonder about it later. It's almost time to go."

Chapter 8

The run-down burgundy van pulled up to the plaza around the knoll, turned into a service drive, and kept going, out onto the grass. The driver remained seated, as two men, one in scruffy black denim with several days' growth of beard, the other man clean-shaven, in immaculate tan coveralls, got out. They went to the back of the van and started unloading a pallet of sod.

Moments later, the two men and the pallet of sod had vanished, and the van was pulling back into the street.

* * *

"Tiln," Echo told his mobile Botanoid cocoon as it carried him along—Echo presumed—just underground, "I need a spot where I can see, but stay unnoticed."

I really wonder what this looks like from outside, Echo thought, intensely curious. *Is it even noticeable? Or do we look like the world's largest mole? If Meg's watching, maybe I can ask her later. Tiln was right. His camo technique is hard to explain. He's doin' it right now, and I still don't get it.*

"Understood," the rustling voice answered from all around him. "Eb'vuv wants to know the time...again."

Echo glanced at his wrist chronometer.

"Eleven twenty-one," he replied. "Five minutes later than the last time he asked, though you don't have to tell him I said THAT. But we're in good shape, time-wise."

"I will tell him...only what he needs to know."

"Good. And thanks."

"Zzs asks if you are...lonely..."

"No. I'm fine."

"Here," Tiln sighed in annoyance, as a cavity opened in the wall of Echo's green capsule, "this is a communications device by which each of you may contact the others. I tire of passing messages." Echo reached out and took the small communications mechanism from the cavity, dropping it into his shirt pocket.

"Thanks, Tiln," Echo said. "Is everyone almost in position?"

"Everyone for whom I am responsible is already in position except you. Eb'vuv is near, perhaps some twenty of your meters away, and the Zargothians are on the very top of the knoll, where they will have the best angle for their weapons."

"Are you keeping them hidden?"

"Yes, of course. I will have to open in order for them to fire or be injured otherwise, but they will remain hidden until we depart. And now you are in place."

The pod around Echo opened, unfurling like giant flower petals, and he found himself crouched in a dense clump of shrubbery—it was under the copse of trees at the rear of the knoll, a little way past the top near the fence, but it now had a thick landscaping hedge, most likely comprised of Tiln, he presumed. He glanced about, and discovered he had a clear view of the entire area, while remaining secreted himself. But if he needed to hook up with Omega quickly, he was in trouble: It might as well have been miles to the nearest sidewalk, and with Tiln on duty, having anything even remotely plant-based in proximity could prove deadly. And there was a reason it was called the GRASSY knoll.

"Echo?"

"Yeah, Tiln?"

"Eb'vuv says you may need these as well." The disembodied voice sighed around him even as a small green mound formed beside Echo, and its top cracked open like a seed pod, revealing a compact pair of electronic binoculars. "This is for lookout duty. He also requests yet another time report. He cannot be bothered to use the communications device, it seems."

"Thanks again, Tiln," Echo said, pulling the comm radio out of his pocket and the binoculars from the pod. He tried not to think of how much the communications device looked like the device from a certain classic television show, otherwise he was apt to use a quote from it, and confuse the hell out of the assassin team. *Not that that would necessarily be a BAD thing,* he considered, *but it might not be all that healthy for me.* "Eb'vuv? It's Echo."

"Go ahead, Echo."

"I got the binocs you sent; they're pretty sweet. Requested time tag is..." Echo glanced at his wrist chronometer again, "eleven twenty-eight. Thirty-two minutes to go..."

* * *

At the hotel, Omega had put her personal worries out of her mind and was coordinating the President's departure.

"Let me assure you, Mr. President," she told the head of state, "we will take good care of you. I know we aren't who you're used to working with, but under the circumstances, we are far and away your most qualified protection against this threat. My team is composed of hand-picked, highly-trained, extra-special forces agents. I'm proud of 'em, and I have due cause to be. You're in excellent, very capable hands, I swear."

"Why haven't I been informed of your organization's existence until now?" he demanded to know.

"Plausible deniability, sir. It keeps us able to function, and you—and numerous other heads of state—able to deny our existence."

"But I know now. And so does the rest of my security."

"Mr. President, do you trust me?"

"After what you've shown me, and what you're trying to do for me? There's ...something about you. Yes. I trust you."

"Ask everyone else to leave the room," Omega told the President.

"You heard the lady," the President responded, glancing around the room, and the other agents, Division One and Secret Service alike, left.

Omega produced a small gold device, similar in appearance to a pocket photometric chemical analyzer but considerably smaller. She activated it, and swept the room.

"All right, if there are any observing devices, whether audio or video, they don't work now. And anything they've transmitted in the last ten minutes just got irretrievably corrupted."

"I thought your colleagues already did that."

"They did. Just making sure. Now, John, let's talk for a second..."

* * *

"Again?" Echo wondered, surprised.

"Again," Tiln's voice—his distinctly annoyed voice—responded from the foliage around Echo.

"That guy's on pins and needles, isn't he?"

"I think you would express it, 'No shit,'" Tiln replied. "Were his pay not so good, I should not still be here." There was a sigh like wind in the trees, then he added, "No. Never mind the pay. He is not a worthy leader. I wish I had known that at the outset. Now...it is impossible to back out."

"...Sorry to hear that. I'll...watch my back."

"That is a good plan, where he is concerned. Well, you had best call him, before he blows his xylem."

"Right."

* * *

"How's it coming, Eb'vuv?" Echo asked over the communicator moments later. "Per your request, it's eleven forty-two. The Prez oughta be leaving the hotel in about three minutes. Are Birdy and Lu'vin'du'v in place yet?"

"No, Echo, they are not. There appear to be some Division One agents that you did not anticipate, and they are blocking the planned route to the building roof."

"Really? Oh, well, be patient. They'll probably move in a few minutes, once it's a little closer to time for the Prez to come by."

"They had better..."

* * *

"WHAT?!" Omega cried, as she read Tare's text message on her cell phone. She grabbed the headset from her jacket pocket and put it on, placing it on the speaker setting so the others could hear as well.

"...Blocking the planned route to the building roof."

"What? Oh, well, be patient. They'll probably move in a few minutes, once it's a little closer to time for the Prez to come by."

"They had better..."

"Jack! What the HELL do your people think they're doing?! They're gonna blow the whole thing! Get them out of there! NOW!!" Omega yelled across the room at the Secret Service chief, and he scrambled for his comm, appalled.

* * *

Echo watched through the binoculars as the Secret Service agents—he could tell they weren't real Division One agents because of the particular style of sunglasses—answered cell phones, then rapidly moved away from the side of the building. Within moments they had vanished from the rooftop altogether.

Way to go, Meg, he thought. He smiled and pulled the communicator.

"Eb'vuv? The coast looks clear now. Get our boys to the roof."

"Done."

* * *

"Mr. President? It's time. Let's go."

Omega led the President of the United States to the limousine that would be used for his travel, as Alpha Two followed him closely, and they signaled the other Alpha teams that would fill in the rest of the motorcade. Romeo climbed into the driver's seat; Omega placed the President in the back seat and got in beside him. India took the seat on the other side of the President.

"This doesn't look like my usual limo," the President remarked, as he settled into the back seat.

"Well...let's just say that nothing is as it appears to be," Omega said quietly. "We brought something in, special, for the occasion."

* * *

Omega sat beside the President and mentally reviewed strategy and position, looking for anything she and the rest of Alpha Line might have overlooked.

The sniper was on the roof of the office building to the northeast of Dealey Plaza, accompanied by an undercover Division One agent from Va'du'sha'ā, prepared to stop the sniper using whatever means necessary. The assassins' backup firepower—some four beings strong, emphasis on strong—hid near the top of the grassy knoll, along with her partner and a mutant Botanoid, capable of morphing into the indigenous flora as camouflage. The electronics engineer and the getaway driver both hid in the transport van, one block over from Dealey Plaza. And Omega and her team—plus one; said Glu'g'ik undercover agent as adjunct—were responsible for neutralizing all of them...and seeing to it that her partner and the Glu'g'ik agent were safely extracted.

The motorcade was making good time from the hotel at the international airport, headed downtown on the interstate. The motorcade route had been diligently cleared by Dallas police, and everything was on schedule. The President would pass the grassy knoll at precisely twelve noon, slowing down for a photo op, en route to a planned twelve-fifteen arrival at campaign headquarters.

The Secret Service patrolled the perimeter, moving along with the motorcade.

Omega and Alpha Two occupied the limousine with the President; a significant number of the other motorcade members—including most of the 'motorcycle cops'—were other Alpha Line teams, undercover in one form or another. Fox and several more Division One partnerships would be waiting at their destination, tag-teaming Omega's group.

Echo, of course, was at the grassy knoll, undercover himself. Virtually in the middle of the backup firepower, not to mention the living camouflage. Where it would be the most difficult to extract him. At least, in one piece. And that worried his partner intensely.

Echo, you're awfully quiet now, Ace, Omega thought hard, listening to the loud silence on her headset. *I sure would like some sign everything's all right on your end.* But if he received her mental message, Echo made no response.

Omega sat beside the President and tried not to fidget.

* * *

Omega was intently listening to Echo's body transponder via the wireless headset, as the motorcade approached the grassy knoll from the west. The transponder had become intermittently active once more as the limousine had neared. Everything sounded as if it were proceeding according to plan.

Omega continued to mull their status: All of the Secret Service agents that would normally be in the motorcade had been replaced by Division One agents—largely pulled from Alpha Line—and the Secret Service was specifically stationed around the periphery, as decoys and observation posts. Romeo drove the limo, and India sat on the far side of the President.

She herself was still sitting in the back seat of the Presidential limo, beside the Commander in Chief himself, and she had carefully positioned herself on the left, between him and the unusually-verdant terrain under scrutiny.

If anybody gets hit, it needs to be me, she had decided, long since...though she had told no one of her decision in that regard. *I'm not keen on it, but better me than anybody else I love. Never mind the President. 'To protect and serve,' and all that.*

Just then, her morbid thoughts were distracted by Echo's comm coming to life again.

* * *

"...Any more sign of Division One, Echo?"

"Yeah, Eb'vuv. There's a couple agents up on the bridge... at least one on the roof of the book depository...several in the street crowd. Just like we figured."

"What about in the motorcade?"

"Hang on and lemme take a look. These are some really

nice virtual-image binocs, by the way...I didn't know you could get these on the street...no, I see nothing but standard Secret Service around the Prez. The Agency must have figured they had everything sewn up so tight, they didn't need to put any-body that close."

"Their mistake."

"Yeah."

* * *

"Good job, Echo," Omega murmured, giving the other oc-cupants of the limo a reassuring thumbs-up. "We're in good shape, y'all. Mr. President, you're gonna be just fine. My part-ner—the guy that's infiltrated the hit squad—is one of the most experienced Agents that Division One has got, and he's right on top of things. Romeo, stay close to that control. I'm expect-ing the signal from Echo any minute."

"You know it, pretty lady."

* * *

Just then, Echo's voice said in the earphone, *"Birdy—are you and Lu'vin'du'v in position?"*

"Affirmative, Terran." Birdy's voice dripped hostility. *"We are both here, and both ready...to be done with this, and off this trrrblrn excuse of a world. A sentiment I am sure you share. All is in readiness on your end?"*

"Yep. Eb'vuv, tell the Zargothians to stand by."

"I'm ready any time, Echo," Zzs's voice said, as sugges-tive as the alien woman knew how to make it...which wasn't much, really. *"Just say the word."*

Faint hisses from the male Zargothians sounded in the background.

Omega raised her hand.

Romeo watched carefully in the rearview mirror.

"Okay, boys and girls," Echo's voice said, *"commence Operation: High Noon."*

* * *

"NOW!!" Omega cried, bringing her hand down sharply, and Romeo hit the control in the limousine. Instantly the limousine shed its outer body panel camouflage, revealing a special black Lincoln limo—one of the Agency's own diplomatic vehicles, 'hot-rodded' by Fox himself—in mid-morph. A faint yellow flicker briefly formed a truncated ellipsoid about the vehicle, then faded.

The President's unusual vehicle shot through the opening that suddenly appeared between the other vehicles of the motorcade, and out of harm's way, just as the pavement—where the limo had been—exploded like a mortar round had hit.

* * *

Echo was moving by the time the word 'noon' had left his lips. As soon as he'd seen the first panel spring off the limo, he'd known what Fox and Omega had come up with, and he also knew the assassin team would realize he had double-crossed them. So Echo was headed for the nearest non-botanical cover he could find. Fortunately, there was a concrete memorial pavilion only a few yards away with extensive paving, and he made a beeline for it.

Abruptly Echo was knocked off his feet and flat on his face by the 'grass.' But the grass did nothing else, which he found interesting. *Maybe I made the discord work for me better than I thought,* he considered.

Before he could even catch his breath, however, he felt himself lifted bodily into the air, as a harsh, grating female voice spoke from behind him.

"Look here. It's the Division One Agent who talks so heartbrokenly about betrayal. I feel so sorry for you, Echo. Or I will—later. Right now...you're MINE."

Zzs wrapped her short, thick arms around Echo's waist and began to squeeze like a boa constrictor, forcing the breath out of him. Echo's eyes widened in horror as he realized the particular position into which Zzs was maneuvering him, and he knew he was in big trouble.

He struggled, systematically trying several different tactics, but without his feet—or some part of him—on the ground, he had little leverage against the incredible force the lustful, angry Zargothian woman wielded.

Damn, damn, damn, he thought, as her arms tightened. His body shifted position against hers—revealing a disturbingly-shaped bulge in her body—and he realized he was running out of time to escape. *The supposed top agent in Division One is about to get raped. And I dunno if they CAN put me back together again after she gets done with me. Let alone if I'd want to be. I gotta do something!*

Just then Echo heard his partner's voice yelling his name from somewhere in the Plaza.

"ECHO!! Kiss her! Then try Bravo-two-four!"

"What?!"

"Trust me! Just do it! Go for the roof of her mouth!"

"Aw, damn, Meg! You've gotta be kidding!"

"DO IT! NOW! Unless you'd prefer a little MORE intimacy!"

Echo immediately twisted around in the Zargothian woman's grasp, caught Zzs's face in his hands, closed his eyes, and kissed her hard.

Shit, he thought, as the tip of his tongue contacted the roof of her mouth. *Meg better know what she's doing. Kissing her is bad enough, but Zzs could bite my tongue clean off like this. Of course, that might be better than having to pull it back into my own mouth right now. Gargling with fluoro-antimonic acid is definitely on the schedule after this. Assuming I survive long enough.*

Suddenly Zzs jerked away with a hissing laugh, and Echo realized what had happened.

It tickles! he thought; jerking her head back toward him, Echo went for her palate again. Zzs let out a series of hisses, the Zargothian equivalent of a giggle, and quickly tried to adjust her grip on Echo's middle, in an attempt to put an end to the kiss and keep him from tickling her further.

"NOW, Echo! MOVE!" Omega's voice urged, and Echo thankfully broke the kiss, twisted around, and instantly kicked back with both feet, contacting Zargothian shins hard, using his attacker's own body as the leverage he had lacked. Simultaneously he arched his spine to slam the back of his head into Zzs's face with as much power as he could generate.

With a grunt of unexpected pain—Zargothian facial tissues were almost as sensitive and nerve-filled as any other humanoid's—Zzs loosened her grip enough for Echo to bend forward, doubling up and gathering himself in preparation for a leap, spring-boarding off Zzs's shins. Just as he leapt, he heard the whine of a blaster discharge shoot by overhead, and suddenly he was sprawled on the grass, rolling down the slope, gasping, spitting, and holding his bruised sides. Hands slipped under Echo's arms when he reached the sidewalk at the bottom, pulling him gently to his feet, as a familiar voice behind him murmured in his ear.

"Are you all right?"

"...Y-yeah," Echo panted, sucking in air.

"She didn't get—"

"No."

"Good." A hand patted his shoulder, then pushed lightly. "C'mon, big guy, you need to hightail it outta here, as fast as we can get you away. Make tracks."

Recognizing Omega's soft voice and gentle touch, Echo never looked back. He just headed in the direction she nudged him—which was across Dealey Plaza toward the courthouse— at an all-out sprint. He heard a couple of blaster shots from her weapon, then her running footsteps fell in behind him.

"You won't be dating her any time soon. I do hope you're not too broken up about it," she told him then, measuring her breath in order to speak without slowing.

"Not hardly," Echo answered in kind.

"Right! Over the railing!" Omega panted, and Echo vaulted the metal fencing and dove right, behind a concrete abutment leading to an underground storage area. He rolled and came up in a crouch behind the abutment, trying not to grab his bruised sides in pain.

Romeo and India, both wearing headsets, were waiting for

him there. The morphed Lincoln had gotten the President to the conference center in well less than a minute, while allowing plenty of time for Omega and Alpha Two to unload him into the hands of Fox and Company—with rather less pomp and ceremony than the head of state was used to, but he accepted the matter without complaint—and still return the trio of occupants in time to extract Echo.

Romeo handed him a headset and a fresh blaster; India checked his ribs carefully, and surveyed him for serious injuries with a handheld medscanner. Echo put on the headset as he glanced around, spotting a hoverpod tucked behind the abutment.

"Where'd Meg go?" he asked, not seeing her.

"Listen," Romeo told him, tapping his own headset, and Echo recognized Omega's voice barking orders into his ear.

"She said to tell you—and I quote—'Ah'm headin' up this posse, Ace,'" India told him with a smile, and Echo grinned.

* * *

"All right, the President's safe and ready for his speech, and Echo's extracted!" Omega, standing in the middle of the action, yelled into the mouthpiece of her transceiver headset as she fired off a round at a fleeing Zargothian. Both blasters were in hand, and she wielded them as necessary. "Alpha Seven, that means you are now free of monitor duty! Top-floor units, begin rooftop mop-up! Alpha Five and -Six, sweep the hillside! Don't forget the Botanoid! I wounded him, but he is still dangerous! Glu'gu'ik unit, rendezvous with your undercover cop A.S.A.P.! These are not playmates, people! Lethal force authorized if surrender refused or resistance encountered! Alpha Seven, apprehend the getaway van. Do not harm the driver—repeat, DO NOT harm the driver. Brain-bleach only; remember, he's an innocent civilian and did NOT know about the assassination conspiracy. The Delzantian with him is another matter; take him into custody! All teams, stand by for containment ops and brain-bleaching of civilian bystanders. Alpha Two, report on Alpha Chief's condition!"

"Echo is fine, Omega," India's voice answered in her ear. "A little banged up, and he could use a couple hot meals in him, but he's in good shape. He's monitoring."

"Good! Alpha Two, join Five and Six, please."

"On it," Romeo replied.

"Echo, I need you overhead in the hoverpod, Ace, to start picking out the participants in this caper so we don't miss anybody. It's got a force field if it turns out you need it, and you probably ought to go ahead and use it, just in case. We don't need anybody taking pot shots at you, at this point. Can do?"

"On my way, Meg," Echo responded.

* * *

"Hey, Meg," Echo murmured into his headset, as he performed lookout duty high over Dealey Plaza in the force-shielded hoverpod.

"Go, Echo."

"How bad did you wound Tiln?"

"Who's Tiln?"

"The Botanoid."

"Oh. Bad enough to slow him down, but not bad enough to stop him. Zzs, on the other hand, isn't gonna be bothering anyone else, ever again. As soon as you broke free and started running, she drew down...on me or you, I'm not sure which. Either way, I made sure not to miss."

"Roger that. I'm not sorry about her. But try to avoid hurting Tiln any more than you can help; I think his heart wasn't in this operation...or the Botanoid equivalent of a heart, whatever."

"You think he was coerced?"

"I think several members of the assassin team were coerced, Zzs at the top of the list, although I suspect that was more to keep her reined in than anything. Tiln...didn't want to be there at the end game, I'm pretty sure; he just didn't have a way out by that point. He had an opportunity to kill me, but he only slowed me down instead. He might work with us."

"Alpha Line teams! Do you copy? Try not to wound the

Botanoid if he'll come peacefully. Coercion may be involved. We may be able to convince him to turn Coalition's evidence."

Several variants on, "Copy," "We read you," and "Roger that," came back on the comm, and Echo nodded to himself.

* * *

When it was all over, Romeo and India took Echo back to the hotel.

"Where is everybody?" Echo asked, looking around the empty suite. "There was a small army at the plaza. Where'd they all go?"

"Handlin' security—and cover-up—at the Prez's speech," Romeo told him. "General mop-up. But Meg figured you'd rather have a chance t' get cleaned up, after several days 'ridin' the range' as it were. Nice hot shower an' all. Even a soft, clean bed, if ya wanna stretch out for a few."

"Mmm," Echo murmured his appreciation, "leave it to Meg to think of everything. Yeah, that sounds great. I was getting to where I couldn't live with myself. Hope I'm not too offensive in that regard, guys! Point me toward the shower."

"Thataway, cowpoke." India pointed with a grin. "A transponder extraction kit is waiting for you on the vanity countertop, along with a disposable personal hygiene kit, with antiperspirant, toothbrush, and the like. If you're as grubby as I would be after several days of what you've been through, I recommend shower, THEN implant extraction. You're less likely to get a localized infection that way."

"Got it. Mouthwash?"

"Huh? Why? What do you need with mouthwash?"

"Dammit, India, YOU try kissing a Zargothian sometime... shit..." Echo almost spat. He DID make disgusted smacking sounds with his mouth, as he remembered the incident in question. "Bleh," he added, for good measure. Romeo and India grinned.

"Check the hygiene kit an' th' cabinet, Echo," Romeo suggested, as his ex-partner entered the master suite, en route to the shower. Echo was already peeling out of the faded black chambray shirt as he headed through the bathroom door, closing it behind himself. Moments later, the bathroom door opened partway, and a pile of 'dirty black denim was tossed out, onto the floor. A hand, attached to a bare arm, reached out and carefully, respectfully, laid a certain black cowboy hat and tooled belt with silver buckle on the nearest cabinet surface within reach. The door closed again.

"Aw," India noted with a smile. "He wore the belt we gave him, and the hat that Fox and Zebra gave him."

"Yeah, an' don't touch 'em," came Echo's voice from the other side of the door, over the gurgle of a tap being turned on. "I know they're dirty as hell now, but I got people can clean 'em good as new."

"Okay," India agreed, as the gurgle changed to a hiss. A wisp of steam filtered under the door, rising in the cooler air of the bedroom.

"Hey, Echo," Romeo called, staring down at the pile of filthy denim, "whaddaya want done with th' rest o' your clothes?"

"Burn 'em," came faintly over the sound of flowing water.

* * *

The President's speech was just concluding when the rest of Alpha Line, fresh from mop-up operations at Dealey Plaza, quietly entered the convention center and rendezvoused with Fox. They unobtrusively spread out around the large room, relieving the Secret Service agents that had been involved. Omega moved to stand beside Fox and looked across the room at Murphy, who nodded in understanding, then gestured to his agents to follow as he left the room. As the thunderous applause died, Fox turned to Omega.

"Is everything ready? Did the plan go down properly? All civilians brain-bleached? Is ECHO okay?"

"Yes, Fox," she answered, confident. "To all of that. It all went down perfectly, right according to plan. All of it. Echo's a little bruised and banged up, 'cause Zzs grabbed him before I could take her out, but that was as much as happened. He's safe, most likely back at the hotel by now. And with his help, we even got one of the assassin squad to surrender, and turn Coalition's evidence for us. Everything's under control."

"Very good, tekhter. Let's go."

They moved forward through the crowd, and met the President as he stepped down from the podium.

"Congratulations, Mr. President," Fox said. "Excellent speech. Pity I can't vote."

"Why not? Oh, because of the, um, special job you do?"

"No; I'm an Israeli citizen. And a dead one, at that. Come with us, please."

"It's time, isn't it?" the President asked in a subdued voice, as Fox and Omega led him into the 'green room,' where the Secret Service had assembled.

"Yes sir, it is," Omega said, as she and Fox pulled their goggle-glasses.

"Before you...do what you have to do," the President said, stifling a sigh, "let me say how much I appreciate what you've done today. I've never seen a better-run operation. You saved my life, and I'll always be grateful—even if I won't remember it."

"Thank you, Mr. President, but it's all part of the job description," Omega said with a smile. Murphy moved over to stand before her.

"You're telling us that this sort of stuff is all in a day's work for you?" he asked, voice quiet.

"Yep. I'm afraid so," Omega responded, still smiling.

"If this is what you do on a regular basis, how do I sign up?" he murmured.

Omega glanced at Fox, who nodded and pulled an extra pair of goggle-glasses from inside his jacket. Fox swept his gaze around the ranks of other Secret Service agents, querying, but no one else came forward. The President watched as Murphy turned and donned the special glasses, taking his place with the ranked Division One agents; then the head of state extended a hand. His expression was sober, and sincere.

"You've been a good bodyguard, Jack. Thanks for everything. I'll miss you."

"Likewise, sir," Jack Murphy said for the last time, as Omega pulled out her brain bleacher. "Godspeed, Mr. President."

"And to you, Jack."

A multicolored, holographic flash lit the room.

* * *

A clean-shaven Echo emerged from the hotel bedroom straightening the tie of his fresh Suit just as the rest of the Dallas Office task force entered and started packing equipment. The newest Division One member, Agent Mu, followed Fox in the door.

"Hello, Echo," Fox greeted his department chief in passing. "Good work, zun. Glad you're back in one piece."

"Yeah, Fox. That was...an interesting 'vacation'. Speaking of which, where's Meg?"

"Right here, Echo," said the tall, brown-haired, dark-eyed woman with the pixyish hairstyle entering the room.

Echo stopped dead in his tracks, stupefied, as he got his first good look at his partner since their abortive time off.

* * *

Omega walked up to him, studying his dumbfounded expression, puzzled as to its cause.

"Oh, that's right," she said, suddenly realizing what was provoking his reaction. "You haven't actually seen me since you 'killed' me. I came back as a brunette."

"Aw, damn, Meg," Echo said quietly, putting out a hand and almost, but not quite, stroking her hair. "So that was you sitting beside the President. I didn't look that close; I assumed it was India."

"Yep." Omega nodded. "It was me. Don't like it, huh?" she asked.

"It's your hair. Do what you want to with it." Echo shrugged. "I'll...get used to it."

Omega turned away.

"That's not what I asked..." she grumbled under her breath. Echo leaned over and murmured in her ear with conviction.

"No. I. Don't. Like. It."

"Okay. Fair enough. I'm curious, though: why not?" Omega wondered, then caught her breath. "Oh, blast an' damn, Echo! I didn't think...it reminds you of Chase, doesn't it?" she asked, as gentle as she knew how to be.

* * *

"No. You're just supposed to be..." Echo paused, remembering a certain muddled dream, "a palomino," he finished, with conviction.

"I think I prefer being called a girl, to being called a horse." Omega snorted as she walked into the bedroom, over to the mirror, and stared into it. Echo turned in the doorway to watch. "I can fix this, at least. Besides, I gotta peel 'em out before they drive me crazy. Well, craziER, anyway." She fished tinted contacts out of her eyes, throwing the disposable lenses in the wastebasket and rubbing watering blue orbs. "Ahh... that's much better."

"Yeah, it is. Dammit, you just don't look right, Meg."

"Be patient, Echo," Omega told him with a smile as she walked back to his side and laid a teasing hand on his shoulder. "I'll get back to looking normal. Truth to tell, I didn't think you'd even notice." Echo briefly looked astonished, covering it quickly; Omega did not appear to see the expression. "I know it's a little disconcerting—I don't even recognize myself in the mirror. But the hair color's temporary—well, they call it 'semi-permanent,' because it doesn't IMMEDIATELY wash out—so it'll wash out eventually."

"But you CUT it."

"It'll grow," she grinned. "This from the man who wanted one of us shot."

* * *

At that remark, Echo jammed his hands deep in his pockets and leaned against the wall, pulling gently away from her hand. Instead of responding, he studiously looked across the suite at the Alpha Two and Seven teams, carefully packing his command center. A distinctly indigo wave of dejection, capped by a light foam of shame, washed through him. After several moments, he offered commentary.

"Have you talked to Fox about it yet?" He avoided the blue gaze.

"Talked to Fox about what?"

"Your transfer."

"Wha-huh?"

"You know. For...the whole shooting thing."

"Oh, that. No."

Echo glanced at her, and Omega shrugged, the hint of a satisfied smile in her eyes.

"I don't see anybody shot," she told him. A tsunami of relief hit his mind, gut, and heart, in that order of impact.

"Thank God," he muttered, deeply sincere.

"Amen," she added, as the smile reached her lips. She elbowed him gently, affectionately; fortunately, it nudged his arm, rather than his ribs. Warmth followed the relief.

"That," he agreed. He offered her a half-grin, the left corner of his mouth quirking up a little bit. Then he lightly hip-checked her, and she snickered.

"A whole lotta that," she amended, and they both grinned.

* * *

India walked up to the bantering, teasing pair just then.

"Meg? I just got word from Headquarters, about, um, about your medical tests. You know, the special ones?"

Both members of Alpha One sobered immediately, and Omega felt her insides lurch with apprehension. India started to draw Omega aside, but Echo straightened up and laid a light hand on his partner's shoulder.

Omega glanced over that shoulder into troubled, expectant brown eyes.

* * *

"Go ahead, India," Omega said then, turning back to the former ER physician while edging closer to Echo, and he rec-

316

ognized her carefully-hidden anxiety in the move—she was subtly requesting support and comfort from him. "We're listening."

"Both of us," Echo added, and stepped forward to stand close behind his partner, still holding her shoulder and giving her the moral support she needed, as they waited for the news. The position and light touch implied, *I'm here for you, baby*. Omega drew a deep breath and nodded. India, seeing the interaction and apparently comprehending it, waited until they had both settled before launching into the results.

"Well, the medics say your metabolic processes ARE accelerated—quite highly. 'To an amazing degree,' were Zarnix's words. But," India continued, as a worried Echo brought both hands to a staggered Omega's shoulders then, steadying her as she swayed for a moment, "evidently your various bodily systems—all the way down to the cellular level—were also altered to compensate. That way, you wouldn't...burn out...before you were needed. Kinda like what the bastard did with the snake venom, I guess. To confirm it, the medics said to ask you something."

"What?" Omega asked, voice low and so quiet that India and Echo both had to lean forward to hear.

"Have you ever had weight problems?"

"Well...yeah, I suppose you could put it that way, but not like what most people have. I usually don't gain it, I lose it. Have to eat like...a horse," Omega grinned lopsidedly over her shoulder at Echo, "to maintain an Alpha Line activity level."

"I can vouch for that," Echo averred. "Damn, can I vouch for that. Some days, she can out-eat me. And she's nowhere near the size of my frame; I've been wondering where she stashed it all. It just depends on what we've been doing."

"That's what they thought. Must be nice," a rueful India smiled, and Echo grinned in amusement and relief. "Here I've been envying you your ability to eat pretty much anything, anytime, and never gain an ounce. But it turns out that you have to, just in order to fuel that hyperdrive body and brain. But the medics say as long as you take reasonable care of yourself, you should have a normal, human life expectancy. As healthy as you are, and with your body's ability to compensate for things, you might even outlive some of the rest of us."

Echo felt Omega's shoulders sag slightly in relief, and he squeezed them gently, comfortingly. It translated as, *See there, baby? Everything's gonna be okay.*

"All right," she sighed. "Thanks, India. It's really good to know. I was kinda—"

"Echo, Omega," Fox interrupted, entering and heading across the room, "your vacation never really got going, at least not properly. Would you like to head back to the Ranch and re-start the clock?"

Echo and Omega looked at each other for a long moment. Then, as one, they both reached for the command center case that Tare held, saying, "Here. Give me that."

* * *

"There IS one thing we need to do back at Headquarters before we return you to your previously-scheduled vacation, though, I think," Fox decided. "India? Do you have an update on that?"

"Yes, Fox, I do," India said, looking up. "Sorry. I meant to tell you, but what with Mu coming on board, and Meg's results coming back, and all..."

"Not a problem, yung froy. The last couple of hours have been...hectic. I assume, based on your faces, that Omega's medical news was good?"

"It was, Fox," India averred. "She's ramped up, yes, but everything else is, too. It all compensates. Meg's fine."

"Excellent. What about the other news?"

"Things should be ready by the time we all get back to Headquarters, according to Zebra."

"Very good then. Echo, Omega, please accompany the rest of the team back to Headquarters, and I'll personally see to it you get sent back on that vacation just as soon as matters resolve there."

Echo glanced at Omega, who looked back at him, raised her eyebrows, and shrugged.

"Sure thing, Boss," he said. "If you need us, we're there. You know that."

"Let's go, then," Fox decreed. "You both probably need to grab some more leisure clothing from your quarters, anyway."

"That's a good point," Omega agreed. "I dunno if that pair of jeans I wore across half of Texas would ever get clean again. Never mind one leg getting sliced wide open to treat a snake bite. And there wasn't much left of the shirt, either, by the time I got done leaving markers for Echo to find."

"Yeah, I hear ya. I just had 'em cremate mine," Echo averred with a shrug. "It was a lost cause. C'mon, baby, let's go."

* * *

Upon arrival at Headquarters, Fox took Alpha One straight through to the Medical department, brooking no delays and no detours.

"No, this is where we're needed," he told them, when Echo protested.

"But I don't get it," Echo said, mildly irked. "I'm fine. Meg is fine, too. I'll admit, after that rattlesnake bite, I was... well. For a minute or two there, I really thought she was a goner. And I was pissed as hell at that snake. But she's okay. Why do we need to go by the medlab?"

"Because there's someone waiting there to see you," Fox said, raising an eyebrow; his expression said *Don't question it, just do it,* in a look that beings knew—and obeyed—from one side of the galaxy to the other. Echo shrugged, and kept going.

Omega caught Fox's eye from where she walked behind Echo's back, trailing the two men, and sent him a querying look; Fox pressed his lips together to hide a smile, and gave her the slightest nod. Omega glanced at Echo to ensure his back was still toward her and that he couldn't see her in any reflective surfaces, then she punched a jubilant fist into the air, grinning hugely. Fox bit his lip, bowing his head to hide the answering grin that threatened to give him away.

The trio turned the corner into another corridor, then passed through the big automatic emergency doors leading into Medical. The main lobby was empty, which was unusual... and carefully planned.

"The place is deader than Arplact in a rainstorm. Which I guess is good, after the operation we just pulled off. All right, so who needs to see us here?" Echo demanded.

"Not 'us,' Ace—you," Omega told him, as she and Fox drifted back.

"There you are," a smiling Zebra said, coming out of her office into the main reception area. Behind her were two others—Zarnix in his usual black scrubs and lab coat, and a smiling woman in black medlab scrubs who appeared to be around 40 years of age, her glossy dark hair neatly pulled back and fastened in a long braid, her smooth skin a lovely golden bronze, chocolate brown eyes twinkling. "Echo, I've got someone here that you might just remember."

Echo stopped dead, staring.

"Ma?" he whispered, shocked.

And suddenly the youngest of the Originals, some said the toughest Agent in Division One, was across the room, engulfing his mother in a gentle bear hug.

* * *

It took several minutes for an overwhelmed Echo to ease back from hugging and kissing his mother. Meanwhile, Omega, Fox, Zebra, and Zarnix kept their distance and remained silent, content to watch and smiling in delight at the reunion.

Finally, the woman—who was indeed Nalin Iyaaye Bryant—took matters in hand, grabbing her son by the upper arms and holding him at arm's length, so she could get a good look at him.

"Hóóyíí, son," she said to him then, offering him a proud smile. "Oh, you are every bit the man I had hoped and dreamed you would be, one day."

* * *

"You—Ma—what...?" Echo tried, but he couldn't seem to get an actual thought fully processed through his verbal centers and out past his mouth. "You...look, look like...you did when..."

"When the Agency recruited you," Fox finished his statement. "That's because that's how far we regenerated and rejuvenated her, to ensure the cancer—and all preconditions thereof—would be gone. Or rather, Zebra and Zarnix did so, with the help of the rest of the medlab, as well as Doron's consultations. And they did admirably, I might add. The cancer, and a couple other conditions no one knew she had, put up quite a fight."

"We were kinda uncertain," a slightly shamefaced Zebra admitted. "Okay, *I* was kinda uncertain...which is why nobody was allowed to tell you what we were trying. We didn't want you to get your hopes up, in case it didn't work like we thought."

"You...you mean she...she's healed?" Echo whispered, confused, looking around at them. "No more cancer? She's not gonna die?"

"No, son, I'm not going to die," Nalin told Echo with a soft smile. "More, I'm afraid you're stuck with me, as your father used to say."

"We've recruited her to Medical," a delighted Zarnix said, grinning from ear to ear. "She is one of the most experienced nurses I have ever encountered—in several different modes of treatment, including herbal. She will make an excellent medtech for us."

"So...she'll be staying around," Fox pointed out. "We finally found a way to give you back your mother, alter khaver, and you back to her. Or rather, I suppose Omega did."

"What? She...Meg...you...?" Echo tried again, staring at his partner. "Was that what all that...? You an' Fox running around together, back before my birthday...?"

* * *

"Um, yeah, Ace," a suddenly-shy Omega said, blushing;

she had not expected to be given credit for the situation, let alone to be made the sudden center of attention. "See, I'm the one that found out she had cancer—well, the doctors did that; what I mean is that I'm the one in the Agency who discovered she'd been diagnosed with it—and I went straight to Fox, and we, er, hatched up this." She waved her hand around Medical. "Uh, happy birthday an' all. I know it's a little late, but..."

"Oh, dear God..." Echo whispered, staring at her. "Baby..."

And once more he was across the room in a heartbeat, catching Omega in his arms and spinning her around until her feet flew outward, before crushing her against his chest. Then he eased her feet to the floor, grasping her hands in his and bringing them to his mouth, where he planted an intense, grateful kiss on the back of each.

Without releasing her left hand, he turned and towed her back across the room to his mother.

"Mom, I got somebody here I want you to meet. This is my partner, Omega. Meg, this is my mom, Nalin Bryant."

"Um, Ace?" a slightly overwhelmed Omega murmured; she had been unprepared for the force of Echo's reaction, let alone the depth of affection with which it was given, and she was struggling to contain her own emotions as a result, fearful of revealing too much. "We, uh, we've already met, your mom and me."

"Yeah, but you haven't been properly introduced," Echo declared.

The smile on his face was a mile wide.

* * *

"...Consequently, since she doesn't have very many close relatives on the Mescalero reservation any more, we are simply going to put out word that the 'experimental treatment' that she went for has failed, and she died of her cancer," Fox explained, as they all sat around the table in the medical conference room—he, Zarnix, Zebra, Omega, Echo and Mrs. Bryant. "I've already taken care of setting up the matter—the message should be sent any moment now—and once Zarnix and Zebra release her from their care, and we get her properly settled in here, we'll start training her. Recruitment is already on top of retrieving her things. Mrs. Bryant, have you decided on a code name?"

"Apache didn't really have a written language," Echo pointed out. "And we're already running low on Greek and Hebrew, which don't seem appropriate anyway..."

"I have been considering the name Dihl," Mrs. Bryant murmured then. "It is Lipan for 'blood.' As some say, 'The life is in the blood.' I thought it might be appropriate on several levels, and it is simple. Would that do?"

"That'll work," Zebra said, smiling. "And it's something I can pronounce!"

"Where will she be stationed?" Echo wondered, as Fox annotated the new medtech's files, entering her code name on his electronic tablet. "Here, one of the field offices, off-planet...?"

"Oh, she will be here at Headquarters for a good little time, yet," Zarnix noted. "She is an excellent nurse, but there is much technology for her to learn before she can function at her highest level with us."

"But I am excited to try," Mrs. Bryant added, eager. "As well as to get to know my son all over again. And his partner."

"We're delighted to have you," Fox said, but Mrs. Bryant largely—and rather pointedly—ignored him. Eyebrows went up around the table, but rather than press whatever issue was in question, Fox merely stifled a sigh. "Well, I need to get back to the office and see about winding up the attempted assassination case that Alpha One glommed us onto, and that they led Alpha Line in thwarting so successfully. Not to mention figuring out how to deal with a mutant Botanoid who surrendered himself. I've got a ton of paperwork to get through."

"What ever happened to 'Lord' Eb'vuv?" Echo wondered, as his mother watched and listened with interest.

"Oh, the Division One contingent from Va'du'sha'ā took him into custody, and left with him," Fox explained. "In the Glu'gu'ik equivalent of a strait jacket, I believe; there was a great deal of aluminum foil involved, I know that. I expect he'll be committed to a mental hospital upon his arrival on his homeworld, under heavy security."

"That's good," Omega noted. "Maybe they can actually help him."

"Maybe," Zarnix said, dubious, "but if the files I saw on him were correct, the problem is going to be genetic, and consequently very difficult to correct. Why so many worlds' royal families think inbreeding is a GOOD thing, I've no idea."

"You're going, honey?" Zebra wondered, as Fox rose.

"Yes, bubeleh, the paperwork is waiting," he replied. He dropped a kiss on Zebra's cheek, and clapped Echo and Omega on the shoulder before departing.

"This was your latest mission, son?" Bryant asked, curious. "You and your partner Omega? Stopping an attempted assassination?"

"Of the President of the United States, no less," Zebra murmured.

"Yes ma'am, it was," Omega confirmed. "Your son was very brave. He infiltrated the assassin team and fed us information."

"Call me Dihl," Mrs. Bryant told the younger woman with a smile. "I need to get used to it, anyway."

"Dihl it is, then," Omega said, shooting Echo a grin.

She thought he would pop the buttons on his shirt.

* * *

"No, uhn-uh, no way, Ace, that ain't gonna happen," Omega told her partner a bit later. Zarnix had returned to his rounds, but Zebra remained with her patient, her patient's son, and his partner. "I am not joining you both for dinner. Tonight, it needs to be just the two of you."

"But Meg, she ought to get to know you, too."

"There's plenty of time for that," Omega insisted. "Tonight, it's all about you two. Now, if you want to stay in, I'll be happy to COOK dinner for you, so it doesn't take you away from her, but I refuse to eat with you. You two have way too much to catch up on, and now that she's part of the Agency, you can actually TELL her. Most of it, anyway; I guess some of it's still classified."

"But you can tell her too!"

"ECHO," Omega said, growing stern, and he blinked in surprise. "Take. Your mother. To dinner. WITHOUT me."

"Son," Dihl said, voice soft, "I see what she is trying to do, and I appreciate it. I would not object to her joining us by any means, but she is most kindly trying to provide private time for me to become reacquainted with my son, who is now fully adult and experienced...but who I do not KNOW as an adult. You are truly a Lipan warrior now, and I respect that... and so does she."

"Oh," Echo said then, somewhat blank. "Well...okay, I get that, I guess. I'm not sure I agree with it, but...all right."

"FINALLY," Omega said, grinning at Dihl, who returned it. "Was he always so stubborn?"

"Always," Dihl averred. "And very determined. I take it, adulthood has not moderated it?"

"Not in the least." Omega's grin grew wider.

"Takes one to know one," Echo shot back, mildly irked.

"No argument there," Omega agreed, and softened her expression to help ease his mood. It worked; Echo settled down and shot his mother a sheepish smile. "Now we need to figure out where you're going."

"If the physician might interject at this point?" Zebra wondered.

"Sure, Zebra, shoot," Echo said, holding out his open hand in invitation.

"Echo, your mom hasn't been out of the regen pod very long, only a Division day or so, MAYBE a day and a half—I lost track, we've been so busy. Anyway, we're still ensuring everything is working well," the second-in-command of Medical pointed out. "Now, while Meg had a good bit of physical therapy to do, on account of all the tissue regrowth, your mom, not so much. She's pretty good to go, but I want you to remember a couple things."

"What things?"

"Well, for starters, she's not used to Division days yet, like you two are."

"Um, okay; good point. I can't keep her out too late."

"Right. Second, she'd been confined to bed for something over two weeks before she came here, and pretty much the whole time she's been here, she's been in the regen pod," Zebra noted. "So, while you and Meg might hoof it down to your favorite restaurant without a thought, I'd rather not see your mother walk so far until she's built her strength back up a bit more."

"Ooo, good point," Omega murmured. "Maybe take the 'Vette?"

"Or you could borrow Fox's motorcycle," Zebra suggested. "It's got a sidecar. I'm sure, under the circumstances, he wouldn't mind loaning it. I've ridden in it with him, and it's a pretty sweet ride, as he puts it."

"Ma? Which one would you prefer?" Echo asked, turning to his parent.

"As far as I am concerned, I should be comfortable, either way," Dihl decided, "for your father had a motorcycle when we were younger, and I have ridden with him over half of Texas and a substantial part of New Mexico on it! But can we not take the mode of transport you are most used to using? I should like to see..."

"That'd be the 'Vette, then," Echo agreed promptly. "Meg, what do you think—the deli, the pub, Trifle's Pizzeria, or that Italian place we like?"

"Mmm...I'm thinking the pub would be best, Ace, or maybe the Italian place," Omega concluded. "They both have a nice, wide variety of food to choose from, a big parking lot, and if you go to the Italian place and can get that corner booth in the back, the two of you can talk all evening to your heart's content, about anything and everything, and nobody will even notice. The corner table at the pub is almost as good."

"I was kinda thinking the deli would be good, and we go there a lot, so she'd get to see..."

"Yeah, but it's got a postage stamp for a parking lot in the back, and you'll have the 'Vette."

"True. Okay, Mom, pub or Italian?"

"Italian sounds wonderful, son. I find I have had a craving for spices since emerging from the regeneration procedure."

"She has, that," Zebra said, and grinned. "I'd be worried for her digestive tract, except she pointed out she was already used to the spicier southwestern flavors, having come here from New Mexico."

"The Italian place it is, then," Omega said with a grin. "We really need to find a decent, authentic Tex-Mex place around here, Ace."

"Yeah, I know. But I've been here a while, and I'm STILL looking for something that suits me."

"I hear you. New York Tex-Mex ain't like Texican Tex-Mex."

"Nope. Even when it's somebody from the region doin' it, they end up tailoring it to Big Apple tastes."

"Another suggestion?" Zebra interjected. "Well, a question, first."

"What?" Echo wondered.

"How many people do you want to know that your mom is working for us? And what do you think would be the reaction to the Agency as a whole finding out?"

"Ugh," Echo grunted, and frowned. "That might not be a good thing. It could come across as nepotism, especially if somebody else has a family member in similar shape or something."

"Well, that's not gonna be a consideration for very long," Zebra pointed out. "Fox is already working on trying to trace family members better, and we may be creating a special 'private medical facility' for such cases. Possibly even recruiting from it, like we did your mom," she added. "He and I had been talking about the idea for a couple months already, off and on.

We can always say your mom was a trial run on the concept, which she was, sorta."

"Okay, that works."

"But there's more to it than that, Echo—you've worked hard to cultivate a certain image...among the agents, among the offworlders, and especially among the perps. You have a galactic reputation as a serious badass. Well, both of you do, these days." Zebra glanced at Omega. "All I'm saying here is that you might want to get more in the habit of calling her 'Dihl,' at least in public. If a lot of people start hearing you refer to one of the medtechs as 'Mom' or 'Ma,' it isn't gonna do Mr. Badass's reputation any favors."

"Uh. She has a point, son," Dihl agreed, making a face. "And I suppose, likewise, I need to get into the habit of calling you Echo."

"It would be good," Zebra affirmed.

"Okay, beginning tonight, I'll try," Echo agreed. "Given she looks like she's not that much older than me any more, people might look at us funny if I called her 'Mom' anyway."

"True dat," Omega averred.

"Mo-uh, Dihl, when would you like to go?" Echo asked. "Do you need to freshen up a bit, or change clothes, or anything?"

Dihl glanced at Zebra. "Are these black scrubs acceptable...?"

"Perfectly," Zebra declared. "I go out in 'em all the time. And I know the restaurant he's taking you to; Alpha One discovered it a few months back, but Fox and I go there sometimes...when we can both afford to get away from Headquarters at the same time, at least. It's casual, but good. It'll be fine."

"Then Echo, shall we go?"

* * *

"Did word get put out?" Omega said, later that evening; in the absence of her partner, Zebra and Fox had invited her over for dinner.

"It did, tekhter," Fox confirmed for her. "As far as the outside world knows, Nalin Bryant's desperate attempt at an experimental medical treatment failed; we tried everything, but she is dead. The hospital has asked about dispensation of her body and effects, and have been told it is in work."

"What about dispensation of a non-existent body, Fox?" Zebra asked.

"I need you to find out what her wishes were, bubeleh," Fox said. "Then we'll kluge something together that will work. Hopefully it will be as simple as cloning some tissue, then cremating it and providing the ashes for placing somewhere on the reservation."

"Why me? Why is she not really talking to you?"

"...I...think she blames me for taking Echo away from her."

"But you didn't. You weren't even in charge, and—based on what you've told me—you argued for brain bleaching, but Lord Entiyti didn't want to use the technology on Earth yet."

"That is precisely correct, my dear, but I am in charge NOW, and...well." Fox sighed.

"You're the figurehead," Omega realized. "And since she knows you're older than you look, she thinks it really WAS you."

"I believe so, yes," Fox murmured, turning his attention to the meal in front of him. "Bubeleh, the tzimmes is especially good tonight. You have learned kosher Yiddish cooking excellently well."

"Thanks, honey," Zebra said, casting a worried glance at Omega, who returned it.

* * *

Echo escorted his mother into the Italian restaurant, nodding at Gianna Ricci, the off-world restaurant owner, who immediately came to meet them; it was the same restaurant to which Omega had brought Echo on his birthday, and Omega had called and given Ricci a heads-up at Echo's request as he and his mother departed Headquarters.

The restaurateur smiled and personally escorted them to

the much-desired back table; it was isolated relative to the rest of the dining room, and they could talk without fear of being overheard. The white tablecloth was spotless, the rolls of silver flatware substantial in their linen napkin shrouds.

"Enjoy," Ricci murmured, placing their menus in front of them. "If I can do anything, just have the waiter fetch me, Echo. Oh, and speaking of which, heads up: The waiter is a homeboy—he was already assigned to this area when I got Omega's call."

"Ah. Thanks, Gianna."

The owner departed, signaling the waiter, who came over immediately.

* * *

The waiter placed two goblets in front of the diners, filling them with ice water from a pitcher on his tray, then he looked up.

"May I get you something to drin— Oh!" the waiter exclaimed. "Ace! This is not your girlfriend Meg...?"

"No, this is Dihl," Echo responded smoothly.

"Did you and Meg break up, then? Is this your new lady friend? I thought you and Meg were so well-matched...no offense..."

"No, no," Dihl murmured. "Nothing like that. I am his, um, cousin. We haven't seen each other in years, and I just moved to the city recently and made contact. So we wanted to get caught up."

"Ohhh. I see the family resemblance, now you mention it," the waiter decided. "Where is Meg, then? Is everything okay?"

Echo was sorely tempted to tell the nosy waiter that it was none of his business, but maintained a diplomatic veneer.

"She needed to do some stuff around the apartment," Echo noted smoothly, "so she insisted Dihl and I go out and talk to our hearts' content."

"She would be unlikely to know of many of the childhood escapades we remember, in any event," Dihl filled in facilely.

"Aw, that's great," the waiter said then, giving them a smile. "I'm looking forward to seeing all three of you coming to dinner in the future! What can I get for you? A nice bottle of wine to celebrate, perhaps?"

Echo ordered an agéd bottle of Barolo, and the waiter nodded and departed.

* * *

"Finally," Echo muttered. "Sorry about that."

"Girlfriend?" Dihl wondered, puzzled. "Omega? I thought she was your partner...?"

"She is," Echo confirmed. "That's a cover story Meg and I use sometimes. It's easy to play to it, and it gets the least amount of suspicion of just about anything we could come up with. Not all the waiters here are aliens, see." He jerked a thumb at the departing back. "That 'homeboy' remark Gianna made was a code. He's human. With no clue his boss isn't from anywhere around here."

"Aha. I see." Dihl shook her head, a wry, amused grin on her face. "I'm thinking I have much to learn, in addition to the new medical techniques..."

"Er, probably," Echo agreed, rueful. "If Meg and I can help, though, just yell."

By the time the nosy but solicitous waiter had returned with their wine, the pair had determined their entrées, and Echo ordered for them both, selecting a chicken and mushroom risotto for himself, and the spicy balsamic pork his mother had chosen.

Moments later, the salad course had arrived, and they launched into 'catching up.'

* * *

"...And so that's what really happened," Echo finished explaining the details of how he had been effectively drafted into the Agency, from his point of view.

"Oh my. What a convoluted situation! And so Director Fox was NOT director then, and he was rather co-opted along with you," Dihl noted, seeming mildly surprised. "While try-

331

ing to work matters so that you could actually come home to me safely."

"Yeah. Only he wasn't quite successful with that last."

Dihl shook her head.

"Then I need to rethink matters. I had thought HE was in charge when it happened, and..." She broke off, then added, "I thought it was his decision to force you into this organization."

"No!" Echo exclaimed, shocked, and wanting to defend the Director, his oldest living human friend. "Fox is a good friend. He's always tried hard to help me preserve my options! Not to mention open up more opportunities, whenever he could, of all sorts."

"I see. That...puts a different light on things."

"So that's why you were giving him the cold shoulder earlier! He probably didn't tell you, but his employer at that time, the HEAD of the Pan-Galactic Coalition, pretty much put him into the organization without asking him, too," Echo told her. "And he wasn't very happy about it either, but there wasn't anything he could do about it, any more than I could."

"But he said..."

"That's because he's the current Director," Echo noted. "The buck stops with him. Just like it'll stop with me, the day after he retires."

"YOU are in line to be the next Director?! Son!"

"Yeah, Ma, er, Mom—uh, Dihl. Fox made that call a couple years back. I've already been named his successor, and it was approved by the Ennead—that's kinda the, lessee...maybe like the galactic version of the UN Security Council? Sorta kinda. Anyway, it's the core ruling body of the galactic government," Echo explained. "And the eventual promotion of me into the Directorship has already been approved by them. They do that so, if anything ever happens to Fox, the chain of command, the line of succession if you will, is already established, and there won't be any hitches. I step into the role and we keep going, even if there's a major emergency—which there might well be, if something ever happened to kill Fox."

"And what happens to Omega?"

"Oh, I'll most likely promote her to my current position, heading up Alpha Line," Echo explained. "She's already my assistant chief now. And damn good at it."

"But what about...would that not be viewed as...nepotism?"

"What do you mean?"

"Isn't she...I mean," Dihl tried, "are the two of you not... together? No, no," she murmured, considering, "you did say it was a cover story...and now that I think of it, while you were very close, and while you both watched each other, neither of you gave any indication that you have an intimate understanding..." Echo's mother turned a sharp gaze on him. "Why not?"

"Huh?"

"She is a beautiful woman, so— er, Echo," the former Nalin Bryant pointed out. "You share a job. You seem to share interests. You are very close—twice now over dinner, I have heard you refer to her as your best friend; that is usually how the strongest marriages begin. I would have thought you would have settled down by now, be married, have a wife and perhaps children."

"Aw, M-Dihl, don't do this," Echo grumbled. "We haven't been back together hardly an hour yet. Don't you dare start in with the, 'When are you giving me grandchildren' litany."

* * *

"Well, no; but the notion had occurred." She offered him a pert grin. "You always seemed to prefer ladies; has this preference been superseded, perhaps? With maturity and a better knowledge of yourself?"

"No," Echo sighed. "It's, um, it's a long story, Dihl. This..." he glanced around the restaurant, "this is maybe not the best place to talk about it. Back table notwithstanding."

"Ah, yes," she agreed. "Well, once we arrive back at Headquarters, perhaps you can show me around your apartment and we can chat in private? I would suggest you come to mine, but I have none as yet, though I have it to understand that one has been assigned, and my few things are being brought in to help furnish it. But Zebra has preferred I stay in the medlab until my...my post-regeneration therapy, is perhaps the correct terminology...is complete. That should only be a few more days," she added hastily, seeing her son grow alarmed. "I am fine, she says she is simply being cautious. I had it to understand there were some complications that cropped up during the procedure, and she wants to satisfy herself that those complications have been eliminated. She and Zarnix seem quite happy about the way the procedure went, for that matter. But I gather most of my things have been quietly brought from the reservation already, and merely await me to put them where I wish, in the apartment assigned to me."

"Most likely," Echo agreed. "And sure, we can go back to my quarters and talk, though I'll probably start telling you about Meg's...background...in the car on the way back; it'll take a while. It's...complicated. And doesn't need to be overheard, including by Meg; it'll just depress her. Then, when we get back to my place, we can sit and talk some more, and maybe listen to some music and junk. Meg might even come over and join us...after I've finished explaining to you about her."

"I think I would like that."

"Good." Echo smiled. "Hey, look, be thinking—are you maybe gonna want some dessert, after we finish our entrées? They do a killer cheesecake here. Meg loves the crème brûlée, though it isn't strictly Italian, and she says the tiramisu is good, too. I generally just get the cheesecake, though sometimes we split..."

* * *

Later that evening, Echo knocked on the partly-closed back door between his and Omega's quarters, then pushed it farther open; she had closed it earlier—in case he wanted to spend some additional private time with his mother when they returned—leaving only a couple of inches' space, so she could hear a call.

"Hey Meg," he said, as she looked up from where she read

a book on her couch.

"Hi, Ace," she said, swinging her feet down and sitting up. "I wasn't expecting you back quite yet. Did you have a good time?"

"Yeah, we're back, and yeah, it was great," Echo said with a smile. "I've put some music on the sound system, and we're gonna just talk some more. There's a pot of coffee brewing, too, though it's decaf—Zebra doesn't want Ma having caffeine until she can verify everything is safe to have it. Seems there had been some arrhythmias that standard medicine couldn't detect, and which should be fixed now...but you know Zebra. Anyway, Ma-dammit, I gotta remember to call her Dihl! Dihl and I wondered if you'd like to come over and join us."

"Echo, hon, I get that you want to try to involve me," Omega said, wishing she could, but feeling it would be inappropriate, "and I appreciate it, but I really think—"

Just then, Dihl appeared, peeping under Echo's arm, where he leaned against the door frame.

"No, Omega, he truly does mean both of us," Dihl said with a gentle smile. "We have spent several hours in each other's exclusive company, and it was wonderful, and thank you for your thoughtfulness in giving us that opportunity. And I have no doubt but that we will spend more; I am very proud of this warrior that James and I bore. But for now, I would very much like to see how my son and his partner interact, and to get to know his very special friend, as he has told me."

"Aw." Omega felt her cheeks heat. "He told you about the 'best buds' thing, huh?"

"That, and more," Dihl replied, and Echo looked startled.

"Ha!" Omega chortled, watching. "I knew it! All moms have some sorta, like, eighth sense about their kids! Watch out, Ace! All that stuff you keep to yourself? She'll read ya like a book!"

"Then she better be as good at keeping it to HERself as you are," Echo decided, eyeing his mother with a slightly suspicious gaze in which was more than a hint of *Keep your mouth shut, Mom.*

"You never knew your father was fiercely ticklish, or that your grandfather had a fling with the next-door neighbor's widowed mother, so I guess I can handle it," Dihl said, calm.

"WHAAT?!" Echo exclaimed, shocked. "Dad was...and Shiitsooyee had a what, now?"

"Okay, yeah," Omega decided immediately, putting aside her book and standing. "I'm gonna accept that invitation to join y'all, just to watch THIS conversation unfold!"

* * *

The subsequent visit was delightful, bordered on hilarity at certain points, and all three were relaxed and comfortable with one another by the time it ended, many hours late into their sleep period.

Rather than take his mother back to the medlab so late and have the doctors and medtechs fuss over her, Echo made his own bed with fresh linens and saw his mother off to bed there—after brushing his teeth and grabbing lounge pants and a t-shirt to try to use as pajamas, as well as his bathrobe—while Omega called Zebra to explain the arrangement.

Zebra approved, and was happy to discover that mother and son—and son's partner—were getting along so well.

* * *

"There you go, Ma," Echo said softly, as he turned down the covers on the freshly-made bed. Then he turned to his dresser, opening a drawer and yanking something out, unfolding it as he did so. He handed the garment to her as he nudged the drawer closed with his thigh. "And here's one of my t-shirts you can sleep in for pajamas, if you want to."

"Thank you, son," she told him with a gentle smile. "You are as thoughtful as you are strong and brave. Your partner is a lucky woman."

"Well..." Echo felt himself flush. "I dunno about THAT. Besides, I mean, we're...partners. Just...partners."

"And the best of friends. And you love her; even though you never used those words to me, I could see it in your eyes, on your face, when you told me about her past, as well as about the various adventures you have had together. And," Dihl added, "you are special to her, as well; I would stake my life on it."

"Yeah, but not in that way, I guess," Echo sighed.

"She has not said so? Or at least indicated? Hinted?"

"No. Nowhere close. I can't even tell if she'd like the idea or not. So," he said, with a shrug and a wry glance, "I'm sorta guessing not."

"Do not sell her short, son. She, too, is reserved and proud, and given her background and what was done to her, well..." Dihl broke off and shook her head. "Alex, son—yes, yes, I know I should call you Echo," she said, as he started to protest, "but it is only we two, and I MUST speak to you as your mother now, so Alex—you told me about her, and then I spent time with her this evening. And it hurts her, son. Having once been made aware of her situation, and with my experience in the healing professions, I could see it, though it is not obvious at all."

"So that's why you said some of the things you did. You were skirting around it, to see how she would react."

"Yes; it is a technique I learned from old Dr. Padillo, for assessing patients' mental states. I was careful, though, son; I did not want to upset her any more than you did."

"Okay. And?"

"She is, I think, struggling with her identity because of it. Oh, she puts on a good face, but Alex, she no longer knows who she is! She no longer knows WHAT she is! I would bet everything I possess on that."

"Well...that assessment does fit in with some comments she's made..."

"I am not surprised in the least. Give her time, son. Whatever she has told you on the subject, I seriously doubt that she is in a mental and emotional position to like herself, let alone love herself, her body, her abilities. Not yet. In all probability, she feels betrayed by it. And if she feels like that about herself, how can she ever believe she could be loved by another? She

is not in a place to accept your love yet, let alone return it...
although I suspect she may, but will not permit it."

"But why wouldn't she let herself feel love for me?" Echo
wondered, pained.

"Stop and think for a moment, Alex," Dihl advised. "Put
yourself in her place. If you suddenly discovered that you had
been kidnapped, attacked, torn apart and reassembled and
made something DIFFERENT from who and what you have
always been, what you have always believed yourself to be,
would that knowledge not shake you to the core of your being?
Even you, who are so strong a warrior?"

"Well, yeah...I guess so..."

"Would you feel right, letting the person you cared for
most in the world, get close to you, tie herself to you? Not
knowing what the future ramifications might be? You have already told me about the scare only a day or two ago, when you
all thought—feared—she might 'burn out' within a few years,"
she reminded him. "If you were in her position, wouldn't you,
instead, try to protect her from any potential repercussions?"

"Oh..." Echo said, expression going blank as understanding dawned. "Oh. Yeah, Ma, now I see your point. No, I
wouldn't be comfortable letting her close, under those conditions. Not until," he paused, considering, "not until I got a better handle on what-all it was gonna do to me, to us. I wouldn't
want to risk her getting hurt."

"Exactly. And from what I have gathered this evening, it
appears she, and the rest of you—her friends, colleagues, her
medical caregivers—are still 'getting a handle on' that," Dihl
pointed out. "The ramifications are still manifesting, because
no one—at least, to the Agency's knowledge, as I understand
it—has ever had such a thing happen to them before, and we do
not know what to expect. SHE does not know what to expect."
She paused, and watched her son for a moment, seeing the understanding on his face. "Now, then. Add to this uncertainty
her inability to trust her body, to like it, let alone love it...and
her likely belief that no one else could love it, love her, either.

Especially if, as you have mentioned, others—even within the Agency—find it off-putting, even frightening, as well. Where does that leave her, mentally and emotionally?"

"Well, damn, Ma."

"Hush, son. Give her time. Support her. Help her to understand, as much as you can, what has happened to her. Be there for her." Dihl nodded. "And I will help as much as I know how, as well. I think I plan to tell Zarnix and Zebra that I would like to work on Omega's case, to help them figure out what happened to her and what the repercussions will be, in future. Would that be all right, do you think? Would Omega mind? Would YOU mind?"

"She's pretty private about it," Echo said, uncertain. "There's stuff that I guess only Zebra, and maybe Zarnix, know. India is our field medic for the department—and a close, trusted friend—but I don't think even she knows everything about Meg's medical records."

"And that serves to confirm for me my suspicions on her feelings about the matter. She does not wish it known...because I suspect she is ashamed of it, for various reasons that it does not take great intellect to guess...though perhaps it takes a certain mindset to extrapolate them," Dihl added, watching her son's mildly-puzzled face. "If I had had such genetic experimentation done on me against my will, I would be very unhappy. But it likely also means, IF I am permitted to work on her case, I will not even be able to tell you."

"Unless it's a downright emergency, yeah, I expect so. Not even Fox knows all of it. But," Echo added, "we respect her privacy, and neither he nor I is asking, either."

"That is gentlemanly of you both."

Echo sighed.

"I can't speak for Fox—I've always thought he was a very old-world, European-type gentleman, though he can be badass, too, when he has to be—but I try," he told his mother. "Especially since I got Meg for a partner. She's a Southern lady, so I try to be a Southern gentleman, for her sake."

"You had no need to try," Dihl told him. "Your father and I raised you as one, and it appears to have taken, rather well."

Echo felt the heat of his flushed face, but he grinned.

"Thanks, Ma," he said, with a nod. "For...everything. All that. You and Dad both. Chances are, I wouldn't still be here if it hadn't all 'taken,' as you put it." He waved a hand at the bed. "Now I need to get outta here, and you need to crash, or Zebra's gonna kill me, keeping you up this late."

"I'm fine," Dihl said with another pert grin of her own, then her face grew wistful. "Alex, do you remember when you were a little boy? How I always came into your room to tell you good night?"

"Yeah, I do," he said, voice soft, as a warm memory washed over him. "You wanna do it now, only kinda reversed?"

"Yes, but...I can't reach any more!" she said, stretching up on tiptoes and still falling short of his face.

"Here." Echo went down on one knee before her.

Dihl cupped Echo's face in both hands, then leaned forward and tenderly kissed his forehead. A tear escaped her and trickled down her cheek. Echo reached up and brushed it away with gentle fingers, then offered her a slight smile and gathered her into a brief hug.

"Welcome home, Ma," he said softly. "It isn't the Ranch, but it's still home. Because now we're all here."

Dihl gave him a wobbly smile and nodded affirmation, as he rose, grabbed his sleepwear, and turned for the door.

* * *

"And now you're going to crash in my bed," Omega told her partner when she got off the phone and he emerged from his bedroom.

Echo blinked. *Did she just say what I thought she...oh wait,* he broke off the thought. *She means for me to take her bed the same way I gave mine to Ma. And then she'll take the recliner or the couch or something.* He tried not to facepalm at his original misinterpretation. *I gotta try to stop my mind from going there, every time Meg says something like that. Besides,*

*if she really meant to SHARE the bed, we wouldn't be gettin'
any sleep. And I kinda think Ma would notice THAT, come tomorrow morning. So would Fox, for that matter.*

"Nah, I'll just take the recliner," Echo decided then.

"Nuh-UH! You've spent HOW many days either in the
saddle, sleeping on the ground, or on the floor of that warehouse? Leastways I got to sleep in a comfortable, clean hotel
bed, once I met up with Fox. Besides, you're never gonna get
any decent sleep in those, if you're still wrestling with a pair of
boxers—and I know you are." She jabbed a finger at the lounge
pants and shirt over his arm, then turned for her bedroom. "This
way, at least you can strip down and get comfortable. Let me
go change the bedclothes, and I'll sleep on my couch. Good-
ness knows, I've fallen asleep there a buncha times before. It
sleeps pretty good. And if I scoot the coffee table up against it,
it'll keep me from falling off if I roll over in my sleep."

"All right," Echo sighed, recognizing the signs that his
partner was not going to accept NO as an answer. "It does
sound good, to sleep in an actual bed for a change. Lemme
come help you remake the bed, at least."

"Okay," Omega agreed, and he followed her through her
quarters and into the bedroom, where she fished out a fresh set
of bedsheets from a dresser drawer, handing them to Echo, who
started shaking them out as she stripped the bed and tossed the
used linens into the laundry chute. "I guess I shoulda done this
before we left on vacay, but I didn't know things were gonna
time out like they did."

"You mean Mom was already in the medlab when we
left?"

"Yeah. Remember when I popped down to pick up a new
bottle of Rejuvic before we headed out? She'd just arrived. I
really went by to see her, before they put her in the regen pod."

"You're kidding."

"Nope."

"Why didn't anybody TELL me?!"

Omega sighed.

"Fox and I wanted to, so bad, Ace!" she confessed then. "But Zebra was thirty-nine kinds of worried. And to be honest, I think she was actually scared. She was afraid they couldn't get the regen fluid composition right for cancer, let alone pancreatic cancer—which is a really nastybad kinda cancer, it turns out—and that it wouldn't work, or would only partly work, and just end up delaying the inevitable or something. And this was your MOM. So she made us promise NOT to tell you, so you wouldn't get your hopes up, in case your mom...didn't make it, after all."

"Oh."

"I'm really, really sorry, hon. I didn't WANT to; it was Zebra's conditions for doing it. And...I understood it. There was a logic there; I just felt horrible, keeping it from you." She stopped and gazed at him, expression solemn. "Are...you mad?"

"Nah. I get it. Probably better that I made my peace with things, just in case."

"Okay. Great. I'm...relieved."

"No worries, baby. We're good. We're always good."

"Yeah, we are. Okeydoke. Let's get the bed made, so we can both zonk. Otherwise I'mma fall over in about ten more minutes. An' I dunno why you're even still standing."

"All right. And I'm still runnin' on adrenaline, I think, from getting Ma back; I'll prob'ly crash hard, soon as I get horizontal. While we're doing this, though, Meg," Echo said, handing her one end of the fitted sheet, "I had an idea. Lemme ask you about something..."

* * *

"Sure, Echo, I think it would be wonderful," Omega agreed. "I say let's do it."

"Have I mentioned lately that you're awesome, baby?"

"Nah, but you can tell me any time you feel like it," she said, and they grinned. "Now, let me get ready for bed, and then you can crash in here, and I'll take the couch."

"That works," Echo said, heading for her kitchen. "While

you do that, I'll fix us both a bedtime snack. Gotta keep that souped-up metabolism of yours properly fueled, after all. An' I got a couple days' worth of meals to catch up on, myself."

"Yeah, you do; you've dropped some weight in the last few days."

"I know. So I'm gonna fix a pretty big snack, if that's okay with you."

"It's a deal."

* * *

The next day, after a hearty breakfast for three that a secretly-delighted Dihl watched Echo and Omega coordinate in making, Alpha One escorted the newest medtech back to the medlab, then headed for the Alpha Line Room to see about winding up the paperwork on the thwarted Presidential assassination attempt.

Dihl allowed a solicitous Zebra to check her vitals, and put her through some gentle exercises, helping to ease her back into activity from her previously bedridden state.

"There we go," Zebra said, pleased, as they wound up the light physical therapy. "You're coming along nicely."

"I was very active before the cancer manifested," Dihl noted. "In addition to my duties at the hospital, I also did ceremonial sand painting, hiked the wilderness areas to wildcraft some of my herbals, and I was a fancy dancer at some of the gatherings and pow-wows."

"Ooo," Zebra said, wide-eyed with curiosity. "I've seen videos of the fancy dancers. I'd love to see it in person some time."

"I think that can be arranged," Dihl said with a smile. "But I was wondering if I might speak with Director Fox for a few moments."

"Uh—okay," Zebra said, startled. "Is everything all right?"

"Yes, everything is fine; I simply feel I should speak to him for a bit."

"Let me call him, and I'll see if he's available in the next few minutes, and if he wants to come down here, or for us to go up there."

* * *

It proved that Fox was tired of paperwork and wanted to stretch his legs a bit, so he came to the medlab, and he, Zebra, and Dihl entered the medical conference room and sat down. Zebra closed the door before taking her seat.

"Is everything all right, Dihl?" Fox wondered. "Do you have a problem of some sort?"

"Not now," Dihl said with a slight smile. "I...Echo and I talked for many hours last night. We took our time over dinner, and spent nearly three hours at the restaurant. Then we came back to his apartment and Omega joined us, and we talked until late into the night. About many things. And I find...I had some misapprehensions about you, sir. I thought you had been in charge and responsible for taking Echo from me, when in fact he tells me that you tried hard to return him to me. My son set me straight most emphatically on that point. And he and Omega spoke of you far too fondly for you to be the autocrat I had concluded you must be, to simply absorb him into the organization without recourse, at such a tender age."

"Well..." Fox said, and broke off, uncharacteristically uncertain what to say; he was not sure what was coming next, or exactly what Dihl was trying to express. A perceptive Dihl apparently saw the uncertainty, and understood it.

"Yes, well then, what I would like you to know, Director Fox, is that I am sorry for ascribing to you certain actions and motives that were not yours. And for attempting to find a place to lay blame that," she shook her head, "does not truly exist, based on my current level of comprehension. I suppose I wanted to find someone to blame, someone to be angry with, for taking my son from me all these years, in such fashion as to make me think him dead." Dihl drew a deep breath, then let it out in a sigh. "Echo made very sure that I understood that there was no blame to be laid. It was a delicate situation, and everyone acted honorably, responding as best they could in such a complex circumstance—including him, and you. And

I know that now. I know, too, that my attitude toward you has not been...appropriate, for all you have done for me...and my son. And...I apologize."

Chocolate brown eyes, so like her son's, met a hazel gaze. *She knows, now,* Fox thought. *She understands, she accepts. Perhaps even forgives. This...is good.*

"I...thank you. And in turn, I would like you to know, Dihl," Fox murmured, "that I did all I could to try to return Echo to you that very day. The only option I had left to me, which would have returned him to you, would also have left you both highly vulnerable...to murder or kidnapping, or even secret imprisonment, with no one aware you had gone missing; and since those outcomes were more probable than not, I considered that option unacceptable. But whereas today I am the Agency Director, at that time I wasn't in charge...of anything, really, and I didn't have the final say. Lord Entiyti was in charge, but we were still trying to feel out the fledgling organization that would become the Agency. At that time, we didn't know any of the agents who were there, and we were uncertain how much they could be trusted. He didn't feel it was wise to reveal too much of the galactic technology until they'd proven themselves. I could understand that, and while I pressed hard to try to find a covert way to do it in safety, in the end it proved impossible."

"I understand." Dihl nodded.

"And I've watched out for your son, all these years," Fox added. "I hope you don't find this offensive, but somewhere along the line, I found I came to think of him as an adoptive son of sorts. He and I are two of the last of what are sometimes called The Originals...the original group of agents that day, the agents that became the core of Division One. Echo is the youngest, the fiercest, and probably the toughest..."

"Don't underestimate yourself, honey," Zebra murmured.

"I'm not," Fox said, offering her a slightly mischievous grin. "But just because I don't LOOK my age, doesn't mean I'm not a wily sonovabitch when I need to be. When you're young, you HAVE to be tough, because you don't have the wisdom of experience to fall back on, to tell you how to do a thing without requiring brute force." He drew a breath, let it out. "In the concentration camp, I was tough. Damn tough. I was in my early teens; I had to be. These days? How does that saying go...? Ah—'Old age and treachery will always beat youth and exuberance.'"

Zebra and Dihl both snorted, then laughed outright.

"Mamet," Zebra added, snickering.

"I think it was, yes." Fox chuckled. "At any rate, Dihl, I have looked after your son as if he were my own flesh and blood. To the best of my ability."

"I had begun to realize something like that last night," Dihl said. "And no, I am not offended. I am thankful that he had someone—two someones, judging by what Omega told me of his first partner—to look after him. He respects you, and he listens to you. Last night I realized how exhaustive his knowledge of this place, this life, this organization, really is. But I also saw, whenever Omega or I ever found a limit to that knowledge—which was rare, but we managed it a couple of times—his response was often, 'I'll ask Fox tomorrow.'"

Fox was silent for a moment, struck by the level of faith in him that the statement revealed from Echo.

"That...is good to know," he finally managed, voice a little rough. "Thank you."

"So...I guess we're all good now?" Zebra wondered.

"We are, I think," Dihl said with a slight smile. "Though, with two of my three supervisors here, perhaps now is a good time to ask..."

"Ask what?" Fox queried.

"Well, I have a little favor to request..." Dihl began with a mischievous grin.

* * *

"Oh really?" Zebra exclaimed.

"Yes, I can confirm that," Fox said. "Though that is classified information, as you might expect, for obvious reasons.

And I don't have a problem with it, if they don't, and if Medical doesn't." He glanced at Zebra and smirked. "The ball is in your court, bubeleh."

"I think that'll work all right," Zebra agreed. "After all, she could use the activity and the fresh air. She already knows the therapy exercises I want her to do. And I'm sure the rest of it will do her good, as well." She turned to Dihl. "Would you like me to send along some study materials...?"

* * *

In a certain small impact crater on a corner of The Ranch, Division One forces, screened by various cloaking devices, surrounded a little cluster of three spacecraft in the center of the crater. Alpha Seven stepped into the open at the base of Meteor Mountain. Tare and Yankee exchanged glances, then Tare nodded and Yankee stepped forward a single pace, raising a bullhorn to his mouth.

"This is PGLEIA Division One, Alpha Seven Agent Yankee speaking! You are under arrest! Stand down and come out with your appendages in the air!"

There was silence for a long moment. Abruptly the closest ship, a small saucer, opened fire on the exposed Alpha team.

A yellow force dome around the pair flared bright yellow, as the energy beam spent itself harmlessly on the field. Abruptly all cloaking fields dropped, and the full scope of the Division One forces was revealed: fully one hundred heavily armed agents in body armor, along with some two dozen armored, high-tech personnel carriers with full armament, lined the crater rim...all wrapped in aluminum foil, all weapons trained downward on the three small ships in the center of the shallow crater. A whirring sound grew loud, as all of the weapons were 'cocked' and made ready to fire.

"I repeat," Yankee said, voice grim, "you are under arrest. Stand down and come out with your appendages in the air."

The hatches on all three ships began to open. Two Glu'gu'ik and one Delzantian emerged, hands in the air.

"Take 'em into custody," Yankee growled.

The final mop-up began.

* * *

A departing Division One Agent Bi'hts'e Dh'u of the Va'du'sha'ā Office, Ar'dug department, assigned to the High Council—formerly known as Lu'vin'du'v and now in his true form—met the Alpha One team at the Dallas Station spaceport very early the next morning, as they were en route back to the Ranch, and he was headed home. Dihl, accompanying Alpha One, stayed in the background, but watched with patent interest.

"Ah, the complete Alpha One team," Dh'u remarked with a smile. "But, Agent Omega, you do not appear as you did when your companion infiltrated the assassin team!"

"No," Omega grinned, "but none of you recognized me in the bar, either."

"Ah! True. That was a smart move, then. You are glad to have your partner back at your side?"

"Oh, he's useful to have around..." Omega glanced at Echo with a mischievous smile. Echo snorted.

"And you, Echo?"

"I suppose I could quote from the Earth musical, *My Fair Lady*, and say, 'I've grown accustomed to her face.' Her hair is another matter," Echo deadpanned. Omega stuck out her tongue.

Dh'u smiled sadly as he observed the two Agents' cheerful banter, teasing each other with good humor.

"You do not know how fortunate you are," he told them in a soft voice. "You still have one another to depend upon. Enjoy each other's presence. Take each day as it comes, and notice the small things—about each other, about those around you, and about the world—the universe—through which you move. If you do this, then no matter what happens, at least there will always be...fewer regrets."

Two brows—brown, and brown with blonde highlights—creased in sympathy. Brown eyes met blue for a long moment, thinking. At last, each gave brief, punctuated nods at the other.

Dh'u watched, and nodded, satisfied. In the background, Dihl also saw, and smiled to herself.

"Goodbye, Omega, Echo. Remember."

The two humans stood silently side by side as the lone—and lonely—Glu'g'ik departed.

"Yes..." Omega whispered as the saucer hatch closed, and Echo nodded once, in agreement.

* * *

"He gave wise advice, your Glu'g'ik friend," Dihl said, as they arrived at their designated gate and awaited boarding. "I had...much the same feeling when James died so unexpectedly."

"But you and Da-uh, James were always so close," Echo murmured.

"Oh, Echo, of course we were," Dihl responded with a gentle smile. "I loved him dearly, and he loved me as much. But..." She broke off and shook her head, as Echo and Omega watched. "I think, for humans...and for many other species, too, it appears...there will always be regrets, where death is concerned. Something not done, not accomplished, left unsaid. My biggest regret? I could not tell him goodbye at the end," Dihl sighed.

"I couldn't, either, and I was already there," Echo reminded her. "It happened too fast."

"I know," Dihl said with a sad smile. "But I regret it, nevertheless." Her gaze grew distant. "I would have held him, and stroked his hair, and told him I loved him, one more time. And then I would have kissed him, as he departed this life." Solemn, she looked at the Alpha One pair. "So I, too, recommend that...you say the things that are important, the things that need to be said...when you can, while you still can."

Echo pondered for a moment, then nodded. Dihl turned to Omega, and Echo kept a surreptitious watch on his partner's face, as well.

Omega's face had crumpled a bit in sympathy for the other woman, and it crumpled further when Dihl offered her advice.

349

There was a troubled look in the blue gaze, and when it met Dihl's gaze, it became almost imploring, before Omega raised one shoulder ever so slightly in a half-shrug, and looked away.

Echo and Dihl looked at each other; Echo was surprised, but Dihl raised a knowing eyebrow in an *I told you so* glance, and a thoughtful Echo nodded receipt of the message.

Chapter 9

The unmarked ebony helicopter dropped the black-denim-clad Alpha One team, plus one, off at the Ranch in central Texas not so much later that morning; like all their other forms of transport, Agency helicopters were far from ordinary. As the Alpha One team climbed out, Echo grabbed a black, hard-sided suitcase and set it on the ground, then turned back and helped a certain woman with a long dark braid exit the chopper.

A ranch hand met them and caught up the hard-sided suitcase, carrying it into the main house nearby. Several more ranch hands extracted the regular luggage from the cargo hold under the tail, departing with all of it toward the main house, as well. Dihl, Omega and Echo got clear of the rotor blades, and Echo gave the Agency pilot a thumbs-up. The craft lifted off and disappeared into the distance.

"Oh my," Dihl whispered, staring about herself at the landscape, and Echo smiled.

"Just like you remember?" he asked.

"Almost exactly," Dihl murmured, then pointed. "That building is new. A guest house?"

"Yup. For the time being, this is a working guest ranch."

"I love it. And you are certain no one will mind if...I take the master suite?"

"Not in the least."

"All right. Let me go find this Joe person and check in with him..." She headed for the main house with purpose. Echo turned to his partner.

"Well, we're here...again," Echo remarked.

"Yep," Omega said, taking a deep breath and smiling. "And the summer wildflowers are still in full bloom."

"Yep. So whatcha gonna want to do first? Once we get everybody settled back in, I mean."

"Guess."

* * *

"Oh, there he is. Hey, Joe," Echo called with a smile, as he headed over to the ranch manager. As he went, he turned and gestured at his mother, and moments later, Omega and Dihl were following. "I got somebody I want you to meet."

"Sure thing, Echo; whatcha need?" Joe said, meeting the Agent partway. "Whoa, Omega! What th' hell did ya do to yer hair?! No offense, an' pardon th' language, but..."

"I needed to look different, in case the perps saw me after we got Echo infiltrated," Omega explained with a sigh. "Judging by the look on your face, you don't like it, either."

Joe snorted.

"Ain't none o' my business, ma'am," he noted, "but I gotta confess, I think ya look better as a blonde. I reckon, based on that 'either,' Echo don't like it none, neither?"

"I do not," Echo declared, in no uncertain terms. "I prefer—"

"Don't you dare call me a palomino again," Omega threatened, glowering. "I like horses too, but there are limits."

A good-humored Echo grinned, aborting the statement he'd been about to make, and Joe and Dihl laughed. "Blondes," Echo finished his statement, producing another round of laughter, even in Omega this time.

"Waaall, they do say gennelmen prefer blondes," Joe drawled, laying the regional accent on with a trowel, then he snickered. "An' I've always known you was a gennelman, Echo. So I reckon it'll do."

"Anyway, Meg and I brought somebody along with us, this time," Echo told Joe with a grin, getting back to the original point of business. "This is Dihl. She's a new recruit to the Medical department. Dihl, this is Joe Beck, the ranch's current manager."

"I'm very pleased to meet you, Mr. Beck," Dihl said, stepping forward and shaking Joe's hand, as Omega moved to Echo's side. "You and your colleagues have done an excellent job, maintaining the place."

"Thankee, ma'am," Joe said with a smile, missing the significance of the statement, couched in the wording. "It 'uz a fine place ta begin with. Now, wouldja like a nice room in the guest house?"

"No, no, no," Echo said, shaking his head and holding up a hand. "Put Dihl in the master suite in the main house."

"But...Echo," Joe began, disturbed, "you're the one what set that as off limits f'r guests..."

Echo simply stepped directly behind Dihl, rested both hands lightly on her upper arms, and looked at Joe over the top of her head.

"Look closely, Joe," Omega murmured. "Very...very...closely."

* * *

At that behest, Joe stopped everything, and followed Omega's instructions, scrutinizing Echo and Dihl carefully, aware that something unusual was occurring. *The new lady's sure purty enough. And he's awful familiar with 'er, standin' that close an' holdin' 'er arms an' all. Surely he didn't go an' ditch Omega for this Dihl,* he thought, perturbed. *Not as much as he thought of Omega. Not so fast, neither—he'd 'a had ta gone from a thing f'r Omega to a relationship with this Dihl in a matter of days! But he brought Omega along too, so it ain't like...waitaminit.*

Joe scanned the two smiling faces, one above the other, two sets of nearly-identical dark brown eyes twinkling at him. Dumbfounded, he blinked, and simultaneously, their smiles grew into grins. *Identical grins, too,* he realized. *Eyes, cheekbones, teeth, ears... Oh shit. This ain't a new girlfriend, this is kin. Close kin. An' the only kin o' his that I know of 'ud be... naw. Surely not.*

"Echo," Joe tried, "this ain't really...?"

This time, Echo, Dihl, AND Omega grinned from ear to ear.

"But she ain't near the right age!" Joe protested. "An' the cancer..."

"Ain't galactic medicine wonderful?" Omega noted then, and Dihl and Echo both laughed.

"Put her in the master suite, Joe," Echo reiterated. "That's where she belongs. She's waited a long time for this."

"Yeah," Omega agreed, "she has. But...you don't have to spread it around exactly who she is. Ace, here, has a certain... reputation...to maintain."

"Not to mention, I don't need her becoming a target for somebody trying to get back at me," Echo added, sobering, then he glanced at his partner. "I've already had plenty enough of that for one lifetime."

"Aw," Omega and Dihl murmured at almost the exact same time.

"I follow ya, pal," a highly-sympathetic Joe agreed. "Mum's th' word, as Madrid likes ta say."

Echo snorted, and stifled a laugh.

"Huh?" Joe said, confused. "What did I say?"

"Mum is indeed the word," a cheeky Dihl noted. Joe decided he must look as sheepish as he felt, as the others all exploded into laughter, and finally he joined in.

"Awright, awright," he scolded mildly, good-humored. "So I made a pun without meanin' to. It ain't like English is my first language, ya know. Never mind havin' ta learn how ta sound proper cowboy, so's th' tourists are satisfied! You bunch behave."

"You know Madrid, Joe?" Omega wondered, when she could talk for laughing.

"Sure. This here Ranch is one 'a his favorite vacation places. Don't tell 'im I said so, but Maker have mercy, how he goes off on alla that Western shit! He's got a silver belt buckle that I swear is th' size of a dinner plate!"

"You're kidding," Echo said.

"Nope. Ask 'im—just don't tell 'im I toldja. Anyhow, back t' business. Now be aware, y'all, iffen ya put Dihl in the master suite, the boys an' girls are gonna figger it out on their own, given the fam'ly resemblance."

"Then they figure it out," Echo acknowledged. "We don't have to confirm it."

"And you really never heard us say WHO she was," Omega pointed out, "other than she's Dihl, and she's a new recruit for the Medical department—which sorely needs new recruits."

"Well, that's true," Joe agreed. "Okay. Omega, Echo, you're back in th' same jack an' jill rooms we put ya in before...well, before alla that shit with th' illegals went down, pardon my language, Miz Dihl."

"Just Dihl will do," she replied, sanguine. "And your language is perfectly understandable, in the circumstances. Echo and Omega have told me about their little...adventure."

"Awright, then," Joe said, turning toward two small suitcases sitting on the back porch of the main house. "That must mean 'at that's your luggage, then, huh?"

"Yes sir, it is."

"Aw, jus' call me Joe," the Haepergen grinned. "Ah reckon as how Ah work f'r you an' Echo, as much as f'r th' Agency, when ya git right down to it. Th' Ranch b'longs t' y'all; you're just lettin' the Agency use it. Y'all c'mon with me, an' let's get y'all moved in, proper-like."

He picked up the suitcases and headed inside, followed by a delighted Dihl, a happy Echo, and an intensely satisfied Omega.

* * *

While the two women settled in, Joe knocked on the door of Echo's bedroom.

"Yup," came the response from within. "C'mon in, whoever it is."

"It's just me," Joe said, opening the door and slipping inside before closing it behind him. He cast a glance at the closed bathroom door, paused by it to listen intently, then nodded to himself.

"So," Echo said, looking up from where he tucked away clothing in the drawers of the dresser that had once been his, and now was again, if only for a short time. He caught the procedure at the bathroom door, and nodded. "You wanna talk to me in private."

"Yeah," Joe said. "I 'membered what you 'uz talkin' about before, about havin' your mom and your partner meet, an' here at th' Ranch, an' all. I s'pose you're purty happy now, 'bout how it all worked out."

"I am, Joe, yeah," Echo admitted. "And the coolest part of it is, Dihl is here and alive and well...BECAUSE of Meg."

"Huh?"

"Meg's the one who found out she'd been diagnosed with cancer, Joe," Echo said, sitting down on the edge of the bed, while Joe pulled out the desk chair, turned it backwards, and straddled it, facing Echo. "She hatched up a whole plan to get her to Headquarters and into a regen pod, then working for the Agency. And Fox agreed, and the medlab did it. They just didn't tell me beforehand, in case things didn't turn out as well as they hoped."

"Aw man. That's...just cool." Joe grinned. "I'd say that partner o' yours cares an awful lot about ya, there, pal."

"Mo-Dihl thinks so, too," Echo agreed. "She thinks Meg just needs time to come to grips with what Slug did to her. I mean, it's really only been about a year since Meg—since all of us—found out what happened. And we're still encountering repercussions, not just in the sense of 'who-all was involved,' but in the sense of how this has affected Meg's health, her abilities, an' all kinds of shit like that. Anyway, once Dihl explained it from...from the 'inside,' I guess you could say—as a healer interpreting a patient's reactions to bad news—well, it made sense. I'm gonna do my damnedest to be patient and wait, while Meg comes to terms with it. And THEN maybe I can make some headway with the relationship I want to have with her."

"Yeah, I get where you're comin' from on that, I think," Joe agreed, thoughtful. "Fox briefed me on her afore y'all came down here th' first time, just so's I'd know if somethin' unusual

happened, not t' mention keepin' th' staff from sayin' something wrong that might hurt or offend 'er, all accidental-like."

"Oh—you mean the staff knows, too?"

"Well, there 'uz rumors last year, pal, like I toldja before,"
Joe said, waving his hand. "This just put 'em all to rest with th'
truth. An' you saw how they acted at th' barbacoa."

"Yeah, that's true. Okay." Echo shrugged. "I just don't
want her hurt."

"I know. An' we ain't about to, if we can help it. She's a
nice lady in 'er own right, not t' mention your partner."

"Good. And yeah, she is."

"Now, how have things changed since the last time y'all
was here, what with Dihl along this time? You want we should
include her on all th' stuff you an' Omega do, too?"

"Oh, no, that isn't necessary," Echo noted, then gave the
other man a wicked grin. "Given I plan to, uh, try to increase
the closeness in the partnership, it's kinda NOT a thing, if you
get me."

"Ha! I do."

"But I know she'd love a tour of the place, to see how it's
held up and how y'all have taken care of it, and what changes
have been made. She rides horseback, so you can always take
her around to see the herds and stuff, too. And we might even
join y'all on some of that. Don't let her overdo, though; she
was bedridden for several weeks, there."

"Gotcha. I won't let 'er stay in th' saddle too long the first
couple days, then. An' I'll pick a quiet horse to start."

"Exactly. Oh, and don't be surprised if she starts in with
design changes in the herb garden, or the landscaping, or whatnot," Echo warned. "She always loved that stuff. And Shiitsooyee—my grandfather, her dad—taught her herbal medicine, so she's the one that put in the garden in the first place. I
remember when that happened, from when I was pretty little.
Though I think Great-Grandma Bryant already had a little patch
of the Celtic-type herbs, now that I think back. But M-uh, Dihl
really expanded on it."

"Ooo. I think I'll take advantage of the expertise, then. There's a couple places th' current shrubs just ain't workin' no more—too big ta fit, not enough water, shit like 'at—but I ain't been able to figger what t' do to change it. This way, we kin update the landscaping around th' place, an' know it'll meet y'all's approval."

"Good plan. Anyway, just let her explore and look around, help her out with stuff here and there, and help me make sure she doesn't do TOO much. I'm sure there's some stuff we'll all do together, and some things we won't. But we'll probably all go to meals together in the dining room, all three of us."

"Right." Joe rose from his seat. "Then I'll let ya get back to it. Ya got two right purty, distinguished, elegant ladies t' bring t' dinner each night, too. One on each arm."

"I do, that," Echo agreed with a smile. "Thanks, Joe. For everything."

"It's been my pleasure, pal, and it'll continue t' be, f'r as long as y'all want me here."

Joe slipped out of the room.

* * *

They had a late breakfast in the dining room, since it was still only mid-morning, and dinner would be late that night because the hands caught on to certain unspoken familial relationships, and decided to celebrate with another barbacoa— Echo, Omega, and Dihl gathered that any excuse would do, and this was a rather large one, after all. More, the Ranch's three visitors were to be the special guests of honor at the informal cookout.

So Joe shifted all of the mealtimes for the day, and Omega, Echo, and Dihl met in the big dining room while Cook brought out platters of full-on huevos rancheros filled with rice, refried beans, fresh-made guacamole, sour cream, shredded cheese, and home-made salsa; this came with sides of pan-fried breakfast potatoes, sweet corn pudding, black beans, smoked sausage, thick-sliced bacon, and a sautéed blend of vegetables that included onions, carrots, red and yellow bell peppers, mushrooms, asparagus, garlic, and jalapeños, along with fresh, strong coffee and grapefruit juice.

"Joe, won't you join us?" Echo wondered.

"Nah, I best not," Joe responded. "Thanks f'r the invite, though. But not only have I got a ton o' stuff t' see to around th' Ranch, I don't feel right, joinin' y'all this time."

"Why not?" Omega wondered. "You joined us for dinner the last time we were here."

"That 'uz a little diff'runt," Joe pointed out. "Weren't none but you two, comin' at it as partners, an' you, Omega, not knowin' where you was quite yet. This time, I'd be interruptin' th' fam'ly's first meal together at th' ranch. Leastways, in a long, long time f'r some of ya's." Unseen by Omega, Joe winked at Echo to let the male Agent know he'd given him an opening, then slipped out to get to work.

"Oh, no, I'm not part of the family," Omega murmured, casting her gaze down to her plate. "Maybe I should..."

"Don't you dare give me that," Echo gently but firmly chastised her then, before she could withdraw—either physically or mentally. "You're as much a part of this family as I am of the one you've managed to put together around you at Headquarters."

"Not...really," Omega said, still staring at her plate. "It's not the same. This...this is a REAL family."

"I beg to differ," Dihl said, voice soft, seeing the interaction and understanding it. "As much as Echo has told me about you? What you have done, how you have stood by him regardless of the difficulty, how you rescued him from those dreadful slavers, very nearly at the cost of your own life? And more besides? 'Loyal' does not begin to express it, Omega. And now I know you, too—and you rescued me as well. No, no, child. You may not have been born to the Bryant household, but you are a member of this family nonetheless, believe me."

Echo and Dihl exchanged a meaningful glance over Omega's head, and it was Dihl's turn to wink at her son, who bit his lip to keep from grinning; he knew exactly what kind of family member Dihl meant.

"You...you mean that?" Omega wondered, voice barely above a whisper, as she finally raised her head long enough to peek at Dihl, then at Echo. "Both of you?"

"Of course, baby," Echo noted, calm. "As long as we've been together now, and as much as we've gone through together? Honestly, Meg, sometimes I think *I* trust you more than YOU trust you!"

"And if Echo considers you family, then of course I do," Dihl averred. "Besides, my interactions with you agree with his assessment, and I don't see that changing. Welcome to the family, child." She offered the younger woman an affectionate, warm-hearted smile.

Omega beamed, and Echo grinned.

* * *

"Mm, I recognize the corn pudding recipe," Omega mumbled around a mouthful as the trio chowed down. "It's almost identical to yours, Ace."

"Well, you know who taught it to me, right?" Echo observed, glancing at Dihl.

"Indeed, and this is a very delicious rendition," Dihl agreed. "Made even better by the fact that I didn't have to make it!" They all laughed.

"Which makes me think," Omega said. "I never did thank you, Echo, for giving permission for the kitchen to share the family recipes with me. I hadn't quite got it in my head at the time that this was your home—I mean, I'd figured it out, I just didn't have...it hadn't sunk in yet, is maybe the way to say it—and when I realized what I'd done about two seconds after I saw Joe send you that querying glance for approval, it was too late to back down. And um, Dihl, I hope you don't mind that he did that..."

"Not in the least, child," Dihl waved away the half-apology. "As much as you cook for him, and he cooks for you? If you can manage to make some of his old favorites for him, I can only think he would appreciate it."

"I just wish there was some way to return the favor," Echo sighed.

"Well, Mom was a really good cook," Omega admitted, "and I learned a lot of recipes from her, and I was working on the whole repertoire. But she learned from HER mom, and her mom never used recipes, so nothing was written down. There's some recipes that...were just lost, when they, when they...died."

"I know. That's...what I mean," Echo murmured.

"Well, it cannot be helped, sometimes," Dihl decided. "Family traditions can be like that. Perhaps between the three of us, and your memories, Omega, we may make a project out of trying to recreate some of them."

"I...think I'd like that," Omega said, offering a shy smile.

* * *

Right after breakfast, Joe called the trio into his little office, where a small package waited for Dihl. He delivered it into her hands, then escorted them into the den, where Dihl sat at one end of the overstuffed sofa, package in hand. Echo sat next to her, then patted the empty space next to him with his right hand.

"C'mere, baby," he told Omega. "Have a seat while Dihl opens this. Joe, what is it?" he queried, as Omega did as she was bidden. Echo handed his knife to his mother, and she slit the shipping tape on the package, then commenced unwrapping it.

"No idea, Echo," Joe said. "Something that Fox an' Zebra sent on, outta her personal effects, accordin' to what Fox told me on th' horn a few minutes ago. He an' Zebra seemed ta think it'd be good ta have, while she 'uz here. Only it didn't show up until after y'all had already left Headquarters." The phone rang, and he glanced back into his office. "Y'all 'scuze me."

"Go ahead, Joe," Echo waved the other man off. "Go do what you need to do."

Just then, Dihl got the last of the paper removed. She gaped at the object in her hands.

"Oh...my...goodness," she murmured, drawing Echo's attention.

"Wow. That's the old family photo album, isn't it?" he asked.

"Yes, Echo, it is," Dihl confirmed with a delighted smile. "Now when we reminisce, we can even show Omega some pictures of it."

"There better not be any butt-naked baby pictures in there," Echo warned, glowering.

"Not this one," Dihl said, giving Omega a mischievous glance. Omega's grin was a mile wide; Echo noticed the fact.

"Dammit," Echo grumbled. "Meaning there's others."

"A perfect little work of art deserves to be recorded for posterity," Dihl noted, flipping open the album. "And you were certainly that. At least, as far as your father and I were concerned. Shitaá, too, for that matter."

Omega, who was leaning partway into Echo's lap in order to see the album—much to Echo's pleasure, though he was having a hard time figuring out where to put his right hand—suddenly gasped in surprise and pointed.

* * *

"Who's that?!" she asked, her index fingertip fractions of an inch from a photograph of an older man. The man in the image had long gray hair pulled into a thick braid, with bronzed, weatherbeaten skin. He was dressed in well-worn jeans, a plaid flannel shirt, and cowboy boots; his belt was tooled leather with silver conchos and matching buckle, but he sported no cowboy hat. His eyes were dark, cheekbones broad and prominent, and his features told the female Agent that he was some relation of Echo's and Dihl's.

"That? Oh, that's Shiitsooyee," Echo noted, leaning over to get a better look at the photo. "Yeah, that's from, I dunno, quite a while back. But that's him. That's Ma's dad."

"You...you're kidding, right?" Omega said, stunned. Echo shook his head, and Dihl gave her a slight nod of confirmation. "Oh, that's so cool."

"What? Why?" Echo wondered.

"You r'member, after the rattler bite, how I told you about a local Apache elder who taught me some herbal lore, so that if I ever found myself in a bad way while I was out and about, I'd know what to do?"

"Yeah?"

"That's him! It was your grandfather that taught me! I didn't know he came back over here to visit."

"I...didn't, either," Echo murmured, glancing at Dihl with a slight smile. Dihl raised an eyebrow, seeming puzzled. "You're right. That's cool, baby. But..."

"But?"

"I didn't think you were even in Texas that much, until about five years ago or so..."

"I wasn't," Omega confirmed. "At least, not this part of Texas. I got sent to Houston every once in a while, when I was working out of Huntsville. But I didn't start coming over here until I transferred to Houston."

"Wait," Dihl interjected. "Then...when did you see Shi-taá?"

"Oh, not quite a year after I started observing on the dry playa on the south end of the Ranch, so about three an' a half, four years before Echo and I met, ish," Omega considered. "An' yeah, now I know...it WAS the Ranch I was on, an' all that hadda been part of Slug's manipulations, Ace."

"Kinda figured, baby," Echo said, seeming absent, to Omega's puzzlement. He threw a meaningful look at his mother, and Omega frowned, concerned.

* * *

Oh shit, Echo thought. *How was THAT possible? But she positively identified him, and I've never shown her a picture of him. Then again, I never showed her a photo of X-ray either, and she nailed him. Maybe she pulled it out of my mind without meaning to.*

"What's wrong?" Omega asked then. "You both look... funny. Like something's not right."

"Baby, what was happening when you saw Shiitsooyee?" he pressed, throwing another concerned glance at Dihl, who returned it.

"Oh, well, I'd just had kind of a near-miss with a rattler, like the night before," Omega said, thinking back. "I managed to kill it, though, and I didn't get bitten...THAT time. He came through on a hike, wildcrafting herbs. He was friendly; said that Mr. Gonzales had told him he might run into me out there, and to say hi if he did. And he saw the rattlesnake body under the brush, where I'd thrown it, and asked if I was okay. I was, so he asked if he could have the body and the skin, to take care of it properly, and I said yes. I hadn't wanted to kill it to begin with, but it was it or me." She shrugged. "He cut off the rattle and showed me how to turn it into a pendant or fob, and said it was good medicine to keep around. I had it on a keychain for years, but I guess it got lost when Cartman crashed my setup that night we met, Ace."

"Hm," Dihl murmured, seeming thoughtful, and Echo knew what she was thinking: Rattlesnakes were revered in most Amerind cultures, and the bodies of those which had to be killed were to be handled properly, lest it prove unfortunate for the one forced to kill it.

"What happened next, Meg?" Echo asked.

"Well, then he asked if I had a snakebite kit or a medical kit with me. When I said all I had was a first-aid kit—I did later put together a pretty decent field medical kit, complete with snakebite stuff, but I didn't have anything then—well, he started showing me various plants and telling me what they were good for." She shrugged. "That's how I knew to use the dotted blazing star root as a poultice on the bite. He showed me how."

"That sounds like him," Dihl breathed.

"Then he asked if I'd like to learn a little, how to identify 'em, how to best use 'em in an emergency sitch, stuff like that. And I said yes," Omega told them, smiling. "So he came back every morning for several days—I was on vacation, observing—and taught me each morning until I got too sleepy. Then he helped me fix a meal over my campfire, and he left while I bedded down. He was really good at the whole 'walk silently' stuff and everything, too. I'd look down at the skillet, and when I'd look back up to say something, he would be gone. And the next day, I'd be reviewing the previous night's data take and I'd suddenly sense someone watching me, and I'd look up and he'd be there."

"And...this was no more than four to four and a half years ago, Meg?" Echo verified, his voice strained despite himself.

"Yeah..."

"And it wasn't a dream?"

"No."

"You're sure?"

"Positive," Omega declared.

"I'd say that confirms her as a member of the family, son," Dihl determined.

"Sure sounds like it, Ma."

"Why?" Omega asked, perturbed. "What's wrong, Ace? You and Dihl look so...odd..."

"Because, my dear girl," Dihl told her, very, very quiet, "Shitaá died ten years ago...on the reservation in New Mexico."

An astonished Omega stared at them.

Echo shrugged, then gave her a slight grin.

"Welcome to the family, baby," he told her.

* * *

The three spent some time after the late breakfast, wandering around the yards, exploring and—in the case of Dihl and Echo—reminiscing. Omega learned almost as much about her partner as she had the day he opened his personal files to her, over a year prior. And she loved every minute of it.

"I bet he was a cute little boy," Omega told Dihl, when Echo had turned aside to check on the site of an old childhood memory.

"He was," Dihl agreed. "I had had hopes of one day seeing him replicated in his own children, but that dream went away...

only, perhaps, it has come back, in some form."

"Um, has he, uh, told you about Chase?"

"You mean the woman he dated for a time, who married another? Yes, he told me of her."

"Well, then you probably understand why...he isn't likely to be giving you any grandkids after all," Omega mumbled.

"Why? I don't understand. Oh, look at the lovely blooms on that prickly pear! That will make some good fruit later in the year."

"Um, he, uh," Omega stumbled over her words, wondering how to explain. "I think Chase was The One, if you get me."

"Hm? No, I don't think so," Dihl considered. "He was grieved by her death, of course; anyone would be, in his place. But no, I am very certain he is past that relationship now, Omega. He as much as told me so, that first night. Don't be concerned for him on that account."

"Oh?" Omega murmured, thoughtful. "Oh..."

Just then, Echo walked back up.

"Was it there?" Dihl asked. "The climbing tree? Is it still alive?"

"Yup, it's still there." Echo grinned, brushing bark off his jeans. "Still strong and sturdy. Even taller than I remember."

"You climbed it!" Omega exclaimed, delighted.

"Mmmaybe..."

* * *

Echo found his mother in the garden, where he had expected he would. She was sitting on the old stone bench under the venerable old pecans, looking thoughtful, with a smile on her face that, had it been on his partner's face, Echo would have called dreamy.

But just because it's Ma, he realized, *doesn't mean she can't dream about stuff too, I suppose. It's gonna take a bit of getting used to, I guess, relating to my mother as adult to adult. Especially when we haven't seen each other in so long. But she's trying to do it for me, so it's only fair.*

"Hey there," he said, keeping his voice soft. "Am I interrupting?"

"No, never, Echo," Dihl murmured, looking up and smiling at him. "I was just...reminiscing."

"About putting in the garden? 'Cause I was telling Joe earlier, I remember when you did it."

"Yes, among other things; and how you 'helped' with that!" She laughed. "Oh, my dear son, do you see that sprawling patch of blue sage in the corner, and the way the other sages are in rows?"

"Yeah? Did I do that?"

"You did," she said with a huge smile. "You accidentally upended the bag of seed I had so carefully harvested from my wildcrafting, right there. So...I left them there, and simply raked them into the soil. I concluded that the One who created the sages had created myself and my son as well, and knew where it needed to go. And there it is, to this day, growing magnificently."

"I was a handful, huh?"

"No, not really," Dihl decided. "Just intensely curious, and always wanting to help. James and I did our best not to stifle that in you—any of that. I can see the fruit of all of it in the man you have become, and I am very proud. Your father would be, too. And if I know James, he's right here with us, agreeing with me."

Echo chuckled.

"I kinda hope so," he agreed. "Him and Shiitsooyee both."

"I think they probably are, son. Chances are, James has been watching over you from the beginning of your strange odyssey, and I'm sure your grandfather has done the same, since he passed over. Just like he did for your partner."

"This isn't a good time for it, but remind me some time to tell you about how Shiitsooyee helped me survive a dust storm in the Outback. I shoulda said something when Meg recognized his photo, but I was kinda blown away."

Dihl raised a curious eyebrow, then settled back on the

bench, leaning lightly against the trunk of the overhanging pecan tree.

"I'll do that. Perhaps tonight? After dinner, around the campfire Joe promised?"

"That oughta work, yeah. Can I ask you something?"

"Of course."

"You always loved sitting on this bench under the pecans..."

"Ah. You know why, don't you?"

"No..."

"These pecans are older than your father. Older than his father, I think. I am not sure how many generations back they go, but they are as much a legacy of the ranch as any Bryant. Your father proposed to me here. With his parents' full blessing, I might add."

"Aw."

"Yes. Sometimes, when I sit here...on the rare occasions I was able to—for the ranch kept me busy—and...not at all in many long years...well, it feels as if he is still here."

"Then maybe I need to go, and let you alone."

"No, no, you are fine. He will still be here, I think. He still IS here, only...quiet, to allow for our conversation, is perhaps a good way to put it. Did you want something?"

"Well, Meg and I are gonna go for a picnic along the creek, for lunch. I was planning on taking her down to the Pool, maybe eat under the willow trees Grandpa set out when he was a young man. By the looks of all the stuff Cook is throwing in the saddlebags, there'll be plenty to eat. We wondered if you'd like to come along with us."

"That is a lovely spot; I think she will enjoy that. And so I think I shall NOT come," Dihl said with a smile, her eyes twinkling mischief. "It will give the two of you some alone time, in a beautiful setting that is NOT work related, for a change. See that you make good use of the time!" She winked at him, and he grinned. "In any case, Joe has asked my opinion of what modifications that I would make to the herb garden, and I have been pondering that...with your father, as it were."

"So...rain check?"

"Rain check."

"Okay. Take it easy, and don't overdo."

"I won't."

He kissed her cheek, and headed for the barn.

* * *

"She's not coming?" Omega wondered, as Echo entered the stable area, alone.

"No, she wants to make sure we have our own time together, I think," Echo decided. "Besides, she was sitting in the herb garden, remembering Dad."

"Aw. Was she sad?"

"No, I didn't think so; she was telling me stories on myself."

"Then I'm goin' to the garden!" Omega exclaimed with a grin, headed for the door. Echo caught her around the waist before she could get past him.

"No, you're not," he declared, knowing she was just teasing him...mostly. *But she'd probably get a kick outta a few more stories like Ma told her, that first night,* he decided. *I dunno if that's a good thing, or a bad thing, at least for me. But right now, I think Ma just needs to be with her memories of Dad, and this place. I guess I never really realized that she loves it as much as I do.* "Leave her be right now, baby, if you don't mind. I think she wants to be alone with...with Dad, for a while. It...was a special place for them."

"Oh. I'll behave, then. I was mostly teasing you anyway, like you didn't know. But, um, do me a favor?"

"Sure. Whatcha need?"

"Well, you know I want to get to know your mom an' all, but...I don't wanna get in the way, either. I get that she's trying to reconnect with her past, and with you, and the ranch, and all that. So...if there's a special place, or a special time, or something like that, TELL me, so I don't go puttin' my foot in it?" Omega scrunched her face.

"Nah, don't worry about it. You're not gonna put your foot in it, Meg," Echo offered, "because I figured out a long time ago that you've only got my best interests at heart, and she's already figured out the same thing—you care, about both of us. And that means a lot—to me, and Ma, both. And...the feeling's mutual. So she's not gonna take offense, and neither will I. Still and all," he said, holding up both hands in a halting gesture as he saw her open her mouth to protest, "I get where you're coming from, and that you don't wanna interrupt fond memories an' reminiscences. So yeah, I swear I'll do my best to let you know about things like that, in so far as I recognize 'em myself."

"Okay. Good. Um, thanks."

"I reckon it's just us, then. Wanna come help me tack up?"

"Like there was ever a question?"

* * *

Big, strong, faithful Ditok was carrying the two off-duty Agents out for a picnic. Echo was in the saddle, and Omega was riding behind, as they'd done on the chase. The difference this time was that they were taking their time and ambling along, instead of racing fast enough to lift off if they held out their arms. As usual, the big horse was tacked with a Texas hackamore, complete with lead line, so that the Alpha One team could tie him to a fence or tree when they arrived at their destination.

Echo glanced over his shoulder at his partner, and Omega caught the gleam in his eye just in time to fling her arms around Echo as he spurred Ditok into a full gallop. As she tightened her hold, however, Omega heard an involuntary hiss from Echo, and he automatically reined in the big horse.

"What's wrong?!" Omega exclaimed, concerned.

"Damn. Sorry, Meg," Echo said, rubbing his side. "I'm afraid I've got some pretty good bruising where the overly-amorous Lady Zzs—and I use the title really loosely—put her bear hug on me. I guess I shoulda made India take a closer look at it before we left, but it wasn't bothering me then."

"Ooh, and I just grabbed onto you in the same place. Let's see," she said, gently pulling his shirttail out of his jeans waistband and raising it to look at his side. "Echo!!"

"What?"

"You're thirty-seven shades of black and blue! I'm getting Dihl to have a look at this when we get back! What do you think you're doing, letting me ride with you, let alone hold on?? In fact, what are you doing even riding?"

* * *

"Aw. Don't fuss over me, Meg. I'm fine," Echo said quietly, averting his face. "I just bumped the bruises, that's all."

"I'm sorry," Omega said in a low tone.

"For what?" Echo twisted stiffly in the saddle to look back at her. She looked down, past where her boots dangled at the horse's flank. To his surprise, Echo thought she looked ashamed.

"You trusted me to extract you safely, and I let you down," she told him. "I didn't get there fast enough."

"Hey, I don't see any body parts missing or...otherwise violated," Echo told her. "You had plans for every contingency, Meg. It's not your fault I got a little banged up, any more than it's my fault Celeste threw you, that first day here. You're only human."

"So to speak..."

Echo winced.

"It's true, Meg."

"No, it's not, Echo. If I were 'only human,' we'd both be dead, because the assassins would never have bought our infiltration story. Never mind the damn rattler bite."

"All right, you're enhanced. But still human."

* * *

Omega grinned, rueful.

"I'll say it again: You're good, Ace. I almost believe you mean that."

Echo blinked, as something that might have been hurt flickered through his eyes.

"You think I'm lying to you?"

"I think you're trying to make me feel better about myself," Omega said, her voice gentle.

"What will it take to convince you that I'm serious?"

* * *

A light flared in the blue eyes, seeming almost of passion; Echo saw it, and sat stock-still in the saddle, almost holding his breath, waiting—hoping—for her response. But the light died, and Omega looked away as Echo barely heard her remark.

"No. No, I can't...it's not fair," she murmured under her breath, and he blinked again, finally starting to understand her mindset and attitude toward what had been done to her, at least to some extent. "Nothing, Echo," she continued in a normal voice. "It's okay. Just...look, just forget it. I'll...believe you. I'm glad you're in one piece, though."

* * *

Echo watched her averted face for a moment, wearing an enigmatic expression that Omega couldn't interpret, then he turned around and nudged Ditok forward—at a slow walk, this time.

"Well, that makes two of us," he remarked, "but you owe me one, Meg."

"Oh, really?" she asked, wrapping her arms very loosely around him to stabilize herself, being careful not to bump his badly-bruised ribcage. "Why?"

"Next time some alien female-type has the hots for me, try to come up with some other plan than telling me to kiss her, okay? Shit," Echo tossed over his shoulder. Abruptly he turned his head. "Ptu," he spat into a nearby clump of prairie sage. "Ugh."

It was Omega's turn to wince, unaware that a look of rejection crossed her face momentarily—though she was very aware of the feeling behind the look.

* * *

Echo, whose head was still turned, caught a glimpse of it, and his eyes went wide in surprise. Swiftly he turned to look forward, pretending not to have seen, and pondered what her expression had meant.

That looked like...rejection, and, and pain, he decided. *But why would she feel rejected by my disliking having to kiss Zzs? I would have thought...if she were interested at all...that she'd be glad I didn't enjoy it. Never mind compatibility issues capable of killing me.*

He mulled over that subject for a split second before the answer came to him.

Wait, he thought, shocked. *She doesn't think I mean HER, does she? Oh, damn—she does! She's almost got to, after what we just finished talking about. I never think of her like that... but SHE thinks of herself like that. 'Some alien female-type with the hots for me' could, in her mind, describe HER, if she's secretly interested...and Ma AND Fox think she is, but won't admit it, 'cause she's afraid to. Shit shit shit. Echo, son, you just screwed up. Now I need to figure out how to—*

But before he could get farther, Omega responded.

* * *

"Ah do th' best Ah can with what Ah got ta work with, Ace," she drawled, after a few seconds to gain control of her emotions. Then, in a softer tone, she offered, "Like I said, I'm sorry."

Echo turned his head slightly; Omega saw the crease of pain between his brows as he responded.

"I know. It's okay," he told her. She eased her hold on him for a moment, and saw Echo's face relax almost imperceptibly. "I, um..." he began.

"Echo..." she interrupted him, worried, "riding back here, I have to hold on..."

"So?"

"I'm hurting you."

"I'm fine, Meg." But the faint frown was still there. Omega studied his profile for a moment.

"It would be way more comfortable for you if I 'drive'..." she offered softly.

"That's...not a half-bad idea, actually..."

* * *

"This is where I had in mind, Meg," Echo told his companion over her shoulder, and she brought Ditok to a halt. Echo released the careful, firm grip he had around his partner's waist, and slid to the ground as Omega spoke.

"Ooo. This is a really pretty spot, Ace. I love all the wildflowers. And the stream makes it just about perfect."

Echo took the reins from her and looped them over the saddle horn before loosing the lead line and tying Ditok to a handy tree, after thoroughly checking the area for 'critters.'

"Yeah, I thought you'd like it," he told her. "Take a nice deep breath of that wildflower scent you enjoy so much."

"I have been, believe me. It's glorious."

As Omega dismounted, she felt hands catch her waist.

"Thanks, Echo," she murmured...

...But he didn't set her on the ground. Instead, he carried her down the slope toward the stream, thrown over his hip, her legs dangling behind them, while she stared in shock at the ground as it went by.

"Echo?! Put me down! What are you doing?"

* * *

Echo pulled a small bottle out of his jeans pocket. He had prepared for this very thing, careful to wear old clothes, even old, worn-out boots and belt that wouldn't matter if they got wet...and Dihl had helped, by ensuring Omega was attired similarly. And the little bottle—with its specialized contents—had been procured by Dihl herself, at Echo's request, from an off-world supply in Medical.

"I'll tell ya what we're gonna do, baby. We're gonna scrub until we wash all that brown shit out of your hair," he told her. "I want my palomino partner back, even if it's gonna take a few weeks to grow it out long enough to braid again." He popped the cap and squeezed a big blob of the special shampoo on top of her head, then strode straight into the water's edge. Omega's eyes widened in disbelief.

"Come on, Echo, put me down! Be patient! It'll come out!"

"Yep. It's coming out, all right."

* * *

"Echo! Put me down!!" Omega cried, poking him in the ribs. Echo flinched noticeably.

Oh boy, she thought. *Well, it's not quite how I intended to take first advantage of it, but I better do SOMEthing, otherwise I'm gonna get a ducking!* She poked him in the ribs again, pretending to discover his reaction for the first time. Echo flinched again, and Meg exclaimed, "Ah-HA! You ARE ticklish! Just like your dad!"

"Ah! No, I'm not! It's the damn bruises!" Echo protested, swiftly trying to shift his grip on his partner as Omega vigorously attacked his ribcage with her fingertips in an attempt to get free. "Ah! No, stop it! Aha! Ow! Haha! Cut it out, Meg—ha!—or we're both gonna—"

* * *

There was a loud splash, and Ditok gazed solemnly across the stream as two heads bobbed to the surface.

"Aw, hell. Dammit, Meg, I tried to tell you—"

"So it's okay to dunk me, but you play by different rules, huh?" Omega grinned, splashing water at him. "I didn't know you'd melt."

A mildly-disgusted Echo, sitting in a chest-deep pool, absently splashed water back at her; then, as a sudden flurry of water headed his way, accompanied by infectious laughter, he retaliated with a grin.

A playful Omega lunged at him, and Echo neatly flipped her over his shoulder. Omega landed flat on her back with a tremendous splash, soaking them both again, and came up gasping, choking, and giggling. Silver highlights now gleamed in the sunlit, light-brown hair.

Echo raised an eyebrow, then dove at her, pushing her under again, and ruffling her hair for all he was worth, as it foamed and fizzed, the foam breaking down to harmless constituents as the stream washed it away. This time Omega came exploding up with short, silver-blonde, dripping locks, and unexpectedly shoved him backward into the water, all the while laughing fit to burst as she slipped and fell backward herself.

Echo stood up, streaming water, and slogged over to his mirthful partner, grinning down at her and offering her a hand. Omega took it and stood, and together they slipped and slid their way over to the bank.

Laughing the whole way, the waterlogged Alpha One team climbed out of the stream and made their way up onto the grassy slope. There, they flopped down on the ground, still snickering, and Echo promptly pulled off his right boot and upended it. Water gushed out, and Omega burst into fresh gales of laughter as he repeated the scenario with his left boot.

"Here, give me your foot," Echo said to his companion, who lay on her back, holding her belly and giggling. Wordlessly, she stuck her foot at him, and he pulled off the boot, then solemnly tipped it upside-down over her head. A cascade of water caught Omega full in the face, and she sputtered as Echo grinned from ear to ear.

Omega sat up indignantly, staring him in his gleaming brown eyes for a long moment. Then they both exploded with laughter, falling back onto the fragrant, sun-warm grass and doubling up. Finally their hilarity subsided into soft chuckles.

"When we get back in this condition, Dihl is gonna have a cow," she decided.

"Nah," Echo demurred. "She's used to it, outta me. Besides, she knew what I was gonna do."

"She did?"

"Yeah. Who do you think gave me that special shampoo crap? Never mind got it from Zebra and brought it along?"

"Y'all are gonna gang up on me every chance you get, aren't ya?"

"What do you think?"

Omega snorted in amusement, and they grinned at each other.

"Thanks for comin' along on my vacation—and bringin' me here, to your boyhood home, Echo," Omega told him then, with a gentle smile. "I'd have been in a world of trouble—and probably bored stiff, instead of just plain stiff—without ya."

Echo shrugged, still grinning.

"What are partners for? Are you having a good time on our vacation, Meg?"

"The best, Echo," Omega said with a grin. "The best. Let's eat."

Author Notes

There are, as always, the usual suspects to thank: my husband, Darrell Osborn, who also does the cover art for this series, and my parents, Steve and Colene Gannaway, who staunchly support my efforts at writing. There are also my beta readers, Dr. James K. Woosley, Evelyn Hively Zinn, and Larry Bauer. In addition to reading the finished manuscript and helping me polish, they all helped me brainstorm several things at various points in the story development. Larry is also by way of being something of a manager for me, so more thanks to him for putting up with all my crap, which crap often includes panic attacks and bouts of, "What do I think I'm doing? I can't write!"

I'd also like to especially thank Dan Hollifield, Michael Thirion, Susan Powers, Susan Baker Farmer, John Farmer, Laura Runkle, Robert R. Murphy, M.D., and the other members of Lady Osborn's Pub and Sarah's Diner, groups on Facebook, for the brainstorming they did with me on a few things here! So many thanks.

Those who have known me as a horsewoman may recognize the horse that Omega rides through much of this adventure. Celeste was one of my horses; a retired Thoroughbred racehorse, she was a lovely 'flea-bit gray' mare that I spent a good deal of time riding, once upon a time, before my body decided not to cooperate any more. I have owned other horses, but none were like Celeste. We rode trails, played polo, and such like together (though I never rode hunts myself, not being drawn to the sport), and she was that one in a million horse that every rider dreams of: the horse with which you make a connection. We understood each other. I could read her, and generally knew what she was going to do, and she did her best to take care of me, even to the extent of doing her best to keep under me, no matter what happened. (And some really wild things happened, from time to time.) Turning her loose on a practice racetrack was the nearest I have ever come to flying without an aircraft.

She was an incredibly intelligent horse, and even delighted in playing pranks and practical jokes on me. If I ever sit down and write a book on animals who have owned me, an entire chapter will have to be devoted to Celeste.

Celeste finally died of old age a few years back, and I miss her dearly. I thought I'd include her in the story by way of remembrance.

~Stephanie Osborn
May 2018

About the Author

Stephanie Osborn is a former payload flight controller, a veteran of over twenty years of working in the civilian space program, as well as various military space defense programs. She has worked on numerous Space Shuttle flights and the International Space Station, and counts the training of astronauts on her resumé. Of those astronauts she trained, one was Kalpana Chawla, a member of the crew lost in the *Columbia* disaster.

She holds graduate and undergraduate degrees in four sciences: Astronomy, Physics, Chemistry, and Mathematics, and she is "fluent" in several more, including Geology and Anatomy. She obtained her various degrees from Austin Peay State University in Clarksville, TN and Vanderbilt University in Nashville, TN.

Stephanie is currently retired from space work. She now happily "passes it forward," teaching math and science via numerous media including radio, podcasting, and public speaking, as well as working with SIGMA, the science fiction think tank, while writing science fiction mysteries based on her knowledge, experience, and travels.

For more, go to http://www.stephanie-osborn.com/.

Don't miss any of these highly entertaining SF/F books by Stephanie Osborn!

The *Division One* series by Stephanie Osborn:
Alpha and Omega
A Small Medium At Large
A Very UnCONventional Christmas
Tour de Force
Trojan Horse
Texas Rangers
Coming soon:
Definition and Alignment
Phantoms
Head Games
Break, Break, Houston
The Division One Agents Handbook
The Division One Cookbook

Alpha and Omega (ISBN: 978-0-9982888-0-2 ebook/ 978-0-9982888-1-9 print) by Stephanie Osborn

Dr. Megan McAllister was already a pretty unusual human—NASA astronaut, professional astronomer, polymath—when she encountered the man in the black Suit that night in west Texas. What Division One Agent Echo didn't know, when he recruited her to the Agency, was that she was even more special.

But he'd find out, soon enough.

Stephanie Osborn, aka the Interstellar Woman of Mystery, former rocket scientist and author of acclaimed science fiction mysteries, goes back to the urban legend of the unique group of men and women who show up at UFO sightings, alien abductions, etc. and make things...disappear...to craft her vision of the universe we don't know about. Her new series, Division One, chronicles this universe through the eyes of recruit Megan McAllister, aka Omega, and her experienced partner, Echo, as they handle everything from lost alien children to extraterrestrial assassination attempts and more. [First book in the *Division One* series]

* * *

A Small Medium At Large (ISBN: 978-0-9982888-2-6 ebook/ 978-0-9982888-3-3 print) by Stephanie Osborn

What if Sir Arthur Conan Doyle was right all along, and Harry Houdini really DID do his illusions, not through sleight of hand, but via noncorporeal means? More, what if he could do this because...he wasn't human?

Ari Ho'd'ni, Glu'g'ik son of the Special Steward of the Royal House of Va'du'sha'ā, better known to modern humans as an alien Gray from the ninth planet of Zeta Reticuli A, fled his homeworld with the rest of his family during a time of impending global civil war. With them, they brought a unique device which, in its absence, ultimately caused the failure of the uprisings and the collapse of the imperial regime. Consequently Va'du'sha'ā has been at peace for more than a century. What is the F'al, and why has a rebel faction sent a special agent to Earth to retrieve it?

It falls to the premier team in the Pan-Galactic Law Enforcement and Immigration Administration, Division One—the Alpha One team, known to their friends as Agents Echo and Omega—to find out...or die trying. [Second book in the *Division One* series]

* * *

A Very UnCONventional Christmas (ISBN: 978-0-9982888-4-0 ebook/978-0-9982888-5-7 print) by Stephanie Osborn

It's Christmas in NYC, but for Alpha Line it's anything but a Silent Night: The Agency has a mole, leaking classified information to toy manufacturers and film producers alike, and the Agents are in danger of losing their anonymity. To compli-

382

cate matters, the Prime Minister of Lambda Andromedae III, complete with entourage, has arrived to negotiate a new trade agreement with Earth. Worse, the more paranoid Division One field agents look at Omega's recent history with the Agency and suspect they have identified the mole!

Simultaneously, the discovery of a grim countdown in the most incongruous place possible—the Christmas tree at Rockefeller Center—augers the threat of horrific events on Christmas Eve itself.

Meanwhile, Omega is struggling to adjust to her very first Christmas in the Agency, made more difficult by the exposure of parts of her past long hidden from her conscious mind.

Will Omega be able to refute the accusations, or be punished for crimes she did not commit? Will the internal conspiracy expose the Agency? Or will efforts to thwart it see Echo—and Fox—caught up in the accusations as well? What is the meaning of the countdown to Christmas Eve, and will any of Alpha Line survive it? [Third book in the *Division One* series]

* * *

Tour de Force (ISBN: 978-0-9982888-6-4 ebook/ 978-0-9982888-7-1 print) by Stephanie Osborn

Alpha One is participating in Omega's very first First Contact diplomatic operation. Unfortunately, it's going to split up the team—the Cortians, a race from the Sagittarius Dwarf Galaxy, have stringent requirements, and that narrows down the list of "candidate exchange students" to...Echo. ONLY Echo. PGLEIA's top Division One Agent, the man being groomed to be the next Director...and Omega's partner. A plum assignment, for the pick of the crop.

But Omega doesn't see it that way, though she can't—or won't—explain why. She is determined to stop the mission from going forward. At any cost.

Why is Omega trying to scuttle a diplomatic mission? What is she seeing that more experienced Agents aren't? Why won't the others listen? Is something bigger, more menacing, happening to her—to them? Will—CAN—Alpha One survive? [Fourth book in the *Division One* series]

* * *

Trojan Horse (ISBN: 978-0-9982888-9-5 ebook/ 978-1-947530-00-3 print) by Stephanie Osborn

After returning the healer Doron to his homeworld of Edeptis, Echo takes Omega on a training run to make her a PGLEIA-certified starship pilot—celestial navigation, extravehicular activity, emergency repair, planetary surveys, you name it. And he secretly delights in seeing Omega's joy at finally fulfilling a childhood dream.

But when the Cortians show on the scene, intending to take Alpha One into custody for crimes against the Cortian Amalgam, the resulting dogfight severely damages the *Trojan Horse*, causing it to crash on a primitive protoplanet. Both Echo and Omega are badly injured, and it will take both of them working together to survive in the wreckage, while more Cortian vessels search for them overhead, and Fox and the rest of Alpha Line try to fight their way through to rescue their friends and colleagues. [Fifth book in the *Division One* series]

* * *

Texas Rangers (ISBN: 978-1-947530-01-0 ebook/ 978-1-947530-02-7 print) by Stephanie Osborn

It's time for Alpha One to take a vacation! Traveling to the Ranch, a field station in western Texas near the famed Pecos River, the pair relax and unwind, riding horseback, picnicking, and generally having fun...

...Until they discover a team of alien assassins sneaking across the landscape and headed to Dallas, to take out the President of the United States on a campaign junket!

Meanwhile, back at Headquarters and unknown to him, Echo's estranged mother—who believed him killed years before, when he entered the Agency—lies unconscious in a regeneration pod, while the medlab staff, led by Zebra, works frantically to save her life: Shortly before their vacation, Omega discovered that Nalin Bryant had developed a particularly virulent form of cancer.

Can Alpha One infiltrate the assassin team without being killed? Can Alpha Line stop the assassination of the U.S. President? And can Zebra save Echo's mother's life and return her to her son, or will Echo lose one—or both—of the two women who mean the world to him?

* * *

The *Burnout* series by Stephanie Osborn:
The Fetish
Burnout: The mystery of Space Shuttle STS-281
Coming soon:
Escape Velocity

The Fetish (ASIN: B007YATGG8) by Stephanie Osborn
In *Burnout: The mystery of Space Shuttle STS-281*, Dr. Mike Anders buys a small spaceman fetish from a Zuni elder at a trading post. But there's a story behind this little lapis spaceman carving. What is it, and how did it come to be?

* * *

Burnout: The mystery of Space Shuttle STS-281
(ISBN: 1-60619-200-0) by Stephanie Osborn
How do you react when you discover the next shuttle disaster has happened...right on schedule?

Burnout is a SF mystery about a Space Shuttle disaster that turns out to be no accident. As the true scope of the disaster is uncovered by the principle investigators, "Crash" Murphy and Dr. Mike Anders, they find themselves running for their lives as friends, lovers and coworkers involved in the investigation perish around them.

* * *

Sherlock Holmes: Gentleman Aegis series by
Stephanie Osborn:
Sherlock Holmes and the Mummy's Curse
 Coming soon:
Sherlock Holmes in the Wild Hunt
Sherlock Holmes and the Tournament of Shadows

Sherlock Holmes and the Mummy's Curse
(ISBN: 1-51888-312-5) by Stephanie Osborn
Holmes and Watson. Two names linked by mystery and danger from the beginning.

Within the first year of their friendship and while both are young men, Holmes and Watson are still finding their way in the world, with all the troubles that such young men usually have: Financial straits, troubles of the female persuasion, hazings, misunderstandings between friends, and more. Watson's Afghan wounds are still tender, his health not yet fully recovered, and there can be no consideration of his beginning a new practice as yet. Holmes, in his turn, is still struggling to found the new profession of consulting detective. Not yet truly established in London, let alone with the reputations they will one day possess, they are between cases and at loose ends when Holmes' old professor of archaeology contacts him.

Professor Willingham Whitesell makes an appeal to Holmes' unusual skill set and a request. Holmes is to bring Watson to serve as the dig team's physician and come to Egypt at once to translate hieroglyphics for his prestigious archaeological dig. There in the wilds of the Egyptian desert, plagued by heat, dust, drought and cobras, the team hopes to find the very first Pharaoh. Instead, they find something very different...(First book in the Gentleman Aegis series)

Sherlock Holmes and the Mummy's Curse is a Silver Falchion Award winner.

* * *

The *Displaced Detective* series by Stephanie Osborn:
The Case of the Displaced Detective: The Arrival
The Case of the Displaced Detective: At Speed
The Case of the Cosmological Killer: The Rendlesham Incident
The Case of the Cosmological Killer: Endings and Beginnings
A Case of Spontaneous Combustion
Fear in the French Quarter

_*The Case of the Displaced Detective: The Arrival* by Stephanie Osborn is a SF mystery in which brilliant hyperspatial physicist, Dr. Skye Chadwick, discovers there are alternate realities, often populated by those we consider only literary characters. Can Chadwick help Holmes come up to speed in modern investigative techniques in time to stop the spies? Will Holmes be able to thrive in our modern world? Is Chadwick now Holmes' new "Watson"—or more?

And what happens next?   [First book in the *Displaced Detective* series]

* * *

The Case of the Displaced Detective: At Speed by Stephanie Osborn

Having foiled sabotage of Project: Tesseract by an unknown spy ring, Sherlock Holmes and Dr. Skye Chadwick face the next challenge. How do they find the members of this diabolical spy ring when they do not even know what the ring is trying to accomplish? And how can they do it when Skye is recovering from no less than two nigh-fatal wounds?

Can they work out the intricacies of their relationship? Can they determine the reason the spy ring is after the tesseract? And—most importantly—can they stop it? [Second book in the *Displaced Detective* series]

* * *

The Case of the Cosmological Killer: The Rendlesham Incident by Stephanie Osborn

In 1980, RAF Bentwaters and Woodbridge were plagued by UFO sightings that were never solved. Now, McFarlane, a resident of Suffolk has died of fright during a new UFO encounter. On holiday in London, Sherlock Holmes and Skye Chadwick-Holmes are called upon by Her Majesty's Secret Service to investigate the death.

What is the UFO? Why does Skye find it familiar? Who—or what—killed McFarlane?

And how can the pair do what even Her Majesty's Secret

Service could not? [Third book in the *Displaced Detective* series]

* * *

The Case of the Cosmological Killer: Endings and Beginnings by Stephanie Osborn

After the revelations in *The Rendlesham Incident*, Holmes and Skye find they have not one, but two, very serious problems facing them. Not only did their "UFO victim" most emphatically NOT die from a close encounter, he was dying twice over—from completely unrelated causes. Holmes must now find the murderers before they find the secret of the McFarlane farm. And to add to their problems, another continuum—containing another Skye and Holmes—has approached Skye for help to stop the collapse of their own spacetime, a collapse that could take Skye with it, should she happen to be in their tesseract core when it occurs. [Fourth book in the *Displaced Detective* series]

* * *

A Case of Spontaneous Combustion by Stephanie Osborn

When an entire village west of London is wiped out in an apparent case of mass spontaneous combustion, Her Majesty's Secret Service contacts The Holmes Agency to investigate. Once in London, Holmes looks into the horror that is now Stonegrange. His investigations take him into a dangerous undercover assignment in search of a possible terror ring, though he cannot determine how a human agency could have caused the disaster. Meanwhile, alone in Colorado, Skye is forced to battle raging wildfires and tame a wild mustang stallion, all while believing that her husband has abandoned her. Who—or what—caused the horror in Stonegrange? Will Holmes find his way safely through the metaphorical minefield that is modern Middle Eastern politics? Will this predicament seriously damage—even destroy—the couple's relationship? And can Holmes stop the terrorists before they unleash their outré weapon again? [Fifth book in the *Displaced Detective* series]

* * *

Fear in the French Quarter by Stephanie Osborn revolves around a jaunt by no less than Sherlock Holmes himself—brought to the modern day from an alternate universe's Victorian era by his continuum parallel, who is now his wife, Dr. Skye Chadwick-Holmes—to famed New Orleans for both business and pleasure. There, the detective couple investigates ghostly apparitions, strange disappearances, mystic phenomena, and challenge threats to the very universe they call home.

It was supposed to be a working holiday for Skye and Sherlock, along with their friend, the modern day version of Doctor Watson—some federal training that also gave them the chance to explore New Orleans, as the ghosts of the French Quarter become exponentially more active. When the couple uncovers an imminently catastrophic cause, whose epicenter lies squarely in the middle of Le Vieux Carré, they must race against time to stop it before the whole thing breaks wide open—and more than one universe is destroyed. [Sixth book in the *Displaced Detective* series]

www.ingramcontent.com/pod-product-compliance
Lightning Source LLC
Chambersburg PA
CBHW050609170726
48283CB00001B/173